EXILES

Chronicles of the Reclamation: Book One

Brandon J. LeBlanc

Cover art by Robert Williams

Published by Jackson Auto Publishing
ISGN (eBook): 978-1-7780597-0-4
ISBN (paperback): 978-1-7780597-1-1

For B.C.

CHRONICLES OF THE RECLAMATION

A Time to Reap

As per his last will and testament, the guest list was kept to a strict limit. I still think he would have been embarrassed by the attention.

I was assigned a seat on the chancel with the officiant facing the rows of pews in the sanctuary. I hadn't anticipated that. Everyone would be facing me directly. Most of the women wore traditional black mesh veils concealing the stoicism, the grief, and the reverence, depending on their relation to the deceased. One notable exception was Dr. Sheppard, escorted to her place in the foremost row alongside her veiled sister-in-law. I couldn't bear to make eye contact with either of them. Not yet anyway.

Entering through the wide oak doors, I was greeted by the sweet scent of incense and fresh varnish. From the soft tones of the polished wooden handrails, to the benches and the inner décor, the renovation of the church was stunning. I was glad to see they'd stayed true to Cadlen's original drawing. It didn't matter who you were or what you believed: anyone walking into a building like this would find solace, at the very least. Answers, after all, are best found when one's guard is down. The atmosphere inside the chapel was completely disarming.

Solace. The deceased didn't know the meaning of the word—which is why his request for the service to take place here surprised me.

Officially, fewer than two dozen people were expected to attend, yet as the crowd flowed in, I counted more than forty. Some were accompanied into the sanctuary and to their seats by staffers and security. It made sense, given the nature of their respective positions. The rest huddled in groups to the side, presumed friends and relatives of the deceased, or hangers-on looking to make a point of being in attendance.

New Inland Chair Karyn sat on the right side of the aisle next to her staff. Reekan's security remained outside the building out of respect, while Joy took her seat near the back of the sanctuary. From here, she could slip out discreetly if necessary. Filling in the spaces on both sides of the aisle, visitors from far and wide paid their solemn respects. I knew some, but I would be meeting others for the first, and likely only time.

Out of respect, the balcony was closed to the public. That was where Cadlen sat all those years ago when he drew. To the left of the altar, the small cluster of hooded Ansati filed in, flanking an older man, bent and frail. They guided him to a seat that was close enough for him to view the service but allowed him to remain unseen if anyone were to look up. The arrangements for their attendance were fraught with complications. As a result, the Council of Regents were not represented in person, but rather, by a generous dedication of the ceremonial wood for the consecration. Another detail he requested that I didn't understand.

All of the focus inside the church was on the casket. Closed per the family's request, it was displayed at the base of the altar steps, framed by an arrangement of candelabras adorned with cream-coloured wax candles. The candles' soft flames wavered each time a guest opened the doors. The spirit wood upon which the simple casket rested was strictly for aesthetic license. The burning would take place later in a private ceremony for the immediate family.

The officiant of the service waited for a few moments before stepping up to the pulpit. To his right stood an oblong canvas concealed beneath a crimson velour drape. The guests would have to wait until later in the ceremony to see it.

Turning to face the congregation, the officiant welcomed the guests before reading a passage from *The Chronicles*, recited by our order for generations and approved for the ceremony with the family's blessing. As for me, it was a privilege to be an active participant in this tribute to a remarkable life that was often misunderstood and at times vilified. I will never forget the aura in the church that day. As I looked at the casket—which was bathed in light radiating from high above the altar and through the *crux ansata* staring down with arms open wide—I resolved to tell the world his story so that it might truly live forever.

As the service began, I looked upon the family, friends, and dignitaries, and then quickly glanced to the balcony. The old man kept his hood down over his face, trembling as the officiant spoke.

"The journey continues. It is a journey without end. The only beginning is the instant the eyes open, the tears of rebirth, salt mixed with honey, as those first rays of light penetrate the retina and draw us from the darkness. The first flutter from these windows of our awakening, from eternal slumber, greets this world with the awkwardness of a young fawn too feeble yet to stand on its own. The Light pours over us; it is thus followed by the air and the waters. We are sheltered from all of these as we are swaddled tightly in the fabrics of the looms and the weavers. Nourished from the breast, we are adored as we adore..."

Chronicles of the Ansati 1:1-6

☥

Book One:

EXILES

Born into This

Domingo, 7 marzo NE 267 (Sunday, 7 March
AC0245)
32 Kilometers, 232° Southwest of Motherland
Lieutenant Paolo Desantos

Paolo Desantos was born for this.

The cruel sun had yet to reveal itself above the eastern horizon, and the platoon was in motion. As the Motherland forces pressed onward across unforgiving terrain, the blazing orb in the sky stalked them without mercy until it was above them at midday. Paolo marched at the front of the colonnade, but he wasn't in the lead. He had dispatched Commander Yael two weeks earlier with a squad of sappers to plot the course and remove any obstacles. As the lush forests gave way to thinner, drier land, the likelihood of encountering brigands increased exponentially. Paolo's father had done well to secure the lands immediately around the Motherland territory. The walled city-state had never exerted its influence this far into the Lake Region before.

The destination was calculated by Yael and the sappers to be a five-day march. Even with reconnaissance, the journey was too dangerous for vehicular transport.

At 1500 hours, Paolo felt the platoon slowing behind him. The men had moved confidently through the thicker woods along established trails, the rising sun not yet punishing them. By noon, the taller growth had given way to spindly pioneer trees fighting to survive in drier, less fertile land. Lush greens were replaced by sickly yellows and browns. Rusted wrecks of motor vehicles decomposed on fallow ground as though their drivers had turned off their engines and walked away. Paolo knew that any human remains would have been long harvested. As the lieutenant pressed on, he wondered how many Reaper eyes were following them from a safe distance.

An open field surrounding a farmhouse with dangling wood siding and a crumbling stone foundation was as good a place as any for the platoon to rest.

"Fifteen minutes, commander." The platoon would have enough time to apply sunblock ointment, rehydrate, and piss, but nothing more. The commander hollered Paolo's order.

Paolo scanned the ground. The dry dirt showed evidence that anywhere from twenty to thirty pairs of boots had passed through days ago. The patterns of the boot outsoles confirmed that Yael and his sappers had passed this way, but there was no indication of any encampment. There were, however, tracks leading to the farmhouse. Paolo squinted through slitted eyes at the derelict building. Without a word, he approached it with slow, steady strides.

"Lieutenant, do you need backup?" The inferior officer would have gone ahead and taken a bullet for him; Paolo knew this. He raised a hand to indicate he would investigate alone. The place was run-down, but someone had been tending to the fields. Someone lived here. At least before the sappers arrived.

Paolo pulled open the unlocked door. "Show yourselves. We mean no harm." The sidearm in Paolo's hand would indicate to anyone watching that this may not be the case. As he stepped inside, the stench hit him instantly. The scurrying of rodents meant the building was likely unoccupied. Movement in the kitchen caught Paolo's eye, and he spun to face it, weapon drawn. A raccoon, gaunt from starvation, gnawed on a bag of grains that had spilled onto the floor. Cupboard doors hung open; their contents ransacked.

Yael had been here. He and his men could have found salvageable provisions before marching out. Still, the acrid stench hanging on the air seemed out of place. Reapers don't leave bodies behind. So, what was causing the stink? Likely, wildlife had crawled into the abandoned building to die. It was still worth a look.

Paolo didn't have to go far to find a crime scene. In what was once a common room where a family would gather at the end of a hard day's work, furniture was overturned and broken. Wide swaths of dried brown blood indicated a vicious attack on no fewer than three people, but no bodies were left behind. A Reaper cross, scrawled in blood on the far wall, met Paolo's scrutiny. Maybe the people who lived in this house were adherents of the Reaper religion.

What he knew for sure was that the Reapers didn't commit the crimes here. They would not have left a gruesome murder scene, and they certainly wouldn't have scrawled their symbol on the wall. Paolo loathed the filthy creatures, but he knew the way they operated. And this wasn't it.

Paolo retreated from the house as the platoon lined up for disembarkation. He pulled his handheld from the utility pouch around his waist and motioned with one hand for the men to march. Plotting the course his sappers had provided before leaving, he motioned with one hand the direction the platoon would follow. The farmhouse and its secrets disappeared behind them as the fat sun bore down on the marching troops for hours. They would pass several other similarly ransacked settlements on that first day before making camp for the night, having survived the punishing sun overhead for the first day of the mission.

At dawn on the second day, the Motherland platoon

broke camp and pressed further into the harrowing lands southeast of the Lake Region. Just after 1000 hours, Paolo's handheld buzzed in his grip. Without stopping, he swiped open the device with his left thumb. The radiation in the area had spiked but was staying within a safe level, at least for now. After about an hour, the level dropped again, and it remained normal the rest of the day. Yael had indicated that there would be brief intervals of heightened radiation, but none strong enough to require medication. The water table between the Motherland Forest and their destination was also expected to be safe for refilling. Paolo wasn't sure.

As the platoon made camp at dusk near a rocky outcropping, Paolo instructed his sappers to find nearby water springs and to test the potability.

"Lieutenant, we have one spring that is reading borderline levels of arsenic, selenium, and microbes. We can purify for our purposes." The officer swallowed as he reported to Paolo the chemical findings of the local water table. Paolo nodded his approval, and the officer corps ordered all water canteens to be filled. The next few days may not be so fruitful: on the fifth day, the clean water table of the Lake Region would be plentiful enough for the men to shower for days, but it wouldn't matter if they weren't healthy enough to get there.

Paolo's sleep was interrupted in the early hours of the third morning by a band of brigands passing through. The night watch made easy work of the intruders, but the encounter made the troops anxious. Before breaking camp, Paolo instructed that the bodies of the brigands be buried deep in unmarked graves. There was no need to draw the attention of the Reapers if they were in the vicinity.

The third day was hotter than the previous two. Paolo would have given his own canteen for even a few hours of cloud cover. The land was barren at this point, with only dead trees, gnarled and cracked, poking out from parched earth and rocky ground. Yael and his sappers had navigated a narrow trail through the badlands, but there was nothing they could have done to make the terrain more even. Worse, Paolo's handheld indicated spikes in radiation that were beginning to concern him. At midday, his men were unable to find any safe water sources. Mercury and lead levels were too high for even their water purification tablets to have any effect.

"Commander, we will not break for the evening. We need to pass through this region as quickly as possible. Inform the platoon to tighten water and food rations by half."

The commander nodded. Paolo was given five days to reach the Lake Region. They were going to do it in four. The troops marched through the night.

And as if the sun held a grudge against him, the fourth day was the most punishing yet. Paolo's handheld guided him to turn north. The platoon could reach the southernmost Lake Region by 1800 hours if they kept a steady pace and didn't encounter any unexpected enemies along the way. The third day had passed without any incidents. The sun would surely punish the brigands just as much.

Around 1300 hours, the commander spoke. "Lieutenant, our men are exhausted and water rations are running low. A break, perhaps? Fifteen, if you please?"

Straining his eyes, Paolo could see ahead that sloping hills were forming in the wavy heat. Faint green hues were beginning to reemerge in the distance. Vegetation meant water. Here, there was no cover from either attack or the sun above. They couldn't afford a break.

Paolo turned to his officer, four days of scruff stained with a mix of dust and sweat on his face. The officer's eyes were narrow and bloodshot. Paolo imagined he was looking in a mirror.

"We continue, commander. The men will rest well tonight."

A look of pained resignation crept over the officer's face as Paolo turned away from him. His handheld indicated lower radiation levels. Between here and the foothills in the distance was a long trek under a stifling sun, but the goal was in reach. His father would be proud. Yael and the sappers would be amazed at how quickly Lieutenant Paolo Desantos had led a thousand strong through such unforgiving land. Still, Paolo only wanted answers. What had happened back in that farmhouse? Since he had made the discovery four days ago, the question never left his mind.

Halfway to the foothills, Paolo heard a low hum between his ears, piercing him like thin needles. He still had a quarter of his canteen left, but it hadn't touched his lips since morning. Dehydration can play tricks on the body, his father once told him. Reaching for his water pack, Paolo realized that the hum was growing into a buzz borne on the air. Whooping from the rear guard alerted him to something approaching in the skies.

"Drones!"

The men broke into a hollering cacophony as Paolo spun around, dropping his canteen onto the cracked earth. A dozen black dots peppered the sky southwest of their position.

"Marksmen, take them down!" Paolo barked as he retrieved his sidearm from its holster. The colonnade dropped to a defensive position as guns blasted in the direction of the approaching mechanical craft. One shot pinged a lead drone, causing a short burst of light. The flying machine, not much bigger than a large dinner plate, plummeted to the ground. Paolo motioned for one of the troops to retrieve it.

"Lieutenant, it appears to be a surveillance drone,"

the officer reported, clutching a broken metal contraption in his hands. The shot that downed it had struck one of the propellers. A small camera lens confirmed the officer's appraisal. The Lake Region was known to harbour more sophisticated settlements. Brigands were known to be more brazen, attacking magna-rail trains often in the spring. If they had been spotted, a well-armed posse in armoured vehicles could tackle a fatigued, dehydrated army platoon of any size.

"Take down those drones!" Paolo shouted, his parched throat causing his voice to crack. Wheeling about, he aimed his pistol at the nearest flying intruder. One shot exploded the drone in a burst of gray smoke. One by one, the Motherland shooters eliminated the buzzing machines. Paolo motioned the troops to pick up the pace.

"Double-time. March!"

The platoon pressed on, staggering through the last miles as though they were programmed. Paolo demanded silence so that any approaching motor vehicles could be heard well in advance of a sneak attack. The foothills grew into swaths of green as the Motherland forces approached, and the sun crept across the sky into the West. Clouds moved in, and when the first droplets of rain started to fall, Paolo smiled. The light had not defeated him on this day.

Before the sun had fully set, Paolo led the platoon into an oasis of lush green shrubs and trees deep in the valley between two loping hills. Wisping smoke guided them to what they presumed would be Yael's sapper camp. They would have been here for more than a week at this point. Paolo ordered his troops to secure the perimeter before settling in for the night. Yael and his sapper crew had yet to reveal themselves. The smoke had proven to be the burned ruins of a small cabin of some sort, smoldering in the square stone foundation that remained.

"Sir, we are within radio range of Commander Yael. Shall we summon him?"

Paolo didn't answer, instead retrieving his own transistor.

"Commander Yael. Acknowledge." Only white noise responded. Paolo turned to his officer. "Gather the first column, we're moving north. The rest will make camp here."

"Sir." The officer barked to the fifty troops who made up the first column. With a wave of his hand, Paolo led the small squad into the darkening woods beyond the settlement. It was nearly 1900 hours before a commotion ahead halted Paolo. His well-trained men drew their firearms and, on his command, moved stealthily through the brush until the lights of a camp perimeter glowed. Hollering and commotion followed.

Kneeling in the darkened woods outside a small community settlement, Paolo spied a horrific scene. In the center of the village, Motherland troops held rows of captives, their hands bound behind their backs. A large bonfire lit the area bright enough for Paolo to recognize the uniforms of Yael's sappers, all of whom had weapons drawn upon the prisoners. Creeping closer through the brush without making a sound, he could see that the prisoners were elderly, women, and young children, all weeping or pleading with their captors. No boys or men old or fit enough to defend themselves, only the vulnerable.

And no sign of Yael.

Whistling a sharp, shrill signal, the sappers turned to Paolo, their weapons drawn. To the relief of the sappers, Paolo stood and revealed himself from the shadows. One sapper whom he had never formally met stepped forward.

"Lieutenant, you're ahead of schedule. We weren't

expecting you for—"

"Where is Commander Yael?"

The sapper gulped. "He and his command crew are handling the last of the resistors, sir." He motioned between two houses to a looming barn at the edge of town, bordering on a field hidden in the twilight shadows.

Something wasn't adding up.

"Where are the men?"

The question appeared to startle the sapper. He looked from side to side, parsing his words carefully before speaking.

"Commander Yael gave us the order, sir. We were told to secure the village and neutralize the threat."

The threat? Paolo looked around. The village was simple—no sign of advanced farm equipment, let alone any technology. It was in far better repair than the poor, decrepit settlements they had seen along the way. These people were subsistence farmers, hardly brigands.

Paolo looked at the row of prisoners. One woman had fallen to her knees, despondent over the loss of her loved ones, mumbling over and over for the sappers to finish it. He turned to the sapper and seized him by the throat, causing the officer's eyes to bulge.

"Lower your weapons. None of these people are to be harmed."

The sapper squeaked in Paolo's tight grasp, enough for Paolo to see he understood.

Paolo strode across the village center toward the barn. A tiny glow through the slatted boards guided him as the squad behind him loosened the bonds of the prisoners who continued to wail in the darkness.

The barn door was open. Paolo dropped his backpack and drew his weapon, peeking around the corner into the open bay. A team of oxen were secured in stalls to the left, rustling as though they were frightened by the events of the day. At the rear, beneath a lantern dangling from a crossbeam, two figures were writhing in the haymow. Paolo inched closer without making a sound until he was an arm's length from Yael and the woman fighting beneath him. He cocked his gun and the woman shrieked. Yael whipped around to see the barrel trained between his eyes.

"Lieutenant... You weren't expected for—"

Paolo pulled the trigger, splattering the back half of Yael's head all over the mow. The woman passed out, her naked body wilting into the bed of hay as her attacker crumpled in a bloody heap. The oxen bellowed in a deep baritone in their stalls. Paolo reached for the torn blouse and draped it over the young woman's torso.

You are to secure the settlement without bloodshed, Paolo had instructed Commander Yael before the sappers left Motherland. *Defend yourselves, if necessary, but do not harm the peasants. I will assess the situation upon my arrival.* Yael had agreed, but Paolo never fully trusted him. The colonel had assigned Yael to lead Paolo's advance sappers. Paolo had relieved him of his duty.

As he turned to leave the barn, he spied a heap to his left, the answer to his question of the whereabouts of the men. There had to be thirty or more twisted bodies in the pile. With Yael dead, the surviving sappers were going to have to answer for the crimes committed in this place. And for all the crimes committed on their path of devastation.

On the haymow, the young woman whimpered. Paolo approached her softly, holstering his weapon. As she gained consciousness, she shrieked at his sight as he raised his hands in a gesture of surrender.

"I am not going to hurt you. Your youth and elderly are safe now, I assure you." Paolo felt the hollowness of his words.

The woman shook her head violently as she fastened

her shirt and readjusted her skirt. Paolo noticed open gashes on her cheeks, and her left eye was swollen almost shut. There was nothing he could do in this moment, or ever, to calm her or reassure her that the danger had passed. Paolo looked down at his uniform, the same issue as that of Yael. Except Yael's pants were around his waist, and he was soaked in the blood of his gaping gunshot wound.

This was a mission to secure potable water. Motherland's table was showing increasing levels of contaminants, the same as the neighbouring communities who were suffering from New Inland industrial runoff. The Motherland ancestors hadn't traveled thousands of miles, following *La Golondriña* to their new home, only for the neighbouring superstructure to render it uninhabitable. It was a noble mission.

Paolo couldn't allow it to be tainted by the actions of a rapist and murderer. He didn't know how to make it right, either.

The sun rose on the fifth day through thin cloud cover. At Paolo's instruction, the survivors were gathered into one of the houses and given medical care, food, and water. The remaining sappers from Yael's command were assigned to the other farmhouse under strict guard from Paolo's first column. The interrogation that followed left Paolo with more questions than answers.

"Commander Yael started out just fine," one of the sappers explained to Paolo as he twiddled his fingers and glanced about nervously. The engineer was pale and sweating profusely. "We were just coming into the badlands and some brigands attacked. We lost one of our own, but we killed the lot of them, ten—no, eleven in all. We buried the bodies and made camp for the night. But when we awoke, the bodies were dug up. Reapers, sir.

They're everywhere! And Commander Yael wasn't the same after that."

The sapper went on to explain that the commander insisted the poor settlers in the old farmhouse were Reapers and ordered their slaughter immediately. Yael painted the Reaper symbol on the wall as a warning to the hooded creatures to stay away. "It was like he was offering up a sacrifice to them," the sapper babbled. "We took what little food they had and moved on. The commander just got worse and worse. And we all started to feel feverish, one by one. We lost two from sickness, but Yael wouldn't let us bury them. So, we laid them to rest in that cabin and burned it to the ground so that the Reapers wouldn't have anything to steal." Paolo's stomach churned.

"Those Reapers, they gave us red tide, sir. You need to get away from here. The water source... It's not safe."

Paolo heaved his chair and stormed out of the farmhouse. He summoned his officers to test the local water table. Within the hour, the tests confirmed his worst fears. Too many microbes.

All of this, for nothing.

Worse, there was no water source to replenish the canteens. Paolo gathered his senior officers. One thousand had left Motherland five days ago; seventy-six had not survived the march through the badlands. And they were at least two days out from the next passable water source.

Five more days for the journey home, and he knew his casualty count would increase. And what to do with the sappers? They were all showing early signs of red tide illness. It was only a matter of time before the Reapers would arrive in numbers, surround what remained of the settlement, and raze it to the cruel earth.

Paolo made the decision and carried it out on his own. Once all the sappers had ingested the cyanide, he looked upon their bodies in a neat row one last time. Lighting the farmhouse ablaze, he ordered the platoon to free the survivors before beginning the long trek home. He never saw Yael's victim again. She had fled sometime in the night.

Paolo Desantos was born into this.

The New Normal

Tuesday, 3 April AC 0245
Government Office Tenement, 0050-Block,
Capston
Phil Fox

The echo of the explosion could be heard clear across the city, from the spires of the core business sector, washing like a tidal wave through the tightly packed downtown, and through the suburbs, until it resonated off the high walls of the New Inland dome. The sound was muffled slightly in the upper levels that ringed the inner ceiling that arched above Capston, the billowing smoke rising to the gantry platforms that joined the Hanging Gardens to the superstructure's central support column. In the highest reaches, life continued, routine as always for the green thumbs, farmers, and other agriculturalists who kept the food supply synchronized with the demand of the populace below. The average citizen would be more alarmed to hear the air circulation units shift into a higher pitch. That only happened when there was a serious smoke problem.

This marked the fourth time in as many months.

Beneath the sky-high sector too distant to be seen in any detail, the panicked city folk reacted as anyone would. Cadenced cries and wailing sirens drowned the low hiss of transit vehicles as traffic snarled and chaos bloomed. Some pedestrians ran toward the epicenter. Most tried to flee the debris-littered perimeter, keeping as safe a distance as they could. Within minutes, emergency personnel outnumbered gawkers as the smoke began to clear, quickly rushing skyward as the fans worked overtime to expel the fumes.

When the fire crews finished extinguishing the blaze that devoured the exposed, fractured frame that remained, there was no trace of the four-story office complex that had occupied the space. One by one, cars slid to a stop near the police barriers, their drivers spilling into the street in hysterics, demanding to see their loved ones who had begun their workday behind desks on the second or third floor. Frantic wives pulled their hair in despair; husbands barked at the guards until they were drooling. Paramedics relayed commands and coordinated responses while dodging debris and news reporters.

From his office window, Phil Fox could swear he smelled the burning. It was impossible. The complex was airtight, adhering to strict codes, so when events such as this took place, the fire would have minimal opportunity to expand. Capston was a densely packed city, perhaps more so than the other four in the Federation of New Inland. Generations of additions to the tourist infrastructure had led to a congested downtown, pushing the residential suburbs further to the fringes of their allotted space. More residences were being built upward, with more citizens preferring to rent townhouses from the deep-pocketed business owners than build traditional-style houses. When space to build is finite, you can only look up.

The previous three incidents had caused Phil's heart to sink into his abdomen. This one did not. And that notion scared him the most.

The bombings are now commonplace. Reekan isn't wrong. This is the "new normal."

Phil continued to watch the citizens of Capston respond to the latest crisis in exasperation for nearly an hour. He'd tried every option at his disposal—at least every legal one. There was nothing more he could have done to stop it.

The buzzing of his handheld resting on the glass side table in the den had not caught his attention the first half dozen times it sounded, as he had muted the ringer so that he could pore over the digital paperwork in front of him. The document was lengthy. Reekan had prepared a diligent report, significant portions of which Phil had preferred to be omitted. Half of his work painted a grim picture of a government that couldn't ensure the safety of its people. The other half promoted the political ambitions of the chief of security. He wasn't ready to display Capston's dirty laundry to the DHC.

Phil knew what was coming. They had argued about it at length more than once.

Forty-eight hours later, Steven Reekan officially declared his candidacy for mayor. Phil Fox found out on the evening news.

A Few Repairs

Tuesday, 3 April AC 0245
Sheppard Family Inn, Capston, New Inland
Robbie Sheppard

"They hit another one, Robbie! That's the fourth, and it's a biggie—office tower on the four-hundred block! You can see it from the parking garage!"

Robbie Sheppard turned in his seat at the commotion. There was a crater where the doorknob smashed the wall every time Lorrie barged into his shop. Robbie always meant to repair it, just like a lot of other jobs that seemed to be piling up since his father passed. And there were really no excuses. Plenty of scrap sheet metal was lying around the shop, left over from countless projects over the years at the Sheppard Family Inn. Four years later, the haphazard mess was only partially reorganized, with half the square footage comfortably open for Robbie's bike repair bench. "Would you please watch the door?"

Gasping for breath, Lorrie leaned his left side into the doorframe, ignoring his brother's plea.

"Come on, Warren's filming it. They have the Defense Corps responders coming in and everything! This is the closest one yet!"

Robbie sighed, dropping the ratchet on the table beneath his upside-down Velo racing bike. Lately, the only thing that snapped Lorrie out of his perpetual sixteen-year-old attitude was the news of terrorist attacks, the only source of excitement on this side of town, it would seem.

"You do realize people are dying, right?"

Lorrie huffed, hunching his shoulders as if he were

saying, "What can I do?"

"Come on! The others were too far away to see, but this one you can smell the smoke—it's that close! And you could stand a break from that bike anyway."

"Fine, fine..." Robbie gave up and followed his brother up the stairs. He grimaced again at the damage Lorrie's entrance had inflicted on the wall.

Emerging from the front office and into the lobby, Lorrie raced ahead. He blasted past his brother Cadlen and thrust the plexiglass double doors open wide. Cadlen's ash-brown hair rustled in his wake. Not that the youngest Sheppard noticed or cared about the commotion; he just sat there in his favourite plush chair, scribbling away in his sketch pad. Of course, he was used to his brother's dramatic entrances and departures. They all were.

"You don't want to go see the disaster out there, Cad?" Robbie asked.

Cadlen dismissed the notion with a slight shrug. His expressions were often louder than the words he chose not to say.

"Yeah," Robbie said. "I hear you." After four explosions in four months, the whole thing was starting to feel like a routine.

The doors were closed by the time Robbie arrived in the lobby. Lorrie had already disappeared into the crowd gathering in the street outside the Sheppard Family Inn. Despite its name, it was actually a hotel. Robbie's father once claimed that an inn sounded cozier, like the ones he'd visited in his youth. In reality, it was a two-story unit with fifty empty guest rooms full of missed opportunities and disappointment. It was easy to dismiss the lack of guests as a direct result of the attacks, but Robbie couldn't lie to himself. The business had been dipping long before any of that; his mother and father's business acumen was sorely missed.

Robbie opted to stay inside. He peered into the growing chaos on the street from behind the safety of the durable, transparent plexiglass door. The television monitor mounted above the faux fireplace ran emergency footage of the unfolding situation. For a second, Robbie thought he saw Lorrie's sidekick, Warren, in the crowd, aiming his handheld at the first responders diving in and out of the billowing smoke and debris.

The scrolling news ticker along the bottom fourth of the screen alternated between market stocks, the ongoing coverage of the fourth Capston attack, and the latest speculation of Le Renard's involvement.

Le Renard's crime syndicate was known to operate outside the New Inland dome, but it had yet to be implicated in the three prior attacks. Talk television loved a juicy angle. The notorious human trafficker and contraband smuggler known only as Le Renard was easy to blame when it appeared the city council had scarce other leads. Robbie wasn't convinced the Reapers were involved, despite their cross-shaped symbol allegedly appearing at the blast sites. That just made for good tabloid reporting.

Robbie looked around the lobby. Apart from his silent brother, all he saw was more maintenance that was not getting itself done. The paint was out of fashion, more in line with the early 0200s when the inn was built, well before his parents, Robert and Julia, had taken possession. The fireplace no longer displayed artificial dancing flames, as it had when all four Sheppard kids used to cuddle around it. It had been four years and a few months since the siblings last lived under the same roof.

Or in the same city.

Or under the same dome.

"Cad, make sure you're drawing pictures big enough that you won't be able to see the unfaded paint underneath. I can't afford to repaint this year!"

Cadlen smirked.

"I'm going back down to the shop. Let me know if anything important happens."

Flashing a thumbs-up at Robbie, Cadlen continued his artwork in silence. Despite countless options in the avatar bank, Robbie couldn't set his handheld to read Cadlen's messages in a believable voice simulation. None carried the right tone. On those rare occasions when his brother chose to use his own voice, it felt like something special. Robbie couldn't remember the last time Cadlen used his words. It was most likely before their father passed.

Opening the shop door, Robbie propped a brick behind it. That would stop Lorrie from causing further damage. That scrap metal his dad had insisted on keeping was a bandage solution. His handheld buzzed on the workbench, vibrating the ratchet and its loose attachments.

With a swipe of his thumb, the screen blinked to life. The secure channel required a six-digit code, which Robbie easily keyed with his index and middle fingertips. He swallowed as the code was accepted. Every time Crystal sent money a knot formed and tightened in his stomach.

3 April AC0245 — Deposit: C Sheppard $4,500

Nowhere in the abrupt communiqué did the Allen Consortium identification appear. Nor did the source of the transfer. But this was by design. Earnings skimmed from Crystal Sheppard's tutoring would be filtered through secondary accounts, dressed up as business revenue. Any alerted inspector would surely prove them fraudulent. The key was to make certain no one was alerted. The Allens were nothing if not meticulous.

Within seconds of the confirmation, the message deleted itself, not so much of a wisp of digital smoke to be traced.

"Thanks, Crys," Robbie whispered to himself as if anyone on the outside preoccupied by the terrorist attack would be concerned in the slightest about his exiled sister. Or her efforts to keep the Sheppard Family Inn afloat despite its fiscal and spiritual drowning.

The Accuser

"One more, Mr. Garcia."

Only a few patrons in the tavern remained as Elbi Garcia wiped the unoccupied tables. The lights were dimmed in the lateness of the day, bathing the quaint establishment in a soft glow but leaving the rear booth section in darkness. The slow rain outside kept Captain Tomás Alvara inside for one last drink. It was a long walk home to the barracks from the less-advantaged east side of Motherland.

The barkeep nodded and ducked behind the counter, littered with empty beer mugs and appetizer baskets. Tomás couldn't imagine many of the locals could afford food. The dregs of the ale kegs would be more than enough to keep them coming. It was a convenient arrangement. Most of the recruits for the Motherland armed forces came from this side of town. Cheap ale and patriotism. Whatever it takes.

"One more before you ship off?" Garcia placed a tall stein frothing above the rim onto the table.

Tomás wiped the foam from his lip. "There won't be a decent drink from here to the badlands. May as well enjoy it while I can."

Garcia laughed. "Come now, surely the colonel will supply you and the troops with cold beer?"

Tomás nearly spit out the next mouthful. "Last I checked, my family name is not Desantos." He made certain the tavern was empty before offering his sarcasm. Garcia was trustworthy. These may be the only four walls in the city where Tomás was truly free.

"Well, if the colonel changes his mind, I'm sure we could work out a deal!" The barkeep winked and retreated to the pile of dirty dishware on his bar.

Fat chance.

Two weeks ago, while Paolo was leading a doomed mission into treacherous territory to find clean drinking water, Tomás Alvara was seated at this same table with four other young men from the neighbourhood. All eager recruits, with nothing to lose and immortality to gain. He was tasked with transitioning half-witted labourers into cosmopolitan transplants. They would be assigned new names. New backstories. New trades and skills, at least on paper. And they would be given the means to communicate covertly from inside New Inland via the Allen Consortium. Months of screening, weeding out the duds, and rehearsing. Mostly conducted in Elbi Garcia's establishment, long after hours and often through the night.

His recruits were successful in three campaigns of terror inside the city of Capston. The fourth, which would be the crowning achievement on Tomás's resume, was delayed until after Paolo had returned. And despite the high casualty count, Paolo, the colonel's son, was receiving a *promotion* before any blueprints for the final assault could be drawn. The nepotism reeked worse than the privies out back.

"Check, Elbi." Tomás gestured with a hand wave as he swallowed back the last gulp, silt must and all. He swore that most of the alcohol hid in the haze of the last drops.

Outside the tavern, the rain began to pick up in intensity. It was half-past midnight, and his dispatch was slated to leave by six. "Come on, Elbi, what's the holdup..."

The barkeep appeared like a phantom on his right side rather than from the bar. "Oh, sorry. I didn't see you there."

Elbi smiled and set a small wooden serving tray on the table. A paper slip was perched on top of a metal coaster of some sort. Without a word, the barkeep retreated behind the bar and down the stairwell into the wine cellar. Tomás felt the hairs on his neck rise. Something wasn't quite right.

Snatching the paper bill, Tomás narrowed his eyes to read the faint handwriting.

I'm sorry, old friend. Drinks are on the house.

On the serving tray, what Tomás thought was a coaster was in fact a pendant shaped like a cross, only the topmost stave was rounded like a loop being swallowed by the rest. He spent so much time learning to hate the Reaper symbol that he forgot how much it terrified him.

"Show yourself." One of them was lurking in the shadows. Possibly more. Tomás's skin crawled at the thought of their proximity. Poor Elbi; the man had to have been scared out of his wits. No matter. If the filthy creature made a move, he was only a few feet from the bar where Elbi kept a loaded firearm. Reapers may have been impervious to radiation and diseases, but they could take a bullet like anyone.

"That won't be necessary." The voice could easily have been reading his mind. "Just pretend I'm not even here, Alvara."

"*Captain* Alvara, Reaper."

The voice emanating from the darkened booths chuckled. "And to you, I would be *Brother of the Ansati*, but who cares for formalities?"

Swallowing dry, Tomás turned to face the darkness and the lurking specter. In the farthest booth, he could see the outline of a hooded character, hands folded gently on the tabletop.

"How many?"

"I am alone, captain. You have my word."

Tomás didn't trust his word.

"What do you want, *Brother*?"

"That's more like it. I have information that may prove valuable to you."

The captain leaned back into the wicker. "So valuable you had to seek me out in a dive bar?"

The figure nodded his hooded head. "You could say as much. Suffice that it would be best served to reach *your* ears, not the lieutenant's."

Is that so? You're on a short leash, Reaper.

"Out with it."

Though the interloper was still veiled in darkness, Tomás imagined a smug look of satisfaction on his face.

"I know plenty about you, captain. Purebred Motherlander, lineage back to the exodus—what, eight generations? Your family blood surely forms a trail that followed *La Golondriña*. Yet..."

The pause was deliberate, for dramatic effect. "Yet, you follow the command of an *orphan*. You are aware the colonel was an adopted ward of His Eminence, are you not?"

It was common knowledge that Colonel Tirel Desantos rose through the ranks from his position among the wards, those adopted by the sovereign and groomed for service within the royal palace and the Council of Regents. It wasn't unheard of. But it was indeed rare in Motherland history.

"Go on."

"How unnerving it must be to watch all your effort, all your fealty to *your* country, be cast aside by an adoptee and his mongrel son."

"Your point—and make it fast."

"I have information that will be of considerable benefit to you."

Tomás felt a pit growing in his stomach. He panned around the room for unseen witnesses. He would have given anything for Elbi to come back upstairs right now.

"Relax, captain. The door is locked. We are alone."

Tomás exhaled. "You were saying?"

"As you know, my brethren are well connected. We see and hear more than you could imagine. The Allens wish they had our eyes and ears! I have it on good authority that your colonel's son means to betray his father."

Paolo Desantos, a turncoat?

"Impossible." Even Tomás wasn't convinced by his own tone.

"Is it? What if I told you Tirel Desantos murdered *his* own father? Apples rarely fall far from their branches, captain."

Tomás had heard the tale, whispered among the youth in years past, only to be hushed by Tirel Desantos's ascendancy to De Léon's right hand. But it was all just urban legend; a fairytale designed to build his cult of personality. Tomás never supposed it could have been true.

"That's just a folk story. You wouldn't be so brave to tell it to the colonel, would you, Reaper?"

The hooded man shifted and stood from his seat, emerging into the faint light. The hood still veiled his face, but his earth-coloured tunic and trousers revealed how easily he could have moved about the streets undetected. It was the nature of his kind to take on the guise of locals and mingle in the crowds. His hood and cape were standard issue to the field workers to protect them from blazing sun and driving rain. Tomás wished he had one for his walk home.

"As a matter of fact, I have indeed told it to him. And for my efforts, I received a sound beating and a week in a cell, if you'll remember."

Andreas.

The beating had been more than sound. He had watched the colonel pummel the Reaper within a gasp of his last breath. Shackled to the stone wall, the silver pendant, now resting on the serving tray, was hung over his neck. Just being a Reaper was punishable by public display. But to accuse Paolo Desantos of *treason*—surely that would have warranted a death sentence. Upon his release, the colonel had warned Andreas the next offense would result in public shaming in the pillory. It was still too lenient, as far as Tomás was concerned.

"I'm not buying it, Andreas. If I were the colonel, you would have been skinned alive."

The hooded man shrugged. "Must have been my lucky day."

That was an understatement.

"Let's say that you did look into the colonel's eyes and utter that garbage. Surely you're mad for even suggesting as much."

Andreas laughed, but not in a manner that suggested madness. "I've spent years in the Ossuary of *Moab*, surrounded by the dead, captain. You know nothing of madness. But what I offer you tonight is true. You can believe me, or not."

Tomás didn't know what an ossuary was, let alone "Moab." For all he knew, it could have been part of Andreas's fantasies.

"Make it quick. It's a hard rain out there, and I could use your cloak."

Andreas leaned forward, throwing back his hood. His hair was scraggly, matted as though he slept in muck. His hazel-green eyes, darkening by the second, glared back at Tomás.

"Paolo Desantos is receiving his promotion in a few short days. It's like this, Captain Alvara. If you don't expose him before his coronation, I will do it for you."

Eclipse of the Son

Sábado, 7 abril NE 267
(Saturday, 7 April AC 0245)
L'Estadio Real, Free City of Motherland
Captain Tomás Alvara

From his vantage point high on the uppermost rim of *L'Estadio Real*, Captain Tomás Alvara panned through the Motherland spectators. They peppered the sloped seating from the nosebleeds to the arena floor. Fluttering flags and a patchwork of coloured shawls created an oval mosaic that funneled to the stadium grounds where the parade passed by. The music of the percussionists, interjected by the brass section, echoed around the rim, the sound waves washing into each other like shifting tidal waters.

Tomás pivoted the sniper rifle on its tripod as he stared through the scope. He lingered for an extended second on a small cluster of revelers and cursed under his breath. Their wide-brimmed hats made it difficult to note the features of any one individual. As low cloud cover rolled in, only a few removed their headwear. The perimeter of unseen soldiers throughout the stadium kept scanning for anyone who didn't fit the Motherland profile. Tomás's eyes strained as they moved from person to person.

The radio bud crackled in his left ear.

"Copy that. Continue to sweep your sections."

Tomás was one of five sharpshooters with sights trained on the section of the stadium floor closest to the raised stage, upon which the podium and microphone stand awaited the introduction of Colonel Tirel Desantos, who was still making his way through the tunnels of his sanctuary. As the marching band passed the royal balcony, midway along the oblong southern side of the oval and directly across from his position, Tomás panned to His Eminence De Léon. Slouched in the deep plush cushions and surrounded by the Regents in their own rigid, pedestrian seats, De Léon grinned as he waved his index fingers, like an off-tempo metronome, to the rhythm of the bass drums. The four-starred lapel on his ceremonial military dress drew bile to the back of Tomás's throat.

Colonel-in-chief. Right...

Refocusing his sight, he set it on the section nearest the stage. This section was reserved for the wards of the state. They'd already been ushered in before the colonnade began to cycle around the grounds. The colonel had been very clear: "The children are the future, our most valuable resource." This philanthropy was a crucial element in the sovereign's brand power, even if Tomás wasn't convinced. In practice, however, it had proven a valuable recruitment apparatus. "Give the most vulnerable the most hope, and they will be yours forever."

Whether that philosophy came from De Léon or from the colonel was never clear. Either way, the menagerie of orphans was an expensive liability.

Hovering above the dais was the insignia of *La Golondriña*, wings outstretched as the profile of the bird's head gazed left, ceremoniously arranged to look not only in the direction of His Eminence's box, but farther south. Looking beyond the walls of the city, over miles of crooked forest and fledgling settlements. Past the ruins of Allentown. Past the shorn perimeter of the superstructure. Past the filaments of magna-rails and graded roads splayed like spider webs. The gaze of the winged symbol of Motherland fixated on the towering dome-shaped superstructure of the Federation of New Inland. The spread-eagled swallow never took its eyes off the menacing colossus. If only it could spot an intruder in the sea of colour on the stadium floor.

The colonel emerged from the shadows, alone. He walked onto the stage to the explosion of cheers from the wards beneath him and the congregation in the stands, while the band ushered the infantry, twenty abreast and kicking high with every step. Tomás watched the cavalry follow, sabred officers jostling along with the trotting of their mounts, as they looked toward His Eminence. Roaring combustible engines heralded the arrival of the artillery vehicles, crawling two by two, canvas topped and deep forest green. It took several minutes before the exhaust wafted to Tomás's perch, at which point the colonel had stationed himself at the microphone, squealing feedback careening off the stadium walls.

"Oye! Oye! El Canto de la Golondriña!"

The band burst into the anthem of the nation as the spectators stood, hands on hearts, while the chorus filled the overcast sky, loud enough to be heard all the way to New Inland. *Hear our song...*

The colonel mouthed the lyrics as though every voice were pouring from him. At least his broken accent couldn't be discerned that way. Tomás swiveled his rifle to the box of His Eminence De Léon, then aimed it high above the opposite side of the stadium.

In the distance, the specter of New Inland emerged into view through the magnified scope, rising above the deep southern horizon like a smoothed-over mountain. The feat of the Five Cities' engineering didn't need to eclipse any sun to cast its shadow. Tomás refocused the sighting on his section, praying none of his subordinates noticed.

At the conclusion of the anthem, the band relaxed and the infantry fell into ease at the beckoning of the drill sergeant. The colonel placed his hands on the slanted surface of the podium, which held no notes for his imminent speech. The wards, ranging in age from five to fifteen, were the last to settle, falling into their predetermined positioning in front of the stage. Tomás lingered over every single ward—male, female; short, tall; hatted, shawled—scrutinizing them with about half the care expressed by his superiors.

If the colonel expected him to find Reapers, they would almost certainly not be among the children. They weren't even known to count kids in their numbers.

"Your Eminence, *El Regencia*, brothers, sisters, and children of Motherland, I bid you welcome!"

The stadium erupted once again with applause. The colonel, trim in his sharp-cut and pressed deep-tan fatigues, which most likely saw zero field action, smiled as the adulation roared from the masses.

"On the eighth day of *marzo, nuestro año de eminencia* 267. The fourth battalion dispatched on a mission to secure a water table, untainted by the New Inland elitists." Colonel Desantos turned his head in the same direction as *La Golondriña*. Tomás watched as the crowd did the same, as though all their necks were synchronized.

The crowd erupted once again, attuned to the cues the colonel had instilled from his past speeches; the audience had been as well-trained as the armed forces. These outbursts of cheer were shorter and fell into attentive silence in a matter of seconds.

"Through broken land, under a cruel sun, harried by brigands and Reapers from behind every rock and bush, we marched on until our mission was accomplished. One thousand of our bravest left our gates that day. But not all made it home."

Everyone knew that the lowered tone of the colonel's last statement meant for silence to be maintained. Tomás continued his surveillance of the wards as the pause lingered for maximum effect.

"On the fourteenth day of *marzo*, two hundred forty did not come home to their families. To *our* family! Those who did, returned no longer only men, but heroes." It was no coincidence the colonel failed to mention that of those two hundred forty, an entire squad of sappers and their commander did not survive. Most of the adoring crowd were ecstatic over the prospect of clean water. Tomás still wondered about the cost in Motherland lives paid to achieve it.

Tomás trained his scope on a taller ward, hat removed to expose his close-cut walnut-brown hair. It was unusual for a ward his age and height to still have hair so short. Assessing the unnamed youth to be no threat, Tomás moved on to the next ward. The radio in his ear cackled as his senior officers reported, none of whom was alerted to anything suspicious. The air began to warm as the cloud cover thinned from grey to white.

"On this day, we acknowledge those who gave their lives in defense of our nation, and we celebrate the achievement of one man who coordinated this operation to ensure our survival."

The wards could hardly contain their excitement, tittering amongst themselves as the colonel looked over his right shoulder, back at the shadowed rear of the stage. Tomás panned back across the youths.

"Today, His Eminence Santiago De Léon confers the rank of lieutenant colonel upon…"

Every pair of eyes widened in anticipation. Every breath held on the light breeze as the sun burst through the thinned cloud layer as though it were switched on by some divine lever.

"…Paolo Desantos!"

Tomás had learned how to roll his eyes without losing focus. Only a few years ago, it was he who was standing to the colonel's right, on a day very similar to this one and after a speech nearly as eloquent, only delivered with more restrained conviction. His promotion to captain promised an eventual transition to lieutenant colonel. That promise remained unfulfilled. Babysitting His Eminence's "children" was not getting him any closer.

Of course, if you were the son of Colonel Tirel Desantos, promotion was going to be a path less difficult. And so, for Paolo Desantos to leapfrog from lieutenant to lieutenant colonel, bypassing the rank of captain entirely, the line of succession was in place, as if there were any doubt. In the highest reaches of the stadium, Captain Tomás Alvara could almost touch the ceiling of his career.

Stepping out from the shadow and into the pouring light of a high morning sun, Lieutenant Colonel Desantos stood, hands clasped behind his back, expression hidden behind wide, silver-mirrored aviator glasses while the masses frothed in jubilation. Colonel Desantos applauded along with the spectators as Tomás carried on with his surveillance of the unbridled wards, arms in air, shawls bunched at shoulders.

The glint of light off Paolo's sunglasses nearly distracted Tomás from another shining sparkle in the crowd at the foot of the stage. Training his scope toward the second source of reflected light, he passed the short-haired youth to the left and rested on a shorter figure who, upon closer inspection, appeared much older. With the crowd around him bustling and dancing, the intruder remained transfixed on the colonel as he pulled a metallic silver pendant from his waistband and held it high in the air.

Reaper!

Tomás's eyes widened, and he barked into the commlink. "Twelve o'clock to the colonel, ten paces out, do not shoot. Bring him in—"

Before he could complete the command, the crowd of wards took notice of the interloper holding the familiar cross-shaped Reaper insignia, its chain dangling around his wrist. The man was facing away from Tomás, but the visible lines of his raised cheeks indicated laughter.

Andreas. The Reaper was here to make good on his promise. Tomás cursed him under his breath.

The colonel must have caught on to the commotion. Tomás watched him turn to the Reaper as the band fell out of rhythm and harmony in a discordant mess. Cheers switched to panicked cries as the guards descended through the masses. A swarm of shielded troopers filled the vacuum of retreating wards, surrounding the Reaper with weapons drawn. Colonel Desantos barked over the swiped-aside microphone stand.

Tomás trained his crosshairs on the lieutenant colonel. Paolo turned and strode back into the shadows as chaos broiled throughout the stadium.

Slither back into your hole, lieutenant.

Andreas would most certainly find himself in the stocks this time. Detaching the rifle from its tripod, Tomás looked one last time toward the distant, looming superstructure of New Inland beyond the now-shuttered balcony of His Eminence De Léon. The outline faded from view as the cloud cover descended once again.

Streetcleaner

Sábado, 7 abril NE 267
(Saturday, 7 April AC 0245)
Eminence De Léon Square, Free City of
Motherland
Captain Tomás Alvara

On orders of the captain, the Motherland soldiery dispersed the crowd, filtering them from the arena and into the maze of streets. A light rain had begun to turn the dusty, mud-covered streets into muck, wagon ruts and hoof prints splotching and scarring the ground as the people veered to the grass-lined shoulders. Tomás felt the mass panic diminish with the thinning of the crowd. As the rain intensified, the chance of a large gathering in the town square lessened. It was probably for the best. After the fiasco in the stadium, he was fine with a sparse crowd to supervise.

The courtyard of the square was cobbled with soft-grey stone in a circular mosaic pattern, like a wheel if seen from high above. At the center, a raised wooden platform replaced a fountain of a swallow in flight. Indeed, throughout the town, where swallows once swooped and soared, carrion birds had taken over the skies.

Tomás entered the open space guarded by two-storied buildings, ringed with balconies and slotted window shutters. A smattering of the angriest peasants gathered as Tomás's men half-dragged the hooded Andreas across the stone-paved expanse. Up on the wooden platform, the pillory, designed for three, already secured one prisoner in the center slot. The guards rattled and unshackled the locks, lifting the topmost plank straight up. Andreas's head, tucked into the hole between those for his wrists, noodled from weakened muscles as he fell to his back. A hooded guard yanked him like a rag doll from the wooden floor, clamping him into the pillory holes farthest to the right.

Mumbling, Andreas offered no resistance, what with his hands and head jammed into a set of half-circled wood cuts. His blood hadn't had enough time to be washed away by the rain. The guards were forced to carry all 180 lbs. of him from the arena through the streets and into the stocks. One of them slid the top half of the pillory down, restraining Andreas in place, catching and pulling his hair and forcing his head skyward. The other clasped Andreas's ankles in iron shackles, ensuring that he would be limited in his ability to kick if or when he was to be loosened from his public ridicule.

"Make way! Make way!"

The crowd parted as Colonel Desantos and his flanking guards filed through, boots striking the stone like a marching band's timpani. The rain intensified as though the colonel himself had summoned it. Ascending the stairs to the surface of the gallows, Colonel Desantos stood in front of the Reaper. The two men stood eye to eye. Tomás had felt the gaze of both sets of eyes. He couldn't decide which was more intimidating.

From his vantage point at the base of the gallows, Tomás couldn't see the colonel's eyes, but he heard the words he spat at Andreas.

"You didn't believe me last time? Or do you have a death wish?"

Andreas cackled, his throat bulging and leaking blood from the splintered stock wood.

"Death... You either seek it, or you deal it!"

The colonel shifted his weight from one foot to the

other and swung at Andreas's face with an open palm. The restless crowd, sopping from the downpour, began to settle at the sight of the colonel's strike.

"Declaring your cult in plain view—now if that isn't seeking death, I don't know what is."

"Come on, colonel, I'm just trying to help make your job a little easier! So many men and women you've strung up here, so few of them actually guilty..."

Andreas shifted his eyes as far to his right as he could. The other prisoner continued to moan as the Reaper taunted him.

"Hey there, sport! Have we met? I don't remember seeing you in the graveyards digging up corpses."

The colonel thrust a gloved hand into Andreas's face, readjusting him to look forward.

"You needn't mind him. He is no Reaper."

Andreas's eyes widened. "Ah, this is the guy who claimed your boy was a Reaper, am I right? I have to say, friend, you have balls of steel!"

Tomás was present when the soldier had been dragged into the street three days earlier, fastened to the whipping post for a scourging for the ages before he was fastened into the pillory. A sideways remark that Paolo Desantos himself could have been a Reaper was enough for his platoon mates to turn him in. Tomás watched as the rain dribbled over his face, flowing red as the bleeding from his mouth coalesced. It wouldn't be long.

"Why come back, Andreas? Why today?"

Tomás wondered the same. Andreas knew he would be captured, then tortured in the public pillory. So many times, the colonel threatened a death sentence, when everyone knew the Reaper wasn't really going to face the ultimate penalty. But what if this time it was different? Colonel Desantos's glare was deadlier than Tomás's crosshairs, or at least for better men. Something had to keep Andreas more valuable on this side of the dirt.

Tomás didn't dare look away for fear of missing out on the big reveal.

The slanderous prisoner began to wheeze.

"You may as well let this one go, colonel. You have your main attraction now—why not release poor Barabbas here?"

The colonel burst into laughter. "I'm familiar with your fairy tale. You think you get to play the part of saviour, do you?"

Forcing his irises down from their skyward gaze, Andreas narrowed his eyes into slits.

"I could have saved you, colonel. But it's hard to do that with your neck in a noose."

"I'm not the one who needs saving."

The colonel lashed a backhand across Andreas's face, leaving an open gash on his cheek. The man clasped into the torture device only laughed louder. Tomás felt increasingly uncomfortable with the resilience of the interloper. Reapers were often described in folk tales as supernatural beings. Andreas's resolve only served to confirm those fears to the crowd that had gathered, huddling under their shawls.

"There's room for one more. Perhaps you could bring your boy in to fasten here beside me—before he does it to you!"

Tomás expected the colonel to strike Andreas with enough force to cleave his head from his shoulders. Instead, he calmly reached into the right pocket of his jacket. The silver pendant did not shine as it did when Andreas clutched it in his clenched fist earlier in the arena.

The colonel stepped close to Andreas until the words the pair spoke to each other were no longer audible from the foot of the gallows. Tomás watched as the colonel placed the sharp corner of one of the cross-shaped pendant arms against the soft tissue between Andreas's brows. With surgical precision, he carved into the flesh a crude rendering of the cross, gushing a torrent of blood over Andreas's face, bubbling in the froth of spittle on his lips.

Andreas gargled in a cacophony of ecstasy laced with agony. The colonel stepped back, looping the chain of the pendant over his head as the bloodied symbol hung with the weight of his cruelty. The prisoner to the left no longer made any sound, his body limp behind the wooden slats of the pillory.

"Any last words?"

Andreas blinked blood from his eyes.

"Fitting act from such an apostle…"

The rain fell hard on the dispersing crowd. Colonel Desantos motioned for the guards to remove the other prisoner. As they lifted the plank, Andreas's head loosened from its forced incline.

"Your kin can have your Barabbas. In a few days, they can have yours as well," said the colonel. Tomás sighed. Andreas's fate was sealed. The colonel meant for him to suffer in his restraints, under the elements, until he hung lifeless like the dead prisoner the guards were dragging away. Tomás would personally drag Andreas's corpse out of the city for the Reapers to claim, as they did with all disposed bodies. The colonel spat in front of his quarry before leaving the platform.

"Bathe in the rain, Colonel Desantos! Let it wash the streets clean. And remember, after the floods, the final cleansing is fire…" Andreas croaked as the top slat clamped tighter around his neck. The colonel ignored him. Tomás couldn't. The Reaper's words made his skin crawl.

Tomás stayed long enough to ensure the crowd had completely vacated the square, since the spectacle was over. Blood from the open wound on Andreas's forehead leached in thin veins off the edge of the platform and onto the stone. Tomás vowed to himself he would return at the break of dawn, to be there when Andreas drew his last wretched breath. The carrion birds overhead would surely pluck out his eyes if they had half the chance.

At sunset on the third day, Andreas was still alive.

Tomás unlocked his leg shackles, and with two hefty guards, hoisted the top pillory board away, freeing the weakened Andreas to collapse to the gallows. Neither of the guards made any attempt to support him. The Reaper was, after all, a carrier of disease, both in the blood and in the soul. The shiny silver pendant that dangled around his neck clattered to the platform. If left where it had fallen, it would have remained there for days. Who would want to touch it?

Andreas reached for his talisman with the shaking of a dementia patient, curling his cracked hand around its shaft and tucking it into the band of his waist. Tomás informed him that the imminent exile to Kayewat would be his last. Upon arrival, Andreas would be stamped with the permanent Kayewati emblem, marking him as a citizen of the frozen, lawless dome on the northern frontier, yet preventing entry into any other civilized structure on the continent The colonel's mercy had saved him from the buzzards, but his cruelty had condemned him to something worse. Short of execution, Tomás accepted this fate as the next best thing.

"I don't know why Colonel Desantos doesn't eliminate you, wretch. But if I ever see you again, know that I will." If Andreas ever summoned his Reaper ability to escape Kayewat and return, it would be to his doom. Tomás wouldn't wait for the colonel's approval. Tomás's threat was a thinly veiled dare.

With sheer willpower, the freed Reaper found his balance and stretched upward onto his feet, hobbling to the stairs like a newborn calf, only to tumble to the paved stones below. He waved off the guards before they could help him up, not that they had any desire to touch him. Tomás didn't have to make the travel arrangements for Andreas's shipping to Kayewat. Colonel Desantos had already taken care of contacting the Allens and paying for the weeklong voyage.

"Just be sure you report your good deeds to your new superior," Andreas wheezed as the guards dragged him to his feet. Tomás laughed. If only the Reaper knew how much he wanted to clear the air with Paolo Desantos. For three days, the captain kept his vigil at the pillory, through much rain and little sun. The new lieutenant colonel did not show himself even once. How could Paolo be so indifferent to Andreas ruining his promotion?

Tomás decided it was time to pay the colonel a visit. He had many questions.

Reprieve

Martes, 10 abril NE 267 (Tuesday, 10 April, AC
0245)
Residence of Colonel Desantos
Free City of Motherland
Captain Tomás Alvara

The guards saluted and each pulled one of the heavy
doors to Colonel Desantos's private chamber. Tomás had
been inside once before. His encounter with the Reaper
in the same tavern where he met with his operatives
incognito was a little too discomforting. The message
delivered that night was even more so.

The colonel once confided in the promising young
captain that he had a credible, if slightly disturbed,
contact among the hooded druids. Promises of safe
passage through Reaper lands, intelligence on which
nearby settlements could be taken with ease or left alone.
It all sounded fine, except for the *Reaper* part.
Generations of Motherland children were raised to fear
them. And suddenly, one of them was trustworthy.

The Reaper's name was Andreas.

Tomás's first visit to Colonel Desantos's underground
office was to inform him of his encounter with Andreas.
The message was an ultimatum. Tell the colonel that his
son was a traitor, or else. Those chickens came home to
roost in the middle of the allegedly traitorous Lieutenant
Paolo Desantos's promotion ceremony. He wouldn't dare
show himself, the colonel had boasted. Tomás had been
almost convinced by the colonel's bellowed voice. Still,
there was a tinge of uncertainty, which was confirmed
when Tomás was assigned to lead the security for Paolo's

big day.

Bring him to me, *alive*, the colonel had ordered.

Alive?

Colonel Tirel Desantos had no problem executing dissenters for lesser crimes. Tomás failed to see how any value the filthy creature might have had justified leniency.

It was three days ago that Andreas was bound, blindfolded, and heaved into the back of a cargo truck, shipped out of Motherland to an airstrip for his condemnation to Kayewat. Three nights Tomás spent at Elbi Garcia's tavern, staring into the booth Andreas had occupied that night they had spoken. Three days to be sure the Reaper hadn't escaped his guards only to come back and haunt the city. Kayewat was a fitting destination, in a way. An entire dome filled to the skylight with criminals and lowlifes. With any luck, the Kayewati would swallow the vermin whole before his stamp ink dried.

Tomás heard the heavy double doors clang shut, reducing the dimness of the light inside Colonel Desantos's chamber to a single track in the center of the room. On either side, Tomás couldn't tell if the bookshelves contained anything, let alone books. At least His Eminence De Léon kept volumes open on his desk to give the illusion that he was a man of letters. The colonel was indifferent at best when it came to history.

At the rear of the room, behind a table draped with fabric of some camouflaged dark colour, the colonel hunched forward in a high-backed, rigid throne. The furnishings appeared to have been salvaged from an old church. When the colonel spoke, his voice shook, echoing louder in the empty, airtight chamber.

"Captain Alvara. I would like to speak to you about a number of concerns I have."

There was no formal greeting, no platitudes, no

cordiality. Tomás swallowed. Andreas had managed to not only infiltrate the city walls, but appear in a crowd of wards at the foot of the stage. The colonel had not broached the issue with Tomás until now. Almost a full week had passed, and no summons.

Tomás paused to be sure his next words were safe enough to say, even if it was pointless to worry.

"Colonel, I take full responsibility for the breach in security. I have disciplined the men harshly—"

"If I were interested in discipline, Tomás, you would have been in the empty pillory hole beside the Reaper." Colonel Desantos stood, allowing the light to reveal his face. His eyes were naturally wide, but the captain knew they were even wider when he was suppressing any sort of rage. Instinctively, Tomás broke eye contact.

"You were right to make a public example of Andreas, sir."

The colonel's chest expanded as he drew a deep breath. Tomás felt his temperature rising despite the cool climate of the underground chamber. The colonel didn't answer, so Tomás continued.

"Surely, he has arrived in Kayewat by now—never to return, I hope. But if I may, colonel?"

"Spit it out, Tomás." The colonel was giving him rare latitude. It was now or never to ask.

"Why did you let him live?"

For any common man, hanging in a pillory out in the elements for three days would have been a death sentence. For Andreas, it was an inconvenience. For three days, Tomás had watched the Reaper laughing as blood poured out of the carved symbol on his forehead. The prisoner cackled through frothing crimson spittle, amused by his captors' efforts to break him. Andreas would have been in for quite a surprise when the Kayewati stamper injected the poisonous concoction of inks into his right forearm. Or maybe he would enjoy the searing under his skin. No one of sound mind should, anyway.

Seconds felt like half an hour before the colonel responded. He began to pace, shifting his blazing eyes away from the light.

"Andreas is a dangerous man, Tomás. But he also has access to information that is impossible to source otherwise. Even the Allens don't know what the Reapers know."

There was logic behind that reasoning. The Reapers flitted in and out of sight like wisps of smoke. They raided graveyards, stole bodies, erased history, and wiped their tracks clean in the process. As a boy, Tomás shuddered under his blankets in fear of the imaginary Reaper in his closet. Perhaps the colonel kept a delicate balance by allowing Andreas to stay alive. Still, the picture was unclear.

"Once inside Kayewat, travel anywhere else will become difficult," Tomás reasoned. "The stamp will guarantee passage into the domes impossible."

"If only that were true."

Tomás blinked. "Colonel?" Everyone knew Kayewati stamps were detectable by all other domes on the continent. Once Andreas was inked, he was marked for life.

Colonel Desantos ignored him. "I am disappointed that Andreas was able to fool your men so easily. But I understand, Tomás. Reapers are ghosts. And you can't keep ghosts out if they want in badly enough."

That was a relief. Tomás wasn't used to the colonel showing understanding.

"You have punished your men enough. The threat has been mitigated, Tomás. It is time to refocus on our goals."

Relief washed over Tomás and he straightened, eager to move on from the incident. Thrice he had led incursions inside New Inland, in the city of Capston, where tourism drove the local economy. Three different targets. An office building, an eatery, and a shopping center. Each with its own challenges, and each successfully hit. The time for rehearsal was finished. The real target was imminent.

"I agree, colonel. We can begin to plan the operation immediately."

Colonel Desantos stopped pacing and smiled. "Yes, Tomás. In fact, the planning has already begun."

Tomás cursed himself under his breath. Of course, the colonel was already thinking ahead. If his men had been able to capture the Reaper ahead of Paolo's promotion, the mission could have been underway. Tomás could have been using his New Inland alias to slip through the main entrance, and again in the central causeway that connected the five cities under one dome. He would have been established in the abandoned hotel. His team would be finalizing details and arming the explosives. It had taken months just to secure the materials necessary to assemble them. The devastation would be magnificent. Tomás sighed at the fantasy.

"Captain Alvara, you will meet me tomorrow, at 1600 hours, at the gymnasium."

Tomorrow? *Why not here? Now?*

"1600 hours, of course, colonel." Tomás's voice trembled, and he hoped the colonel didn't notice. If he did, he didn't say as much.

"You have something else you would like to say, captain?"

Tomás had plenty he would like to say, but the moment had passed. He knew he didn't have the courage to ask if what Andreas had suggested about Lieutenant Colonel Paolo Desantos was true. What actually happened on the march? How did Commander Yael die? Why did so many not come home? Tomás asked the colonel none of these questions.

Four successful missions into the belly of the New Inland beast, and none of his men suffered even a scratch. Yet *Paolo* received the promotion. Tomás swallowed his questions like a fistful of razor blades.

"No, colonel. Tomorrow, 1600 hours, sir."

"Very good. Dismissed."

Tomás stiffened and raised a salute as Colonel Desantos sat back on his throne. As he approached the chamber doors, they creaked open as though the guards outside were listening.

He would not ask the colonel any of those questions. But Paolo would have to answer them one day. Once Captain Tomás Alvara returned from Motherland's greatest victory, he would look the lieutenant colonel in the eye as an equal.

Biological Machine

Tomás expected to meet with the colonel and the Kayewati in the colonel's office: standard briefing of the logistics, cursory introductions, then dismissal to make the preparations. So, when he received the message that the meeting would take place at the gymnasium, Tomás wasn't sure what to expect. He skipped supper and brought along his athletic gear. Perhaps his new partner would work out with him for a few hours as they got to know each other.

Inside the gymnasium complex, Tomás made for the weight room. At 1700h, the facility was atypically empty. Usually that was a sign that Paolo was on-site—he preferred to exercise alone. The colonel always saw to it that the facility was empty for his son's training regimen.

Prone, on a padded bench and midway through a rigorous set of 40 lb. dumbbell flyes, Tomás spied whom he presumed was the Kayewati. Trying not to stare, Tomás noted his taut physique, unblemished by tattoos or stamps. Whoever he was, he was focused on pushing his workout to the limit, which evidently was high. The man didn't look up. Tomás wasn't sure if he should introduce himself without the colonel present. Rather than hang on an uncomfortable silence, he passed through the weight room and into the shower area.

Through the lockers and around the maze of shower stalls, he emerged into the high-vaulted, glass-ceilinged pool chamber. The smell of chlorine and the hum of an electric motor filled the room as Tomás's attention was drawn away from the still water of the large pool to a smaller endurance lane. It was no more than ten meters in length, and only wide enough to occupy one swimmer at a time.

Carving his way against the controlled current, Paolo stroked in a mechanical rhythm. Tomás had never seen the lieutenant colonel in the middle of one of his legendary workouts. The summoning from the colonel had temporarily pushed his desire to confront Paolo to the back of his mind. Now that the opportunity presented itself, the circumstances were all wrong—most notably due to the presence of Colonel Desantos, standing at the control panel while his son strove to beat the current.

Tomás estimated the default current on the machine was sixty seconds per one hundred meters. Never an enthusiastic swimmer, he had set his own personal best at eighty-five seconds per hundred. The man currently in the training lane was capable of much faster than that.

"Captain, join us."

The colonel motioned Tomás to come closer. The hum intensified and water sloshed in hollow receptacles at the rear of the lane. As Tomás approached the edge of the pool, the form of Paolo in a textbook front crawl plied the water. A metronome could have timed his stroke to the millisecond. No doubt he was forced to train against such an oppressive device during his younger years.

Tomás observed on the monitor that Paolo had been in the pool for nearly 15 minutes at a dead heat, and as he had predicted, he continued to attack the current at a comfortable 60s/100m.

"He is remarkable, wouldn't you agree, captain?"

Tomás stood to the colonel's right, watching Paolo gaining against the current. The swimmer's skin-tight flesh-tone cap concealed his chestnut hair and his silver-tinted goggles concealed his eyes. His head bobbed to the right with every left stroke.

"He is indeed, colonel." There was no other answer.

Colonel Desantos gazed at his son in the pool with an air of accomplishment, akin to succeeding in building an impossibly high tower, or solving an unfathomable riddle, or curing the red tide disease. Yet Paolo had achieved none of these. Leading armed incursions into surrounding villages and building a reputation as a silent and deadly soldier, perhaps. It seemed to Tomás that Paolo's greatest accomplishment was building his image with as little visibility as possible.

"The lieutenant colonel had a productive retreat, I presume?"

The colonel continued to stare at Paolo, silently clocking his pace as though he were the metronome. "As always, yes. We continue to expand our influence in the Lake Region. Paolo ensures the locals comply."

The door of the showers opened and the stranger from the weight room emerged, shirtless and skirted with a light blue towel.

"Have you been introduced, captain?"

The man approached the pair on the deck alongside the training lane while Paolo continued to press on. His light-tan hair was still damp from a post-workout shower, ruffled into place by his hand. A hand he didn't offer to the captain. It wasn't a great first impression.

"Grant."

The man spoke only one name. Tomás introduced himself in kind.

"*Mr.* Grant, I presume?"

"My name is *Grant.*"

The reiteration of his singular name reeked of impatience.

"Grant here is in my employ for a very special task. You see, he has an ability that few of his kind possess."

Tomás remembered the absence of a stamp on Grant's arm.

"A Kayewati without a stamp? Who could imagine such a thing?" Grant opened his arms, rotating them in every angle and slant of light. With a motion of his finger, the agent invited Tomás to approach him. Tomás declined, and Grant shrugged indifference.

"For the fifth mission, we need someone with extensive experience in subterfuge," the colonel continued. "The Kayewati were generous to take Andreas off my hands. They were fascinated with the prospect of stamping a Reaper. In exchange, they offered the services of an experienced Le Renard agent. I couldn't refuse, especially the prospect of one who could pass the security scans of New Inland."

The Kayewati stamp was a tattoo, impossible to conceal from the scanning detection all travelers were required to cross upon entrance to or exit from New Inland and its five cities. And here was a Kayewati agent *without* one, able to come and go at will.

"So how did you conceal your stamp, *Mr.* Grant?"

Grant smiled, ignoring the formality. "Let's just say that my former employer bought some fancy technology that can masque it pretty well."

Tomás stared at Grant's right forearm where the inked marking should have been visible. This time, and without invitation, he touched the agent's unblemished skin, which had no sign of any artificial covering, then pinched it. Grant flinched.

"Careful, now! It's still healing."

Still healing?

"Is this synthetic skin?"

The agent cupped his left hand over the pinch mark Tomás left. "It's all who you know, captain."

Tomás turned back to the colonel, who was watching the exchange with mild amusement. He cast all fear of reprisal aside. What could Grant do that Paolo could not?

"With all due respect, colonel, you hire a criminal from Kayewat to do a job, while the lieutenant colonel hikes and swims laps?" He immediately regretted the statement but was relieved that the colonel allowed his insolence to slide.

"You're right, Captain Alvara. I would never trust a rogue like Grant to *lead* the next insurgency in Capston."

The colonel thrust a finger onto the control panel, intensifying the current to a staggering 45s/100m. Any other man would have been blown to the back end of the lane and into the collecting troughs.

Paolo Desantos was not any other man. He adjusted his stroke to the rapid current and appeared to even gain on the it, reaching for the impossible front end of the pool. Even Grant looked impressed.

"You've been wondering when my son would take the reins. That day has arrived, Tomás. And a mission of this magnitude certainly deserves some private time to prepare, wouldn't you say?"

Tomás's stomach churned. The colonel wasn't giving him the lead on the fifth mission. He was giving it to his son.

Paolo intensified his stroke, gaining on the current until the tips of his fingers were brushing the head of the lane. Colonel Desantos turned to Grant and began to discuss the details Tomás was expecting to hear in an office, not poolside while Paolo outpaced him yet again. The colonel and the Kayewati retreated to the lockers.

Finally, he was alone with Paolo Desantos, but the words weren't forming on Tomás Alvara's tongue.

"Congratulations on your big assignment, lieutenant colonel." It was all he could manage to say, even if he wanted to say this wasn't over yet. Not by a long shot.

The Paper Enemy

Viernes, 13 avril NE 267 (Friday, 13 April AC
0245)
Armoury and Firing Range, Motherland
Lieutenant Colonel Paolo Desantos

By late morning, the sun had melted the last of the cloud covering away and the murky water troughs in the wagon ruts began to dry. Paolo walked along the grass edge to avoid the suction of muck under his boot treads. His new rank entitled him to assign cleaning of his gear to subordinate officers, but it was pointless to saddle officers with menial work. They would be better served practicing target shooting. Besides, his boots were going to see plenty of muck in the days ahead.

Beyond the concentric-circled city streets and vectored blocks, the lieutenant colonel stalked toward the armoury and firing range. Wood-paneled stockade blockhouses rose into view on the outermost perimeter of the walled city, tall forest trees dusting the horizon on the north end. Squadrons conducting morning exercises marched in tight formations around the weapons depot where the land was firm and flat. There were no personnel inside the range today. Paolo was glad he didn't have to order the facility closed for his practice today.

Entering past two stiff guards with fingers flat at their temples, Paolo startled the quartermaster behind his office counter. The major, with grey-lined hair pulled back into a tight ponytail, awaited the captain's signal to relax.

"*A gusto*, major."

Paolo paused at the entrance, panning around the office from door to door until the firing range came into his view. The quartermaster remained at attention despite Paolo's order to relax. The officers always remained at attention around him, even before his promotion. The colonel's shadow loomed large, extending over his son. Still, there were advantages in wielding so palpable an aura.

Paolo sat in one of the three rigid chairs opposite the counter where the major continued to sweat under the duress of the moment. Unlacing his mud-stained boots, he took them into his hands and thrust them in his subordinate's direction.

"I want these clean enough to see my reflection in the shine, major."

"Aye, sir."

Paolo reached into his left breast pocket and produced a folded piece of paper. "I am leaving the city this evening. Everything I need for my trip is listed here. I would like them pressed and packed in a standard-issue rucksack."

The laundry list was sufficient for fresh clothes for five days, but Paolo could make them last far longer if need be. He would have preferred to pack his own gear, but it was just as well the major had something to do. He didn't want the old man to watch him on the monitors as he practiced his shooting.

With Paolo's boots and list in hand, the quartermaster retreated down the corridor and to the tailoring rooms.

Paolo slipped through the doorway and into the arsenal chamber. Vertically arranged combat shotguns, some sawn short; assault rifles with and without wood trim; and a miscellany of rocket-propelled grenade launchers lined the columns and rows.

KL series. 74...

Paolo's eyes came to rest on his weapon of choice. KL-

74s were standard field issue, but more importantly, they were comfortable in his grip. When he held it, the rifle became an extension of his hands. His father bragged that Paolo's marksmanship was owed to hours of daily practice dating back to when he was old enough to hold a gun without dipping the muzzle. But that wasn't it. Paolo always felt the bullet discharging in a flash and arriving precisely where he wished. He couldn't explain it. He imagined the result, and his finger on the trigger made it so.

He didn't target-shoot for need of practice.

He would be spending the next week in the wilderness, en route to a community specializing in high-tech electronics. The Allens provided the information as compensation for information Paolo had relayed to them about the water table fiasco. This was his last opportunity to relax. He selected his weapon and a small crate of ammunition. Two hundred rounds would be enough. He proceeded into the range, selecting the lane farthest from the surveillance camera. The facility may be empty, but so long as the electric eye in the corner was on, he could have an audience of anyone, even after he was finished. Paolo craved solitude, but he demanded privacy.

Mounting the paper silhouette, he pressed the release button, and the target flew to the end of the lane. Slipping two bulky sound mufflers over his ears, the lieutenant colonel knelt, aimed his rifle, and let his skills do the firing. Every twitch of his index finger on the curved trigger was like a blink of an eye. In slow motion, his eyelid would shut, and reopen to a bullet hole exactly where he intended it. Through the sighting scope, Paolo counted round after round piercing the heart of the paper enemy at the end of the lane.

But that's all it was—paper. No one he would encounter over the next seven days would be two-dimensional, pale, and black and white. Commander Yael hadn't been any of those things. He was alive, moving, and able to fire back, if he hadn't been too occupied with the girl in the hay mow.

Paolo gritted his teeth and chose a different target. The muzzle of his KL-74 shifted to the paper target's groin. Pop after pop caused the lower section of the paper sheet to become riddled with holes. The mufflers on his ears couldn't block out the young girl's screams, echoing in his memory. The black outline of the target began to emerge into the commander's form. Yael's look of indignity stared back, daring Paolo to stop him from having his way with the girl.

Paolo aimed the muzzle between Yael's eyes. With a blink like a camera shutter, Paolo ended his life. Over and over again. Every time he strung up a new target sheet, Yael was there, taunting him. He couldn't kill him dead enough.

Paolo continued to shoot until the final round was spent. Retrieving the shredded target, he crumpled what was left of it and discarded it into the shredder just as the quartermaster returned. The rucksack was compacted and loose. The old man had done a good job pressing his clothes.

"Your boots, sir."

The quartermaster stood as close to attention as possible while still clutching a pair of immaculately shined boots.

Paolo saluted the old man. "Thank you, major. I will be checking out my sidearms. That is all."

"Sir." The quartermaster nodded and left the range for his post at the front counter. One last stop in the armoury to retrieve his sidearms and clean his KL-74, and he would be on his way. A brief message on his handheld was sufficient notice to the colonel. When he returned, he would have a new and improved device. A handheld that had the ability to scan others in the vicinity, with all sorts of handy functions.

More importantly, one that couldn't be hacked by any other Motherland devices. Including the colonel's.

Paolo demanded privacy, and he was prepared to travel into dangerous outsider territory to the small settlement where such technology could be purchased to get it. The colonel didn't need to know that part—as far as he was concerned, Paolo was going to scout out another water source. Only this time, he didn't have hundreds of lives depending on him.

The Wages of Sin

Monday, 16 April AC 0245
11:45 PM
New Mills, Federation of New Inland

One more job. That's all any of us really want. One last assignment that will earn us enough to be able to walk away for good. We all have our own ideas of the perfect retirement scenario. CF is happy enough to live out his last days in the Abattoir betting on the races and fights. The boss himself always talks about hiding away in a cabin in the woods. Not exactly my idea of fun, checking for ticks and lugging firewood.

Me? I honestly don't care, as long as I don't have to keep looking over my shoulder. I've been Walpurgis for more than half my life. Kayewat has been home for more years of my life than not, but even in retirement there won't be any escape. What I've done… It carries far.

And I carry it all. Every day.

Retirement won't change that.

It was the job in Haven that made me realize it. So much death. The fires were so intense and widespread that I still smell the smoke in my clothes. It should have been simple. Regular cargo shipment. We had the means to carry it out, no problem. The town was dying anyway. In a matter of months, all that would be left was blackened earth, and soon grass would start to grow. In a year's time, there would be a nice green field where there used to be homes, businesses, and people living out their lives.

All of it, gone. Forgotten forever.

But I'll never forget it.

I'll never forget the screams of the children. They will echo in my ears no matter how long I'm retired, no matter how far away I travel. If I live for a hundred years or more. Whether I cross the ocean, or I live in a cabin, or I'm drunk on Aquavit beside CF in the Abattoir. Nothing can undo the life I've led. What do the Reapers call it—the wages of sin, or something?

So, I made a decision today. While waiting in an abandoned hotel in Capston for my last assignment, my retirement fund just fell in my lap. I couldn't believe my luck! No weapons deals, no drug shipments, no children. Only information, and it was juicy.

I could sell it to the Allens and make quite a purse. But if I can get it to Le_Renard, that will change everything. Of course, I'll need the Allens to get back to Kayewat, and that will mean I'll have to deliver something—probably to Hyacynthe since New Inland won't trade with them anymore. I wonder if the New Inland DHC realizes just how much trade still flows back and forth between the two domes? These are some crazy times, when a birthday card between two kids is as illegal as a shipment of kids.

As soon as I realized what I was sitting on, I ran from the abandoned building so fast I might have left the alleyway door open behind me. Capston has been under siege from unknown terrorists who have the whole city on edge worrying what's going to blow up next. Over a hundred dead in four separate bombings.

But the next one, that's going to be a game changer. And they won't see it coming.

I know this because in my abandoned hotel, I happened to overhear them planning it.

I already have too much on my conscience. If I can move quickly, and if Le_Renard sees the big picture that I'm seeing, I can retire with something the Allens could never give me.

Peace of mind.

This file is doubly encrypted. It's important that I chronicle this job in case I'm unable to finish it. The timestamps will be able to verify that I'm telling the truth as it happens. I have embedded instructions to transmit the files to Phil Fox in Capston, Le_Renard, and the Allen Consortium if three days lapse from my last entry. While I wait for confirmation of my meeting with the Allens, the commercial city of New Mills will make a better place to squat. I figure it's best to buy some new clothes anyway.

Walpurgis

Wednesday, 18 April, AC 0245
2:45 AM
New Mills, Federation of New Inland

I would have liked to be back before midnight, but when you're operating on Allen time, you put up and shut up.

I've traveled all over this continent, from the mountains to three oceans and all points between. I've met people who live in megalithic biospheres, and others who live in holes in the ground. There were times I was terrified to close my eyes at night in both New Inland and Hyacynthe. I never slept most nights in Kayewat. And there were others when sleep was so natural under the stars, I could have stayed forever.

If it weren't for the Reapers.

My luck, they'd mistake my peaceful sleep for a permanent one. They'd carry my carcass away and do whatever it is they do with the dead. I'll die happy if I never know.

If there's any positive aspect about traveling through Allentown, it's that the Reapers avoid it like a plague. Or at least a plague they don't carry. The Allen

Consortium guarantees safety from the hooded druids to all clients. It's probably the reason they've become so successful. You can work with other outsider traders. But everybody knows your best bet is with the Consortium, if only because you won't have to worry about your body being harvested if you stop and take a nap.

Inside the city limits where the ruined suburban buildings are still broken and crumbled, and far from New Inland sensors, I was greeted by a man and woman in disheveled outfits and messy hair. They didn't even have to speak. I knew they were Allen agents. We nodded to each other, and I submitted to the opaque hood. Whatever fabric they used, it was heavy, black, and kept my breaths short. Two hands guided me onto an open-air buggy that rattled as it rumbled along the broken road.

The vehicle slogged through uneven streets, broken concrete, and asphalt, heaved and hewn by generations of patchwork maintenance. A keen eye would recognize newer debris among the decay. Freshly turned earth where machines were stored or moved. The faint smell of burning petrol. The almost inaudible hum of electric cables. All of these, the only traces of life in this ruined artifact of an ever-fading past.

And I saw none of it. Every image of the

ruined city came from photographs and filmed footage. You can't just go for a stroll in Allentown.

I spent nearly an hour as human cargo. The irony wasn't lost on me. I could feel the air souring as we descended into one of the entrance tunnels below ground. The Allens have hundreds of shortcuts and passages out of sight from sky surveillance. I once heard that all five New Inland cities were in so deep with them, they had their own access points. The buggy came to a halt and the exhaust fumes sucked up under the hood. My guides removed it before I could suffocate. The artificial light glowing from semi-translucent shades made my eyes strain to focus. They led me through a series of doors and corridors until we reached Mr. Allen's office.

Mr. Allen, of course, is every male agent. Anonymity is crucial to their business model. Still, if I somehow found my way up in the streets, lost, and I came across someone who wasn't going to imprison me for trespassing, they would know which 'Mr. Allen' I was seeking. As if the way I pronounced the name was distinct. I have only ever dealt with my personal Mr. Allen. One is enough.

Inside, the office was decorated with cultivar plants from the Hanging Gardens and enlivened by gentle chamber music. A lone figure was seated at a wooden desk, poised behind a thin, square monitor. His eyes blinked as if on a programmed timer beneath neat, straight hair parted directly in the center of his forehead. His posture was perfect. It's been said that the Allens were trained to keep their clientèle slightly uncomfortable, to detect insincerity.

Mission accomplished.

"It is my understanding, Mr. Walpurgis, that you have procured the desired assets?"

It wasn't hard for me to 'procure' anything in the Hanging Gardens. Whatever the buyer in Hyacynthe wants to use those seeds for is their business. I cleared my throat.

And the agreed commission remains, I hope?

"Of course." The agent smiled, typing at his keypad and gazing at the monitor as the magic of Allen business unfolded. Within seconds, accounts were updated and settled. "As is our policy, any change in fees will be noted in direct correspondence with the primary customer. You would then be informed by your clients."

I was often tempted to ask how the Allens could so easily access people inside domes but remembered that it was impolite to impose. It could jeopardize future business. As uneasy as it feels moving through this cemetery of a city, skulking through underground tunnels and hidden trails, only the Consortium could pay for the services he required. If I hold up my end of the deal. Sometimes it was as simple as smuggling out a few plants. Other times, it was trickier.

The agent clicked along his keypad to a crescendo, then swiveled the monitor so I could verify the transaction.

"There you have it, Mr. Walpurgis. The credit has been transferred. The parcel will arrive in Hyacynthe on time. And most importantly, your identity in the New Inland database has been extended, as per our compensatory agreement."

The agreement included my continued access to the Consortium and invisibility in New Inland. Until the next assignment. With any luck, there will be no need once I'm back in Kayewat. Le_Renard will pay me enough that I won't have to be an Allen errand boy any longer.

"Is there any other business you would like to discuss, sir?"

As a matter of fact, there is. I need transport home. Can this be negotiated into my terms?

The agent smiled in an uncharacteristic, emotional response.

"I expect so. You understand it will take upwards of two weeks from today before you set foot on the frozen tundra?"

I understand, sir.

"We can quicken departure, but we would need you to make a delivery."

I see.

"Oh, nothing of the dangerous sort, I can assure you. Correspondence to a foreign national. That would be all." The agent leaned onto his elbows. "We are fortunate that you are willing to go. Our other operatives would do so for a price, but it always requires careful planning, rearranging of schedules. How long will you be staying in Kayewat, Mr. Walpurgis?"

A few weeks, tops. I'll contact you when I'm ready to return. My visit this time is personal.

"It makes no difference to us. We only expect that if you wish to continue on our payroll, you return in accordance with our predetermined flight times. It would be difficult to extend your citizenship in New Inland beyond that."

I understand. So, we can do this, then?

Mr. Allen swiveled the monitor back and started to type again. "I should say so. As you are aware, the board must approve your request, as you plan to travel via our means to a highly sanctioned port of call. Your fee will be in the form of accepted labour, and the terms will be forwarded to your New Inland account within twenty-four hours. I suggest you keep your bags packed; the sooner we can book you a flight, the better for all."

My bag is never unpacked, Mr. Allen. You'll contact me when the arrangements are in place. That's all for today.

"Wonderful. It is a pleasure doing business, as always. I wish you a safe and uneventful voyage. My regards to Le_Renard."

I almost reached to shake his hand before remembering the agent wouldn't accept it, even if there wasn't a plexiglass barrier. There's always a protocol you have to follow with the Allens. They understand DNA theft. They practically invented it.

Walpurgis

Mountains Never Seen

"You're not finished fixing that yet?" Lorrie snarled from one side of his mouth as the other devoured his half-heated lunch. Three Sheppards and one Connelly sat around the dining room table in the Sheppard Inn kitchen. Robbie was surprised to hear Lorrie ask him about his racer. In his sixteen-year-old brother's mind, the only racing sport worth anyone's time was longboarding. Bike racing was for chumps. In any case, Robbie just wanted to eat his lunch in peace before Willits left at 13:00. The reception desk wasn't going to watch itself.

Robbie's shoulder and hip still ached from the collision on the synthetic oval track four years ago. One of his fellow cyclists described wiping out on the Jewel Velodrome like being struck with a thousand kilos of feathers. Two weeks on, and a pillow of ten thousand kilos of feathers still wouldn't allow for comfortable rest. His temperament as sensitive as the soft-tissue injuries, Robbie carried on in the inn as though he were on autopilot.

His competition could afford to replace badly damaged bikes. Robert Sheppard once told his son not to expect sponsorship to fund his dream. Instead of a new set of wheels, Robbie's father built for him a workstation to repair his own racer. The tedium of long hours learning how to reset the gear mechanism, straightening warps in the lightweight aluminum frame, calibrating the chain—he would endure all of it, and more, to have his father back.

And just like his competitive riding dreams, memories of him were receding.

"It wouldn't do much good. I can still barely walk, let alone balance on a bike."

Robbie picked through the serving of pre-cut vegetables he had prepared for the four of them. Robbie and Cadlen were ready to eat half an hour earlier. Lorrie and his tag-along friend held up the meal as usual.

"I told you, brother, you should've gone for the physio. I mean, why else do you pay insurance?"

Picking the broccoli sprigs from his plate, Robbie sighed.

"Because there's a deductible fee, Lor. I thought you knew everything."

Warren smirked, but quickly wiped the grin from his face when Lorrie's eyes darted to him.

"Don't even say it, Warren."

Warren Connelly forked a mouthful of seasoned chicken strips but didn't wait to finish chewing. "I wasn't gonna say a word. I'm just enjoying a nice home-cooked meal."

"Home-heated meal, you mean."

Warren swallowed.

"Have you ever had Clara Connelly's cooking? I'll take Robbie's any day!"

Robbie glanced over to Cadlen, chewing his food as silently as he did everything else. If he could read his mute brother's mind, he imagined the response to be "You already take Robbie's food everyday..."

"How are Mr. and Mrs. Connelly these days?"

"Don't ask," Lorrie snapped.

Warren narrowed his slotted eyes at his longboarding partner and best friend.

"By the amount of order-in food Dad and I are eating,

I'd say Clara's doing just fine. Dad, not so much."

It had been about a year since Robbie noticed Warren referring to his mother by her name, while he still called Charles "dad." He couldn't help but smile remembering Lorrie once trying to call his own father Robert. It hadn't ended well.

"Charlie says she's on business, but we all know where she's really hanging." Lorrie wiped his mouth with the back of his hand, ignoring the cloth napkins at every setting.

"Don't talk about your friend's mother like that."

"He's not wrong, Robbie. Her shuttle's been seen in the Lucky Strike Lounge park lift. New Mills for business, my ass..."

Robbie remembered the first time Lorrie came home from school with his lost puppy friend. Julia Sheppard had come from behind the reception counter and invited Warren to sit in the big comfy-cushioned chaise near the fireplace. It could have been the cookies and milk. It could have been Julia's warmth. Whatever it was, Warren never really stopped following Lorrie home. Thicker than thieves, the pair began to longboard still in their single digits. Julia told Robbie never to let on that the longboard Lorrie received for his twelfth birthday was a token of appreciation from Charles Connelly. Even then, business was showing signs of recession.

"I'm sure that's not the case. You know how people talk."

"Right, bro. But not every shuttle has a pair of pink dice hanging from the rear view."

Warren shrugged in resignation.

Later in the afternoon, Robbie guarded the reception desk while Cadlen settled on the chaise. After a peaceful day of sketching and accounting, the stillness was shattered by the pronounced arrival of two longboarders, wheels still whizzing on each board tucked under arms.

"Whatcha drawing today? Workin' on a still life there?"

Cadlen kept his legs tucked up beneath himself as he nestled into the heavy cushions. Often, guests remarked how lovely it was for a young boy to quietly work on his art down in the common area. They said it added ambience to the small inn. *When* there were guests.

He didn't look up. The small box of oily pastels, some of the primary colours ground down to the labels, sat on the armrest that supported his shoulders. Reaching down and swapping one for another, his eyes never leaving his page. The only time Cadlen ever reacted to Lorrie's taunting was the day Lorrie reached for his pastels. Cadlen leaped from the chair and snatched the red-printed carton quicker than Lorrie had taken it. Warren hooted, but when no further retorts came, he silenced his jeers. Cadlen stood on the balls of his feet, his black pupils gazing in complete defiance at his tormentors.

"Is that a mountain, Cad?"

From the reception desk, Robbie could see the outline of a high peak capped with snow, back-dropping thick forest reflected in still water.

"Are you going off memory or just taking a wild guess?" Warren's thin brow crinkled. "I never knew your folks went to the mountains!"

Lorrie snorted. "You kidding? We've never left New Inland! Mountains, right..."

They trudged off to the back room, Lorrie still jawing about those mythical mountains that may as well have been on the moon. "Mom and Dad were going to take us to the Hudson too, but that's not happening anytime soon, now is it..."

The voices trailed off as the door shut behind them. Cadlen turned back to his sketchbook.

"He bothering you?"

Cadlen didn't look up.

"I can make them come in the back. You can draw there all day if it makes you..."

Cadlen paused, and Robbie was aware he had his attention.

"Happy."

Cadlen pursed his lips and rolled his shoulders slightly. He heard the message.

Robbie puttered around the lobby for a few more minutes. He made sure the wastebasket was fresh. He swept the floor. He dusted the pictures and trinkets that decorated the lobby. He fluffed the cushions on the big armchairs, or at least the ones that Cadlen wasn't using. Satisfied that his brother was okay, he turned and left the lobby. In the back room, Lorrie and Warren were making sandwiches and doing a poor job tidying after themselves. Preserves were still on the table, their lids leaving juice rings of different colours on the scratched wooden surface. The refrigerator was hanging open. Utensils, sticky all the way up the handle, were tossed unrinsed into the basin on top of the dishes they hadn't cleaned from lunch.

"You plan on cleaning that before you leave, right?" Robbie had already sent Willits home. He was the last staffer still on payroll, and by Thursday already on overtime for the week. Robbie had no time to clean up after slobby teenagers when the front desk needed to be tended.

Lorrie snickered under his breath without looking up. "Yeah, I got it, don't stress."

Robbie put on his best fatherly voice. "Why would I stress?"

Warren knew enough not to interfere with this one. It was one thing to take a jibe at Cadlen, who rarely defended himself. Robbie knew Warren held a healthy respect for him, even if Lorrie didn't.

Lorrie gulped back a mouthful of juice. "Because stress is kind of what you do, isn't it?"

Robbie ignored the insult. "You two have a big race soon, don't you? Isn't it the City-Wide?"

Warren spoke up. "Yeah, next month. 29th, I think? We're competing to make the cut. You know, the tour around the other cities? Plus, it's Troy's last race—"

Lorrie cut off his friend, and Robbie knew why. He was always going to beat Troy the next time, except that he was running out of next times. Robbie knew how it felt to face a nemesis again and again, only to go home disappointed. He had never beaten Andrews on the oval.

"We'll qualify as long as we have a clean run. You wanna come down and watch a real sport?" Lorrie's comment cut his brother more than he realized.

"And who will watch over the inn if I go?"

"What about Willits? Don't be so cheap, and pay the man overtime, maybe! I don't know, never too early to train Cad. But you kind of have to talk once in a while. You know, if people actually check in."

Lorrie wasn't wrong. Only five rooms out of fifty today, no bookings yet for next week.

"The guests probably got tired of hearing you two idiots storming around—that's enough to drive anyone away."

Lorrie tossed the cup into the basin. "You can blame me all you want, Robbie, but this place is a sinking ship, and you know it. Why you don't sell I'll never understand."

Because it kept him and his friend fed.

Because they had bills to pay.

Because it kept him boarding in qualification tourneys.

"I thought you did great today, Robbie."

Crystal lay across the bottom of his neatly pleated bed

blanket, on her belly with her head cradled in her hands.

Robbie slumped back against the headboard, legs crossed at ankles and arms folded in a full display of introversion. He was expressionless, but Crystal could read him regardless.

"Everything was perfect—the bike handled well, I was in a groove, Andrews had fallen back, and he was the closest to me for most of it! I just can't believe it came apart."

Crystal rolled sideways onto her right elbow. "I know. It was a fluke, Robbie, it was shit luck, all right? But at least you didn't get hurt."

"I know..." Robbie relaxed his arms. "I went through the checklist with a fine-tooth comb, though. Those lag bolts were as tight as I could get them. Figures it wasn't enough."

"You're so hard on yourself, Robbie. We all can see it. I wish you could too."

Robbie raised his eyes to meet hers. "You really want to help, don't you?"

Crystal smiled. "Of course! You seem really down this time."

"I don't mean just now, but always. You always try to help people, even when they don't want it."

Crystal sat up. "I can go if you want."

"No, that's not what I meant." Robbie saw the disappointment in his sister's eyes. "It's good, you can stay—please, stay for a while."

Crystal lay back down across the edge of the bed. "How do Mom and Dad do it, Robbie? We're so different from each other. Cad won't even talk. And Lorrie... how can anyone deal with him?"

Robbie chuckled, finally allowing a smile to creep out. "Yeah, we're pretty different, aren't we? I'd say Cad's more like me, and—"

"Don't you dare say Lorrie is closer to me!" Crystal's

eyes widened, her gaping smile showing her silver braces, not due to come out for months yet.

With a full-belly laugh, Robbie swung his legs over the edge of the bed. Crystal fell into his one-armed consolation hug. Moments like this weren't frequent. They were the kind of siblings who thrived on an unsaid competition between them, to see who could be less dependent on the other. If Crystal ever moved away from home... Robbie couldn't fathom a life without her.

Crystal left for Hyacynthe four years ago. His mother died only months before that, and not long after, so did his father. One day, Lorrie would move out on his own and stop wreaking havoc on the family business. Cadlen would be selling his art all throughout the five cities.

Why you don't sell...

The two boarders were gone before he could articulate what he meant to say.

Because Mom and Dad would want me to keep it going.

Crystal in Hyacynthe

Friday, 20 April, AC 0245
The River-Way, *La Fédération d 'Hyacynthe*
Crystal Sheppard

All Crystal Sheppard needed was a place to gather her thoughts and focus on what really mattered right now.

Why this night, of all nights, *Le Café Mondial* had to close early was beyond her. The quarterly exams were only days away, and a campus of caffeine-starved night owls, careers in their crosshairs and itching to finish their assignments, needed this place, now more than ever. Back at the flat, Mireil would have her pounding club anthems shaking the windows and rattling the glass cabinets. She needed the peace of the café. She loved Mir to pieces, but never got anything done when she was home.

With the café closed, Crystal found a bench along the riverway. Hyacynthe was the only Dome on the continent that boasted a river that naturally passed through it. The River-Way was a wide expanse of parkland with natural trees and real land. All the comforts of inside, with the flowing breeze of the salty seaway coursing up the artery that pumped life into the superstructure she had called home for nearly four years.

The first thing Crystal Sheppard had noticed when she first came to Hyacynthe was the coldness of the circulating air. One thousand kilometers north of New Inland may as well have been one thousand degrees colder. Her flatmate Mireil had assured her that after a year, she would get used to it.

But Mireil had lied. While she was wearing calf-revealing knickers, Crystal was still adding layers. It didn't matter if they were moving up the turbo lifts on the north or south end of the river-spanning dome, or if they were strolling along the open-air riverway. She would only be warm again when she finally returned someday to the soft down of her own blankets back home in Capston.

The trade embargo between New Inland and Hyacynthe had put all her hopes on hold indefinitely. In the meantime, diving into her studies would have to be her distraction. It was increasingly difficult with two flatmates.

Four years, and the benefit of being straight-out busy with school left her with little time to think about how much time had passed.

It took that first year to muster the courage to venture out along the riverway at all. The air was different here than back in New Inland. During the winter, even with climate control in place, it was heavier, like a weighted blanket on her chest. The cold air took her breath away, much like the sight of the wide river that bisected the twinned cities. Hyacynthe made her feel smaller than New Inland. Home, she looked up and saw only a cyan blue hue where she knew the Hanging Gardens hid above the sky reflector panels. The naked eye saw everything in Hyacynthe, from the apex platforms that joined the north and south cities, and the farthest reaches of the river disappearing into white-light tunnels. She tried to imagine her brothers and her parents, swimming in the summertime and skating in the frozen winter. Robbie would absolutely love it there. Cadlen, he'd have drawn it all. She probably would have thrown Lorrie to the fishes.

And Mom and Dad...

Crystal set her handheld on the bench beside her, and gently shut her *ordinateur*. Monsieur Laurent had never gotten used to calling it a "computer", and Crystal had stopped trying to teach him. Her mom had proposed to her dad right around here, with this same view as the backdrop. She couldn't wait any longer. The Hyacynthe Youth Retreats had been their annual pilgrimage for years, and it served as a vessel for their growing romance. They were chaperoned, but the Retreats were like a tear in the fabric of space and time. Everything came to a halt in Hyacynthe. They would return to the mundane, but while here, they basked in the magnificence and freedom. New Inland was home, but Hyacynthe was their escape. If Crystal could find half as much joy in her stay, she would be lucky.

Her handheld twitched on the bench beside her. Crystal hated being a slave to her pocket-sized communication device. On the one hand, she needed it to receive messages from her professors. There was always the remote chance her brothers could find a way to break the embargo and call her, at least in her mind, anyway. Still, she couldn't truly escape distraction as long as it was there. It would have been nothing to toss it a few feet away into the river. But then, how would Druna or Mireil be able to bother her? Most times, she was glad they did.

Mireil was a good flatmate, and an equally good student, able to balance work and play. Crystal held herself to stricter expectations. Her brief escape down by the river couldn't last forever. But for the time being, the weight of the world on her shoulders could wait while she watched the river's current winding through the superstructure. Crystal gazed out over the gentle ripples on the water and felt her heart rate calming. There were no freighters today. Maybe New Inland cargo was waiting in limbo at the downriver opening. She took comfort in the idea that a whole stack of parcels from her brothers might all arrive at once someday.

It was hard to imagine that at one time, trade between the two domes was fluid. Normalized relations would have made choosing school an awful lot easier. Sure, Heartsburg was under the same dome as Capston. Their pharmaceutical program was exceptional and could even rival Hyacynthe's Lacraie facility. But Hyacynthe had one benefit no other program in the land could offer. For Crystal, there was no other choice.

It's all who you know, her father always said while he was still alive. And her parents knew Monsieur Laurent well. Crystal never wanted charity. She wanted even less for Robbie to have to pay for her schooling while trying to keep the inn afloat.

Crystal opened her *ordi*. One more year, this time as in intern, assuming she passed her quarterlies. Now if only the embargo could hurry up and end before that.

Her handheld buzzed again.

Crystal reached up and fixed her hair, blonde with wisps of faded blue. Neither was a natural hue. The breeze picked up and her locks, held tenuously in a hastily tied ponytail, began to slip free. She was never one to fret over her hair. At least, not until she'd moved in with Mireil. Crystal found herself more worried about her appearance. Perhaps it was because her courses were coming to an end. Video conferences and interviews would begin soon, or at least she hoped they would. Employers preferred an image of someone with a little more self-respect than the archetypal student in her casuals, all unkempt and content to live in student limbo than face the working world.

It was probably Druna. She met another future husband at the *Palais Marée*, and she just couldn't wait to tell how gentle he was. Mireil could feign excitement, but Crystal could barely pretend to be interested. Druna, with her bust barely restrained and her wide eyes accented with too much makeup. Pouty fish lips and wide hips. Her figure was fuller than full, but her love life none the worse.

Crystal shook the thoughts of her flatmates. Even if they weren't there beside her, they were a distraction.

"You should answer that once in a while, *Crystale*."

A voice far more masculine than either Mireil or Druna snapped her to attention. Instinctively Crystal reached for her handheld that was still buzzing, only to brush against a wrinkled hand that had beat her to it. The hand turned over, Crystal's ruby-red encased device resting easily on his palm. She turned to him and closed her fingers over the device that had now stopped.

"Oh, it was you..."

"I stopped by your flat. Mireil told me you would be down here. She figured her music had driven you out again..."

Crystal smiled. After a light-gestured peck on either cheek, the two of them strolled along the fenced boardwalk of the riverway. A rusty-hulled freighter plied the waves upriver beside them. The sky, projected on the high-overhead arches, was a soft blue, clouds choppy and thin at a high altitude. Crystal didn't know how it appeared like magic on the underside of the concrete and steel ceiling that draped across the river. In Capston, the mirrors were arranged to shift with the procession of the sun, allowing people to look up without staring at laser-like beams. Still, the blueness of the natural sky was unique to Hyacynthe. Even the people walking by appeared softer in the filtered glow. Laurent was an elderly gentleman with a soft grey hue in his full head of hair, slouching slightly as he shuffled along beside her.

"Mir's great, but we just need different things to inspire us. I mean, I love her to pieces, it's just—"

"You just need to be... here."

Laurent gestured to the water as the freighter chugged past, unidentifiable cargo crates lashed to the flat deck. Most likely raw minerals from *Le Bras d'Or*. Hyacynthe had the capacity to refine almost anything, from raw materials for construction to precious metals for medical equipment.

"Your parents wandered up and down this trail almost daily. Julia, now she could live without the cold breeze. But Robert..."

The man sighed and seemed to lose his train of thought. It was entirely possible. He was in his early eighties and still remarkably healthy, due in no small part to the expertise of Hyacynthian medicine. An industry in which even an elderly Laurent was still considered a giant.

Crystal attempted to finish it for him. "Daddy, he loved it down here."

Her mentor continued as though he had said the words himself. "Yes, yes. He did love it here. He had a passion for the outdoors and the Retreats soothed that hunger in him. Oh, your mother loved it here too, no mistake there. But she would do just about anything for him. Anyone around them could see."

He stopped and rested his right hand along the guardrail. Crystal stopped, but she knew he was fine. Slow and steady. Laurent had all the time in the world. In retirement, he had no decisions to make, apart from what he might wear or what meals he would order. At last, he could rely on people to help him for a change. Still, he oversaw the correspondence between Crystal and Robbie. It was one responsibility he insisted on keeping.

Laurent leaned out over the rail and gazed out at the river. "Your quarterly exams, do you feel you're ready?"

Crystal leaned onto the rail beside him. "As ready as I can be, I guess. I've had a lot on my mind lately."

Laurent smiled. "No doubt your brothers. Four years is a long time. Do you think you can last one more year for your internship?"

The fifth-year residency in nuclear medicine was required to complete her degree. They both knew her transcripts wouldn't be worth a byte of data to Heartsburg's institute back in New Inland. And transferring to a program in Arctica or Sascota would not be without its complications either. Still, the thought of working in a dome with normalized relations to New Inland was a tempting prospect.

"I mean, I kind of have to, right? I have to keep working where I can earn enough to send home to Robbie and the boys. And I'm not likely going to get Lacraie..."

The old man threw his feeble hands in the air and let out a laugh hearty enough to make him collapse. "*Chère*, must you always be so down on yourself? Of course, you can. Lacraie is no different than any other."

Crystal snorted. "No different? Then how come everyone wants to be posted there? They're only accepting ten applicants, out of what, two hundred applicants?"

"And I have seen your transcripts. You can certainly compete, *Crystale*." Laurent always pronounced her name in his thickest French accent when he was scolding her.

A fishing trawler crawled past, causing a rippling wake to wash along the boardwalk support posts. The sour smell of chum intermingled with the sea-sprayed air.

"If only you were my teacher, monsieur."

"I would treat you no different than the rest." They both knew it wasn't entirely true.

"I'm still grateful to have you nearby. Maybe it's best I stay in Hyacynthe. Lacraie is so far away." The nuclear medical facility of Lacraie was indeed the best on the continent. The nearly four-hundred-kilometer commute to the remote installation on the Lacraie River meant living on campus for the duration of a ten-day run. The compensation for the remoteness and the modest accommodation more than made up for it.

Crystal heard Laurent sigh as though his laughter caught up with him. "Have no fear, *chère*, I will still see you plenty."

It took her a few seconds to process Laurent's choice of verb tense.

"What do you mean, you will still see me?"

The doctor's smile was barely a line between his lips, but the wrinkles around his eyes gave him away. "I told you, you should answer that once in a while."

Crystal squealed loud enough for shore birds to take to the air. Surely the longshoremen across the river could have heard her excitement. It was all she could do not to wrap her arms around the old man and squeeze him out of his blazer.

"I made Lacraie! So, when?"

Laurent opened his arms and motioned for her to hug him, clearly unconcerned for his physical safety in her embrace. She rested her head on his shoulder, staining his shoulder with tears. She was too overcome with ecstasy to be embarrassed just yet.

"Next week. If you're not too busy."

Crystal's laughter sounded more like blubbering muffled into his coat. "I think I can make the time."

Laurent placed his hand on her head. "And you told me Mireil was emotional..."

Best-Laid Plans

Tuesday, 8 May, AC 0245
Holt Tower, Capston, New Inland
Phil Fox

"So, what do you say, whiskey on the rocks for another round? Or do you want me to go digging around for the fancy green stuff you like?"

Phil Fox rolled his reddening eyes to the bartender leaning on elbow sleeves half-crinkled. The "fancy green stuff" was more suitable for celebrations, hardly for losing elections. In a two-horse race, the loser always finishes dead last. It was an idiom he could have appreciated if it weren't that his opponent had used it on national broadcast during the final debate. Pundits were crediting the new mayor's charisma and quick wit for his significant victory. Phil couldn't disagree.

Sliding the glass across the bar, the bartender nodded and topped off the round-bottomed glass with the amber spirit. "Now Phil, I'm gonna have to cut you off if you're driving your own shuttle, right?"

Phil shook his head. "On foot tonight. So, you've got no excuses, Jason, unless I start getting rowdy."

"Now why didn't you show a little of that rowdiness in the campaign? You might still be the man in charge, and I might be charging you double for your imported liqueur!"

Teetering on the barstool, Phil held open his hands, gesturing at the lounge. Patrons were already flooding in, crowding the place, and filling up booths as the early evening set in. "As if you need to make any more money off me..."

"Well, I couldn't make any less off you," Jason said. "At least I'm getting the lease agreement for the new mayor and his council. The 93rd, right above the security-leased levels, so Reekan won't have to walk too far."

As the clock turned over to 20:00, the music livened to a more up-tempo brass swing sound as the patrons crowded around tables and raised their voices to compete with the soundtrack. It was time to call it a night. His only regret was not coming to that conclusion about ten minutes, and two drinks, earlier.

A mob of a dozen ranking officers and personnel from the Security Department swarmed into the lounge. He knew at least half of them. He ducked his head and stared down into the half-empty whiskey glass.

Why doesn't he want them to see him? Jason took his cue and strode across the lounge to escort the party to their reserved tables that were pushed together earlier.

Hell, does the celebration ever end?

A brisk clap on his shoulder gave him the answer.

"Fox, my man, I figured you'd be on your way by now! Where is it again, you have something down in *La Bermude*, don't you?"

Swilling back the last of his drink, Phil clacked the glass on the bar. "Something like that. And I figured you'd be up on the 93rd unpacking all your stuff, or at the very least, working on some new leads."

Mayor Steven Reekan climbed onto a stool and roared for a round of drinks. Phil doubted he would ever get used to Steven's new title. "This one's on me, old friend. What are you having, the green stuff?"

"Jason cut me off, Steven. I was just about to leave, actually."

"Nonsense! What, does Kendall have you on a curfew for your big trip? Come on, just one before you go. Least I can do!"

The least he could do was leave Phil to wallow in his own disappointment.

Miss Kendall had long since gone home for the evening, even if Phil's intention were to return to his half-packed office to stay the night. Steven wasn't entirely wrong, though. She most certainly would have given him a look halfway between incredulity and pity.

"Now, as a matter of fact, we have Simmons and Merrick upstairs trying to break the encryption on a device we found in the 400-block. It's got all the markings of an outside city. And you know what that means..."

"It means you're filling in the gaps on illegally gained intelligence?"

Steven swallowed about half of his taller glass, wiping his chin with the back of his sleeve. "Come on, Phil, that's the DHC talking through you, and you know it. Think about it. Intel inside Motherland goes quiet just weeks before the first bombing. Before that, it's all anti–New Inland rhetoric from the colonel and his figurehead ruler. More and more incidents of hijacked shipments well within their range of land travel."

Phil turned to face the new mayor.

"And not an ounce of hard evidence, only conjecture and theories! And you think the DHC, with Marribel as chair, will agree to a joint expeditionary force? When I already stuck my neck out to increase the defense budget?"

"You know damned well that if even so much as a firecracker went off in Heartsburg, Marribel would have emptied the coffers quicker than she could slam her little gavel. But when it's Capston—when it's only Capston—she has the nerve to stand on ceremony and get all sanctimonious."

Steven waved to Jason, who then slid a second tall glass across the bar, frothy foam listing over the rim.

"Now you're going to have to deal with her and the rest of the high council. And you thought working with me was tough—"

"Tough? No, no, Phil, you weren't tough. A little stiff maybe, but you weren't too bad. I mean that."

The pair settled into an uneasy silence while the happy-hour volume filled the negative space with that end-of-week air of jubilance mixed with relief. Phil pulled his fingers through his mussed, rust-brown hair.

A burst of laughter from Steven's table punctuated the room. Steven raised his glass to the group.

"I'd invite you over for a drink, but I know you're shoving off in the morning. What, two—three hours on the magna-rails? And then on the open water? The shape you're in, you'll be tossing Holt's drinks over the side before you lose sight of the shore!"

Phil patted his left bicep. "Hour and a half. And that's what seasickness patches are for. What are you celebrating, anyway?"

Steven feigned seriousness. "We're dispatching to Allentown. Shore has the lead on this one. We have intel on Motherland presence in the north end of the city, so we're camping out on the south side, but quietly. You know as well as I do the Allens aren't too fond of visitors."

"Just pray Marribel doesn't catch wind of your activities."

Phil fumbled with his handheld, keying the balance owed on his tab. Jason glanced at his own monitor; with the transaction completed, he nodded his approval of the tip.

"And you'd best have your ducks in a row for when I'm back. Sixty days, Mr. Mayor, and then I'm holding you to account." When he returned and assumed his role as chief solicitor, there would be no contravening the DHC. But then again, if Steven Reekan lived up to his own hype, the cases would be solved, and life in Capston would be back to normal. Except for the demoted ex-mayor.

Phil slid off the barstool, leaning over on two of its legs as he straightened his posture and aimed for the door. He couldn't look back; Steven's voice was splitting his skull, deeper with every word.

"In sixty days, we'll have the bastards caught, Phil. Travel safe and tell Kendall the offer still stands!"

Phil's only concerns were walking in a straight line and catching a few hours of sleep before shipping off for *La Bermude*. And from there, the actual destination.

Legal Contraband

Wednesday, 9 May AC 0245
Magna-Rail Transit Station, New Inland
Phil Fox

The last traces of self-induced headache clung on the inside of Phil's temples. He was never more thankful for the soft whispers of transit shuttles as he processed his boarding pass and turned in his travel trunk for screening. The jumbled voices of travelers, punctuated by the tinny crackle of the public address, were enough to keep his discomfort top of mind.

Wide sunglasses, black as night, served to keep the high morning sun out of his eyes, along with the scrutiny of strangers. His trip was technically legal. Marribel had signed off on the release personally. Even Reekan had approved. Phil had committed to sixty days of personal leave. He hoped that for most of those days he could forget about the bombs, the victims, and the guilt over his failure to stop any of it.

Before climbing aboard the train, Phil submitted to the full-body scan just as he had exiting Capston into the arterial causeway, and again at the bay arches that served as the principal point of entry of the New Inland dome. The number of uniformed personnel at each post had more than doubled from the last time he had embarked on this journey. Technicians with tablet-sized handhelds scanned every square centimeter of equipment or goods moving in either direction. The interception of contraband was sufficient to justify increased security, but Phil knew that if outsider terrorism was the cause of Capston's attacks, the perpetrators would be far too clever to just walk in the front door.

Ahead of his own travel satchel's examination, a middle-aged businessman pleaded with security for his wardrobe to be returned. Without the proper documentation and lack of authenticity tags, the clothing was deemed contraband, likely for illegal resale on the inside. A hefty fine and travel ban were in this amateur trader's future. The businessman's sharp protests only intensified Phil's hangover headache.

As the guards guided the protesting man away, Phil stepped forward through the rectangular frame that scanned his body for anomaly signature traces. The scanning technician greeted him on the other side with a familiar list of questions:

> Have you traveled to or from the Hyacynthe Federation in the past three years?

> Have you at any time in your life traveled to and been granted admittance to Kayewat?

> Have you at any time in your life traveled south of the Red Zone boundary?

> Have you purchased any goods outside New Inland within the past six months?

> Are you traveling with intent to sell goods or services to any outside persons, organizations, or political entities?

> Have you ever been diagnosed with red tide illness?

> Have you been medically cleared by a certified physician of any symptoms of red tide illness?

> Have you been cleared by the appropriate government authority to travel outside New Inland?

Phil answered the questions with the poise of a

solicitor and the careful phrasing of a mayor.

"I have never traveled to Hyacynthe."

This was a technical response. If the guard had asked him to specify whether that included any holdings of the Hyacynthe Federation, he would have to clarify that he had in fact visited the Lacraie Medical Research Facility. Although it predated his time in New Inland, the guard would be compelled to note prior travel to an unfriendly location. Phil was comfortable with the white lie.

"Kayewat? Never."

No ambiguity there. The body scan would have detected a Kayewati stamp, in any case.

"No."

Phil wasn't required to reveal his past travels to Ozarck, south and just west of the Appalachian range. Only a fool would willingly travel past the Red Line, where red tide illness was one of many tropical ailments that creatively ravaged the body. Viral mutation occurred faster than the discovery of treatment, so if you successfully dodged one, another would be waiting to take its place. As the son of a red tide victim, Phil had no desire to court that disaster.

"I purchase all my goods and services in the City of Capston."

That was *Mayor* Phil's response. Of course, goods from any of the five cities were legal, and in fact encouraged. As the scanning technicians out of sight were analyzing the contents of his larger travel trunk, they would be looking for manufacture-origin tags. The items would have to match the previously submitted pack list. He already knew that one item in his carry-on satchel would halt the scan for further scrutiny. And with security heightened at Reekan's behest, there would be no dodging it.

"No, I'm not a salesman."

The pack-list manifest would confirm that at least

there was no out-going product. The security would be more concerned about incoming contraband. Phil would deal with that in sixty days.

"No, I have not."

Phil's medical information was always up to date and accessible to security in large part because of his position as a public servant. The nature of his work, traveling throughout New Inland's cities and the common areas that linked them, required extra care in monitoring his health. The mention of red tide still caused discomfort, even after all these years.

"Yes."

Medical clearance was simply a matter of formality. Still, the clean bill of health always came as a relief.

"Yes. I've been approved for travel from Chair Jennings Marribel of the Domestic High Council, as well Mayor Steven Reekan of Capston."

Solicitor Phil Fox declared his credentials without as much as a hint of uncertainty. If he were to wear his mayor hat, he feared his shaken confidence from his failures as mayor would have betrayed him.

"Mayor Fox, we have a question about one of your personal items."

He was waiting for the question. The scanning technicians would have to pry it out of his dead hands. The memories it carried were far too valuable.

"Happy anniversary, son!' Lucas Fox knelt beside Phil, resting a hand gently on his shoulder while Elsa captured the moment with a quick snap from her handheld. Five years old already. Lucas had to remind himself that his son was still so young. He had shown an aptitude for reading as soon as he could figure out the combination to unlock the library on his mother's handheld. Elsa had wondered if he could in fact read any of the words he was studying, until he began to repeat them back to her. It's a text far beyond his age level, she thought to herself. Such a wonderful gift...

Lucas never told him that he would have preferred he followed in his footsteps. Phil had shown little interest in the physics of the world. How things worked didn't matter to him. Reading led to questions, and in due time, he would provide his own answers, whether his parents asked for them or not.

The Fox family huddled around the faux fireplace in their downtown condominium. The bustling of Sascota's busiest metropolitan district was muted by the airtight, translucent panes, but allowed the regulated climate to shine in. The suite had a wide-open concept. Contemporary art in mixed straight lines and soft contours adorned the walls sparsely, mimicking the décor of the most sophisticated apartments of Sascotan elite minus the overindulgence and expense of original works. Even as a young boy, Phil found the style of art was fake.

He glowed with joy when his parents revealed the scaled miniature diorama of the Sascotan Federation dome, complete with a cut-away panel to reveal the inner workings of the individual cities within. He correctly pointed out where they lived, imagining his family smaller than fleas. The instructions that came with the model were intended for parental guidance, but Phil needed no help reading them. He was already underway with the application of the inner features when his mother called his attention.

"You're not quite finished yet, Phil," she said softly. Phil had become accustomed to his mother's slow speech, a lingering effect of the long illness she had been fighting as long as he could remember. Her energy seemed to surge that day. He imagined she would be napping later in the afternoon as a result.

"There's more?" Phil tried to determine who outside of his family could have bought him something. The Fox family didn't have any other relations in Sascota, to his knowledge, and he didn't have any close friends. Despite her poor health, Elsa kept Phil at home, reluctant to allow him to start his classes. Indeed, he wasn't lacking for education in her care.

Lucas sat back on his haunches, his wide smile fading. He and Elsa glanced at each other, very briefly, yet Phil never forgot the exchange.

Elsa smiled, and reached behind her back, retrieving a small parcel in an unwrapped and unmarked brown box. The plain packaging was curious. Anything that was purchased from Sascotan retailers came in a fancy package. Phil found the mystery part of the allure, and he reached for the box, eager to solve it.

Lifting the lid, Phil grasped a small contraption that felt odd in his fingers. He held it up, turning it in all directions, tilting his head as he attempted to understand it. It felt smooth, yet unlike the usual toys he had received. The material was quite unusual. And the smell...

"Do you know what it is?" asked Lucas.

Phil wrinkled his brow in a way an older gentleman might. Lucas couldn't help but chuckle at the sight.

"It looks like a transit shuttle, but it has wheels. Is it a shuttle, Dad?"

"Very smart, Phil!" exclaimed his mother. "It's similar, like the ones we ride when we go downtown. But this one's a little different."

The boy set it on the floor with care, the driver's side of the small toy facing him as he slid back to get a wider view of his gift. The car was very well-balanced, wheels perfectly circular as though they had been pressed in a machine. He leaned forward, and with two fingers nudged the toy, causing it to glide smoothly several centimeters. Phil narrowed his brows again as he pushed it back with his left hand, amazed at its effortless gliding.

"It's an automobile, son. Or at least a toy replica of one. Handcrafted, and not from plastic or metal."

Phil retrieved the toy and held it to his nose.

"Wood?"

Lucas smiled. "That's right. This wasn't made in a factory. A craftsman made it by hand. These are rare, Phil."

He played on the floor with his toy car for about ten minutes, zooming it faster and faster before his father warned him to be mindful of its fragility. Phil smiled, holding it in his hands and examining it like his parents had only seen him interact with his books.

It occurred to Phil that one important fact had not been clarified.

"Who would buy me such a fancy gift?"

His mother knelt beside his father, draping her arm over his shoulder.

"This gift is from your uncle, whom you haven't met yet," Elsa explained. "He lives far from here, and he is very fond of automobiles. I believe he made this for you himself."

Phil's eyes widened. Already a valuable item, the car had increased in value a hundred-fold.

The toy car was painted royal blue, a glossy finish protecting it from scrapes and stains. The shape of the frame was like a bell, the front hood low, arching over the passenger cabin, and lowering again at the rear. Details, like door handles, trim, headlights, and even a tiny steering wheel set into the carved-out driver's seat, were impeccably painted with care. Most notably, the hood was adorned with a curious logo on a shield. A man, dressed like a warrior of old, was crouched, leaning forward, sword in hand above his head, pointed as though he were ready to lunge into battle.

On the figure's helmet, tiny letters were painted in script he couldn't read. He leaned in close, scrunching his forehead as he focused on the strange writing.

"It says FTE," said Lucas. "Front toward enemy. That's your uncle's family crest and motto."

"Wow. That sounds really dangerous! Was he in the army?"

"Enough questions for tonight, son." Lucas laughed. "He would be pleased to know you liked his gift. We can talk about it tomorrow."

Phil knew his father was implying it was bedtime, and that tomorrow would not likely reveal any more answers. Smiling, he curled his hand over the tiny car and made for his room. As he reached the doorway, he slipped in one last question.

"Dad, who is the enemy?"

Elsa looked at her husband. Lucas tightened his lips as he considered his response. Phil spun the wheels as he turned the car around and around in his hands.

"Your uncle has made a few enemies. That's why he lives so far away..."

Aboard the magna-rail train, and three coaches down to the private seats, Phil held the wooden toy with the same wonder as his five-year-old self all those years ago. Anticipating grilling over the unusual trinket's origins, Phil had the documentation of its Sascotan background ready in a shortcut tab on his handheld. If there was a second degree of separation from its true source, there would be no trouble.

The train accelerated, hovering above the

magnetically charged rail line and thrusting forward in dampened silence. The combustible engine roared, jostling the driver's seat as it rumbled over rocky and tree-rooted terrain. As the trees along the rail line began to wheel past into a blur of mottled green, Phil found solace in memories of engines and petrol fumes, of chrome glistening and bone shaking.

Front toward enemy.

So why did it feel like retreat...

Rock Throwers

Wednesday, 9 May, AC 0245
55 Kilometers East of New Inland
Phil Fox

It took almost half of the ninety-minute transit from New Inland to the coast for Phil's headache to subside. In the privacy of his priority cabin, after the car engine in his mind idled to a low rumble, he stretched his legs onto the adjacent empty seat and reclined the backrest. Emmanuel Jackson had returned to the Spruce Grove, unannounced. It was enough for Albert to contact Phil, for the first time since his last visit almost ten years ago. He knew he wasn't going to sleep. Besides, there would be plenty of opportunity for shut-eye on the twenty-four-hour ocean leg of his trip to La Bermude. Instead, out of habit, he dimmed the handheld screen and reviewed last-minute correspondences with Kendall.

Three new messages blinked into his correspondence folder—all from Kendall. Phil couldn't imagine what would necessitate even one new message, let alone three. None were more than a few bytes in size, so none could have been terribly important. He pictured her smug grin when her notification of receipt blinked onto her own handheld. He could even hear her voice. *Off. Grid. My. Ass.* The message from the unrecognizable "Walpurgis" was pushed out of the frame of his screen. By the time he reached the harbour in Gasperro, it would have shifted to the junk file folder, along with all of Kendall's messages.

The magna-rail train hurtled along the rail line through narrower forest lanes. Kilometers of shorn vegetation around the superstructure were reduced to only meters along the conduit lanes. Setting the handheld on the cushion next to him, Phil turned his attention back to the tinted window. Outside, an unseen electrical field provided the ultimate protection from anything or anyone that may come in contact with the cylindrical white projectile. Multi-paned plexiglass kept cabin pressure stable and allowed for observation if the traveler desired to stare at whipping-past trees. Phil's father would have seen the same trees blurring into mottled green on his countless runs from New Inland to Hudson Harbour.

It was about the halfway point that the narrow tree line widened into a shrubby expanse that extended in an unkempt trail off into the woods to the north. There were once buildings, forming a small community, but they had long since been reclaimed. Phil had seen photographs of a long, narrow depot station with a raised deck and ramps for passengers. The long-abandoned train station was once the last stop before the rigorous journey across land to Allentown. Pictures of the vanished settlement still evoked in Phil images of the perils that lurked, hiding in the blur of green that whipped past his window. Few understood those perils like Phil Fox.

"You could have called, son..."

Elsa's voice trailed into a faint wheeze. Phil pulled the door shut behind him and dropped his satchel. The lights were dimmed, and his mother was resting near the faux fireplace, the artificial flames shimmering on her weathered cheek.

"I know, I'm sorry. Just lost track of time."

Phil leaned in and kissed his mother on the cheek,

wrinkled from her relieved smile.

"I'm sure they had to... coax you into packing up..."

Phil slouched back into the plush cushions.

"It's not like I want to read four-hundred pages of case law, Mom. And it's just so hard to concentrate here."

Elsa gently rocked her wicker chair. "It's hard to think of anything else but your father, isn't it?"

Her eyes reflected the flitting of the flames. Phil sighed.

"Yeah."

The pair sat in stillness for more than a few minutes. Elsa broke the wall of silence with a small burst of unexpected energy.

"The police have closed the file... Without new leads, it's unlikely... they'll be able to..."

Phil noticed the medallion his mother cupped in her hands upon her lap. He swallowed the news like the bitter pill it was.

"I'm not surprised. Disappointed, though."

Both Elsa and Phil understood the frenetic pace of his studying was propelled by the desire to understand the legal wrangling surrounding his father's death and subsequent investigation. Three years later, and with no credible leads to pursue, the investigatory funding would inevitably be scaled back. If the day were to come, and the perpetrator were to see his day of reckoning, Phil wanted to be armed with as much knowledge of the legal system as possible. Still too young and unqualified to intern with the solicitor, Phil armed himself like a small child poised to defend his father with a rock in his cocked-back hand.

"I'm sorry I've been out so late, Mom. It's time I stayed in with you a little more."

Elsa's faint smile was a thin line between narrow, dry lips. "You need your rest. But promise me you'll finish your studies."

Phil reached for his mother's hands, trembling around his father's medallion.

"I promise."

Elsa nodded her forehead to his, her flaxen hair seeping strings of grey, shrouding her face. As they met, Phil blinked away a grainy tear. He could hear the shortened breath deep in his mother's lungs, permanently damaged by the red tide. Her half-capacity to do anything rarely deterred her from trying.

"Did your father... ever tell you about the day..."

Phil joined hands with his mother, cradling his father's medallion between them. Lucas Fox was reluctant to retell the events that led to his consecration as a city hero.

"He did..."

Elsa leaned forward as though she were a child listening to an elder telling a story full of magic, heroes, and villains. Since the death of his father, Phil felt the roles between himself and his mother reversing. She knew Lucas had told him the story. Asking him was a thinly veiled prompt to tell it again.

"He was assigned to the Lake Region run for six weeks, starting in late-April when the outsider incidents usually started to ramp up. What did he say...? April showers bring May cowards? Something like that. He used to talk about how before they brought in the electro-field, the crew used to have to clean all the scrapes and dents on the outside. Rocks, sticks, even drones used to be lobbed at the trains!

"Now, hijack attempts were never common, but with the electro-field, it was impossible for someone to storm a moving magna-rail train. The charge was enough to make a full-grown outsider go limp. And if you fell under the carriage into the magnetic field, there wouldn't be much left for even the Reapers to claim."

Elsa suppressed a chuckle. "Your father used to tell

these... outlandish stories about brigands on horses riding alongside the... trains, ropes and hooks swinging..."

Phil laughed. "I think he was ripping off those old Sascotan Western films! Whenever I called him on it, he would always say that's how it was told to me..."

He mimicked his father's gruff voice. Elsa laughed until she coughed.

"One day, on a run through the Lake Region to Hyacynthe Station, he sensed the train was different that day, somehow. The motion was no different, still gliding along its magnetic rails with no resistance. But he just felt something was off.

"See, the movement of the train was so soft that if it were to actually stop, passengers and crew wouldn't even notice. Dad checked all the consoles, and nothing seemed out of the ordinary. Velocity, estimated time of arrival, weather conditions—everything was, for all intents and purposes, normal. But he couldn't shake the feeling that something was wrong. Or so he said."

Anticipating the action, Elsa had straightened in her chair, health limitations forgotten in the moment.

"Dad used the manual override to open the shields on the windows. You see, the trains relied on cameras and monitors for protection from outside collisions, and to keep the cabin pressure tight. He looked outside and saw that the train was at a complete standstill, even though the equipment told him everything was fine."

Phil paused to allow his mother to soak in the details of the story. Elsa interjected, like a child anticipating what would happen next.

"Hijackers?"

Phil nodded. "The only way anyone could hijack a magna-rail would be through hacking the mainframe and altering the data. The coach drivers were trained on how to handle a slowdown or stoppage, but not an outsider invasion.

"Dad was able to reroute the computers, and sure enough, the cameras picked up three outsiders: two climbing on the hull of the passenger carriage—you guessed it—with ropes and hooks, and another still on the ground, nothing more than a flintlock rifle in his hands. Dad wasn't worried about what the gun could do to the outside of the train. He was more worried about what would happen if they got *inside* with firearms. He had to act fast.

"So, as the story goes, he found his way around the hacked commands that had stopped the train. He could see them latched onto the hull as they began to cut into the steel outer protection with circular saws, sparks spraying and everything.

"Dad punched the manual accelerator. And as soon as the train began to move forward, he saw the hijackers start to panic. The third man on the ground dropped his gun, waving his arms at his henchmen, but it was too late. Once the train shifted speeds, the electro-field reignited."

Phil saw a pulse of revitalized energy surge in his mother at the precise moment of the story when the hijacking outsiders were electrocuted.

"Two bandits were sucked under the magna-field between the train and the track. Trying to keep up with the acceleration, the third one grabbed a rock about the size of an apple and threw it at the coach."

A burst of electrical neon outside his window startled Phil back from the daydream. Outside the gliding train, an array of half-built all-terrain buggies scooted alongside, ragged bandits hopelessly hurling hand-sized objects. It was likely a rock striking the invisible field just outside Phil's window which caused the electric light show.

Springtime meant a higher chance of brigand harassment. Lucas Fox's moment of glory happened in the springtime. As did his murder. Phil was expecting to see disgruntled vagabonds up to mischief, but there was no real reason to worry. The electro-field disintegrated rocks, bullets—anything an interloper might hurl at the trains. Phil leaned back in his plush seat, extending his legs again, intent on napping for the second half of the ride to the Hudson docks.

He thought of his mother, exhausted from listening to the story of how Lucas Fox saved a train carrying more than a hundred travelers from an outsider attack. How his quick thinking led to policy change and tightened security.

How Lucas Fox, a simple magna-rail coach driver, became a hero.

Sea Legs

Monday, 14 May AC 0245
L'Isle de la Bermude
Phil Fox

Phil's first documented island stop, *L'Isle de la Bermude*, was five days by sail from Hudson Harbour. The seven-day debacle of his first trip all those years ago still haunted him like a pang of seasickness that wouldn't settle. The adhesive patch on his left bicep would prove to be more effective than the oral medicine that had taken way too long to work that first time he traveled by sea. Having made the trip more than once, Phil shifted his apprehension to the weather conditions, calm enough to foresee no delays, but skies grey enough for skepticism to creep in.

As a paid passenger, Phil wasn't responsible for controlling any of the rigging. Once aboard his own private sloop, he would suddenly oversee everything on his own. He planned to use the longer leg of the trip to distance himself from politics, and to reconnect with the cool ocean breeze and salt spray. Still, when the opportunity arose to trim the mainsail or help the crew gybe, he couldn't help but jump into the action. If nothing else, it helped shake off the ten-year rust.

The wind eased, slowing his nautical speed from ten to eight knots, and stretching the five-day trip into six. On the fourth day, he noted that not one fishing trawler appeared on the horizon, in any direction, despite his course through rich shoals. Late spring and this far south, it was no surprise the red tide warning had been posted.

As a result, *La Bermude* was less bustling than Phil remembered. Trawlers were all secured in the quay, likely being used by their owners as living quarters while they waited for the abnormally early red tide to subside. Any fishing north of the island probably would have been uncontaminated, but health officials rarely allowed for any potential cross-contamination from the tropical reaches and the cooler northern waters. Phil wouldn't be dropping any fishing lines on the next leg. He could live with seasickness, but red tide was nasty business.

Once the sloop was moored, Phil descended the gangplank to the wharf, his travel trunk in tow on a rental trolley and his carry-on satchel slung over his right shoulder. There were no guards directing him to the registration shanty. If you tried to dodge the authorities, they would find you. Once his documentation and his cargo were double-checked by an old seaman who appeared to have never left the docks in decades, Phil could step onto land. A young hand not more than fourteen years old with a deep bronze tan and eager smile piloted the coach that resembled a rickshaw without the need for leg power to his apartment. One full night's sleep on terra firma would do a world of good to his medicated system.

Before sunset, he decided to take a walk along the nestled beach of Church Bay on the southern crescent of the main island. He needed the open air. The instant he stepped outside the gaping maw of the New Inland point of entry, he dreaded being back inside. Phil took advantage of his brief opportunity to walk along La Bermude's smooth, pristine south beach. The shores in Gasperro were much rockier. Only minutes from his rented cabin, the shore was less desirable to wandering tourists, most opting for the more posh, cyan blue waters up the coast.

Standing at the edge of the tidal reach, Phil gazed off

into the southern blue, so peaceful yet so menacing. The same could be said about any of nature's vistas outside the domes. Lush green forest concealed brigands, killers, and vicious animals. The dry, expansive desertscape of the badlands east of Sascota was parched of nutrients, cover for insects and reptiles, and inhospitable for hundreds of kilometers in every direction. Much like the frozen tundra of the North. Despite the dangers, there was always an underlying sense of peace.

But the danger lurking in the deeps, far beyond the southern horizon, was most unsettling.

Phil's sandaled foot dislodged a dimpled, ridged shellfish from half-burial in the tide's wake of beige sand.

"Lucky for you, little fellow, red tide is up."

Phil held the oyster in his hand, rubbing away the sticky clumps of sand. In a safer season, this would be one of many in his bucket, and would have proven a rich supper. With a flick of his wrist, he bounced the closed shell full of poison across the waves, watching as it dropped beneath the surface.

"Keep your diseases." Phil muttered as he turned away from the sea, retreating to his cabin for the evening as the sky deepened into a deceivingly beautiful blue.

"I mean it, you're going to miss your shuttle. And you haven't even had a shower."

Phil strained to open his sleep-crusted eyelids. The swirling motion of the ceiling fan came into focus first, followed by the redirected light pouring through the untinted windows of his office. Deliberate clattering of trinkets on his shelves and wall hangings were daggers through his temples. Kendall stood over him. She had no sympathy for his hangover. In the moment, he hated her for it.

"I'm going to assume you won't need this—what is it again?"

Peeling his bare back from the false-leather covering of the loveseat he had slept on, Phil sat up and stretched his arms wide. Kendall held a polished wooden, spindled wheel, with what appeared to be a clock of some sort in the center, tilting her head and scrunching her eyebrows as though she had just stumbled upon it on the sidewalk.

"It's a barometer," Phil answered through a wide yawn.

"It's junk, that's what it is." She tossed it into an open packing box. Phil protested her treatment of his treasures.

"Careful! That came from Azore. I made a trade with a shipper in *La Bermude*—"

"Yes, I know, and you probably gave him an old handheld that doesn't even work anymore, or something equally useless. So, it goes in storage, then?"

Phil rubbed his aching temples with one hand and waved his approval with the other. All his trinkets had a story. Kendall had heard them plenty of times in her eight years as his office manager. He never once heard her complain. He loved her for it.

"You need to keep your stories straight, Mr. Fox. I remember you telling me that you bought it from a street vendor in Azore, not in a trade with a shipper."

Phil smuckered his tongue from the dry roof of his mouth. Without even guessing it was there, he reached for the full glass of water on the lamp table. Kendall thought of everything. She was the definition of efficiency.

"I won't be long cleaning up. Shuttle lifts off at what, 0700?"

"0659, on the dot. You have forty-two minutes."

Downing the glassful of water and wiping the stray droplets from his chin, Phil sprang into action. Kendall continued to pack away his valuables while he showered in the adjacent restroom, re-emerging a new man. Light auburn hair styled with gel, face shaven with faint traces of foam still along the sideburn area, and his button-up shirt pressed and tucked as he tightened his belt.

"Eleven minutes, not bad. You said you could do it in ten, though."

"I even flossed!" Kendall's rolled eyes congratulated him with sarcasm.

Phil's hangover was still there, but the medicine Kendall would have stirred into his glass of water had already begun to ease the symptoms.

Kendall stopped packing the office décor and stepped in front of him. "You missed one." She slipped the top button through its loop and straightened his collar. "The manifest of your travel chest has already been sent. They may give you grief on the car—but don't blame me, I told you to leave it behind."

Phil slipped his feet into his loafers waiting near the office door. The room was devoid of Phil Fox personality. The bookshelves bare, starving for the knowledge of the packed-away volumes. The walls sterile, culture from the outside world removed, to be forgotten save for the faint, faded silhouettes left behind in the soft brown paint. A work desk accustomed to carrying the weight of his world, now jobless, holding only memories of stacked books and java mugs. Plush carpet with the soft outlines of fossilized footprints from years of pacing. All that remained was Miss Kendall, hands on hips and a knowing look peering down over prescription lenses, hair pulled in a back-to-business ponytail and dressed down in denims and casual tee.

"Once I'm shoved off from the Hudson, I'll be off-grid until La Bermude."

Kendall's eyes narrowed. "Off. Grid. My. Ass."

Phil laughed as he opened his arms. The pair held each other for a moment before Kendall released her grip first, clasping his shoulders as she forced him toward the door.

"Six minutes. They won't wait for you, even if you're mayor."

"Ex-mayor."

"Ex. Right..."

Neither said goodbye. Phil knew she was right. He wouldn't make the magna-rail leg without at least checking his inbox file.

Through the reed-strung blinds over the window, the dusk sky smothered the sunset. Phil tried to relax on the lumpy mattress, wincing his shoulder blades in between clumps of cotton stuffing. It's only one night, he told himself. At least the form-fitted mattress in his sloop was comfortable; well, comfortable enough for the planned four-night third leg of his journey. One night on course east-northeast to Azore, as per his travel manifest. Three north once he was safely beyond the tracking grid of La Bermude, when the rest of the world assumed he was on his way.

Sixty days was the agreed leave. Phil's capable temporary replacement was a former intern who had been groomed as much by Kendall as himself for any necessary fill-in. He tried to imagine his office redecorated with New Inland abstract art; bright, clashing colours in sharp lines hanging over the faded outlines of his naturally curved, earth-tone relics. Already, Phil regretted not bringing the steering-wheel barometer. He predicted a slight rise above the seasonal

1020 millibars based on the colour of the sky and the gentle breeze that fluttered his blinds through the cracked-open bottom pane.

Smooth sailing ahead. Phil's handheld stayed on the mute setting, tucked inside his satchel since his arrival. He drifted into an off-grid sleep, satisfied that this time he proved Kendall wrong.

The Rookie

Tuesday, 15 May AC 0245
Domestic High Council Chamber, Federation of
New Inland
Chair Jennings Marribel

Jennings Marribel had learned a long time ago that it was best not to think how far above the ground level of New Inland she spent so much of her time. It served her nothing to linger along the arched gantry platforms between her beloved Hanging Gardens plot and the Domestic High Council chambers. Leave the plexiglass-floored observation adventures to the thrill-seekers, she remembered telling more than a few people in her time. If she ever felt the urge to kiss the ground floor, she'd prefer to be several kilometers closer to it.

Someone once described the sight of the DHC chamber rotunda as though an enormous mushroom cloud had been detonated at the geometric center of what became New Inland, roaring and expanding for kilometers into the sky before it magically froze. Marribel had seen her fair share of political meltdowns inside the chamber and could even claim a few of her own. Slowing her pace as she approached the facility, she anticipated another as soon as she tapped her gavel to bring the session into order. Once the first DHC meeting with Capston's new mayor was in the books, she could retreat to the Gardens. Life was simpler there.

She entered via the Heartsburg anteroom and into the offices of her home city. Exchanging her gardening attire for business wear, Marribel passed her fingers through her short, grey hair before making her way into the chamber. The bailiffs were already seated; the pages, reviewing the business order of the day on their monitors. Representative Fellows greeted her with a curt nod as the chair took her seat.

Only four months remained of her term. And if she could see beyond the artificial sky of New Inland, she would count her lucky stars that in four months she would never have to leave the Gardens. Jennings Marribel was far spryer than the average seventy-year-old. The lush greenery of the agricultural level in the highest reaches of the Federation of New Inland's dome surely had something to do with her good health.

Above the chamber floor, the viewing balcony was at about two-thirds capacity. Higher than usual. Probably due to Steven Reekan's first appearance as mayor. Anyone entertained by the chief of security during his raucous campaign would be either present or tuned in to the livestream, on the edge of their seats for a soundbite.

Marribel wasn't settled into her high-back throne before a ruckus emanated from the Capston vestibule. The doors thrashed open, and Reekan and his delegation poured into the chamber. It was disheartening to see the rookie mayor take the raised seat of his predecessor. Phil Fox had been an exceptional diplomat and colleague. Marribel already missed his poise.

Introduction protocol began with the roll call, beginning with the city delegation to her left and around the five booths back to her own. Marribel called upon the mayors and their second representatives from the cities of Preston, Arcadia, and New Mills without incident. She forced herself not to show any disdain as she called the next city.

"Capston."

Reekan was already starting to stand up before she had even finished. She remembered feeling humbled the first time she spoke her name and title, back then as chief of Public Health. The new mayor of Capston was beaming with pride, barely able to contain himself.

"Steven Reekan, Mayor!"

The gallery applauded, breaking decorum to the annoyance of Chair Marribel. She opted to leave the gavel in its block as the spectators gradually settled. Reekan waved to them, his deep brown eyes sparkling as his trim-bearded face lit up under the adulation.

"Take it easy on the new guy!"

Reekan didn't receive the hearty response he was expecting, and with child-like disappointment passed to his Second.

"Pax Brien, Agriculture."

Marribel nodded to the soft-spoken representative. "Let the record show, Mr. Brien is serving as interim second in the absence of Mayor Phil Fox, Solicitor."

Reekan cleared his throat. "You mean former mayor, right?"

Marribel glowered. "I'm sure you are aware, the title of mayor is for life, even beyond the end of term."

Pax Brien cupped his hand to Reekan's ear. The realization of his error caused the rookie to laugh nervously.

"Yes, that's right, I apologize. As you were, Madame Chair."

Thank you, Your Worship.

"Heartsburg."

As chair of the DHC, Marribel called for the second of the fifth and final city. Her home.

"Cooper Fellows, Treasury."

"Jennings Marribel, mayor, and chair of the Domestic High Council of the Federation of New Inland. This session is come to order."

With a ceremonial clack of her gavel, the session began. Representative Fellows delivered the Department of Treasury report with succinct detail. Reekan was unable to feign his boredom, despite his best effort to scrutinize the columns of numbers on his datapad. Snickering when the defense budget was read aloud, Reekan drew Marribel's attention.

"If you have something to add, Mayor Reekan, you're expected to submit your question beforehand. I assume you read the budget?"

Reekan appeared offended. "You don't think I would come into my first meeting unprepared, do you? Of course, I read the budget."

"Very good. You haven't submitted a question, so we'll proceed with the order—"

"Pardon, Madame Chair, but I will be allowed to ask my questions when the submission list is finished, correct?"

Marribel could have used a few more seconds to compose herself. One deep breath would have to do.

"The protocol is clear, Mayor Reekan. Submissions are expected before the agenda is released so the appropriate chiefs can prepare for question period. I thought that was explained."

"Clear as muck. But isn't it also in the policy that questions from the floor follow the ordered submissions?"

"That's true, Mr. Mayor. But I will point out, as mayor, and therefore First for your city delegation, you're to submit your departmental questions—"

Reekan interrupted a second time.

"And I will also point out, Madame Chair, that the policy states that questions from the floor are permitted to voting members, and last time I checked, that includes the five mayors, right?"

Marribel turned to her pages, already retrieving the constitution to verify the claim. The youngest, a man in his early twenties, had been an intern in the Heartsburg National Bank—bright and eager to please. His eyeballs darted back and forth like laser pointers. In less than a minute, he confirmed with a glance that Reekan was technically correct.

"Very well. You can ask your questions during the open floor, but I'll caution you to be careful."

Reekan nodded with implicit satisfaction.

"And in the future, I'll make sure I get my homework in on time."

Marribel already wanted to claw his eyes out.

As Fellows fielded questions from the floor, only Reekan raised his hand like a schoolboy, generating audible chuckles from the balcony. Representative Brien pointed out the electronic button that was meant to be used for submitting a request to speak. Reekan's reaction was as though he had just discovered the meaning of life.

"Your question, Mayor Reekan."

The mayor of Capston stood even though no others did for their respective floor time. As a result, the microphone only registered half of his baritone, the other half echoing around the chamber walls before he corrected himself.

"I will keep it short and sweet. Representative Fellows, in your budget it says here that the allotment for defense to the cities has increased by 2% since the last session. If I'm not mistaken, that increase was to be adjusted to 2.5% in the first quarter. Now, you know we presented our defense budget in good faith, and given our current situation, anything that gets trimmed off will really limit us. Representative Fellows, is there a typo here, or is the council going back on its word?"

Despite his unpolished vocabulary and brash approach, Marribel had to acknowledge Reekan's audacity. She stopped short of respecting it.

"As was stated earlier in the report, export revenue fell short of projections in the fourth quarter, and as a result, the Department of Finance has the provision within the mandate to adjust spending in accordance—"

"So, what you're saying is you counted your chickens before they hatched."

Marribel slammed her gavel.

"Mayor Reekan, you're reminded that when a representative has the floor, you are to allow them to finish."

"With all due respect, Madame Chair, I'm not interested in banker jargon. And neither are these people." Reekan looked up to the balcony, where the spectators applauded. Marribel banged her gavel three more times, each a little harder than the last.

"And I will remind the balcony that if decorum cannot be kept, the filters will be turned on to allow the council to continue without noise."

A few jeers coursed down from the upper level before the bailiffs signaled for the boisterous attendants to hush.

Reekan raised his hands in surrender. Fellows cleared his throat.

"The shortfall is from nuclear medicine export. We expected a decline because of Lacraie ramping up production. But as you know, Mayor Reekan, there is no diplomatic tie with Hyacynthe and its holdings at this time. The information we receive about their export is third party at best."

"*Is* it, now? Has the DHC been having small talk with the Allens lately?"

"Steven, you're out of order!"

"That's Mayor Reekan, actually. Okay, I retract."

"This isn't a trial and you're not the solicitor."

"Don't worry, Chair Marribel, your buddy Fox will be back in a few months."

Following through on her promise, Marribel signaled to her pages and the noise from the balcony softened as the invisible dampers hummed to life. Fellows looked to Marribel before returning his attention to Reekan, who was basking in the commotion from his audience despite their muffled reaction.

"We are able to tabulate Hyacynthe GDP based on aggregate totals from the other federations on the continent. Our counterparts in Ozarck have increased spending on everything from radiation to red tide treatment. But Mayor Reekan, you would be familiar with Ozarck, wouldn't you?"

Reekan objected to the jab.

"I thought I was asking the questions from the floor? You already know the answer."

If the gallery above looked surprised at Reekan's earlier insolence, the rest of the council was visibly shocked at the latest exchange.

"Forgive me, but I thought the lease agreement between Capston and Ozarck over Ap-Oz was legally approved?"

The contentious issue over Capston leasing a facility outside New Inland contributed to the blowback of Phil Fox and his handling of the terror crisis. At Chief of Security Reekan's urging, a significant portion of the Capston defense budget was allotted to the leasing of a training and research facility in the Appalachian Mountain range to the south. Marribel still simmered over the DHC's 6-4 vote. She had vehemently argued against further business operations outside the dome. She was far too familiar with the dangers in the outside world. It was poisoned. Water, air, soil, minds. That sentiment remained unchanged.

"This line of questioning falls under the Chief of Defense report. Do you have any further questions, Mayor Reekan?"

"None as long as I get answers to the ones I already asked."

Fellows sighed.

"As I stated, the shortfall is a result of—"

"Yes, yes, Ozarck is buying more medicine from Hyacynthe. Which is better than buying it from Le Renard, I suppose. But still..."

Marribel smashed the gavel, a hairline fracture in the tapered handle creaking in her grip.

"And you were reminded not to interrupt!"

Before he could retort, Reekan yielded as Representative Brien tugged at his sleeve. Closing his eyes and inhaling, he sat down, adjusting the microphone.

"No further questions. For the treasury, anyway."

The entire council chamber seemed to sigh along with him. If that were his only confrontation during the proceedings, Marribel would have considered it a small victory.

It only got worse.

The Hammer and the Anvil

Tuesday, 15 May, AC 0245
Domestic High Council Chamber, Federation of
New Inland
Mayor Steven Reekan

Steven Reekan could handle the rigors of long hours in the Foundries. He could withstand the strict regimen of the foremen. He could carry the weight of the payload on his shoulders. He carried it every day. But no matter how mentally prepared he was, as soon as he entered the chamber, he felt the resolve wilt. It took every ounce of whatever remained to maintain the confident façade that drew cheers from the gallery and scorn from the council. His father once told him an anecdote that would resonate with him long beyond his time working in the metalworks of the industrial sector:

There are two forces. The hammer and the anvil. One strikes and the other resists. The hammer will only swing with as much power as is applied to it. The anvil is designed to withstand whatever force the hammer wields.

Some days you're the hammer. Other days, you're the anvil.

But what is produced between the two... now that's what it's all about.

The Preston second and chief of defense, Blythe Easton, was a worthy anvil. Steven went over the motion of his swinging techniques while the formal address was delivered. Something about more frequent raids on the magna-rail lines from disgruntled outsiders. More about the crime levels in four of the five cities either stable or decreasing while Capston's was on the rise. No surprises there. Reekan's palms sweated as he tightened the grip on his most trusted tool—determination. He would be heard.

"Mayor Reekan, you're up."

Marribel didn't look his way. Steven wouldn't have suffered her the dignity of acknowledgment. He was already homed in on Easton who, by the look in her eyes, was steadying her anvil in anticipation of the first strike. The mayor of Capston cleared his throat.

"Representative Easton, Capston submitted a budgetary proposal outlining our plans to combat the ongoing terrorism within the city, which we continue to stress has an impact on the Federation as a whole. Since our requests for an increase in funding for technological development were not approved, we then applied for DHC permission to investigate any leads outside the dome—we even promised to itemize our plans in the interest of transparency. Again, we were denied.

"My question for you, Representative Easton, is this: How is the Defense Corps expecting us to further any progress following leads when we're blocked from both increasing our spending on technology and pursuing any leads outside our city jurisdiction?"

Easton read along with the pre-submitted question, summarized by Steven as he lobbed his first swing. She appeared unfazed as she signaled the chair for her reply.

"As we have explained in the budget, decreased remittance from Capston has led to a decrease in the Defense Corps budget altogether. Mayor Reekan, you get out of us what you put in."

"Right. You wanted Capston to add to the Defense Corps personnel even though we're facing an unparalleled crisis within our own city walls. I don't see how you can make any argument for Capston to allow more warm bodies to walk around the causeway and issue tickets when we have outsiders blowing our people up."

Easton didn't blink. "Since your alleged outsiders would have to pass through the Federation arches and through the causeway to even get to Capston, wouldn't it make more sense to field more resources there? I'll remind you, Mr. Mayor, the Defense Corps has increased security checks by nearly 50% in the last quarter, as per the request of Mayor Fox. And at *your* insistence, I would add."

"Right. Tell that to the families of the forty-six dead in the 400-block bombing last month."

If he looked up, he knew the gallery would have been on their feet, fists in the air, as they screamed fruitlessly into the still-activated sound barrier. Easton's steely stare met his own with a static charge that should have sent her straight, pulled-back hair in all directions. She absorbed the attack, remaining composed. The exhilaration of the clash washed over Reekan, recharging his resolve for the next swing. Capston was on his watch now. The fourth bombing would be the last if it meant the end of his career.

He opted for a quick jab this time. "So, it is clear that Capston can't count on any further assistance from the DHC."

"Mr. Mayor, you claim you're so destitute when the council is very aware of your operation at the Appalachian-Ozarck complex. Last time I checked, you weren't so excited to share with us the profit margin of your development sales to Ozarck, am I right?"

Steven's single greatest victory as Capston's chief of defense was securing the right to operate inside the mountain fortress several hundred kilometers south and west. Closer to the Ozarck Federation dome than New Inland itself, the facility offered two very important things—privacy and solitude.

"Ap-Oz is a private sector business, Blythe, you know that."

Marribel chimed in.

"*Representative Easton,*" Marribel corrected. "Please follow the protocol, Mayor Reekan."

Steven smirked at the thought that Marribel may have caught a stray spark.

"Of course. Representative Easton, the Defense Corps has previously approved Capston operating in the legally leased facility of the Ozarck Federation, and it has been disclosed that profits from private enterprises are not funneled into public works, as per the DHC ruling."

"So, what are you stockpiling all that profit for, Mr. Mayor? Your retirement?"

Steven pounded his fist. "Any objection to that, Madame Chair, or am I the only one to get my wrists slapped for using sarcasm?"

Marribel swung her gavel. "Representative Easton, reconsider your response in accordance with protocol."

Easton narrowed her eyes at Reekan and smiled. "Of course, Madame Chair."

The anvil had held. *Now we're dancing...*

"Mr. Mayor, the taxable revenue from your business ventures in Ap-Oz contributes to your city budget. Given that we aren't privy to your figures, the Defense Corps is in no position to hand out any more cash."

"One more question, and I would appreciate some rationale with your answer. Our intelligence has provided us a credible lead that would indicate outsider planning in the 400-block bombing. Will the Defense Corps and the DHC grant Capston legal permission to pursue leads outside New Inland in the interest of public security?"

Steven lobbed a two-fisted swing, determined to test Easton's fortitude.

"We would require the source of the intelligence. We would then have to determine if the source were legally obtained. Until then, our position is unchanged. I must ask, Mr. Mayor, does Capston still believe the Ansati are responsible?"

Steven's eyes widened. "Our investigation is ongoing and I'm not going to elaborate on classified information. But the Reapers are only fairy tales, Ms. Easton. Call them what you want, but they're still only fantasy. We're looking for *real* terrorists."

Easton's brow wrinkled. "That's interesting, as I recall your predecessor reported that his chief of security had not ruled out Ansati—Reapers, in your words—after symbols of their order were left at the bombing sites. I assume you've interviewed them since, to clear their good name?"

The representatives from New Mills and Arcadia chuckled as the gallery hissed above the chamber. Marribel once again scolded Easton to follow protocol. Steven was certain steam was puffing from his ears. Real or not, Reapers were no laughing matter.

The former chief of security and current mayor of Capston stood up and opened his arms wide. "You can mock me all you like, but we are pressing forward. Let the record show the DHC continues to stand on ceremony instead of helping the people of Capston! You all should be ashamed of yourselves."

Above, the bailiffs descended into the gallery crowd, restraining the Capstonian observers. Steven heard the screams of his supporters. They weren't bound to any red tape or protocol like he was. Marribel attacked her gavel block as though she had swapped it out for a five-kilogram sledge.

"Mayor Reekan, you are out of order! Retract your statement or face sanction!"

"Seems like we're already facing sanction, Jennings—

rather, Madame Chair. I retract, under protest. Get that in your report." The Capston page nodded as he tapped away at his console. Easton tried her best, but at the end of it all, she was still only the anvil. Steven found great satisfaction knowing this was only the first of many DHC meetings to come. He wasn't going anywhere, and the other four cities had to deal with it.

Jennings Marribel's hawkish face was nearly as gray as her cropped hair.

"Steven—rather, *Mayor* Reekan—the Domestic High Council has given Capston plenty of latitude during your ongoing security crisis. Against our better judgment, we approved your request for naturalization of Ozarckian nationals from Ap-Oz. Mayor Fox argued for your increase in outside personnel to be fast-tracked, all under the banner of security. He put a lot of faith in you. The council placed a lot of faith in you. So, it's time you walk the walk. You have what we're willing to give. Make something out of it—and until you have results, don't come in here demanding anything."

Steven refused to sit down.

"You want results?"

Easton, Marribel, and the other representatives on the DHC glared at the beaming mayor of Capston. He didn't know what the final product of the forge would be. But he knew it would be beautiful.

"Just watch us."

Not Today

Tuesday, 29 May AC 0245
The Causeway, Capston, New Inland
Lorrie Sheppard

Pushing with his right foot, Lorrie coasted along the emergency lane of the elevated high-transit roadway, Warren three longboard lengths behind him. Any closer, and his friend's whining would be unbearable.

"Honestly, Lor, we aren't going to gain any time," Warren protested from Lorrie's tailwind. "First sight of a squad car and we'll…"

Lorrie thrusted himself further ahead, so he didn't have to hear the rest of Warren's worries. He had already explained it to him. If they left two hours early, the police patrol should be quieter before rush hour begins. They would save almost twenty minutes by avoiding the winding, rutted ground-level streets. How come boarders and cyclists have to use the shitty roads when the rich can glide along the smooth-as-glass transit causeways, he had asked rhetorically. Ten blocks and change from the Sheppard Inn to the longboard track, and an awful lot of slums in between. Lorrie would rather take his chances with the police than whatever they might encounter down below.

Hugging the far right of the emergency lanes, the friends glided along the boulevard, four shuttle lanes wide for regular traffic, two for low-occupancy vehicles, and one for both emergency access and illegal skaters. It wasn't like they were the only ones. As far back as he could remember, Lorrie recalled pointing out kids and adults alike in all manner of self-propelled wheels, from behind the window of the mass transit shuttles. They can move much faster with the tailwinds, Lorrie's father once told him. The thought of wind in his face was romantic to him before he had ever stepped onto a longboard.

Around a wide, southbound arc, the boulevard stretched into a long straightaway, passing at least six blocks before Lorrie's sight line vanished between high-rises on either side. Warren coasted up alongside him.

"Thanks for leaving me in the dust!" Warren kept pace, forcing Lorrie closer to the low-occupancy lanes than he preferred.

"Quit crowding me, Warren!" The whooshing of a passing shuttle car proved his point. New Inland shuttles were quiet, and the cause of more than a few collisions with illegal riders on the emerg lanes. Lorrie couldn't tell if the rush he felt was from the sudden gust of the passing shuttle or the danger of riding so close he could have reached out and touched it.

It may have been his nerves, too. The race this afternoon was Troy's last in their age grouping. Lorrie came so close to beating his nemesis the last time. He would not lose today.

Warren backed off a board's length. "Shuttle! Pull in, Lor!"

"And miss another tailwind? I don't think so!" Glancing over his shoulder, Lorrie timed his crouch to the exact instant the car would pass. As it sailed past, Lorrie thrust with a strong push of his left foot and felt the invisible force dragging him forward as though he were being pulled in a wagon. It was all he could do not to stand straight up, open his arms, and bask in the rushing wind. Instead, he closed his eyes and let the longboard do the work for a few minutes.

"Squad car!"

Warren's shriek snapped Lorrie back to reality. In the

opposite lane, a pill-shaped police squad car flashed on its lights. "Damn, Warren, why did you have to wear that neon green track shirt?" It didn't even match his beige secondhand helmet.

Still coasting on the backdraft, Lorrie pushed on as Warren gained on his right side. He didn't look back. "Does he have his lights on us, or someone else?" He already knew the answer. The next off-ramp was about two hundred meters ahead.

"He's coming around! I told you we'd get caught!"

Lorrie looked back to see the squad car crossing traffic, U-turning at a designated connector lane. A transit shuttle whooshed past, occupants waving and laughing at the longboarders. How many times had he laughed at people just like himself, pulled over and fined through the nose for a few blocks of smooth boarding? He could already hear Robbie chastising him.

Not today, Lorrie promised himself as he aimed for the off-ramp. "Looks like we're leaving!"

As the grade dropped in a wide arc under the elevated causeway, the boys leaned hard into the turn. The squad shuttle was about half a kilometer behind, Lorrie estimated due to the distance from the last connector. They should have enough time to get off the ramp and down some alleyway before the police made it to the exit—if Warren's secondhand longboard wheels didn't rattle off their moorings and send him flying first.

The smoothness of the ramp gave way to the rougher surface of the ground-level streets. At first, Lorrie was grateful that there were no cars. A cursory glance around at the dereliction of buildings answered a question he hadn't asked. There must be a reason no one was traveling down here.

"I've been through some slummy neighborhoods, but this is something else!" Warren pulled up alongside Lorrie as the pair took in their surroundings. The entire block, as far as Lorrie could tell, from apartments to stores to offices, was either boarded-up doorways or heavy-tinted glass windows. The streets were clean and devoid of homeless people huddled on corners.

"Oh, wait, this is the 300-block," Lorrie said. "The second bomb went off around here somewhere, didn't it?" He remembered the temporary influx of guests at the Sheppard in the days following the attack, and how almost as quickly, they were gone. It meant a welcome boost in income for Robbie, but not enough to justify hiring more help. It meant more work around the inn for Lorrie.

The police siren sounded, and the boys darted into the nearest alleyway, between what was once a department store on one side and a windowless two-story building on the other. They had to keep moving. The police would catch on to their escape route soon enough.

Boards under their arms, the pair ran between steel dumpsters and discarded debris too large to fit inside them. The end of the alley would lead to better options, as long as the police didn't see where they went. "I don't think they saw us," Warren said as though he were reading Lorrie's mind. The muffled siren of their pursuer echoed in the stillness of the fallow block.

Lorrie's presumed better options turned out to be a dead end. A tall, woven wire fence bisected the alley, blocking their escape.

"We gotta climb!" Lorrie leaped onto the wire, swaying with his momentum. The siren grew louder.

"Lorrie, this one is open, come on!" Warren pulled open a heavy, steel-framed door that should have been barred shut. Lorrie clung to the fence trying to piece it all together. If the neighbourhood is all sealed up, why was this door open?

"If that's open, someone's probably inside! Come on, we have to climb!"

Glancing back over his shoulder, Lorrie saw the reflection of the flashing police lights. The squad car was close. There was no way he could scale the fence without being seen.

"Lorrie, come on!" Warren ducked inside the open door as Lorrie dropped from the fence. As he pulled the door behind him, the siren's echo pulsed up the alley. The door latched and all sound and light vanished into pitch blackness.

As a young child, Lorrie Sheppard was terrified of the dark. He never understood why. All he knew was that when he was curled up in his bed, his mother would read him stories in the soft glow of the nightlight. Robert Sheppard always stepped in to kiss him goodnight on the forehead before turning off the light. "You won't be seeing anything while you're asleep, anyway," he always said. "The lights drain power, and every little bit counts." Those words could have easily been said by either his father back then or his brother today. Only today, his mother wasn't around to sneak back in and turn the nightlight on again with a wink and blown kiss.

Engulfed by a darkness so thick he felt his breath quickening, Lorrie waited for several minutes before calling out to his friend. And when he did, the words stuttered in his dry throat.

"Warren?"

"Do you think they saw us?" The acoustics were muted enough to make it impossible to judge how close or far they were from each other.

"I didn't see the squad car before I shut the door," Lorrie answered. The lapse in time reminded him that they were going to miss their practice runs if they didn't get moving. He swallowed and reached for his handheld. It was too cheap to have a flashlight, but in this room the glow of the screen was at least enough to orient them.

Warren was crouched only a few meters from him, huddled against a pile of furniture draped with fabric. Slowly rotating the small screen around him, Lorrie identified several stacks of armless chairs, and oblong tables stacked in pairs, surface to surface, with legs straight up like turtles on their backs. He turned back to the door and spotted a manual latch bolt, which he turned to secure the door from anyone who might try to get in—police or otherwise. A light switch next to the frame predictably didn't work.

"No power," Lorrie said. At least the building wasn't still in use. Now the challenge was to find another way out, since the police would almost certainly be waiting near the alley. "Come on, Warren, let's go."

The pair shuffled with light steps between more stacked furniture, rows of painting frames stacked vertically against one another, and unmarked boxes until the far side of the room revealed a faint line of light beneath a set of double doors. It wasn't enough to suggest a light source; more likely it was natural light from a distant window beyond.

Lorrie leaned his ear against the doors. The silence that choked him in the storage room extended into whatever waited behind them. He turned the handle slowly, and pushed.

Even though the light in the hallway was dim, it hit his eyes like he was staring into the sunlight mirrors above the city. Warren emerged beside him, rubbing his squinted eyes. "What's this, Lor?"

As his focus corrected, Lorrie gazed down a carpeted hallway, doors on either wall staggered and numbered, odds on the right and evens on the left. Halfway down, a cleaning cart lay still, various spray bottles perched on the top shelf. At the end, two doors were propped open, allowing light from the lobby area.

"Two-story, just like the Sheppard Inn."

Lorrie sighed. Maybe the last guests in this hotel sought refuge at the Sheppard in the aftermath of the 300-block bombing. Or maybe it was already shuttered. There didn't seem to be enough dust on the door handles to suggest it had been closed very long.

Which way, Lorrie asked himself. Behind them, a service elevator and emergency stairwell door capped the back end of the hallway. A hanging exit sign over an adjacent hallway that presumably led to another wing gave them at least one other option. "Come on." The lure of the open lobby was too much to pass up. The emergency exit was probably barred shut anyway.

The pair emerged into the lobby after peeking around the propped doors. The light from the dark tinted windows that lined the street-side front of the hotel gave a slate grey hue, making an already drab space even more stark. At the center of the room, the reception cubicle was an open-concept, round countertop adorned with lifeless monitors and keypads. This is where the abandoned hotel differed from the Sheppard. Reception was a long counter, cutting off the offices from the guest area. In the Sheppard, a long sofa and plush chairs offered guests a place to sit comfortably while they waited for their shuttles upon checkout. Here, the furniture was gone, probably under blankets in the storage room they first encountered. An image of Cadlen curled up in a corner on the floor, oblivious to the emptiness of the purged room, still drawing in his sketchbook: This is the future of the Sheppard Family Inn, Lorrie imagined. Mom and Dad were dead. Crystal had already left. It occurred to him that his greatest fear was of dying in the empty shell of his parents' hopes and dreams.

"Lorrie! Lorrie!" Warren whispered in a hoarse gasp. The police squad car crept the length of the windowed hotel front, lights intermittently flashing without their blue and red passing through the tint. The boys froze as though a spotlight were upon them. Still, the squad car kept moving. If the police officer had seen them, he would have stopped. He couldn't see anything. Lorrie smiled, and approached the tinted windows.

Warren wheezed in exasperation. "What are you doing? What if they have heat scanners?"

Lorrie snorted. "What if they do? Those sliding doors run on electricity. What's he gonna do, smash the windows?" He stopped less than a meter from the sliding doors, opening his arms in defiance. The squad car didn't stop. Lorrie stared as though he were willing it away. "That's right, asshole, keep going. You're not fining us today."

"If they can't get in this way, we can't get out either," Warren observed. He was right. Their best option was to retreat the way they came in and go back through the door they locked by hand.

"Okay, so we hang here for another ten minutes or so, then we backtrack to the storage room. If the cop doesn't pass by again, he's gone on his way. And we can still make it to the practice runs before Troy." They'd lost a lot of time, but they'd at least get in one run before the first heats.

"You let Troy get into your head too much," Warren said, rolling his eyes. "He's just a New Mills pretty boy. I don't see why you get so worked up about him."

Lorrie turned away from the glass doors. "Oh, I dunno. Because he puts in half the effort and still comes out on top? Because he has to flex his body ink every chance he gets?" There couldn't have been more than a square centimeter of natural flesh tone from his neck down to his ankles. The guy was a walking graffiti wall.

"Who cares? Once he's out of our division, we won't have to compete against him for at least the next two years. And by then, we'll be bigger and more experienced."

Warren was right, but none of that mattered if Lorrie couldn't afford the higher fees of the 18-25 division. Robbie couldn't afford to cycle at the Holt Velodrome anymore. Lorrie knew how many stones made five. His longboard career was already on borrowed time.

"I know I can win in a division without Troy. I know it. But it doesn't mean anything if I'll always remember that I couldn't beat him."

"But do you think Troy's thinking about you like that? After today, he moves on, and guys like us are just forgotten stats from his 14-17 stage—"

Warren's eyes widened. "Lor, get away from the windows. Someone's coming." Warren ran to the reception kiosk and leaped upon the marble-topped counter, tumbling to the other side as his board clattered on the floor beside him.

Lorrie turned to face the glass. Across the street, two men in dark jumpsuits and beaked caps were walking briskly. The pair stopped opposite the sliding doors. One of the men held a device that looked too big to be a standard handheld. He turned to face the front of the hotel, and with the touch of his index finger, pressed on the device. A snapping crackle of electricity sounded, and the lobby lights burst to life.

"Oh shit!" Lorrie lunged for the kiosk, sliding across the counter as Warren ducked beneath. He watched from his crouching position as the two men, both bespectacled in wide sunglasses, crossed the street.

"Who are these guys?" Warren shuddered from his fetal position.

"They look like sanitation, from the jumpsuits and caps anyway." It made sense for city crews to watch over the abandoned business. It kept squatters away. But apart from the preying police squad car, these guys were the only signs of life the boys had seen since they boarded off the causeway ramp. Why here, and why now?

Lorrie ducked, and tucked himself as deep under the counter as Warren. The doors slid open, allowing a rush of wind to accompany the footsteps of the two sanitation workers on the tile floor. Lorrie listened for any trace of a siren. Nothing, as the doors shut again. Warren held his hands over his mouth as though he couldn't trust himself not to blurt something.

The pair walked across the lobby floor in the direction of the open double doors. Lorrie could hear soft muttering, but only as they approached the reception kiosk could he discern any exact words.

"...We're wasting our time here, lieutenant—"

"Keep my name out of your mouth, Grant."

"Likewise."

"Since when is careful planning a waste of time?"

"I was hired to get results, not to hide in corners. If I'd been leading the mission, the entire 300-block would have been rubble."

"So you say..."

The voices trailed off as the pair of bickering men passed the kiosk and through the open double doors into the hallway. Warren's pupils peeking through the slits of his eyes were deep and wide. After a few seconds, a bell sounded, and two more automatic doors shuffled open. They're taking the elevator, Lorrie surmised. As the doors shut, both boys exhaled.

"Lorrie, those guys aren't sanitation."

If I'd been leading the mission, the entire 300-block would have been rubble...

Lorrie gulped. "I think you're right. Come on, let's get out of here."

Peeking up over the countertop, they could see that the lights were still on in the lobby. Electricity meant that the sliding doors would still open. This was their only chance.

Grabbing their longboards, the pair leaped over the counter and raced for the doors. The motion sensor drew them wide, and the boys sprinted down the street in the opposite direction the squad car had approached earlier.

"We have to tell the police!" huffed Warren as his longboard wobbled under his arm with every stride. "There's gonna be another attack!"

"But what do we tell the police? That we broke into an abandoned building after fleeing a police cruiser and we overheard terrorists? How's that going to sound?"

The boys didn't stop until more than two blocks later. The whooshing of shuttle traffic above them on the causeway broke the silence of the 300-block slum.

"So, what, we just go to the meet like nothing happened?"

Lorrie dropped his board and mounted it with a hard thrust. "That's exactly what we do. Besides, we don't even know what we heard."

As he pushed on in the direction of the longboard track, Lorrie left Warren catching his breath, panting. "Come on, Warren, we've lost a lot of time," he called back over his shoulder. Troy wouldn't have cared anyway.

The Interlopers

Tuesday, 29 May AC 0245
The Causeway, Capston, New Inland
Lieutenant Colonel Paolo Desantos

The grey jumpsuit was a size smaller than he would have preferred. He couldn't wait to arrive at the safe house to change into better-fitting clothes. Paolo pulled the beak of his grey cap as close to his eyebrow as possible to allow for the wide lenses of his shades to fit properly. Grant, his Kayewati tagalong, insisted on talking most of the time on the shuttle bus. Paolo ignored him, staring out the window as the carriage whisked down the causeway in sterile silence. Something about the elevated highway system off the ground level combined with the muted power train reminded him of hang gliding. No jostling, no exhaust fumes, no bumps in the road to shake him. It would be so easy to lose concentration in such a soft mode of transportation. Paolo preferred to be alert, especially behind enemy lines.

Passengers whooped and slapped their hands on the windows at a pair of teens illegally skateboarding in the emergency lanes. Idiots, Paolo muttered under his breath. *Drift too close to one of these shuttles and you'd never know what hit you.*

"Next stop is ours," Grant said, reaching beneath his seat for his work bag. "At least the cops will be busy chasing those punks."

"Indeed." Paolo gritted his teeth. Grant was too careless with his words. The shuttle came to a stop alongside the emerg lanes, and the pair disembarked.

The spiral, steel stairs corkscrewed down from the causeway to the 300-block, where at least there would be fewer ears to overhear the Kayewati slip up and say too much.

Paolo slung his work bag over his shoulder and took the lead. The artificial airflow up on the causeway died completely at ground level. Living his life in the open air of Motherland, he could not acclimatize himself to the emptiness of the New Inland controlled-climate system. It was like living inside a vacuum.

"What, two blocks from here?" Grant retrieved his handheld and extended his arm as though he were reading a field compass. Paolo sighed. Old-world technology was no good in this world. He pulled on the strap of his bag, its contents jostling against his back. Fortunately, he carried the solution to some of their new-world obstacles.

Two blocks later the pair turned up an adjacent street towards the front entrance of the shuttered Spartan Hotel, only half a block from the second Motherland target. "Talk about returning to the scene of the crime," Grant muttered. "You couldn't have found anything better?"

Paolo glared at his partner.

"Okay, fine, no more until we're upstairs."

A siren trailed off in the distance—probably the same police squad car that was chasing those punks. Paolo wasn't concerned if they were to be questioned. The paperwork was all in order, thanks to the Allens. Any identification scan would indicate that both he and the Kayewati were legal residents of Capston, working for public sanitation, assigned to the 300-block to report on any damage or illegal garbage dumping. Their identities were expensive.

The device in his bag was tenfold more so. Across the street from the dark-tinted plexiglass windows of the

Spartan, Paolo retrieved his latest acquisition. The device wasn't fully assembled, although the electronics inside were live and running. It was just as well. More airflow would keep it running cooler, and they weren't expecting to be caught in any rainstorms, anyhow.

"You paid how much for that, again?" So much for Grant not talking until they were upstairs.

Paolo ignored the question and brought the small screen to life with a click of his left thumb on the side. After a few seconds, the device retrieved a screenshot of the Spartan blueprint, tiny lights blinking over the power grid controls. A blue light signaled the device was synchronized. With the push of his finger, the sliding front doors of the Spartan Hotel slid open, and the lights beamed to life.

"Never mind," Grant conceded as the pair crossed the traffic-less street. "I'll have to get myself one of those."

"I'll let you know if I hear they're on sale," Paolo answered as they stepped inside the lobby. With the lights on and the electric grid humming, he could smell the dust wafting from the air exchangers. Scanning the room quickly, he detected nothing out of the ordinary. His eyes came to rest on the false fireplace, and for an instant he imagined it roaring and crackling artificially, surrounded by wealthy visitors who wouldn't know how to rub two sticks together if their lives depended on it.

"You know, in the event of an earthquake, a fire pit or fireplace would be your best place to hide, unless you're near a bathtub."

"That's fascinating. Let's go." Paolo turned for the open doors of the hallway that led to the elevator. Thanks to his purchase, the lift was operational, which would make it easier to move supplies up and down. And it would give Grant one less thing to complain about.

As they passed the reception kiosk, Paolo slowed his pace. There was a fine layer of dust on the dark granite countertop, except for a few scuff marks. He remembered leaning across the counter the first time he had scouted the Spartan looking for squatters. That was a week ago, though.

"What's the matter, you missed a spot? Want me to call housekeeping? Come on, we're wasting our time here, lieutenant—"

"Keep my name out of your mouth, Grant."

The big Kayewati took off his sunglasses and looked hurt. "Likewise."

"Since when is careful planning a waste of time?" Paolo turned away from the kiosk and continued his way to the elevator.

"I was hired to get results, not to hide in corners. If I'd been leading the mission, the entire 300-block would've been rubble."

"So you say," Paolo muttered as the pair entered the hallway. "Your resume is impressive, Kayewati, but you've yet to prove anything to me."

"I've burned entire villages to the ground, lieutenant colonel. They don't pay me to source out new water wells. Here, if you want to go back and clean up the dust, here's your cart." Grant kicked the trolley out of his path.

Paolo toggled the screen of his device to life and synched it with the elevator. As Grant reached for the second-floor button, the doors slid open, startling the big mercenary. "Okay, now you're showing off."

The pair stepped inside as the doors slid shut. The small living quarters on the top floor offered clean linens, running water, and one-way glass to see up two streets. The pair of twin beds were made as though room service had come to call, short of a complimentary mint candy on each pillow. Paolo returned his device to his pack and removed his cap and glasses, tossing them on the bed he claimed as his own for the night.

"I wanted this one anyway," Grant muttered as he

followed suit, peeling out of his jumpsuit to reveal the snug-fit combat fatigue undershirt hugging his impressive build. Paolo changed out of his jumpsuit into a set of new clothes, still crisp from the factory looms.

"Suppose we call for some food?" Grant flopped back on his mattress. Paolo wasn't hungry, but the rations of dried meats and cereals would be enough to tide him over. They would be leaving tomorrow anyway, and once the job was carried out, he'd have no reason to even think of this place anymore. If the Kayewati was worth his salt, forty-eight hours from now the pair of them would never have to see each other again. For Paolo, it was two days too long.

His thoughts returned to the disturbed dust on the kiosk counter just as his device dinged.

"It's for you, Desantos!" Grant was strewn on top of the covers, his artificially sleeved arm covering his eyes as though he were about to take a nap.

Paolo's forehead wrinkled as he retrieved his device. The screen had come to life and the sliding doors of the Spartan were blinking. "Someone has come through the doors."

"Huh?" Grant sat up, a look of inconvenience in his eyes. "You mean after us?"

"That's what I said," Paolo answered as he swiped menus and tabs across his screen. The surveillance cameras were synched to the power grid, of course, so it would be easy to access them with his new machine.

His eyes narrowed when the camera in the lobby showed two young boys, each with a longboard under his arm, emerging from the hallway into the lobby, goofing off before hiding behind the kiosk counter. They must have been the kids those policemen were chasing earlier. But how did they get in...

"So, what, you want to go back and finish your cleaning rounds, or—"

Paolo spun around, and his fist connected with Grant's jaw hard enough for him to stumble. Shaking off the strike and spitting blood, the mercenary sneered.

"You want to try that again, Desantos?"

Paolo thrust the screen up to Grant's nose. "We had company, you idiot, and they could have heard us. I told you not to talk until we were upstairs..."

Grant wiped his lip. "I thought you had this place secured."

So did Paolo. His predecessors had been using the Spartan since the first attack. Paolo sat on the edge of his bunk and began the arduous process of retrieving surveillance footage from the days, even weeks before they had arrived. It didn't take him long to learn that the alarm system was tied into the main power grid, so when it was off, someone could have had a party throughout the building without detection. Still, all the exits were controlled electronically as well. Except...

"Are there any back doors you forgot to check?"

Grant was really pushing his luck. The service doors in the back locked from the inside. Only a professional lockpick or someone with a device like his own would have been able to get in. Paolo resigned himself to a sleepless night going back over the footage to see if anyone was actively spying on the previous Motherland agents.

"Can you use that thing to identify who those kids were, at least?"

That, he could do. "I'll have their identities in a matter of minutes."

"Good, because before we hit the big job, we need to get rid of them."

They were only children, clearly up to mischief but nothing more. Paolo remembered the huddled children who suffered Commander Yael's cruelty, all those weeks ago that felt like yesterday. He swallowed the image like a bitter pill.

Paolo had a job to do. The screen on his device blinked and a new blueprint similar to the Spartan flashed to life.

"Don't get too comfortable, Mr. Grant. We're going to visit the Sheppard Family Inn."

Family Portrait

Tuesday, 29 May AC 0245
Sheppard Family Inn, Capston, New Inland
Lieutenant Colonel Paolo Desantos

During the long walk through the ground-level streets, the Kayewati never stopped complaining. Paolo had to spell it out for him how it wasn't wise to take public transit to the Sheppard Inn. Investigators would pull all surveillance and manifest records right away. Sunglasses and hats wouldn't be much of an obstacle for a forensic investigator. It was as though in his eyes Grant's synthetic sleeve acted as an invisibility cloak. He carried himself with an air bordering between arrogance and petty annoyance. If he heard him start one more sentence with "In Kayewat, we...," Paolo might strangle him in public and happily accept the consequences.

It wouldn't have been easy to conceal in their travel bags the explosives required to level the Sheppard Inn. So, not only did they have to walk several blocks through winding streets, they had to carry the extra weight, something Paolo was quite accustomed to but was apparently too much for Grant's fragile ego. Were all Kayewati so physically fit yet unmotivated? He had no intention of ever visiting to see for himself. He was content to let Andreas find out.

As they approached the Sheppard, Paolo consulted his device once again. According to the available schematics hacked from the public works database, there was one blind spot to surveillance at the rear of the two-story hotel. It appeared that no one in Capston ever thought to check the back doors. Crouched behind a dumpster in the nearest alleyway, the pair climbed out of their sanitation jumpsuits, transforming into regular workaday civilians in button-down shirts and pressed slacks. Paolo doubted Grant ever dressed so chic. He removed his ballcap, revealing a hairpiece that concealed his longer, wavy curls tight to his scalp to the point he had to fight the urge to scratch. Few New Inland men wore hair at any length below the ears. Grant scoffed at the thought of wearing a wig. Real Kayewati men keep their hair short and sweet.

Now sporting the appearance of Arcadian tourists, the pair crossed the street without any urgency. Traffic was more fluid once they left the 300-block, but it was still thinner than the downtown core closer to the Holt Tower district. Keeping a wide berth, Paolo led his mercenary partner around to the rear side of the building. Checking the schematics one last time, Paolo zeroed in on a door that should have led into the kitchen area, as evidenced by the smell of organic waste in the receptacle on the hinge side. Grant inhaled deeply through the nose. "Ah, now that smells like home..."

Nice.

The door, as expected, was locked from the inside. Paolo swiped to a new menu and the blue light blinked. It was accessible by remote, at least. With the touch of his finger, the door latch clicked. Grant reached for the handle, and Paolo swiped his arm away.

"There is motion detection, idiot."

Grant scowled back at him. "That's twice, Desantos. Touch me again, I dare you."

Paolo didn't turn away from the big Kayewati's glare. It was pointless to fight him, but he liked his odds even if he gave half a foot and fifty-odd pounds to the mercenary. He'd beaten bigger and better. But now was not the time. There was a job to do.

Keying in on the alarm system, Paolo disabled it with

a few swipes and they stepped inside, reapplying the lock so no unexpected visitors would interrupt their work.

Inside the kitchen, Paolo emptied the contents of his bag and began to prepare the palm-sized explosive devices. Small but potent, they were the choice of Motherland insurgents for their portability and concealability. The 300-block bombs had been planted almost two full weeks before detonation. The occupants had lived their final weeks with the cause of their death under their noses. When it was discovered that the Sheppard Inn was not a busy hotel with a staff and guests and was even closed for the day for some unknown reason, Paolo made the suggestion that they take the stealth route once again. Plant the bombs now, then set them off later for maximum casualty count. Grant agreed but stressed how important it would be to eliminate the two boys first before they were able to tell too many people about what they might have heard back at the Spartan. There were too many moving parts. Too many things that could go wrong.

Instead of helping Paolo arm the explosives, Grant wandered over to the refrigerator. Rifling through until he found a container of leftover casserole, he grabbed a dirty spoon from the sink and shoveled a few mouthfuls.

"Ah, this is stale," Grant spat as he hurled the container across the room, shattering it on the tiled floor. "No wonder the place is empty if they serve shit like this."

Paolo glared at the broken dish, spilling with sauce and noodles among the shards. "Maybe you live that way where you come from, but we have a job to do."

Grant laughed. "You really must have been a maid servant in another life, Desantos! We're about to blow up the building and you're worried about spilled dinner!"

The mercenary sighed and took his place next to Paolo. "All right, let's get these babies powered up. You have the schematics loaded on that thing of yours?"

The vulnerable places in the hotel were indicated on the schematics in red. "The load-bearing partitions are here, here, and here." Paolo pointed to them, and Grant pretended he understood. "You set the rear marks, and I'll take care of the lobby and offices."

"Which one is the kid's room?"

Paolo shook his head. "No, none in there. The forensics will ask why we set one there when it's nowhere near a pressure point."

Grant threw his hands in the air. "I thought the whole point was to wipe out the kids!"

"Do you think anything through before you speak? You realize the children have likely already told their story, don't you? If the investigators determine we deliberately tried to assassinate them, it will only confirm the boys' story."

"Fine, fine. Just give me the bombs I need and show me where to put them." Grant swiped four explosives off the counter. Paolo pointed to a fire alarm panel, a vending machine, and two guest rooms close to load-bearing beams.

"I'll meet you back here in, what, ten minutes?" Before Paolo could agree, the Kayewati turned and walked out into the hotel corridor. Paolo sighed. Finally, some quiet time to think.

Paolo finished arming his four explosives and ventured into the empty hotel, following the opposite route until he emerged into the lobby. Time was ticking, so he didn't waste any of it looking around. He was also aware of the surveillance camera and tried to keep his face shielded from its view even with his wide glasses and hairpiece concealing his identity. Using his device to confirm the best places to set the bombs, he moved first behind the reception counter, setting two near the end of a large arch that supported the wide expanse of the lobby from the weight of the second floor. Following the electronic blueprint map, he crossed back into the lobby and armed the second explosive behind a tall vase with artificial plants. The vase and plants were fitting, Paolo mused to himself. Everything under the New Inland sarcophagus was fake.

He stood and turned to face the reception desk. Still five minutes to spare before he was to meet up with Grant if he could figure out for himself how to set the bombs. Paolo shook his head. The man was capable of so much destruction, but despite his list of accomplishments, it was incomprehensible that he was smart enough to have done any of them. From the instant they met back in the gymnasium, Paolo was less than impressed with his assigned partner. Leave it to his father to get wide-eyed at the sight of the big oaf lifting weights and drooling over his accolades. After all, the colonel got Grant in exchange for Andreas. You always get what you pay for.

For the first time, Paolo took in his surroundings. It was a pleasant facility, far more alive than the shuttered and packed-up Spartan Hotel across town. The Sheppard was clearly in need of repairs, he thought to himself. The paint was faded, the furniture had worn fabric, especially the couch, where someone clearly sat regularly. The wooden reception counter had noticeable dents and scrapes. Still, it was tidy and clean. The proprietor clearly cared about his business, but the downturn in business had to mean cutting corners.

Paolo looked above the worn-seated couch to a portrait that hung in a plain brown frame. Six people, presumably a family, were huddled together in a warm pose, all except one of the children, who was standing slightly apart from the rest, a more neutral expression as opposed to the smiles of the others. A husband and wife stood behind a tall teenaged boy, the mother resting her hand on his shoulder. A teenaged girl held a younger boy, maybe six or seven years old, in her arms by the waist. The pair of siblings were beaming, particularly the girl, with full, wavy hair spilled around her cherubic face. Paolo moved closer to the picture. His eyes widened when he realized that it was not a photograph at all, but hand drawn.

"Incredible." Paolo narrowed his eyes to the details of the facial expressions. Whomever drew this was exceptionally skilled. The teen girl's eyes positively glowed. The artist clearly held great affection for her.

To the left, the father, in the back, rested a hand on the shoulder of a boy clearly drawn half a step away from the other siblings. He may have been nine or ten years old, but there was something familiar about the sullen boy's image. A light went off in his memory, and Paolo retrieved his device, swiping back through the blueprint tabs until he reached the bio page.

Lorrie Sheppard. This is the Sheppard family, Paolo realized. But something wasn't adding up. According to public works, the proprietor was Robbie Sheppard. He must have been the older teen boy. So, the adults in the back had to be the parents. Mr. and Mrs. Sheppard?

Paolo checked his time. Three minutes left.

Swiping the bio page away on the device screen, he keyed up Capston public records in the database. Indeed, Robert and Julia Sheppard were the proprietors before they both fell ill and passed within months of each other.

The Sheppards were orphans. Paolo looked again at the portrait.

"Nice picture," muttered Grant, who had crept up behind him.

"We were supposed to meet in the kitchen," Paolo said.

"I've been there waiting for you; figured you were out here vacuuming the rugs or something." Grant snatched the Sheppard portrait off the wall revealing deeper-hued wall paint. "Who's this cutie, now?" Paolo watched the Kayewati ogling the teen girl. He felt his stomach crawl.

"This is the Sheppard family. And it is a drawing, not a photograph."

"Nice-looking bunch. Too bad we have to kill 'em. Especially the girl. Would you look at those eyes!"

They must not have women Grant's age in Kayewat.

"You know, in Kayewat, you'd pay half a week's salary for a piece of ass like this. Too bad she's not home, I could have had her for free—"

Paolo seized the picture from the pervert's hands. Grant laughed. "Easy there, captain. I'd let you have her when I was done. Relax..."

The Kayewati turned for the kitchen. "Come on, let's get out of here before someone comes back. *If* they come back, that is. I don't know why anyone would want to hang around a tomb like this."

Before Grant realized it, Paolo had already activated the sliding doors and slipped outside into the open artificial climate of Capston. As the door slid shut, Grant turned, a startled look on his face at the change of plans.

"Hey, I thought we were leaving by the kitch—"

Paolo pressed his finger on the tab that locked them shut. Through the tint of the glass, Grant grimaced, pounding his clenched fist without making any sound on the outside. All those hours in the gym, and this meathead wouldn't be able to budge the plexiglass. The irony was too much. Grant raged, mouthing profanities and commands to unlock the doors. Paolo smiled and pointed into the lobby to the faux fireplace.

Grant's eyes widened and all bravado vanished from his expression, replaced with terror. Paolo lifted the device so the Kayewati could see which tab he would press next. Tucking the Sheppard portrait under his arm, he turned and walked away, comfortable that he could safely cross the street in the ten seconds before the explosives went off. Paolo smiled knowing that in the same amount of time, Grant could make it to the fireplace. But it wouldn't matter.

Last Curfew

Tuesday, 29 May AC 0245
The Causeway, Capston, New Inland
Lorrie Sheppard

If he had snapped his longboard in half as he'd wanted after Troy beat him in the finals, Lorrie would be walking home. Never had he been so grateful that his parents weren't there to watch him race. He couldn't even bear to open the messages from Robbie earlier that day. How he wished he could have fled Capston, fled New Inland, and gone off to live in the wilderness, away from his family, away from Warren, away from Troy. Instead, he'd have to settle for his bedroom.

Worse still, the money he had budgeted to take the shuttles home—the reason he and Warren didn't in the morning—was spent after their debacle in the 300-block. They had no choice but to take a shuttle to the meet if they were going to get any practice time in. It killed Lorrie that Warren had been right. Still, his best friend didn't say "I told you so," and was kind enough not to say anything at all when Lorrie coasted over the finish line, two board lengths behind the blur of colour that was Troy. Lorrie stepped off the board and let it fly off down the track, unbuckling and heaving his helmet as tears welled in the corners of his eyes. Well over two hundred spectators witnessed him miss his final shot to win. At least it wasn't televised.

Warren didn't say a word when Lorrie, showered and changed into his civvies, reemerged from the dressing room. His longboard was waiting for him in his best friend's hands, though he would have rathered that

Warren leave the damned thing on the track, along with whatever was left of his dignity.

With nothing more to say, the pair left the way they came. Lorrie stopped at the on-ramp to the causeway.

"You're not actually thinking of taking the causeway again—have you completely forgotten this morning?" Warren's board was better equipped for the ride back. After his rear wheels shook loose, costing him his heat in the round of sixteen, the tourney pit crew were nice enough to touch up his bracket and tighten the bolts. It was likely in better repair than when Julia Sheppard bought it for him.

Lorrie strode onto the on-ramp, his board dragging behind him. "Why not? If we get caught again, we'll at least get a free ride home." There were no time constraints at this point. The races and his career were over. They could have walked all night if it didn't mean going back through the slums again. He had forgotten neither their adventures with the police nor the sketchy sanitation workers in the abandoned hotel.

Atop the causeway, the early evening traffic had begun to subside as the automated mirrors high above Capston slowly shifted to allow for a gradual dusk to descend over the city. Lorrie tossed his board ahead of him and leaped upon the deck. Behind him, he heard Warren do the same. As they pushed forward, Warren made no attempt to ride up alongside him, even though he was skating at a leisurely pace. All along the causeway, windows in the elevated structures began to blink to life in the darkening evening. He used to love hurtling along the causeway in the transit shuttles at night. He used to tell his mom that it looked like they were hurtling through space faster than light, stars streaking past. Tonight, the stars were pitiful candles in the eyes of buildings that either pitied or judged him.

The boys arced around the wide turn that led to the

long straightaway, at the end of which a final turn would lead them within a block of the Sheppard Inn. At the vanishing point of the star or candlelight, there was a commotion of some sort too difficult to discern at over twelve blocks away. Warren finally pulled up alongside him.

"Did you ever answer Robbie?" Multiple messages from his brother dinged on his handheld, but Lorrie had no intention of answering him. They had argued about money before he left this morning. Unless his brother was sending along some extra cash, there was nothing to say. His bank tab alarm never sounded anyway, so he was as broke now as before.

"I'm sure he just wants me to pick up milk or bread. Which is funny, since he'd cut off my allowance." The pair had had enough leftover cash to buy a few snacks, but neither had eaten since breakfast. Leftover casserole in the fridge wasn't exactly appealing, but after a day like this, he would have eaten his right shoe.

"Maybe, but what if there was an emergency? What if Cadlen was hurt or something?"

"Hah! Cad? He'd have to get up off that couch to hurt himself. I can count on my hands how many times I've seen him on his feet in the last two weeks, no kidding!"

Warren laughed. "Maybe so. But at least someone is checking in on you, right? Clara is probably still in New Mills 'on business', and Dad is too depressed to do anything but watch rerun pictures and mope about it."

"At least your parents are still alive, Warren." Lorrie shoved ahead to avoid accidental eye contact. Warren caught up.

"Sometimes I wonder, Lor."

His best friend's answer hung in the air. Lorrie wouldn't say as much, but he had to agree. The Connellys were absentee parents at best. As much as Crystal and Robbie used to complain about Warren hanging around all the time, they knew it was a positive environment for a lonely only-child. Without a doubt, the elder Sheppard siblings would have heard Warren speak more than their mute youngest brother. Lorrie always figured they preferred Warren over himself anyway.

His self-pity was interrupted by a siren burst coming up behind them, a reflection of blue and red lights washing over the illegal skaters.

"Oh hell, please don't be the same guy..."

Lorrie and Warren stepped off their boards and turned to face the squad car, now pulled into the emerg lane. A white beam of light blinded them as the silhouette of a uniformed officer stepped out of the car. Traffic swooshed in a wide berth around them.

"Good evening, boys. It's been a few hours!"

Lorrie cursed under his breath. Of course, it was the same guy.

"Sorry, sir, we're just heading home after the longboard races. We shuttled in, but we didn't have enough money for the trip back." It was a partial truth, at least the money part.

The police officer didn't buy it. "Is that so? Wasn't it you two I spotted just off the 300 this morning?"

Lorrie shook his head. "This morning? No sir, we were on our way to the practice runs. We took the shuttles."

Stepping out from the beam of light, the officer smirked. "Shuttles, you say?" He held up a datapad, wider and flatter than a standard handheld. "So, you're telling me these two punks don't look familiar?"

A dashboard freeze-frame clearly showing Lorrie's and Warren's faces was slightly blurred but irrefutable. Lorrie wore a look of frustration, while Warren's mouth was open as wide as his eyes.

"Give it up, Lor, he knows," Warren said, raising his hands in surrender as though he were about to be cuffed.

"Shut up, Warren. Fine, you have us. Today's been the piss, why not cap it off with a fine."

The officer pulled back the datapad and began to tap on the screen with his index fingertips. "Now I have you two on two separate illegal riding charges. Anything you want to tell me about the 300-block?"

Lorrie grimaced. Illegal boarding on the causeway would be a hefty fine, but manageable. He'd do overtime work for Robbie for a few months and that would be that. But if the officer had something to prove they broke into private property, that was another matter altogether. Both he and Warren were sixteen. Juveniles yet, but they would both be eligible for stiffer penalties. With his luck, he'd have to do community service collecting trash in the slums, or cleaning privies in the Foundries.

"The 300? No, we ran from you, but that's all. We were late for our practice runs. That's the truth!"

Before the officer could answer, a rush of identical squad cars sailed past, lights flashing and sirens blaring. Lorrie remembered the faint sight of some sort of gridlock off in the distance. The officer swiped the screen of his datapad and glanced back at the boys. His expression dropped.

"I need you two to come with me, please." He gestured with rapid waving motions of his hands to the squad car. Warren immediately complied. Lorrie wasn't so enthusiastic, even if it meant a ride home.

"What's this about? I'm already past curfew. Can't we make some sort of deal or something?" It was foolish to ask, but at this point his replies were automatic.

"Just get in the car, Mr. Sheppard." The policeman's tone deepened. Lorrie swallowed and followed Warren into the back seats of the squad car.

The officer tossed his datapad in the empty passenger seat and hit the throttle, accelerating to a higher speed than the posted limit of the causeway. From the rear row and behind a layer of plexiglass, it was difficult to see up the road, around the officer's head and his dash equipment.

"Lorrie, I don't want to go to jail," Warren whined.

"Knock it off—something's going on, Warren. Look."

As the causeway wound around the last long turn, heavy fog enveloped the neighbourhood, billowing like clouds over the ground-level streets on either side. Only fog didn't happen in Capston. The squad car was airtight, but Lorrie knew that as soon as it opened, the stench of smoke would hit them straight away.

"There's been another hit, and it's close to home…"

As soon as the last word left his lips, Lorrie's eyes expanded as the burning ruins of the Sheppard Family Inn came into view. Scores of emergency vehicles had formed an arc around the half-collapsed building while police and security corps officers cordoned off the streets and diverted traffic. A crowd of onlookers had gathered.

"No, no, noooo…" As the car came to rest, Warren climbed out into the street, ushering in the pungent smoke and the clangour of the first responders. Lorrie followed, staggering to his feet as he felt the life sucking out of his abdomen. The officer put his hand on his shoulder, but Lorrie shook it away. The man was trying to calm him, but the words were just empty tones.

"You should have answered Robbie." It was the last thing he wanted to hear Warren say. Lorrie lurched and emptied the bile from his empty stomach onto the cracked, uneven pavement.

Silence and Black

Tuesday, 29 May AC 0245
Sheppard Family Inn, Capston, New Inland
Lorrie Sheppard

"My dad! I need to see my dad!" Warren kept shouting to the first responders who crisscrossed the blocked-off street in front of the Sheppard Inn. Lorrie saw blackened streaks of soot-stained tears crawling down Warren's cheeks and imagined his own face looked the same. His eyes stung from the airborne pollutants of the smoke. Firemen aimed high-pressure hoses into the heart of the inferno while security officers controlled the gathering crowd and redirected traffic. Lorrie didn't know where to turn.

"We're looking for your dad," the officer said, shielding Warren from the disaster scene. "Come and get back in the car, it's safer there."

Lorrie scowled. There was no way he was getting back inside that squad car.

"Don't do it, Warren." Lorrie's words were sour after throwing up. "These guys can't help us."

The officer glared at him. "We can't if you don't let us. Now please, both of you, get in the car. We can get you some food and drinks."

Any food he swallowed would wind up back on the ground. He should have been complaining about Robbie's leftovers by now, tossing his dirty dishes in the sink and retreating to his room.

His room. It was gone.

Lorrie didn't own much. The photographs on his walls held the most sentimental value. There was one of him and his mother on their last trip to the Hanging Gardens. They were posed in front of some big-leaved trees with crisscross patterns on their trunks. No Cadlen. Just the two of them in a happier time. Lorrie was already beginning to forget some of the details in the picture.

Warren turned away from the squad car as two officers in full-body, plastic hazard jumpsuits and gasmasks emerged from the darkness. Before Warren could speak, one of them pulled a dark fabric hood over his head while the other secured his hands behind his back. The police officer stepped away.

"Hey! What are you doing! Leave my friend—"

Hands clasped Lorrie before he could finish protesting. A hood draped over his own face as his arms twisted behind his back. His first instinct was to drop to the ground. If he were being arrested or kidnapped, he wouldn't make it easy.

"Warren!" Lorrie hollered, but his voice muffled in the soft fabric. A drawstring tightened the opening of the sack around his neck, restricting his ability to breathe or protest. As a pair of strong hands lifted him from the street, Lorrie's consciousness dissolved into silence and black.

The first sensation he recognized was his body rising quickly, as though he had been launched straight up in the air from a cannon. Drawing a lungful of air, his eyes opened to a blur of residual sleep, a yellowish light soaking it up as he focused on his surroundings. It was an elevator lift, tube-shaped and sterile. Lorrie held his hands in front of him. Unbound, he turned to face the two people standing behind him. One was a tall, heavy-set man in tan-coloured security force gear. His sidearm was holstered at his thick waist. The other was a slender woman wearing the same uniform, her short-trimmed hair peeking from under a beret-style cap that was cocked to her right side. It was the woman who spoke.

"We're almost there, Lorrie." Her voice was direct, with a hint of compassion. "You'll have your answers soon, I promise."

Lorrie pressed his fingers into his eyes, wiping the last grains of sleep away. "How about some answers now? Where's Warren?"

The big man spoke up. "We've got him, he's safe."

The lift whisked higher, lights over the top of the doors streaking white as it passed each floor. His ears popped, causing his own voice to echo inside his head. The same thing happened all those years ago when his mother brought him to the Gardens. Chew this gum, she told him. It will keep your jaw moving, and it will pop your ears quicker. She was right.

"I don't suppose either of you have any gum?"

The woman smirked. "Your ears? You'll get used to it, trust me."

Used to it?

The lift slowed until it came to rest. Lorrie was still facing the officers as a bell sounded and the doors behind him swished open.

"This is your stop, Lorrie." The big man smiled and motioned for him to turn with his fat right hand. Before he could, Lorrie heard a voice out of his memories.

"Lorrie!"

At first, he imagined his mother beckoning for him to step off the lift into the Gardens where they would wander for hours breathing in the soft air infused with the scent of natural plant life. He inhaled and the scent greeted him. But when his name repeated, it was clearly not his mother.

Lorrie stepped off the lift, leaving blackened, soot-lined footprints. He was wide awake, but the black still followed.

Lockdown

Tuesday, 29 May AC 0245
Sheppard Family Inn, Capston, New Inland
Robbie Sheppard

Robbie slouched over the counter, his face in his palms. He would have preferred to take the call in the office while Willits covered the front desk. As luck would have it, getting sick rarely happened out of convenience. Robbie's last remaining employee couldn't make it due to a high fever. He probably didn't have red tide. But after both his parents succumbed to the disease, he wasn't going to tempt fate to add a third statistic to Capston's public health registry.

It wouldn't have been a big deal, except the psychiatrist in Capston recommended by Cadlen's pediatrician called about five minutes later. There was an opening, which hardly ever happens, the perky secretary told Robbie while he wrung his hands and paced behind the counter.

"Today? I don't want to turn it down, but I have no one here to cover my hotel!

"Oh, really?" The lady didn't try to hide her disbelief. "Is there any way you can check, because I have a long list if you decide you can't make it."

Robbie gritted his teeth. It wasn't a decision he could just make. He imagined locking the Sheppard Inn doors only to have a tour bus roll up as he and Cadlen were boarding a taxi shuttle. He bit his tongue and breathed.

"Can you give me five minutes? I have someone I can call." Robbie knew Lorrie wouldn't cancel on his big race against Troy for him. But maybe he would for Cadlen.

"Well, since you're in a bind there, I can give you five minutes, Mr. Sheppard."

Robbie thanked her and swiped the call link off. He keyed open the tab for his direct message chain to Lorrie.

I need a favour. Cad can get in to see the doctor, but Willits is home with a fever. Can you come back and cover? I'll make it up to you. R

In the best of times, Robbie wouldn't have preferred Lorrie to watch the front desk. He was curt with the guests, messed up the paperwork, and complained every time. If he were a little older, Cadlen would have been better, even if he never said a word. In his heart, Robbie hoped Lorrie would find something for himself beyond the Sheppard Inn. His brother was only ever truly happy when he was on the track, weaving around his competition. It wasn't long ago Robbie felt the same rush on the Velodrome oval.

Five minutes evaporated, and the incoming call alert sounded.

"Mr. Sheppard, are you able to come in?"

Robbie looked at Cadlen, legs crossed beneath him as he drew in his sketchbook. His baby brother lived inside his own head. Robbie could have counted on one hand how many times he had heard Cadlen's voice since his father passed away. If Cad were to speak right now, how would it sound? Lorrie's voice had begun to deepen when he was twelve. Cad's voice was still childlike in Robbie's memory.

What choice do I have?

"Yes, we can make it. I can call a shuttle and be there within half an hour." Robbie's worries were a tug of war between Cadlen's health and the survival of the inn.

"Wonderful. We're at 1755 in the business district.

Check in at the front desk and you'll be shown where to go."

The 1700-block was the exact opposite side of town from the longboard track. If they were closer, Robbie might have been able to stop in and ask Lorrie in person. There was no point lingering over a what-if scenario. Robbie thanked the receptionist and scrambled into action.

"Cad, we have an opening with the psychiatrist. The one Mom wanted you to see! We have a chance, but I have to shut the inn. Can you be ready in a minute?"

Cadlen peeked up through his bangs and nodded. The youngest Sheppard gathered his art supplies strewn on the couch beside him. Robbie logged off his server and set the silent alarm. The shuttle arrived in a matter of minutes as the two brothers climbed aboard.

Robbie glanced back at the Sheppard Inn as the taxi coasted ahead. It was quieter than he had ever seen it.

The buildings of the 1700-block formed a cluster of high-rises that could be seen from the Sheppard when the mirrors shifted the light to midday. Robbie and Cadlen gazed up at 1755 as the taxi whisked away. He watched his little brother's eyes widen as though they were gathering as much data as possible for future drawing.

"It might not be as tall as Holt Tower, but it's still impressive, isn't it?"

Cadlen nodded, pursing his lips. Whenever he did that, he was thinking deeply. Robbie wondered if Cadlen remembered watching him race in the Holt Tower's Velodrome track. Cad would have been six, maybe seven. His mother, father, Crystal, and Lorrie, all cheering in the stands as he wheeled past, but Cadlen was face-deep into his sketchbook. Even then, his art offered an escape from the chaos of the world around him. *I don't think we should bring him next time*, Robbie had heard his mother say to his father later that night. She was afraid that the crowds were making him even more anxious. That one day, she might never hear her baby boy speak again.

It was the right decision, Robbie assured himself. He took Cadlen's hand and walked through the sliding doors to the reception area.

"You'll be taking the second lift. Eighth floor, and the office is number 86." The receptionist smiled and motioned toward the row of lifts just beyond the open foyer. Before Robbie could thank him, the receptionist squinted, tapping the small earpiece in his left ear.

"Can you repeat that?" Robbie turned away. It must have been important for the gentleman to turn his attention away from them.

Everything happened so quickly. Lights began to flash, and an electronic alarm sounded in a low volume. Security guards emerged from the lifts, stairwell, and offices behind the reception area. The dozen or so people in the foyer exclaimed in confusion, looking around them and asking one another what was happening. Cadlen pursed his lips again. Robbie turned back to the receptionist.

"Excuse me—"

"I'm sorry sir, there's an emergency situation. Please stay in the foyer, the security team will give you and your son directions."

"This isn't my son, it's my brother—"

"Just over there, please."

The man turned away from the Sheppard brothers and a security guard in taut blazer and pressed trousers interjected.

"If we could bring you over into the center of the foyer, sir. There has been an emergency nearby, but we've been told to lock down the building, and all buildings in the surrounding blocks."

"Lockdown? Does anyone know why?" Robbie's heart

raced. If it were another bomb, wouldn't he have heard it?

"No details yet, sir. We'll keep everyone up to date as soon as we can. Please, this way."

Over the next several minutes, the foyer became packed with evacuees from the uppermost levels. Outside, traffic was being controlled by police officers, allowing only essential shuttles through the streets. A pair of uniformed officers entered and approached the security guard who had ushered Robbie and Cadlen into the foyer. Robbie watched them exchange words and nod back and forth. The receptionist retreated into the offices.

As the crowd became more and more dense, the panic volume increased. Robbie put his hands on Cadlen's shoulders. "Are you okay, buddy? I'm sure this isn't anything too serious."

Cadlen's shoulders were tense. His arms hung at his sides, and he gripped his sketchbook and supply kit in his hands as though they were about to fly away. Robbie remembered the same response from his brother all those years ago in the Velodrome. Only this time his mother and father weren't there to comfort him. They had to get out of the crowd before it got worse. Here they were, only a few floors away from the help he so desperately needed.

Robbie guided Cadlen through the foyer, jostling and apologizing to everyone before the pair cleared the crowd. A police officer was stationed at the reception desk.

"I'm sorry, sir. My brother is extremely anxious from the crowds. We're here to see his doctor, actually! Is there any way—"

"You can bring him over to the benches there," the officer interrupted. "Once we have more information, I'm sure we'll be able to send you on your way upstairs."

If Lorrie had been there, he would have had some sarcastic comeback.

Lorrie.

He hadn't answered Robbie's cry for assistance earlier. But he had to let him know where they were in case anything happened. He pulled his handheld from his pocket, but the police officer raised a hand.

"Sir, we can't let anyone use their devices right now. We're shutting down the wireless grid in the 1700-block for the time being."

"But my brother, he doesn't know where we are. I need to let him know."

The officer nodded. "I understand. Let me take your information. As soon as we're able, we can try to reach him. Please be patient, sir."

If one more person called him sir, Robbie was going to lose his head. He had used the tactic many times to diffuse an angry guest. Sir, Miss. It was so condescending.

The foyer capped its limit of three hundred people while Robbie cradled an arm around Cadlen, still too overstimulated to open his sketchbook. He kept a death grip on his book and supplies, refusing to let go when Robbie offered to hold his hands. As minutes turned into hours, facility staff circulated, offering the crowd small snacks and cups of water. Through the constant commotion, Robbie heard a hundred possible situations unfolding. It was a fire. It was a gas leak. It was a robbery. It was a Reaper invasion. It was a structural failure. Robbie couldn't prevent his brother from hearing the hysterical speculation. As the afternoon became the evening, most of the crowd in the foyer had sat down on the floor. The panic had become exasperation. They would have to be told something soon or the exasperation would descend into discontent.

The public address crackled to life. Finally, some

answers, Robbie sighed. The crowd fell silent.

"Ladies and gentlemen, the Capston Security Corps were informed that an attack was imminent in the area surrounding the 1500-block. While the corps has been investigating, we have been placed under physical and airwave lockdown until the investigation is complete. It may take some time yet. We may be here for the night."

The crowd roared in disapproval. Robbie lost his breath. Would they have spoken to Lorrie yet? Who would stay with him at the inn? Maybe he could stay with the Connellys for the night while all this got sorted out...

The voice from the speaker continued.

"Once we have more information, we will begin to move guests back into the higher levels. As soon as possible, we will turn on the wireless network again."

The public address crackled off and the crowd jeered. At some point, they would have to let people leave if the threat was averted. The seats he and Cadlen had been assigned were contoured for good posture but grew more and more rigid with every passing hour. Cadlen began to lean into Robbie's shoulder.

At the reception desk, a new staffer greeted two combat-ready soldiers. Security corps troops had been patrolling the street outside the 1755 building, but now they were inside. The receptionist turned and motioned to the Sheppards. Robbie's stomach knotted as the pair marched in his direction.

"Robbie Sheppard?"

"I am Robbie." It was all he could say.

"Come with us, please." The second soldier reached to Cadlen to grip his forearm. The boy shook it off with a violent yank.

"It's okay, Cad. Let's just do what they ask, okay?"

Cadlen frowned, his brows wrinkled and his lips slitted. He stood and the soldier stepped back to give him room. The troops guided the Sheppard brothers behind the reception area and through a maze of office corridors to an exit.

"Is everything over now?" Robbie asked as the door thrust open and all four stepped out into the dimming early evening light. "We can go home?"

The lead soldier motioned to a box-shaped military vehicle, deep grey and sharp-edged compared to the usual soft curves of public transit. "Please get inside the transport."

As they walked across the empty sidewalk, Cadlen lost grip of his supply kit and it clattered to the ground, spilling pencils everywhere. Robbie knew Cad wouldn't go anywhere without them.

"Please, let him pick up his pencils," Robbie pleaded as the soldiers ushered him past the spill and into the open side door of the transport. Despite their calm words, the officers carried themselves with quiet urgency. Something wasn't right. "He needs them."

Cadlen dropped to the ground as though he were shot, scrambling for whatever he could grab. The rear soldier knelt and helped him retrieve them. Robbie craned his neck over the soldier guarding the doorway of the transport to see Cadlen and the soldier retrieving the pencils together. Removing his tinted lenses, the soldier spoke to Cadlen, but Robbie couldn't hear the words. He couldn't tell if Cadlen was answering him either. The man smiled, and kind wrinkles formed around his eyes. The pair stood together.

"Commander Shore, we need to get them back now."

"Did you hear that? We have to go now. Can you make it?" Commander Shore spoke to Cadlen softly, but with respect. Cad nodded, and the pair joined Robbie aboard the transport. The first soldier heaved the door shut. As the transport's propulsion system whirred to life, the commander removed his beret.

"My name is Shore. We need to bring you back to HQ,

and I promise we'll fill you in on everything."

Before Robbie could answer, Commander Shore retrieved his datapad. Two swipes of his finger and his face flushed in relief.

"We have your brother and his friend, Robbie."

Scars

Robbie had been to Holt Tower before. The last time he raced on the Velodrome oval track that occupied the entirety of Level 5, both his parents were still alive. Crystal was still at home. It was the first race in his 18-25 age grouping, and he was not ready. The competition was tough, more so than he had expected. His whole family was there to watch him except for Lorrie. "I don't want to be there to see you get destroyed," Lorrie had given as his excuse to waste time with Warren on their skateboards. Longboards, Robbie would have been corrected.

The lifts to the Velodrome level were much wider than the standard ones with mirrors and escape hatches in the ceiling. They were service elevators, designed to carry much more weight, and slower. As Robbie and Cadlen stepped inside the lift with Captain Shore and the doors slid closed, the ascent thrust Robbie's heart into his throat. High-velocity racing speeds and the inertial pull as he rounded the sloped Velodrome track, he could handle. The upward motion in an enclosed, tight space with no windows made him wonder if his insides would slide right out of his body.

Cadlen held his art supplies in both hands. He didn't appear to be as concerned.

Captain Shore had removed his beret and used his handheld to key instructions into the elevator control. Above the door, the glowing light that indicated the floor levels displayed only two blinking zeroes. Robbie didn't ask how far up the tower they were going. He couldn't make an educated guess. After several minutes, it stood to reason they were beyond halfway up the tallest skyscraper in Capston. Maybe they were beyond the highest level and into the sky lift that would bring them high into the artificial sky to the Hanging Gardens. Without windows, who could tell?

None of the three passengers in the lift spoke during the climb. Cadlen, of course, wouldn't speak anyway. That was a certainty. In the transport, Shore was friendly, but not forthcoming with any information. There will be information once we get there. "There" was never disclosed until the transport pulled into one of the service bays of Holt Tower. From there, everything was automatic. Silent, even steps. Rhythmic breathing and heart rates. For a moment, Robbie wondered if this is how it felt being led to the gallows for execution, which was how the outsider communities still carried out their justice.

The lift slowed for the final floors before coming to a halt, jostling Robbie's insides back into place. The display screen above the door remained at double-zero. The doors opened into a white hallway. Men and women in security corps uniforms passed one another, crisscrossing the busy conduit. As they stepped into the hallway, passing officers greeted the captain with informal salutes. Robbie admired the respect Shore's officers showed him. There was an air of professionalism without fear.

"This way." Shore guided the brothers around several left turns. Each level occupied a hundredfold the area of the Sheppard Inn—Robbie knew this from the enormity of the Velodrome so far beneath them. They arrived at a set of double doors flanked by two alert guards. Each saluted before drawing open a door.

Seated at the far end of an ovoid conference table was a stalky man scowling at a datapad screen as he clattered away at a keypad set into the table surface. Unlike all officers Robbie had seen up to this point, the man wore a casual, buttoned tan shirt with no indication of any rank or file.

"That will be all, Shore," the man ordered without looking up.

"If it's all the same to you, Steven, I'd like to stay with the youngster."

Steven looked up, irked by the response. "How about you bring the youngster to the gallery? I don't imagine he will have a lot to say."

Robbie looked at his brother. "What do you think, Cad?"

Cadlen pursed his lips and nodded. Shore smiled.

"This way, then. If you enjoy drawing, you'll have plenty to see in the gallery." Shore looked assuredly to Robbie. "He'll be fine with me, I promise you."

Robbie nodded. As the doors shut, Steven waved him closer.

"Please have a seat, Robbie. I have some questions for you."

As he was about to take a seat across the table, Steven grunted and waved his hand again. "No, no, over here. I don't want to shout across the room at you."

A sensation not unlike the ascent of the lift rushed up Robbie's chest. He sat two seats away from the man at his datapad, leaving a buffer zone of sorts. After a few seconds, Steven finished typing and shoved the screen down until it closed flat on the table. He leaned forward and clasped his hands.

"Robbie Sheppard. You are the proprietor of the Sheppard Family Inn since the passing of your father four years ago. Your mother passed not long before, if I recall. Left to run the business and raise three siblings.

That's no small task."

Three siblings. Robbie hadn't disclosed Crystal back at the 1700-block. It wouldn't have been difficult to research the family through public records. The question was why anyone was researching the Sheppard family at all.

"That's right," Robbie said. His mouth was dry.

"Before you feel like you need to make up something, we know Crystal is studying abroad. That's not why you're here."

Robbie looked at Steven. It was hard to guess how old he was, but there were hints of gray wisps in his short, styled hair. The deep brown of his moustache didn't quite match. The lines on his forehead and around his eyes led Robbie to figure him for forty at least. Steven's eyes were deep and penetrating beneath sharply downturned, bushy brows.

"Robbie, when you left this morning with your brother, who was watching the hotel?"

"No one. The inn is vacant today. Cadlen's appointment was too important to miss, so I closed for the day." The initial disappointment he felt when he had locked up came back again. "My other brother had left for a longboard meet."

Steven sighed. "Yes, your brother. He's quite a handful, isn't he? Ling had to convince Gry to sedate him when we brought him in."

Robbie had no idea who either Ling or Gry was. He didn't care as long as Lorrie was safe.

"I wanted to contact Lorrie, but we were told that the airwaves were offline," Robbie said. "Our plans had changed. I didn't want him and Warren to come home to a locked door."

At this point, Robbie noticed Steven's demeanor shift. He leaned back into his chair and chewed on the words he wanted to use.

"Robbie, I'm just going to say it. Your business was hit today. We had a tip on a different hotel in the 1500-block, which is why we locked down the surrounding neighbourhoods. We didn't have any warning... I'm sorry."

Hit.

The last time anything was hit, Lorrie and Warren ran off to record the chaos of the first responders and the confusion in the streets. Every time the news reported a bombing, the targets seemed to be important in some way. Office buildings, apartment complexes, banks. These seemed to be targets of consequence. It never once crossed Robbie's mind that a failed hotel would draw anyone's attention. If anything, one less failed business would have benefited Capston. Too many shuttered businesses were bad for a city that relied so much on tourism.

Steven's news hit Robbie as if the building had collapsed on top of him.

"It's gone. It's... *gone*?" Robbie verbalized the only thing that he could rationalize. It's gone. When he locked the doors this morning, it was for the last time. Forever. The building was empty, quiet. He remembered a feeling of farewell as the taxi pulled away, ashamed of himself for wishing he didn't have to return. A wave of nausea rushed into his throat.

"Here." Steven shoved a small wastebasket just in time for Robbie to throw up. "Don't worry about that. I'm truly sorry, Mr. Sheppard."

After his stomach emptied and only the raunch of aftertaste lingered, Robbie looked up. Steven's expression had shifted from all-business to compassion. His deep scowl softened, and his face revealed a few scars, some in straight lines, others dotted pockmarks. Each must have had a story to tell.

"At least no one was inside," Robbie said.

"Your family was very lucky. As Shore told you, we have your brother and his friend. I need you to be honest with me. Did you speak to your brother at all after he and his friend left this morning?"

"No, not at all. I messaged him after I got the call for Cadlen's appointment—Lorrie didn't know about it. I thought he could cover the desk while we were out, but he never answered."

"Turns out your brother and his buddy were busy today, not just at the races." Steven opened his datapad and swiveled it so Robbie could see. "They were spotted riding on the emerg lanes, but they fled into the 300-block. As luck would have it, the same patrol car picked them up on the causeway after the races. Once we realized who they were, we brought them in. But not without a fight. Lorrie was causing such a commotion; we had to hood and sedate them."

Robbie pictured Lorrie waving his arms and barking at anyone who would listen. The sixteen-year-old was scrawny, but whomever laid a hand on him would be surprised at the response they would get. Lorrie was born ready to take on the world.

"I told him to stay off the causeway," Robbie said. "I'll cover the fines, mister..."

The man he knew only as Steven shook his head. "Don't worry about that. I'm just thankful that you and your loved ones are safe."

Crystal. She was safe, if only illegally so.

"Our sister, she studies away." How would anyone be able to tell her?

"In Hyacynthe, yes, we know." Steven's eyes narrowed again. "And likely helping you keep the inn afloat. But none of that concerns me right now. The most important thing is that she's safe."

Robbie exhaled. They knew about Crystal. They suspected that she was transferring him money. The separation from his sister left an internal scar that had yet to heal. He wondered if Steven could tell.

"She needs to know that we're all okay. Can you reach her?"

"That's not so easy. Not even for a mayor."

Mayor?

Steven Reekan.

"Mr. Mayor. I'm sorry, I didn't know."

The man smiled. "I'll do my best to contact her. But for now, I'm more concerned about Lorrie and the Connelly kid's adventures in the 300-block. Your inn wasn't a random hit."

The Jewel of Capston

Tuesday, 29 May AC 0245
Holt Tower (Level 93 Gallery), Capston, New Inland
Lorrie Sheppard

If his mother and father had greeted him, Lorrie would have been sure he had died. He never believed in any sort of afterlife. He couldn't think of anyone he knew who did. Still, nagging thoughts of pure white, lush plant life, and loved ones waiting came to mind on those rare occasions he thought about it.

Lorrie stepped inside a space that came close to fitting the description. A wide-open concept chamber, predominantly white with soft blues and greens accented in the furnishings, stretched wide and deep. Behind Robbie, who was greeting him with open arms, a raised level was crowned with soft couches and armchairs. Sure enough, Cadlen nestled against the armrest of the biggest couch, legs crossed beneath him as he drew in his sketchbook.

"You should have answered me, Lor!"

Robbie scolding. Cadlen drawing. He was clearly still alive. But it was time for answers.

"Did they kidnap you guys too?" Lorrie stepped forward and allowed his brother to wrap his arms around him. Robbie squeezed him tight. Lorrie responded with the same force, but when his brother wouldn't let go, he slackened.

"Sorry, I just thought..." Robbie trailed off and Lorrie was grateful that he didn't finish his thought. It would have come off as awkward, and there was enough awkwardness in this room.

"So, what is this place?"

"Steven calls it the gallery." Robbie turned and motioned to the upper level, three long rows of stairs above the main floor. Beyond Cadlen on his couch, the far wall was lush and green, from ceiling to floor. As a forest scene unfolded, Lorrie inhaled the rich air. The exhale brought with it loosened phlegm as he coughed into the crook of his elbow. Robbie retrieved a glass of water garnished with a wedge of lemon that nudged Lorrie's upper lip after the first gulp. As his guard began to fall, a wave of fatigue washed over him. He stumbled to the nearest chaise, pure white, cushioned, and deep. His black steps faded with every successive footfall, but his hands left grey streaks on the armrest. Robbie would probably scold him for dirtying the furniture.

Across from him, Cadlen continued to draw without looking up from his sketchbook.

"I'm glad you're okay too, Cad."

Lorrie's little brother pursed his lips together, a telltale indication that he was listening despite the lack of reply. How wonderful it must be not to have a care. To just immerse yourself in a fantasy world. Cadlen could have been cross-legged in his usual spot when the bomb went off around him, and he would have gone to his grave oblivious to the carnage. Lorrie wondered if Cadlen thought he was in the afterlife too, that first time he saw this place.

"So... This is Holt Tower, then?"

Robbie took a seat next to him, keeping his posture instead of succumbing to the deep cushions. "It is. But you know, no one has ever actually said it is. Clara Connelly can't stop saying how amazing it is to be in the *Jewel of Capston*—so put two and two together."

The Jewel of Capston. All advertisements for Holt Tower contained the famous tag line in some manner.

Whether the luxurious hotel suites, gaming facilities, sports complexes, or any other of the services contained in the tower, every aspect of the Holt brand screamed upper-class. Luxury beyond the common person's understanding. Protected from the natural atmosphere's buffeting winds by the New Inland dome, Holt Tower stretched high enough that any believer in the hereafter might assume it was a direct elevator. The sky lift, of course, only reached to the Hanging Gardens, still inside the safety of the dome. If he had had the courage that day to walk out onto the transparent floor, he and his mother might have looked down at the *Jewel*.

"Wait, Clara Connelly? So, they're here too?"

A voice from the wall of flora startled him.

"Mrs. Connelly is quite taken with her accommodations. She can't stop gushing to Jason about it."

Lorrie turned to the source of the voice. The wall of lush green shrubs and trees, upon closer inspection, was contained behind a pane of glass. Camouflaged until he began to move, the speaker stepped forward, revealing earth-toned brown and green jacket and cargo pants. The voice was hefty as though every word was pushed from deep in his chest.

"I'm Steven."

Steven's eyes were beads, deep brown beneath thick brows turned down as though he were angry. His bushy moustache had wisps of grey whereas his hair, parted in the middle, was a consistent chestnut brown. The man didn't offer a hand. Lorrie wouldn't have taken it anyway.

"Who's Jason?"

"Lorrie!" Robbie barked.

Steven smiled. "Jason Holt owns this place. Maybe you'll show him some gratitude when you meet him."

Jason Holt, the guy who charges almost double for his

boarding lanes and Velodrome meets. *Gratitude. Right.*

Steven turned his attention back to the nature wall. Lorrie stood and approached the paned barrier between the outside world and the white chamber. He couldn't shake the sensation of natural smells, the sounds of trickling water and faint bird song. The air even felt more humid as he walked alongside Steven, peering into the glass as though it were a dimensional portal. The closer he looked, the more details popped to life. Insects scurried on the deadfall and the decaying leaves. A squirrel scurried from the branches of the wider trees. It was as though he was watching nature practicing its magic—more so even than the Gardens all those years ago.

"Remarkable for a hologram, isn't it?" Steven didn't look at him. "The climate controls are a nice touch too. You'd think you were actually there, wouldn't you?"

"I wouldn't know," Lorrie muttered. "Closest I ever got was the Gardens once."

"I don't much care for them. I've been on the outside plenty of times, son. Completely different—"

"I'm not your son." Only one man had the right to call him "son," and he was long gone.

"Lorrie!" Robbie gasped behind him.

"Relax. I meant no harm by it. Your brother wasn't kidding when he said you had a temper."

Lorrie rolled his eyes. Of course, Robbie had to tell him.

"So, the real outside world is better?"

Steven turned to him, eyes glowering. "Oh, not better. Not by a long shot. In the Gardens, at least you don't have to worry about insects, reptiles, bears. Or viruses and bacteria. Radiation. And then you have the brigands, Reapers..."

Steven's voice trailed off as he went over a danger checklist. Lorrie suspected he was listing dangers in order of least to most dangerous.

"Red tide can happen just as much inside."

This time, Robbie didn't interject. That one must have hurt him just as much. The virus that was blamed for both his parents' early deaths was nearly as taboo a subject as the infamous Reapers that skulked in the outside world. Lorrie could dismiss the mysterious druids as nothing more than a folk legend. The red tide, though, was very real.

"I'm sorry about your parents, Lorrie." Steven's voice contained a hint of compassion. This man did his homework. But did he know about...

"We're going to keep you and your family safe here. The Connellys, too."

At least Warren was in the tower. Now, if only Jason let them have access to the boarding lanes. If any silver lining was to be found, it may as well have been in a state-of-the-art training facility.

"So, we get to live here? Who's paying, the mayor?"

Lorrie heard Robbie muttering, and Steven smirked at the glass. With a quick glance, Cadlen pursed his lips again. And then it occurred to him. Steven... He remembered from the news reels.

"You're Mayor Reekan."

The mayor nodded without looking at him. "You can thank Jason Holt. Believe me, my tab is already pretty high."

The two sighed. Lorrie's chest fluttered and he turned back to the lounge chairs, looking for the half-drunk glass of lemon-infused water. It had been refilled. Condensation beaded on the outside of the glass.

"So that's it then, we live here now?"

Robbie spoke up. "We have to stay on this floor, in this building. At least for a while."

"Until they catch the bombers, right? Then we can go home?" To whatever remained of "home." They had insurance. They could rebuild.

"It's not that simple, Lorrie."

Lorrie turned to the mayor. "Nothing's simple, is it?"

"You don't understand. I told you that no one was killed in the bomb, but that's not what the news is saying. The official death toll is *six*."

Six. Three Sheppards plus three Connellys. Lorrie choked on his last gulp of water.

"Wait—the world thinks we're dead?"

A rush of excitement coursed through him. No more school with idiots, no more insufferable teachers. No more ignorant inn guests...

No more contact with Crystal.

"But our sister," Lorrie bit his tongue. How much did the mayor know about her?

"It's okay, Lor, they know."

There was nothing illegal about Crystal living and studying in Hyacynthe. There was a lot illegal about the transfer of money she sent every six months or so. Even the letters and photos sent both ways were strictly controlled. When the Sheppard family was anonymous, nobody paid them any attention. They would be under a microscope now. If they were alive.

"We can't reach your sister in Hyacynthe. Unless you give up your contact with the Allens, but I understand if you don't."

Robbie glared at Lorrie. For once the brothers understood each other. Lorrie's mind raced, trying to figure out how to navigate this impossible situation.

"I don't talk to her anyway, so nothing changes for me." It was a white lie, but grounded in enough truth that he could say it with confidence. "She left us behind years ago."

"And because of that, there's no need to worry about her safety. But when all of this is over, I'll do my best to bring you four back together."

Lorrie was only sixteen years old, but he was already cynical enough to know that the mayor's platitudes were just that. Another silver-tongued politician trying to say all the right words at the right times.

"In the meantime, your brother and I were talking about Cadlen here. Jason has agreed to bring in school tutors, and even a specialist to help him with his speech issues."

Cadlen didn't react, continuing to zero his focus in on the page. Whenever he was nearing the end of a sketch, his attention intensified to the point where a scream in his ear would go unregistered. Steven walked over, leaning against the armrest and craning to see the drawing.

"You have some kind of talent there, Cadlen!"

Cad smiled, already more reaction to a stranger than he ever offered Lorrie. The youngest Sheppard brother set his sketch pad on the cushion beside him, the charcoal pencil atop it. Without a sound, Cadlen stood and left the room.

Robbie narrated the moment. "Mr. Holt told Cad he could go to the kitchen anytime he was hungry. I'll show you around."

Steven picked up the sketch pad, his face widening with surprise and admiration. "He's really good. You have a prodigy here!"

On the sketch pad, Lorrie saw Cadlen's rendering of himself, his brothers and sister, and their parents, all in a wooded scene reminiscent of the holographic wall. The likenesses of Robert and Julia Sheppard were as uncanny as a photograph, always young through Cadlen's memories. It could have been a family vacation that never was meant to be. Robbie, taller than his mother, stood to the far right, Julia's arm around her eldest son's waist. Robert, roughly Robbie's height, draped an arm over Crystal's shoulder, as Cadlen nestled between them, a hand lovingly on each shoulder.

Lorrie was on Crystal's right, but noticeably detached from the group. He had drawn his brother similarly apart in a portrait that hung in the lobby of the inn. He was also the only one in the drawing not smiling. In one sketch, Cadlen said more than any words could express. Lorrie hoped the pediatrician Jason Holt was bringing in could work miracles.

Ghost in the Ruins

Cal Merrick could think of no better place to be than back in the Appalachian-Ozarck facility. The silence deep inside the mountain fortress ensured safety. Capston was very loud, and the Ozarck foreign national had yet to acclimatize to his new city. Not even three months since his citizenship was fast-tracked, the forensic scientist had surpassed into triple digits the number of processed autopsies, all from a total of four explosions. The first had taken place while he was still nestled into the Ap-Oz sanctuary, where biotechnological work occupied his thoughts as opposed to the suddenness of death.

A total of 108 confirmed casualties through the first four bombings, pending the results of the recovery of the fifth site. Not even half were identifiable by facial recognition. The faces were simply not present; in some cases they were burned, and in many the whole head was gone. The victims who were spread upon his examination table in pieces were in fact easier than the others. Without eyes to stare back from beyond life, the samples were reduced to identification numbers and DNA sequences. Data to be entered into software, to be cross-referenced with official New Inland databases. Cal recalled the first identified specimen. He had third-degree burns on almost 100% of his body, save for a small, untouched area beneath his arm. When Cal made the mistake of retrieving a photo of the victim before the third Capston bomb tore his legs from his torso and bathed him in white flame, he noted that the victim's skin tone was deep brown, much like his own. It was a far more common trait in Ozarck. Perhaps this delivery driver in his early twenties had once also immigrated to the prosperous federated dome to the north. Where the work paid well, and tropical diseases were less virulent. No doubt, he wouldn't have jumped the queue without the advocacy of Steven Reekan or Phil Fox.

Cal was relieved that under the brightening skies of daybreak, before the early commute clogged the rerouted streets around the block, the fifth explosion yielded no fatalities. Shonn Simmons' role within their partnership was to take the lead in crime scene forensics, so Cal was more than happy to pass the lead to him.

"Not so fast, Cal. Looks like you have a body here after all."

Well, there; 109.

From his seat at the console of the field trailer that served as the hub of all investigations, Cal sighed as he swiveled to the open sliding door. Approaching from the debris field cordoned off with bright yellow slatted barricades and strung-up ribbon, Simmons suppressed any "I told you so" smirks. Without question it would be brought up before noon.

"Tell me it's at least a foot or a hand." The analysis of DNA would only take minutes to confirm, and then the appendage would be zipped into a plastic bag and sent to the mortuary until the next of kin came to claim it.

"And I thought you'd rather have a body intact!"

And why wouldn't I? If only to verify the numeric codes that matched weren't just glitches? Nope, I'd rather have just a foot.

"All right, then."

Cal eased out of the trailer and waded into the rubble of what was the lobby of the Sheppard Family Inn. The rising refracted sun was shaded by the remaining third of the building that survived the explosion. That was a first in the wave of attacks—all other buildings until now were completely leveled. If the Sheppard Inn had been fully occupied, there was a good chance some might have even survived. He could not imagine the face of a survivor. Only the dead.

"I thought the lobby was already checked."

Simmons' forehead wrinkled. "It was." Cal's partner reached and pulled a blackened frame of what must have been a sofa. The fabric and cushion were completely burned away, baring the coiled springs and the metal rods that reinforced the armrests and back supports. "This gave him just enough protection to keep him from roasting. But nothing was going to save his life."

The body was crumpled in a ball as though the victim had tucked into the fetal position. The cleared debris revealed he was nestled into a shallow cavity of some appliance embedded in a wall.

"Fireplace?"

Simmons nodded. "Only for show—poor guy must have thought he could climb up the chimney. Except there wasn't one, of course."

Of course, there wasn't. Open fires weren't ideal sources of climate control in a domed city. Cal began to piece together hypotheses as to why a man had crawled into an obviously ornamental fireplace. Records already confirmed there were no guests registered, and there were no staff on shift. Robbie Sheppard had taken the youngest sibling and closed shop. So, the fact that anyone was still in the building was already strange.

Who is this guy...?

Simmons and Merrick each slid masks over their faces and pulled the body away from the crevice, stretching the limbs flat. What remained of his shredded beige cargo pants bulged on his left thigh. Simmons reached a gloved hand inside the pocket and retrieved a handheld, lifeless, cracked and spilling electronics. Motioning to an agent, Simmons ordered the device to be analyzed immediately. Cal's hopes weren't high for it or any of its contents to be salvageable.

The exam began despite the burned and lacerated face staring back at him from behind forced-closed eyelids. A file photograph would likely be enough to visually identify the sanitation worker, as the badge on what remained of his navy-blue work shirt indicated. A swab from inside a cheek was fed into Cal's diagnostic tool. If he's a Capstonian, it should only take a few seconds.

Sure enough, the device beeped, and a profile appeared on the tiny screen. Cal squinted in the glint of morning light to read the results.

Grant, Ennis: Male, 34. Registry: Capston

The listed occupation was indeed Sanitation Department, along with a street address from the Heights suburban block. Clear across the city from here, Cal remarked to himself. A search of all public transit in the hours leading to the attack would have to show how he got here. On foot he would have had to walk for hours. His legs were sore at the thought of it.

Cal braced for the profile photo, but it was unnecessary. There was no photo. The square space in the top right corner was white.

"Merrick, you seen a ghost there or what?"

Simmons was crouched behind, craning his neck to see the profile. Ghost, indeed.

"No next of kin. No stock photo. So, either he's a ghost..."

"Or he isn't who he says he is."

The pair locked eyes. Simmons amended his observation. "Or was, anyway."

Cal felt sweat beading under his mask. Traffic began to tighten, and the security formed a perimeter to keep onlookers behind the barricades from overstaying their welcome. A full post-mortem examination was the next step, so the pair waved for their interns to assist in securing the body for transport without contaminating either the scene or the specimen.

Ennis Grant's right arm was tangled in the shredded fabric of the destroyed shirt. Cal swiped a scalpel blade across the frayed threads and the elbow buckled, swinging the limp arm to the side of the elevated spinal board. An intern reached to catch it as though it were going to fall off.

Cal wasn't sure what exactly caused him to stop her. The arm hung by the shoulder socket, the hand broken and blistered, scraping against the rocky debris. The skin along the entire arm from the bicep to the elbow joint was sticky red and streaked with white, indicating third-degree burns. Nothing he hadn't seen before. However, the texture and colour below the elbow on the forearm was different. Blood streaks and exposed veins still splotched the skin, but it didn't appear as wet.

"Now why is this..."

Simmons didn't answer the thought. "Why is this what?"

The aberration made no sense. Grant's shirt was still intact when the explosion happened, and most of the sleeve was still accounted for, even if it was reduced to strings.

Cal Merrick's thoughts returned to Ap-Oz. Not out of any sense of nostalgia or regret. "I want this arm wrapped very carefully. Get him back to the lab."

The interns secured the body and hoisted the spine board waist high.

"Shonn, get Shore on the line. We need Dr. Jarren."

"You can call Jarren from your secure line, right?"

Cal pulled the mask below his chin. "We need Jarren *here. Now.*"

Night Flight

Monday, 30 April AC 0245
1:25 AM
25,000 ft above Ungava Bay

Mr. Allen wasn't kidding when he told me to be at the ready for departure. Usually I snap awake, my body clock far more efficient than my electronic alarm. It was eleven minutes past 0200h, the red lights flickering through my half-open lids, when I realized I had to move. I met the cargo truck on the loading dock. After the retinal scan confirmed me as WALPURGIS, the bay door was thrust upward, and I was ushered into the back where a man greeted me with a black hood. I counted five, maybe six others, already in hoods, slumped and seated for the most uncomfortable leg of the trip. It was unlikely any of them were destined for Kayewat. No one goes there on a whim. Few go on purpose, for that matter.

But home is home.

I feel I need to write about my travel experiences so that if anything happens to me someday—and in my line of work, that's almost a guarantee—the story of who I am will not be lost. One day, the gulf between Kayewat and the rest of the world will not be any wider than the Davis

Strait that separates the island from the mainland frozen tundra. Citizenship in Kayewat will no longer be a life sentence. The poisonous blemishes that mark the skin of the right forearm will become old-fashioned body art, ugly on wrinkled, faded skin, the information contained within only a dead language.

With the hood secured around my head and the gag stretched over my mouth to prevent me from talking to my fellow cargo mates, I slid my free left hand across my arm. I know it's there. It will always be there. I know the name WALPURGIS is hidden inside the concocted ink and salve. I know the scanner will pick it up when they call my number at the Kayewat Ninth Circle.

And even in the exposure of natural light, no one in all five cities under the New Inland dome has ever set eyes upon it. Not once has any security scanner detected it. My employer's pockets are deep enough that not only can I afford to live a clandestine life in Capston, but I can also acquire the means to conceal my Kayewati trappings that would otherwise prohibit entrance. I really ought to visit Ozarck one last time...

The sedative that laced the hood material kept me unconscious for several hours, long enough to be shuttled out of New Inland and aboard a westbound magna-rail.

Neither **WALPURGIS** nor my Capstonian name appeared on the manifest, just like my semi-frequent trips to Allentown. When I awoke, the hood was gone. I was slumped against the plexiglass window in a private cabin, and the only evidence of my movement as human cargo was the itching around my neck from the hood. I always have some sort of allergic reaction to whatever that sedative is. I won't miss it.

The train swished to a halt at the Badlands Junction. The crossroads, as some people call it, are where the four mainlines meet. Sascota in the plains to the west, New Inland in the east, Ozarck to the south along the mountain range, and Hyacynthe north and east of the Lake Region and its barren sprawls. The Hyacynthian customs station is always a hassle. Any travel to or from New Inland in the past four years disqualifies entry to any Hyacynthian holdings—and they have several, dotted all over the river valley and deep into the forested lands north and just shy of the tundra. New Inland claims the French are way too loosey-goosey with their trade. If the other domed federations feel the same, they don't say much.

Still, I can't get home from Hyacynthe. So, there I was, standing on a dock in the sweltering heat of the grasslands where four behemoth empires touch fingertips.

I was spirited away by a private coach that ran on ethanol and chugged and churgled as though it would collapse any second. We drove off, the Junction vanishing from site so gradually that I could imagine it was never there in the first place. As hills began to swell on the horizon, I saw the hangar come into view. The airplane, dirty white and yellow paint fading where the rust leaked along the seamed panels and rivets, napped on a tarmac that stretched to a vanishing point somewhere in the setting dusk. The coach driver says, "Don't even go take a piss, board now," so I grab my travel bag and hop out of the coach, half expecting it to up and die behind me.

My trip was timed perfectly. For such a flat land, it's awfully easy to get shot in that hundred-yard dash from the coach to the plane. Bounty hunters of both the legal and illegal kind know about this airstrip, and where its flights are often charted. I know the Arctican bounty on me is still live. They have a long memory; that was a long time ago and those kids are all grown up now. At least my hidden stamp has helped me stay under the radar, so to speak.

Once on board the plane, a ruckus kicked up outside. I ducked beneath the port-side window and tucked my pack under the seat. Some shouting, a scuffle, and plaintive pleas were all I could make out before the metal door slammed shut. The propellers cranked to life and the noise of the engine's tortured screaming made the coach sound like a lullaby. As we began to taxi down the runway, I saw the man who had made the commotion, on his knees, hands behind his head while the uniformed officers stood around him. I felt the wheels lift off the runway just as the gun flashed and the man crumpled to the dirt. The loud shot I heard could have been one of the plane engines. Either was plausible.

The flight to Kayewat is direct. As long as the plane is fully fueled, we would spend the next five hours at over twenty-thousand feet in the middle of the night. Far too high for any colony brigands in the Lake Region sprawls to send up their drones. Far too distant for Hyacynthe to track. I was the sole passenger. The rest of the cabin was packed to the brim with cargo of all shapes and purposes. Medicine. Drugs. Raw materials. Correspondences too risky for digital transmission. Weapons. Some in bulging sacks, others in wooden or metallic boxes. All of it illegal.

The most important cargo on this plane is in none of these packages.

It's in my head.

Rattling around with the information of dozens of covert operations over the years. I'm certain that this would be valuable enough to my employer that I could maybe even retire.

I never slept a wink.

After three hours, I estimate we're soaring high above Ungava Bay. The plane will touch down at the old-town airstrip in the Horseshoe Bay, and from there another land leg through the Akshay Pass before the Kayewat monstrosity, in all its infamy, emerges into view, multicoloured sections that look as slapdash as they indeed are. I think I'll try to get some shut-eye before we land. The next coach will be a bumpy ride. And sleep back home never comes easily.

Walpurgis

Plus Signs

Steven Reekan always felt the conference room on Level 93 of Holt Tower was too expansive. Even if it was swept for surveillance bugs. Even if it was reinforced for soundproofing. Even if he could handpick the people who would be allowed inside. Save for the round table and eight chairs, one rectangular video screen on the far wall, and a datapad to control it, the room was bare. The track lighting embedded in the ceiling panel that circled the wall crown revealed a bluish-gray interior, glossy and cold. Steven was not worried about anyone outside listening in. Still, he could never shake a feeling that festered in his guts. It was a tomb, in some ways. Life was stifled in this place.

Yet here we are.

We included his second in command, Lieutenant Hayward Shore. Deft in public relations and a tactical genius, Shore exemplified integrity, making him the perfect face for Steven's security business as it became the official police force of Capston.

"Wall was pretty eager to ship out," Shore said. "She said she could even put up with Gry's stink!"

Captain John Gry proved to anyone he met that his heft was deceiving. Gry was surprisingly agile; Steven couldn't believe it until he saw it with his own eyes. Gry could run. He was exceptionally strong. And there was no dance floor in any Capstonian club that didn't know his size fifteen feet. John Gry was equally capable with his lady friends as he was with an assault rifle. Steven wasn't sure which was more startling.

There were precisely two women immune to Gry's charm. Both were in Steven's employ, and one of them was not present. Kenzy Wall never bought into the big man's charms.

"Major Wall is probably the only one who would put up with him. I just hope they have separate rooms at the Grace." Steven crinkled his nose imagining the atmosphere of his quarters after running reconnaissance all day and three meals of field rations.

Captain Ender Ling was the other. She rolled her eyes and continued to toggle her handheld. Steven always worried when Ling was standing in formal attention beside Gry. If he were to faint and fall on her, she wouldn't stand a chance. Ling's torso was about the same girth as one of Gry's legs. Steven knew of no one who could calculate on the fly so quickly. Her mind for big-picture conceptualization made her the only choice to lead the police squadrons within Capston.

"I'd live another fifteen years in the Arctican ghettos if it meant I never had to share a closed space with Gry." Ling's narrow eyes and thin lips gave little indication of her temperament, though her sharp voice more than made up for it.

Steven laughed. "And the poor man isn't even here to defend himself. Anyway..." He settled into his seat at the head of the table. Shore and Ling were joined by a fourth attendee of the emergency meeting. Dr. Kyle Jarren shifted his slender figure in his seat, unable to settle into a comfortable position.

"Good to have you with us, Kyle. It must have felt good to slide right in with that new citizenship cert, hey?"

Jarren appeared eased by Steven's casual comment. "No problems at all. If only I could come and go from Ozarck as easily!"

Steven couldn't imagine why anyone would want to travel to Ozarck in a heightened red tide season. "They're still testing at the gates? What do they do—temperature probes?"

"And you wouldn't want to know where they take it."

All laughed except Ling, who continued to work at her datapad.

"Right. So, here's what we're looking at. Merrick confirmed the identity of the dead body as Ennis Grant. Or at least, that's his New Inland identity."

Jarren's face turned ashen as Steven continued.

"He was carrying a handheld that was damaged pretty badly—mostly from water. Simmons was, however, able to pull up a few files. Jumbled and mostly incomplete, but a few little bits are worth our time."

The screen across the room flashed to life. On it there a confused soup of broken characters encrypted in symbols no one in the room could read.

wUwDPgly%u9LOn#Af4vxS@QgQZltcz7LWwEquhdm5k77Ik9 45$wfxtSTsma

"So, according to Simmons, the key here is... this sequence." Using the drawing tool, he circled a sequence of 10 numbers and symbols.

wUwDPgly%u9LOn#Af4vxS@QgQZltcz7LWwEquhdm5k77Ik9 45$wfxtSTsma

"This crosses with a code that is similar to an Allen encryption we have used in the past."

Shore spoke as the data on the big screen widened. "The Allens change their codes all the time. How can we be sure?"

Good question. Trying to track anything in Allentown is a pain in the ass.

"They do, and we can't. But check this out."

The widened frame brought the sequence to full view. Steven split the screen, placing a second sequence directly beneath it.

"Take a look at the second-to-last character."

The dollar sign was one of many symbols used in Allen encryptions. Nothing out of the ordinary with that. They were all about the money, of course.

"Now take a look at the bottom one."

wUwDPgly%u9LOn#Af4vxS@QgQZltcz7LWwEquhdm5k77Ik9 45$wfxtSTsma
  N5%ke9cBVjl#fgmQ9V35ja523+RDhCU7/2THg2iDr/3NGQZfz 3@SWviwCe7

The plus sign looked completely benign to Steven until Simmons pointed out a fundamental difference when they met earlier that morning.

"I don't get it." Shore scrunched his brows as he gazed at the two codes. Even Ling looked puzzled. At least he had her attention.

"If you bring up any encryptions from Allentown, you will find a sequence of specific numbers somewhere in the code. Accounts—those change all the time, to throw people like us off the trail. The bottom code, it's ours. And we can tell, not just because we know it's ours, but because of the '+'. It denotes our location within the city as an identifier."

Steven hated Grace Hospital in southern Allentown almost as much as the DHC chambers. It was a wreck of a building full of rat shit and mold. And it was the perfect place to establish a covert surveillance center in the ruined city. So long as the DHC was kept out of the loop.

"It's the medical cross." Ling ran a hand through her short-cropped hair that waved to her left side. "So, they identify us with the Grace because we're working there."

Shore's eyes lit up. "The dollar sign, would that mean a bank?"

"I would certainly think so. Now, we know the Nationwide Bank complex on the north side is still somewhat intact, much like the Grace. Gry is going to find out if Motherland is occupying it."

Jarren's faint blue eyes darted from one person to the other as each spoke before he joined in the discourse. "You may have a money trail to Motherland. But Mr. Grant, he's not one of them."

Steven's eyes met Jarren's. The doctor had promised clarification on Merrick's autopsy. The slight-built doctor shifted in his chair as though his clothes were three sizes too big.

"Dr. Jarren, you have the floor."

Jarren cleared his throat like he hadn't had a drink of water since yesterday. "Merrick detected an anomaly on Grant's right forearm. Steven, if you could bring up the footage."

Steven nodded. The encryption codes disappeared, replaced with filmed footage from inside the examination room on Level 90 medical facility, three floors beneath them. Jarren narrated the proceedings.

"As you can see here, there are substantial burns to the skin. Note that the discoloration when under white light is noticeable." The light in the sterile, gray room brightened and a patch of skin appeared, pinker than the red surrounding it.

"Even a seasoned coroner would not notice the subtlety. But Merrick, he's had some experience with this in my lab at Ap-Oz. Watch."

An arm reached into the frame, clutching in its hand a device larger than a handheld with two long prongs protruding from the end. With the push of a button, an electrical pulse emitted from the prong points. At first, nothing appeared to change. Steven felt his impatience rising with his pulse.

"And now, look right... here." Using a laser pointer, Jarren indicated a small area where the red and pink met. Slowly but surely, the pink skin began to wrinkle and regress as though an invisible hand was slowly peeling it back. Blood began to bead, at first in small pinhead droplets before coalescing into rivulets. Steven increased the speed twofold. The covering rolled back, revealing whitened skin streaked with blood before a black shape came into view.

When the full emblem tattooed into the natural skin was fully formed, both Shore and Ling exhaled with audible consternation.

"The Kayewati stamp." Reekan identified in his most dire baritone what everyone in the room already knew. The logo was shaped like a man made from blocks of stone, gripping a straight sword in his hands, hilt chest-high and pointed down.

Ling turned from the screen back to the men at the table. "We have a dead Kayewati. Inside Capston. *Inside New Inland.*" The chief of police spoke with a tremble in the timbre of her voice.

Shore spoke. "Grant was able to enter and move freely inside the dome and presumably any of the five cities, even though he has the stamp. How is this possible?"

Steven looked to Jarren, who picked up the cue. "It's possible because of the layer of synthetic skin you see in this clip. As you know, the stamp of Kayewat is laced with a mixture of trace elements that are *designed* to be detected with known scanning technology. You get the stamp, and you can enter Kayewat—but you can't enter any other dome on the continent without detection. And of course, subsequent arrest."

"But they have a way to get in now, is what you're saying." Ling's eyes flared. "We could be crawling with Kayewati criminals, and we can't detect them."

The room fell silent. Reekan didn't know how to respond. He still had a lot of questions of his own. After a few awkward moments, he asked the first.

"Kyle, you were able to identify the synthetic skin. Maybe you can explain to us how that works?"

"Of course. As you know, Steven, when my team and I were hired by Reekan Security in Ap-Oz, we were developing several biotechnological advancements under the sponsorship of the Ozarck Federation. The Ozarck DHC wanted nothing to do with external scientific study and so they let us out of our contract. And as everyone present knows, my team and I were granted citizenship to Capston in exchange for our services in biotech—"

"Under the provision that New Inland DHC laws are followed, of course," Ling interrupted. "I had no idea the council approved your work in synthetic skin, or whatever it is."

"Bio-synth," Jarren answered. "We are able to artificially grow replica skin that looks, feels, and behaves like biological tissue. And more than that..."

The doctor's voice faltered as he searched for the words. Ling delivered them.

"More than that, it can cover the Kayewati signature stamp. How does the DHC feel about this?"

Jarren turned his eyes to Reekan. In his glare, Jarren was silently asking him how he was going to explain this away. Reekan wondered if his uncertainty was as discernible to the doctor.

"The DHC doesn't know yet."

Ling threw her arms in the air, letting her datapad clatter onto the table. Shore cupped his face with his open palms.

"Steven, you know this is a blatant violation of the DHC covenant on technological advancement, right?" Ling's words stung in his mind.

"Ender, listen. Jarren and the Ap-Oz lab have been

working on this for years—way before we became partners. The developments were not Capston initiatives. So technically—"

"*Technically,* you're withholding scientific advancement from the other four cities. Which is illegal."

Shore looked up from his open hands. "And we have a bigger problem. We have a Kayewati inside New Inland. The DHC is going to want to know two things: how he got inside, and how we figured it out. So, I want to know, how *did* we find out unless *we* actually created the technology?"

"Naturally, Lieutenant Shore, Cal Merrick recognized the bio-synth. He was able to confirm that the molecular signature of the skin does not match ours. Therefore, the technology is out there." Jarren's answer felt well-rehearsed. Steven imagined the doctor repeating the words over and over the whole way from the Appalachian facility to Capston.

Steven felt the room running away from him. "Settle down, everyone. Kyle, you can confirm that the bio-synth is *not* Ap-Oz?"

The doctor nodded in confirmation, but the anxiety on his face was still present. "We confirmed it with our own data. It's not us."

Steven's remaining questions were all about who it could be. Kayewat was not an organization so much as a harbour for crime syndicates and shady operators. The Allens were currency and information brokers. There were a host of criminal gangs working in the outside, but most were small and without the capacity to fund research of this magnitude. One, however, certainly could...

"Le Renard." Shore blurted the name that everyone was surely thinking. "He's still operating across the continent even if we haven't dealt with him lately."

Reekan nodded. "It crossed my mind. But what's the

motive? They typically trade in weapons, drugs, human trafficking—they have no interest in terrorism, or at least as far as we can tell. No, I don't think it's Le Renard. But it could definitely be Desantos."

Motherland was poor enough to float under the radar, just far enough away that any blatant attack would be impractical. But the anti-dome sentiment that had begun to swell along with the ascendance of Tirel Desantos was at an all-time high.

"So, if Gry confirms that Motherland is in the Allentown Nat Bank..."

Shore was interrupted by Ling. "Then we can connect Grant to Desantos. And the Allen Consortium may be the silent backer of the bio-synth that allows them to import Kayewati agents. If something goes sideways, like it did with the Sheppard Inn, Motherland stays clean."

Reekan smiled. He always knew his team was the best he could hope to have, but it was moments like this that confirmed it.

"For the time being, we keep all of this at this table. I'll deal with the DHC over the Ap-Oz science when—"

A commotion in the corridor outside the conference room interrupted Reekan's closing statement. The voice of Clara Connelly protesting loudly drowned out the tempered voices of the officers pleading with her to calm down.

"Don't tell me the mayor isn't in today! I was promised my own suite—if I have to listen to my husband snoring for even one more day, I swear I'll walk right out the front door..."

Shore rested his face in his palms again and Ling returned to her datapad. Reekan sighed. "Looks like we're adjourned. Kyle, I'd like you to stick around for a while. Just promise me you won't bitch about the accommodations."

Dr. Doherty

Monday, 4 June AC 0245
Lacraie Nuclear Medical Facility
Crystal Sheppard

Being an intern at Lacraie Medical Dispensary hadn't exactly turned out the way Crystal had thought. Or hoped. Not even two weeks in, and she was still a glorified receptionist. Not at all what she was expecting, all those nights she fantasized with Mireil. When she was overpacking for her first ten-day rotation. When she was on the magna-rail slithering through the lush forest, nearly 400 kilometers to the Hyacynthian research facility and community. In the letter she had hastily written to Cadlen, it sounded a lot more romantic.

After ten days of nearly twelve-hour shifts, Crystal found very little to reflect upon as the final hours crawled by. She may as well have been back in Hyacynthe. Laurent had yet to call. She couldn't remember any of the technicians' names for sure, but one may have been Lachance. Or Latagne. Heck, it may as well have been Joe.

Crystal was never more excited to get back to her flat.

Her anonymity as just another pharmaceutical student made Crystal pine for Druna's *joie de vivre*, for Mireil's pragmatism. For the salty air. Lacraie offered a new set of sensory experiences. Outside, in the walled-in courtyard high upon the rocky plateau that overlooked the Lacraie River, the deep forest pine scent offered a reasonable compensation. Inside the compound, from the upper levels down beneath the ground, there was an unsettling sterility that hung in the processed air circulation. Crystal always imagined laboratories to smell more scientific. She didn't know what that meant, but it just made sense in her naïve imagination.

"Safe travels, see you next round." An unnamed technician in a white lab coat and thick goggles whisked through the sterile, white customer service lobby and through the secure laboratory doorway without making eye contact.

"Thank you, sir—?"

But the door to the laboratory levels had already slid shut. At least he knew she was leaving tonight. Maybe she wasn't anonymous after all.

Nearly 1800 hours, and she was the last intern on shift. Only the evening shift of pharmaceutical technicians and the armed security outside the complex remained. The janitorial crew left two hours ago. She had filled the final order of medicine for pick-up by the couriers well before that. No one came in off the street at this time of day. Not when the magna-rail was due to leave within the hour. The last hour of the last shift was always the longest. She wasn't wrong.

Files complete, and the cabinet locked. Double checked, so she didn't leave it like last time.

Crystal silently checked off her list. Flicking switches. Shutting and securing cupboard doors. Straightening the small pile of requisition forms that would be waiting for her successor in the morning. The shuttle for the dormitory would leave in about half an hour. Her bags were already packed. She had plenty of time.

The buzz of the security door snapped her to attention. It had to be another technician, either early or late for their shift. She didn't pay any mind and continued to fuss about her workspace. The trash bin— that still needed to be emptied. She bent down to retrieve it, and an unfamiliar voice startled her.

"I apologize for the lateness of the hour. Am I still able to pick up my requisition?"

She looked up to see a stranger appear in the doorway. He wasn't wearing a white laboratory coat. Standing straight but trying to appear casual, the man glanced about the office. Longer hair neatly pulled back, coupled with his accent, indicated he likely wasn't from Hyacynthe. His eyes were narrow and focused, yet pleasant enough. He dressed in a casual style not unlike clients she attended to regularly—midnight blue straight-leg pants and a semi-formal button-up shirt beneath an all-purpose seasonal blazer. Crystal could see crisp creases in both his shirt and trousers. They were either freshly pressed or brand new.

Lateness of the hour? Are you kidding me? Crystal stood, clutching the wastebasket in both hands, her hair rustled from straightening up so quickly.

"I'm sorry, but you'll have to come back in the morning." Time was ticking. Processing a requisition now would leave her only minutes to catch the shuttle.

"Oh yes, I see you're nearly finished your shift." The man spoke with courtesy, but the words read like a script. Crystal looked terribly unprofessional. Shirt untucked, hair undone, and an unemptied trash can in her hands. Please, don't be an evaluator, she silently prayed.

The man stood very still while he tried to appear relaxed. His dimples creased as his eyes widened. "I would have arrived earlier, but I was delayed."

Crystal set the trash can down near her feet. As frustrated as she was, she still had to be professional. Subconsciously fixing her hair and straightening her shirt, she scrambled to reply. "Oh, that's just the worst. The last shuttle back to the station leaves soon, too. I'd hate to make you backtrack. Especially if you've traveled far."

"I'm not dependent on the shuttles, but I can see that you are. Again, I apologize."

The man began to walk about the office casually, looking at the abstract artwork on the walls, browsing the information pamphlets beside the guest chairs. He dropped a leaflet and rapped his hand on the bottom shelf of the display. Crystal gulped and her heart began to quicken. Charise had gone over various protocols on how to deal with unusual situations. She wasn't certain if this were the time when she'd need to reach back into her memory for what to do. Especially if the seemingly pleasant man who had arrived so late were to become less pleasant. She was grateful for the plexiglass barrier between them. For now, he only winced as he kneaded his hand, seemingly more embarrassed than upset.

"I'm sorry, I hope I didn't alarm you." He raised his palms forward in a gesture of surrender. "If you prefer that I speak to a manager, I can wait outside."

Crystal couldn't help but feel sorry for the late-coming client. If she was quick, she could fill the requisition, and both would be on their respective way. "No, it's fine. I just don't have clients arrive unannounced. I mean, I can help you, of course! You're here for a requisition, you said?"

The client relaxed his hands, sighing with relief. "Yes, it was filled two days ago, if I'm not mistaken. I'm under strict orders to retrieve it in person."

Crystal sat at her console and switched on the screen. She hadn't yet logged off for the day. Had this client not arrived, she would have forgotten. A lock of hair fell loose over her cheek, but she ignored it as the program loaded. "I will need—"

"223567-889B." The man rhymed the numbers as though he were reading them. "That's the number I was quoted."

Crystal was about to ask for his name when the name listed as the supervisor of the request appeared:

Supervising Technician: Dr. Jonathan Doherty

Dr. John Doe. Crystal got it.

She may yet be a fresh-faced intern, but she knew that any requisition attributed to "Dr. Doherty" was encrypted, beyond her clearance. *Don't ask questions,* Cherise had told her.

"Right. I see it, just a moment."

889B was stored with the other 889 products, and Crystal had already secured the cabinet. Fishing for the keys as she wheeled over to the long doors, she repeated the number to herself so she wouldn't have to write it down. Time was ticking.

She inserted the key, only for it to snag and slip, clattering to the floor. Anywhere but in Lacraie she would question the use of physical keys and locks. The security she had to pass that first morning of orientation, and every day since, was enough to ease her mind. She bent down and scooped up the keys, fingering through the half-dozen brass wands until the 889 key was in her grip. The client was conspicuously looking away from her, as though trying to spare her any further embarrassment. Mireil and Druna would be howling if they could see it.

The cabinet clicked open. Crystal flipped through the filled requisition envelopes until she reached 223567-889B. She paused just long enough to skim the label:

Potassium iodide
Radiogardasse
Diethylenetriamine

She knew what this medication treated, even though

it was never purchased by individual clients. Only for mass shipments. Crystal averted her eyes as she tucked the envelope under her elbow, closing and locking the cabinet. Whoever this client was, he was involved in something dangerous to need these medicines.

Walking back over to the counter, she set the envelope in front of the client, who did not immediately reach for it. Crystal made eye contact by accident. His were grayish blue, disarming despite their sternness. Faint reddish streaks in the corners told her he was either light on sleep or fighting an allergy of some kind. He rested his heavily calloused hands on the counter, just centimeters away from the parcel.

"Will I need to sign anything...? I don't have a pen."

Sign anything? A *pen*? What century was this guy living in, exactly?

Crystal squinted, trying to understand. The man smiled.

"I am joking, of course. You need my palm print, correct?"

Crystal laughed uneasily. "Yes, of course, you'll need to scan your palm, just let me grab the handheld. It's just over... here..." A sinking sensation crept in as she realized the handheld was already locked away. Time was still ticking. She was cutting close to the shuttle's departure time.

She went for the file drawer at the far end of the counter. Fumbling for the third time for the right key, Crystal prodded the key at the lock. It opened with a soft click. Retrieving the handheld, she nearly cursed as she realized the device needed to reload. It dawned on her that she would easily miss the shuttle at this point. In her rushing, she hadn't noticed that the man had followed her the length of the counter. His features were even more striking up close. Startled, she nearly dropped the datapad.

"Crystal, is it?"

"How do you know my name?" For the first time, something about the stranger was off-putting. He couldn't have been an intruder, as the guards would have cleared him to enter. Still, he moved around the office at once quiet and clumsy.

He pointed to her. "The name tag, of course." Crystal hoped he couldn't read the embarrassment that was surely on her face. "I've made you late for your ride home. I'm truly sorry. Please, let me make it up to you."

Crystal's eyes began to swell. The client's courteous demeanor almost made her forget that she would have to wait another night in the dormitory before the next shuttle midday tomorrow. He retrieved a small handheld device of his own, keying it to life with his thumb. After a few swipes and finger taps, his pupils widened in the soft glow of the screen.

"Crystal *Sheppard*, I presume?"

In her lab coat pocket, her own handheld buzzed. On the notification menu, she saw the missed alarm for her shuttle departure, two messages from Mireil, and one from her ethics professor. A new memo flashed above the others, this one from her bank. Crystal's eyes widened when she saw the amount of money that had been forwarded to her.

"There is more than enough to hire a private taxi." The client switched off his device and pocketed it. "I understand they can be very expensive after hours."

The sum was staggering. It had taken her months to save up the last lump sum she'd sent to Robbie. Tutoring didn't earn much. But this was a game-changer. She could pay for the quarterlies all up front without Laurent's help. She could hire Lorrie a professional trainer. Speech therapy for Cadlen...

Robbie...

Her brother could sell the inn. Finally, he could do

something for *himself.*

While she daydreamed in shock, the client had taken his parcel and was nearly at the door. She could imagine Mireil scolding her, *"Thank him, you idiot!"*

"I don't know what to say! I mean, thank you, Mister... I didn't even ask you your name!" Once her eyes saw Dr. Doherty as the supervisor, she didn't bother checking the client's own name.

The man turned his head and nodded. Crystal blinked a tear onto her cheek, hoping her makeup didn't leak with it.

"Ian."

Crystal smiled. "Well thank you, Mr. Ian. You are very generous."

Ian raised his right hand in a farewell salute. Even if his mouth didn't smile, she was certain his eyes did. As soon as the door latched shut, Crystal reached for the office datapad. Ian had pressed his palm to the screen while she was fumbling for her own device, and she hadn't even noticed. The account was still open. Crystal glanced past the name of the supervisor and confirmed his identity.

She sighed, hoping she hadn't given radiation exposure treatment to just anyone. There was enough to last a full-grown adult almost two weeks after exposure to around 500 millisieverts of radiation. Crystal Sheppard was still a fresh-faced intern. But she knew enough. And she hoped that in his travels Mr. Ian Null wouldn't require even a fraction of that amount.

Everywhere and Nowhere

Tuesday, 5 June AC 0245
Hyacynthe Station
Crystal Sheppard

The cycle at Lacraie was ten days. The eleventh day was due to the eleventh-hour visit by Ian Null. Waiting another twenty-four hours may as well have been another full cycle. Still, Crystal had plenty to occupy her imagination.

The small dormitory in the residential quarter offered no frills. She was given a bed, and a set of sheets and blankets to keep her warm over the cooler Lacraie nights. Cooler than she was accustomed to in Capston. Her room was further furnished with standard bedroom furniture. A view screen with a modest selection of programs. A charging dock for her handheld. A small private bath accessed through a door barely wider than her shoulders. She kept pictures of her brothers along with a collage of snapshots of Mireil and Druna tacked onto the dimpled cork board above her one-drawer desk.

Crystal only needed to pack about half of her clothes, since she didn't unpack all of them upon arrival. Any idea of socializing in her scant spare time was always suppressed by fatigue. The mundane work was more exhausting than her most difficult exam-studying breaks. While the internship was a tremendous opportunity, it came at a cost. In Hyacynthe, she missed her brothers. In Lacraie, she missed everyone.

She was even looking forward to the clangor of her roommates' lives. No doubt they would be in a rush to catch her up on everything she missed at the clubs. They would be doubly pressing to find out about Crystal's love life. Druna was drooling over the legendary dashing young men from the untamed frontier lands. Girl, you'll have an endless buffet, Druna had gushed. No thanks, I'm really not that hungry, she had replied.

No stories to tell anyway, girls.

Except...

So many clients in her first ten days pestered her for requisitions and complained about every detail. And her thoughts returned to the last one, who had arrived impossibly late.

Ian Null. How would I even describe him?

He was so serious, yet there was a charm she had never encountered in anyone she met during her time in Hyacynthe. She did everything wrong except give him the wrong package. She began to second-guess even that. Her gracelessness cost her the final shuttle back to the dormitory. It was an absolute disaster.

And then, Null more than made up for her loss.

Crystal opened her account every few hours just to confirm the money was still there. She did this so many times that she had to recharge the handheld hours earlier than usual. Should she contact Laurent? She was avoiding him for fear he would break her the news that the funds in her account were illegal or were not allowed to be kept by interns. There had to be a loophole. The shoe had to drop eventually. But not if she didn't ask, or so her panicked logic informed her.

She scanned the room one last time. The taxi would be leaving for Hyacynthe Station in less than an hour. The five-hour journey back to Hyacynthe would be occupied by reviewing the latest assignments from her professors and replying to missed correspondences. Maybe even catching some sleep. Life with her roommates never guaranteed rest. One final glimpse of her photos on the wall, and Crystal flicked off the lights.

Her taxi was waiting.

The terminal for the magna-rail buzzed with activity. The station served as a relay between all Hyacynthe's scattered business interests in the region, as well as a departure point for Arctica and Sascota north and west, respectively. Almost entirely walled in heavy plexiglass, the facility was naked from an outside eye. The heavy presence of armed, black-clad soldiers on the grounds and in the surrounding rampart towers kept the travelers inside confident of their safety. Crystal didn't like the guns, but she hoped they were bigger than those of any would-be invaders.

How big was Ian Null's gun? He must have had one.

Crystal made her way to the teller window and held up her device for the attendant to confirm her identity. Voices of travelers washed through the terminal as she pocketed her handheld. Forty minutes before boarding, and her stomach gurgled. She hadn't eaten since breakfast. *Something light, maybe? I don't want to sleep too deeply and be groggy when I get home.*

She settled on a half-portion smoked meat on rye, a staple of the region for centuries. Sascotan rye and Hyacynthian beef. She requested a smaller portion of meat and more vegetables, with a hint of tangy mustard to hold it together. A small cup of java from beans harvested in the biomes of Ozarck washed it down. She forgot her tooth-whitening paste back in her water closet. Crystal groaned reflexively about buying a new tube. Only now, money wasn't an issue. She still felt guilty about frivolous spending.

None of these things were cheap in New Inland. Hyacynthe products were simply impossible to purchase. New Inland's hard stance on cooperation with non-domed political entities may have kept them secure, but it ensured that they would need to be self-sufficient in all production. None of this made Crystal feel any better.

Every time Laurent informed her of an attack inside Capston, her heart sank until he assured her the Sheppard brothers were just fine. When she waved goodbye four years ago, she never imagined it could be for the last time. And the longer she lived away, the more plausible it became.

Crystal held the sandwich at eye-level. None of the ingredients were from home. Nor was the clothing she wore. All Hyacynthian. Same with her handheld. Nothing around her as far as the eye could see. Home was a construct, only alive in the echoes of her memory.

Her luggage checked in, Crystal made her way to the dining courtyard with an earthenware cup in one hand and a multicultural sandwich in the other. The cleaning staff were hurriedly wiping up spills, gathering used dishware, and sweeping floors. Crystal spied a freshly cleaned table for four. She sat and began to eat her lunch, scanning the terminal. She was usually in too much of a hurry to take in her surroundings.

From her vantage point, she saw the magna-rail tubes for all the major destination routes. The magna-rails dipped beneath the surface through burrowed tunnels that would reemerge beyond the transparent walls. All four major arteries were visible to some extent. The Arctican artery was farthest, but such a major highway was constantly bustling with pedestrian traffic and regularly scheduled bullet trains. Twelve hours at highest velocity would get a traveler to the largest dome on the continent, and within striking distance of the corridor across the Bering Strait and to the Far East. Transportation to Kayewat in the frozen Northeast was possible from Arctica if one knew whom to contact. Why anyone would wish to go there, of course, was beyond her.

Next closest was the arched entry to the tunnel that would ferry travelers to the dome on the plains. The

Sascotan Federation was a powerhouse in agriculture, tens of thousands of hectares of arable land lying within their jurisdiction, domed over with the most sophisticated artificial climate system anywhere. Their medical school could have been a contender, except for the high tuition and the lack of connections Laurent afforded her in Hyacynthe. Crystal watched as the magna-rail cars slid silently through the opening, lights flashing to warn pedestrians of the next departure. Almost instantly, an arriving train slid parallel to the outbound rail. How does the train stop so quickly without violently jostling its passengers?

The Ozarck terminal was even busier. More robust trade between the mountain folk and the rivermen had developed in the vacuum of the New Inland embargo. She sat close enough that she could easily hear the passersby conversing with one another. Talking about how flat the land looked around here. How sumptuous the cuisine tasted. How clear the air felt off the water. How eloquently the accent rolled off the tongues of the locals.

Her java cooled enough to take longer gulps. Crystal washed down the last bite of her sandwich as she spied the shuttered terminal that once led to New Inland. Vendors kept shops open outside the terminal, but the ticket counter was bolted shut, the magna-rail was void of trams or trains, and the plexiglass walls were mostly obscured with hanging plastic. She imagined dust was beginning to accumulate where travelers no longer trod. Unclaimed luggage was likely still on the baggage racks. Small rodents and insects were more than likely reclaiming the abandoned terminal for their own security from the elements.

She imagined standing in the queue, flashing her identification to the attendant, and boarding the sleek vessel. It would have ferried her home to her brothers in a matter of hours, quicker than the train that would be bringing her to Hyacynthe.

Out of the corner of her eye, she spied a young boy alone at his own table. His dishware was pushed aside as he hunched over a notepad, hastily scratching away with his pencil, his hood drawn and his eyes turned downward. Cadlen would be about the same age as this youngster. She didn't stare long enough to arouse his sixth sense, for fear that the eyes that met hers might even be Cad's same deep brown.

Crystal snapped to attention at the sound of commotion. A group of young men in their late teens were causing a fuss at the cafeteria counter. Something to do with misunderstood dialect. Arctican kids were known to be somewhat arrogant. The youth yelling the loudest sounded just like Lorrie screaming at Robbie. The attendant took the verbal tirade with the same resignation as her older brother.

"Excuse me..."

Startled, Crystal sent the earthen java cup crashing to the floor. She remembered how silently Ian Null emerged as she was emptying the trash bin. That sophisticated yet clumsy charm. His hair tied back, and his shirt still pressed as though fresh off the loom. His voice rang in her memory as though it were a recording held to her ear.

The man lurched back upon the launching of her dishware projectile, clearly apologetic for startling her. Crystal held her hands over her mouth, reliving the embarrassment of yesterday. Nearby, black-suited guards turned their attention to her, quietly assessing the situation and turning away.

"Oh no, I'm so sorry! I didn't mean to scare you! I was just..."

Crystal sighed and lowered her hands, her cheeks reddening. "No, I'm sorry. I was daydreaming. I didn't hear you."

The man who had startled her looked nothing like Ian Null. He was in business attire, carrying a small satchel and his own handheld, lost in the maze of terminals looking for the boarding ramp for Sascota. After she gathered herself, she stammered through directions to the station three tunnels away. The traveler gently nodded in appreciation, apologizing again before he turned and shuffled to the gathering queue for the next departure.

Only fifteen minutes until boarding. Crystal stood and pulled the handheld from her pocket; keying open the boarding pass. Returning from the direction she came, she noticed security guards had intercepted the loud man who was yelling at the ticket agent. As she walked past, she could tell the traveler was protesting the seat he had purchased. *No surprise. Arctica.* His friends stopped jeering as the black-clad security guards admonished the brash young traveler. Glancing over to the table where the young person was drawing, she saw that only the dishware remained. He had packed up and left during the commotion she had caused shattering her mug. Cleaning staff were already sweeping up the shards. Maybe he was never there in the first place.

She would continue to see her brothers the rest of the trip home. A team of cyclists occupied the cabin next to hers. *Did Robbie ever race against them?* Loud-mouthed teens could be heard cackling in the dining car. Younger children with their hoods drawn seemed to be in every second seat. She could have sworn the usher had a New Inland twang to his accent.

Ian Null was nowhere.

He was, of course, *somewhere*. Crystal only saw him stubbornly lingering in her memory.

Dirty Boots

Le mercredi, 6 juin AN 231 (Wednesday, 6 June AC
0245)
Le Café Mondial, South End, Hyacynthe
Crystal Sheppard

Le Café Mondial, like many of the businesses and housing units in the South End district of Hyacynthe, clung to the vertical rises, overlooking the mighty river that flowed through. Crystal felt the palpitations of her heartbeat that first time Monsieur Laurent guided her along her first tour four years ago. For a moment, she worried a gust of wind off the river would whisk her away. And then she saw the view—kilometers in every direction. The width of the entire South End to her left and right. The North End twinning it across the river, joined by connecting platforms in several junctures. One of them had segments of transparent floors, Laurent told her. In four years, she had yet to experience it for herself.

And true to her elevation-fearing self, Crystal always chose booths farthest from the wide windows and terrace outside. It had taken Mireil a year to stop teasing her. Druna still did from time to time. Of the hundreds of restaurants, cafés, and other social establishments, *Le Café* was the best watering hole this side of Capston, boasting a great spirit selection and better ambiance for after-school relaxation.

"What is this band playing?" Druna cocked her head sideways as an organ cooed through a rhythm section keeping mid-tempo. Two musicians in floppy hats held their brass instruments ready to interject with their solos. Half a dozen patrons were turned in their chairs to face the live entertainment.

"I don't know, I kind of like it!" Mireil blinked her long lashes and swayed to the music. "I wasn't sure what to expect from 'fusion night'!"

Druna rolled her eyes. "If we came on Wednesday like I wanted to, we would have heard the Pop Revivalists, but *someone* was too tired."

Crystal parried her roommate's thinly veiled jibe. "I was up over twenty-four hours finishing my term report. Sue me!"

"Sue *me* for getting my beauty sleep!" Druna downed her drink and motioned to the server for another. "Life isn't all about tests and reports, you know."

"Maybe not." Crystal shifted and straightened her blouse. "But a solid GPA will get me a job quicker than a long nap will make you prettier!"

"Bitch!" Druna's gorgeous brown eyes widened. "You're lucky I love you so damn much!" Crystal admired Druna's self-awareness, even though it drove both her and Mireil nuts.

"Besides, Dru. We know when you were at Remy's — is that his name? There was no sleep happening!" Mireil's brows were thin and sharp, narrowed into an accusing look under her bouncing, curled hair. Dru laughed and nearly knocked the drink from the server's tray as he was leaning in.

"So jealous, Mir. So jealous." Druna winked to the handsome server, causing him to smile. "Don't stray too far!"

Crystal wanted to warn him to stay away from her maneater roommate but didn't want to draw their attention. It was more fun to watch Mireil pushing her buttons anyway.

"And what if Remy saw you flirting with the server?"

"Remy knows a good thing when he has it. And besides, maybe *you* should be getting this guy's number!

When was the last time you got laid?"

Mireil almost spit out her drink. "Easy! And how would you know anyway? You're hardly ever home overnight these days..."

Crystal laughed. It was true. At least Druna wasn't hogging the washroom.

"I'm not wrong, am I? Oh Mir, I just want you to be happy. Whatever happened to that one we met last year? Jérémie, wasn't it? He was a nice guy."

"Nice guy" in Druna-speak meant that he was friendly but not attractive enough to sleep with. Crystal remembered him. She didn't think he was Mir's type. Then again, she wasn't sure if Mir even had a type.

"He was a nice guy. But I don't know..."

"Bad in bed?"

This time Mireil did spit out her drink in a burst of mist that caused people in the next booth to look. "Not that it's your business, but he just wasn't... *mature* enough."

"Well, you aren't gonna find maturity on campus. Besides, it's overrated anyway. You need someone who likes to live a little. It would do you some good."

Mireil sighed. "I think you're more worried about my love life than I am."

The brass instruments jumped into action and the audience politely clapped for the organist. Crystal laboured over her drink, expecting Dru to beckon for the server to bring her a second.

"And what about you?" Dru turned her attention to Crystal. "Anyone catch your eye out there in Lacraie wilderness? Something like 70% men I hear! No excuses if you can't find one there!"

Crystal's reply was well-rehearsed. "No time. And besides, everyone is either too old, taken, or not my type."

"Or, someone's just not trying!" Dru flashed an

accusing glare.

Or, they appear out of the blue and vanish again just as quickly...

"What's this? Uh, oh! You *did* meet somebody!" Someday Druna was going to make a great counsellor. Or fortune teller. Crystal was afraid she would pick up on her body language and force a story out of her.

"Go on, you may as well tell her and get it over with," Mireil urged.

Crystal had confided in Mireil her encounter with Ian Null at the dispensary. How he arrived late enough to cause her to miss the shuttle home. How he was handsome, but awkward. Crystal left out the little detail of the money he transferred to her for compensation. It was best to keep it simple, anyway.

"I did meet this customer. He was really good-looking—strong, tanned, broad shoulders. His eyes, they were like blue and green, but not quite hazel. Dressed like he climbed right out of a storefront window display!"

"Wow, in four years I have never once heard you describe a man like that! So, did you get his number?"

"Dru, she was *working*, right? You can't just ask out clients at the counter!"

Mireil jumped to Crystal's defense, thank goodness. It gave Crystal time to process her answer.

"It was late—I almost didn't make it back to the dorm in time to catch the magna-rail home. Besides, I don't think he was from around here."

"How could you tell? Too mature?"

Mireil smacked Druna in the arm. "Very funny."

"I mean, he had a slight accent, but I couldn't tell what it was. Nothing I've ever heard in Hyacynthe, that's for sure. And he had longer hair, pulled back and very neat. We don't see men grow it out too often around Lacraie."

"Ooh, maybe a frontiersman! But you said he was dressed well." Druna had often gushed about wild-eyed, untamed outsider men. Something about not kicking them out of bed for wearing their dirty boots.

"Anyway, I doubt I'll ever see him again, so it doesn't matter." Crystal finished her lukewarm drink and was resigned to a second. "Like Mir said, it's not like I can just hit up a client."

Druna waved for the server. The young man, in his early twenties, with styled, short-cropped brown hair and dimples, came over with two more drinks on his tray.

"Thanks, hon! Hey, are you single? My friend here thinks you're cute."

The server blushed as he set the drinks on the table. Mireil slapped Druna's shoulder again, this time harder. "Leave the poor man alone!"

"Sorry, I'm taken." The server began to collect the empty glasses onto his tray. "My partner would be upset if he found out I was calling someone else!"

"Well, then..." Druna squinted to read his name tag. "Marcell, is it? Your partner is a lucky man! Can't blame a girl for asking!"

Marcell smiled. "I'm flattered! Can I get you girls anything else?"

"Unless you can find my friend here the man of her dreams, or you can get her back home for a visit, we'll just take our check."

"Ah-ha-ha, well! Can't help you with the man, but I could call you a cab to anywhere on the South End."

Home. If only she could crawl under the table, close her eyes, then appear back at the inn. Even if it was just for a day.

Druna's drinks were loosening her lips. "Ha-ha, no chance you'll find a cab to bring her back to Capston."

Marcell's face darkened. Mireil turned to Crystal with a look of concern. Most Hyacynthians tolerated New Inlanders, who at this point must be stranded there by the embargo. Crystal braced herself for the server's reaction to her revealed home city.

"I wouldn't want to be in Capston these days. Five bombings, now! Pretty scary."

Five?

Crystal swallowed dry. "Four, you mean?"

Marcell shook his head. "No, five. It's on the news."

The talking heads on Hyacynthe news programming were without a doubt reporting on the latest New Inland misfortune with an air of mockery, as they had in the past. Crystal never understood the details that led to the cutting of ties between the two domes. Laurent once tried to explain that trade and tariffs were a big part of it. Security was another. Lacraie, as an example, was trading and selling to outsiders, and New Inland drew a line in the sand over their alleged lack of business ethics. Chair Marribel resented Lacraie, her biggest competitor when she was head of New Inland's Department of Medicine and Research. Crystal's supervisors still complained about it.

Crystal thumbed the tabs on her handheld. Laurent had not messaged her. *Calm down, Crystal. Laurent would tell you if the boys were in trouble.*

He would if he knew anything. And for all she knew, Marcell was just a pretty face unaware of the facts in the news.

"You're killing the vibe, Marcell!" Dru continued to flirt with him even though he was obviously never going to be interested in any of them. "My girls are going to go home and probably watch a film with a tub of ice cream."

Crystal knew Druna was going to Remy's flat again tonight. She also knew that instead of a tub of ice cream, she was going to fall asleep with her handheld on. And no dirty boots on the door mat.

Head of the Table

Martes, 3 marzo NE 221
The Village of Jude
Tirel Desantos

"Quickly, Tirel, dinner is almost served..."

Emerging from his room, Tirel raced around the corner but stopped short of entering the dining room. He turned to the long mirror that hung in the hallway. Peering at his own image, he plied his hand over his tousled hair, straightening it as hastily as he could. His shirt tails were untucked. He crammed them into his waistband, slackening them as naturally as he could.

Satisfied that he was presentable, the young boy took a breath. His pulse quickened as he rounded the corner.

The dining room was not as decorated as the family was attired. Luther had already taken his place at the head of the table. A small handheld rested in his left palm, occupying his gaze. Hazel milled about, filling their glasses and adjusting the cloth kerchiefs. She had lovingly plied them into a fancy folded pattern, and each was set at precisely ninety degrees from the silverware.

"Shoes."

Tirel skidded to a halt at the stern voice of his father. Luther had not even looked up from his handheld, yet somehow he knew Tirel's shoes weren't tied in a proper bow. He always knew. He was always watching.

Kneeling carefully, Tirel unlaced first his left, then his right shoe, taking extra care to be certain the bows were taut and even. While he was at it, he took a moment to wipe a small smudge from the toe of his right shoe. Oddly enough, his father hadn't noticed. He could have sworn his father had smiled in approval. Under his breath, the boy cursed his wishful thinking.

"Come now, Tirel." Hazel's voice cooed. "Luther, he has done his best..."

Luther looked up at his son. Tirel shivered in the gaze of his father's piercing grey eyes. He wouldn't see a glare as fierce until many years later.

"M... m..."

"Speak up, son."

Tirel nearly wet himself when Luther interrupted his stutter. Swallowing hard, Tirel cleared both his throat and his inhibitions.

"May I be seated..."

Luther continued to gaze, as he did so many times before. All those years, all those meals the three shared together. How could he have never imagined how Tirel had been molded by his rigidity? How could his father be so oblivious?

Tirel couldn't stand it for a second more.

"Tirel, aren't you forgetting something?"

Hazel turned her back and was making her way towards the kitchen to retrieve the meal she had so carefully and lovingly prepared. Safely out of view, Tirel stepped to the table. Luther watched, confused that he had not received a compulsory answer.

"Tirel, I asked you, aren't you forgetting—"

The boy moved with startling speed. So much so, Luther didn't have time to find the words in the back of his parched throat to process what was happening.

And all this time, Father, you thought the shaking was fear.

It turned out the boy was not afraid in the slightest.

In one swift move, Tirel swiped the cutting knife that

was so neatly arranged next to his mother's kerchief. With the hilt firmly in his left hand, his motion arced the tip of the serrated blade into Luther's throat. Instinctively, he pulled the blade free, unleashing a stream of deep crimson blood gushing onto the dressed setting.

Luther made to scream out, but he wheezed, more blood pulsing from the gaping wound. The boy knew exactly what he was doing. Hazel was still out of the room. Tirel breathed a deep sigh of relief, thankful his mother didn't have to see it taking place. She'll be better for it, eventually. They would both be better for it. Tirel's heart rate was already starting to slow, a significant burden dissipating faster than the bloodletting of his father.

Tirel grabbed the knife from his mother's place setting. He looked into the terrified gray eyes of his father for one last time. The fierce gaze was gone, pupils narrowed to pins as Luther's confused, panicked look silently pleaded with his son for amnesty. The fear now radiating from Luther's eyes only served to anger Tirel. The knife blade thrust cleanly and without mercy into first the left, then the right. The soft, membranous spheres flashed into abrupt scarlet darkness. Tirel's victim pressed his palms into the ruptured cavities in nervous reaction.

Luther tried to stand, and immediately slipped on the blood that had pooled around his chair. Wheezing uncontrollably from the wound in his throat, Luther flailed, his hands still tight against his dead eyes. His head smashed against the table, making the first loud sound since his own voice sharply grilled his attacker. Tirel wanted to think that the last thing his father thought was *"all of this, over untied shoes."* He couldn't bring himself to believe it.

Hazel dropping the dishes and screaming in terror

was all Tirel could hear behind him. He couldn't see her expression as she entered the room to the gruesome scene. It's a shame Mother's diligent work had been soiled by the gore. Of course, it had been soiled for years before that, only this time it was visible in the deep red Tirel had always seen. Now, all over the floor for the world to see.

This deep red I've kept to myself my whole life.

Stepping back, tracking the blood with his perfectly tied shoes, Tirel replied at last.

"May I be seated, Father?"

A Prayer for Rain

Tirel never understood how his mother and father could stand and sit without rustling and bunching their robes like he did. How the coarse fabric chafed under the tasseled rope. How the overhand knot dug into his belly. It never looked as straight and trimmed as Luther's. He could swear his father's eyes were drawn to him every time the attendees rose and knelt. The officiants were surely judging him every time he moved a muscle.

Tirel knew his father was.

The sanctuary was cavernous to his young eyes. Sloped downward toward the altar, two rows of pews steeped behind for the brothers to sit while the lead officiary delivered the sermon. Behind him, the gown-draped and veiled Sibylline sisters waited in the shadows for their role in the ceremony. There was plenty of space in the bench pews for them to sit, yet they kept to their assigned placement. Tirel had no memory of a time when the seats were filled, but in his lifetime the attendance had noticeably dropped. These were lean times, Hazel reminded him when asked. There was too much work to be done. Fewer prayers for rain and more strong backs to haul clean water from a new source, miles away.

One of the Sibylline sisters emerged from the

shadows and delivered the sermon. This part of the ceremony was spoken in English. It was always a story or parable of some sort that was meant to provide *illumination*. Or so Luther said. Tirel didn't understand the meaning behind burning bushes, the dead rising, or water turning to wine. The soft tone of the Sibylline's voice was rife with deceit.

Fires always burn themselves out.

The dead don't come back.

Given the choice, Tirel would choose clean water over wine every time.

When she finished, the veiled woman retreated into the darkness and the officiant stepped to the pulpit to recite the prayers. They were recited in a language Tirel didn't understand. Even if they were in English, he still wouldn't have understood.

"Requiem aeternam dona eis, et lux perpetua luceat eis. In memoria aeterna erit iustus, et non faciet male."

The chorus echoed in antiphony three times. The requiem hymn bellowed from the tall brass pipes, towering needled spires behind the seated monks. The music rang dissonant to Tirel. His clenched teeth vibrated together, leaving a discomforting chalkiness on his tongue. The monks' hoods were drawn low over their faces, revealing only their bearded chins shifting up and down as they sang the chorus in loud unison with the organ. The robed men were joined for the final sequence of the ceremony by the veiled women, shuffling from their place in the shadows, up the aisles along the walls to the dais. They formed two arcs on either wing, one step in front of the men. Their harmonizing voices were loud enough to hear all the way back into the heart of the village. The requiem repeated in full three times. Tirel was convinced a fourth would cause his head to explode.

Hazel reached her gentle hand to Tirel. His own were crammed under his thighs to keep him from covering his ears. Luther scolded him once for wringing his hands during a service that required stillness. The punishment for covering his ears was worse. His mother was also forbidden to hold his hands. How else would he learn, Luther bellowed in the other room before an awful silence descended over the house. Tirel had scars from the leather belt on his palms to remind him. Hazel's glassed-over eyes and forced smile were hers.

"Ut supra, et infra. Et dum vivet, non morietur in aeternum. Perfundit lumen semper et in latitudine pelagi oculi..."

This passage signaled the benediction, which meant the end of the ceremony. He remembered asking his mother once what it meant.

"It means '*As above, so below. They shall live forever as they shall never die. The light pours over them always, in the width of an ocean or the breadth of an eye.*'"

"But Mother, what does it *mean*?"

She never answered him. Tirel wasn't convinced she understood it herself. He didn't dare ask his father. True belief will reveal the secret behind the requiem, or some other nonsense.

Tirel was brought back to the present by the scent of the wafting incense. The smoke offering drifted a pale blue, hazy through the dim lights while the organ reignited into a piercing wail. The congregation rose row by row and filed humbly to the waiting officiant in front of the draped altar, where the incense rose from two globular decanters. Each worshipper bowed their head as the robed monk offered his right hand.

Tirel stepped closer and closer to the officiant as though the solemn march was a death processional.

Ahead of him his father, then his mother received their blessing. He stepped forward and looked up to the robed man. Above his full beard, two eyes glowed in the shadow of his hood. The older man reached a veined hand forward. Tirel didn't offer his own at first, but when he did, the old man cupped it between his own.

The old man must have felt the ridged scars.

"What is your prayer, young man?"

From the corner of his eye, Tirel saw his father and mother retreating down the outer aisle. He swallowed.

"Rain."

The officiant nodded his head, squeezing Tirel's punished hand before releasing him. The prayer didn't really mean anything. Rain was either going to fall or it wasn't. The robed Reapers had no direct line to the weather, or to any make-believe spirit that could turn it on or off. It was all lip service.

No one spoke a word until they left the sanctuary. Even tiny infants seemed to know not to whimper until their mothers had ushered them out. Once outside, Luther stopped to speak with a fellow parishioner. Hazel began to walk Tirel back through the dry, dying woods to the village.

"Mother, why is the chapel so dim? If the light pours over us, why do we sit in the dark?"

"*We* are each of us the light we seek." Hazel pointed to her chest. "Our journey through life is the way. When the doors of the chapel open and the light from outside greets us, we are home."

None of that makes any sense.

Hazel smiled.

"One day you will understand, Tirel. I promise you."

"I don't think I will ever understand."

Hazel's expression turned to alarm. She glanced back

to Luther, still conversing with his friend, thankfully out of earshot.

"Please don't ever say that to your father..."

Jueves, 7 junio NE 267 (Thursday, 7 June AC 0245)

The Chapel of Saint Jude sanctuary was not so vast now to Tirel Desantos, visiting as an adult. He leaned over the backrest of a pew where he once sat on his hands to keep them out of trouble. The altar was bare of its fancy drapery. Shards of broken glass crunched beneath his quiet steps as he walked up the center aisle. The sweet incense in his memory was overpowered by the richness of mildew. Tirel was alone. No congregation. No Reapers.

No ghosts. Nothing.

"I'm here, Mother. It's been a year already—forty years, to be exact."

His voice echoed in the empty chamber. Tirel hated speaking out loud without an audience.

"It will be the last. Every year, I return because you promised me I would understand. Just another promise you didn't keep."

You will see her again, Tirel. Your mother will keep that promise to you. The Reapers that occasionally appeared to him always told him the same message. When he returned with De Léon's men to raze what remained of his village, they urged him to spare the chapel. Of all the decrepit buildings, the chapel deserved to go up in flames first. So many people went unfulfilled for so many years because of this rotting hovel.

It was time to look forward.

"I sent him away, Mother. Andreas is gone, north to

Kayewat where he can live out his days among the liars and thieves."

Andreas was different from the other Reapers that came before. At first, Tirel admired his candour. His willingness to offer real proof, real evidence about his mother, instead of riddles and rhymes.

Of course, when the cost was too high, he knew Andreas had become a liability. The mad monk was as poisoned as the village well. No rain would ever wash clean his childhood home. And it would not come from prayers in a crumbling chapel.

The well is filled and covered. Andreas is banished.

Paolo left that morning for Allentown. *He will bring the rain...*

Mr. Null

Friday, 8 June AC 0245
Allen Consortium Complex, Allentown
Mr. Slava Allen

Null.

The only name he would provide to the Allen Consortium upon first contact, nearly six months prior, was a simple four-letter word that meant nothing. Anonymity as literal as it was figurative. The unflappable Allen agent, who like all others revealed himself as only Mr. Allen to clients, monitored his breathing with care. He did not want the client to perceive his apprehension.

"Now, Mr. Null. The requests are as follows."

The list glowed on the screen. The client was looking at an identical one opposite the barrier.

```
> Access to closed-circuit surveillance
within a private structure
> Access to the network surveillance in
various spot locations along public transit
corridors
> Access to press databanks
> Dissemination of footage and assembly of a
montage
> Broadcast of said montage to various points
of specific destination both inside and
outside the private structure
```

"That is correct." Mr. Null spoke with a soft, unsettling confidence on his side of the opaque plexiglass.

"As you can see, the task is extraordinary. Access to a network to which we have no established link is certainly possible, but will require significant labour for our field agents, not to mention significant risk."

Of course, the best field agent for the job was Walpurgis, who happened to be in Kayewat. Who still hadn't made contact with the Allens for either his next assignment or arrangements for his return. Mr. Allen hoped Walpurgis wasn't too incapacitated on Kayewati Aquavit to do his job.

The agent continued clicking the keys as data blurred across his screen. The client on the other side was so quiet Mr. Allen questioned if he was even there.

"As you can see on your own monitor, Mr. Null, the invoice indicates the fine details, itemized as such for your convenience."

The silence from beyond the screen was slightly unsettling. Null did not answer.

"The cost is significant, however there is flexibility in the price depending on the time frame you are seeking. For example, we could employ fewer agents to your assignment if more time were available. Conversely, if time is of the essence, we could employ more people, reducing the time, but of course costing accordingly—"

"What is your name?"

Mr. Allen sighed silently to himself. Clients often asked him his name. He understood their motivations, much like he did their desire for anonymity. It was standard procedure to explain to clients not to attempt a personal connection to any agents they would meet during the process. Still, some couldn't help reaching out for a personal liaison, to find common ground with the person with whom they were conducting their business. The barriers, both physical and interpersonal, were in place for very good reasons. For a moment, Mr. Allen began to let down his guard. *Perhaps Null may be human after all...*

"Mr. Null, as you are aware, it is against our policy to

identify ourselves as anything other than Mr. or Ms. Allen. I am sure you can understand and respect our—"

"Your screen, Mr. Allen."

The agent peered down. A second field had emerged, cascaded over the lower-right quadrant of his spreadsheet software. A fund transfer link with Null's given credentials had appeared, with a large sum in the taskbar. The agent raised his eyebrow slightly.

Oh my.

"Go on." Mr. Allen was sure Null could hear him gulp.

"The sum on your screen for your *name*. Something I can ascribe to *you*. You alone."

Years of training in protocol vanished. The agent had never before reached this point in discussion with a client.

"Mr. Null..."

"As you know, I have a true name, but I choose to identify myself to you as *Null*. Even 'nothing' is something. No one, anywhere, can match it to my real name. I can assure you, Mr. Allen, it cannot be matched in any other database in the known world."

Kayewat has a deep database that the Allens had yet to breach. And there were of course small servers peppered across the continent where upstart organizations hid. But most of those were amateurs compared to the Consortium. With enough time and money, any of them could be hacked. But that would be like finding one pixel from a thousand screens. Null continued.

"Whichever name you choose to provide me, I will accept without question. I, of course, have no ability to track you, even if I were to set up my own residence within this complex. So, Mr. Allen. Your identity, or I am afraid our transaction will be as null as my name."

The agent remained silent. There was no need to react too quickly. He was aware that the man sitting on the other side of the privacy barrier needed Allen services more than he needed the sum of money glaring back at him on his monitor. Without knowing his actual identity, he surmised that this person was significant to the organization to which he belonged. If a deal couldn't be reached, the repercussions could be severe.

All that money, though. Talk about one in a million...

"Slava"

The agent spoke the name with feigned confidence. Mr. Null did not respond. Likely he was also processing the name, perhaps trying to make some sort of connection, maybe to reason the significance behind it. Slava was not prepared to divulge any more than that. He hoped it was enough.

"Create a proxy account, Slava. Twenty percent of the sum will appear within twenty-four hours. The remainder of your commission will be transferred upon completion of the tasks, to my satisfaction. The Consortium will of course receive the full amount as well upon successful completion. Those are my conditions, Slava."

Null repeated the name with emphasis as though it were more real when spoken aloud. The agent sighed silently to himself. The work necessary to create the proxy account was valued at a fraction of its reward. Still, as omnipotent as they were, the Allens could not add time to a day. Alter chronometers, create illusionary gaps in time to fool computers and their operators, they could do these with ease. They were not, however, magicians. Slava knew that his workload became that much more prescient with this new, albeit profitable task. He had created countless proxies for clients, but this would be the first for himself.

As he set to work, Slava began to daydream.

The easiest, and probably most satisfying, would be to create an identity inside a dome. Perhaps in Hyacynthe.

How lovely to have a home along the mighty river that flowed beneath it! To feel the comforts the structure offered while the salty sea breeze gently coalesced into every corner, like the human lung drawing a deep breath...

Or maybe he would go for a challenge and establish himself in Arctica, that supermassive structure to the northwest, along the mighty banks of the Great Slave Lake. That center of multiculturalism, the gateway to the Far East...

Perhaps Sascota. Where agriculture reigned over all aspects of life in the mostly flat lands. He found the kilometers upon kilometers of visible flat horizon that surrounded it very comforting, safe from outside incursions...

Slava knew what kind of folk made their living in the spotted colonies beyond the walls of the superstructures. He would have been lying to himself if he admitted he had more of an aversion to primitive life than cosmopolitan. *But maybe someplace near the ocean...*

"There is another request."

Slava snapped back to reality, not expecting his client to persist with more business. "Of course, Mr. Null. Please, continue."

There was another awkward silence, but Slava could hear the faint clicking of Null's keypad on the far side of the barrier. The man typed with deft speed, clearly skilled in data processing to move so fluidly across his keypad.

After several minutes, a new window appeared on Slava's screen. His eyes widened. A weight pulsed in his abdomen at the gravity of what he was reading.

"Mr. Null, I..." Slava couldn't find the words to answer, even though they were swimming in his mind.

"Mr. Allen, what I propose to you is not nearly as

tasking as my first request. However, the names involved make this somewhat delicate."

Slava gulped. "Indeed. Might I surmise then—"

"I would advise against that," interrupted Null. "This request is of the utmost importance. And I request that you pursue it personally. Are we in agreement, Slava?"

The agent now known as Slava never entertained the notion of planning his own anonymity beyond "Mr. Allen". He wondered if there was even one small corner, craggy outcropping, or harbor he would be able to call home if he failed in this second request.

"Very well, Mr. Null. I will set my agents to work on your primary task immediately. And I will personally fulfill your second. Now, as for the fee..."

A number flashed onto the screen in a separate bubble.

"I trust this figure should more than cover the costs. You would be able to reroute to a second proxy account if you felt it necessary. I would have no quarrel with you if that were your choice."

Slava Allen sighed, at this point unconcerned if his client detected his emotion. "It will be done, Mr. Null. Is there anything more you require of us, sir?"

He could almost smell the ocean air of his retirement home.

The Profile of Mott Wrengel

Sunday, 10 June AC 0245
Allen Consortium Complex, Allentown
Mr. Slava Allen

Wrengel. The deeper Slava delved into his file, the less about Mott Wrengel he actually wanted to know:

```
Wrengel, Mott Peirs.
Born: NE (Nuestro año de eminencia) 233;
25 marzo, Age 34.
Height: 1.83m
Weight: 86.12kg
Hair: Ash brown
Eyes: Hazel
Build: Well-built, minimal body fat
Blood type: O-
```

Rare blood type, particularly among the colonists of Motherland. Slava did not run a scan for a total count among the population; he figured, based on his surface knowledge of blood types, there would be fewer than a few thousand. It would certainly have made for a difficult task if ever Mr. Wrengel were to require a donor...

```
Parents: Garret James Wrengel (d); Teresah
Corazon    Wrengel (n. Reyes) (d)
Siblings: Nil
Offspring: Nil
```

The Allen agent read on to learn Wrengel's parents had both died during the red tide outbreak of 211.

Teresah Corazon succumbed to the illness itself, and within months Garret James was killed in the mines north of the city from methane exposure. Media reports were scant, but Slava found a brief article in which it was speculated Garret had been reckless under an announced methane advisory. Was the writer suggesting the senior Wrengel knowingly breached protocol? In the wake of such a heart-wrenching tragedy as the loss of his young wife, no less? Slava wasn't sure. He dealt in black-and-white facts; inference in print was not first nature to him.

All reports indicated young Mott suffered immeasurably. Orphaned at age twelve, he was placed into the care of the state as a ward of His Eminence. Slava had dealt with these unfortunate souls before. On the surface, wards were paraded as children of the sovereign, His Eminence De Léon, a loving father to a multitude of souls he had fostered in the absence of biological parents. The wards were often seen about the city tending gardens, landscaping, making small repairs, and grading roads. They wore royal-coloured tunics which made them stand out. Colonists, as per custom, always greeted wards with smiles and a courteous bow, as though they were addressing a member of the royal family. The wards, however, could attest to their true standing; were they unafraid of reprisal.

Slava squinted his eyes and continued to scan the profile.

While a ward, Mott suffered a predictable fate. Petty crimes kept him in and out of detention centers before he was finally charged with a violent assault during an altercation with a shopkeeper over stolen goods. So little value for his own life to risk the pillory over a satchel of groceries...

Slava clattered away at his keypad, drawing more and more sources. Two years in the reformatory appeared to have paid off; he received recommendation for enrollment in the armed forces upon reaching legal age at fifteen. Physical and psychological aptitude tests revealed a highly functioning young man in remarkable shape and with a remarkable presence of mind, although it was noted he was quiet with an almost icy comportment. Upon completion of the tests, he was assigned to the platoon of...

The clattering stopped. Slava pieced it all together instantly.

"Mr. Null, you are full of surprises..."

Rats

The reason Major Kenzy Wall tolerated the funk of decay in the sodden streets of Allentown was her experience working in close quarters with John Gry. He had arrived a few days earlier in an attempt to establish a link with assets on the ground. Reaching the safe house in the old Grace Hospital would be easy. Gathering intelligence within the ruined city, against the laws of New Inland and within the tight requirements of the Allen Consortium, would be more complicated. Kenzy figured that finding definitive proof that Motherland was responsible for the Capston attacks was about as likely as finding a bar of soap in Gry's pack.

Two full days by off-road vehicle to avoid public transport, and a hike on foot through dense brush, before the outskirts of the city began to emerge from the overgrowth. Her squad of five men and four women kept a tight formation as they climbed piles of ruins, avoided open pits, and watched for watchers. The Allens were watching. That was never in question. Whoever else was watching, however, may be doing so through crosshairs.

Once inside the Allen perimeter, signs of prior movement in tall grass and footprints in the dirt became clear, and more plentiful deeper into the city. None of these signs of life were from Allens. There remained a robust population of squatters all over the city, none in any hurry to hide from anyone. Most were destitute vagabonds, who looked the part in tattered garments and ill health. Gry had once joked that if you came across someone in Allentown with all their teeth, they were probably an Allen. Kenzy had yet to meet someone with all their teeth.

The squad was well into the city before any signs of life appeared. Kenzy's heart skipped a beat when a ragged figure darted from one window cavity to another in an abandoned plaza devoid of glass. Reaching for her handheld, she thumbed the device to life and toggled through the tabs. The tiny screen flashed and dimmed to black before a thin luminescent maze emerged. A blinking cursor indicated her position. Only about twenty meters...

"Watch for a metal grate, fifteen or twenty paces." Kenzy motioned with her gloved left hand up the street, mostly concrete broken by hardy shrubs and weeds. Sure enough, she felt a concealed panel creak under the weight of her step. Kneeling, she pocketed the handheld and dusted away loose dirt revealing a rusted metal panel that served to hide the grate her handheld indicated was there. The squad circled Kenzy as she pulled the grate off the tunnel opening. She inhaled one last, long lungful of fresh air before stepping onto the iron-doweled ladder. One by one the squad descended into the gaping hole, the last pulling the grate back over, leaving the panel askew. Before the last officer stepped off the ladder into the tunnel, the natural light through the grate was stifled by the panel being replaced by some unseen figure. The Allens made good on their pledge to conceal the route. They were indeed efficient. Wall ignited the lantern light of her handheld and the team pressed on.

Boots splashed in the puddles that coalesced in the dank corridor. The route to the sub-levels of the Grace was full of sharp turns, heavy doors with creaky hinges, and rodents so numerous the floor seemed alive. Echoes of footsteps indicated there were others in the catacombs. Kenzy always chastised Gry for calling the sub-surface squatters *rats*. They were people, after all, right? Still, she imagined the frightened vagabonds skittering away at the sound of the marching boots, retreating into crevices before any artificial light flooded the chamber.

The handheld served as a treasure map. Instead of finding buried riches at the electronic "x," their great reward for navigating the old sewers was an open door into an established safe house where the must and mold was a little less pungent. Wall estimated there were another hundred meters to go when the officer at the rear whistled, calling the party to a halt so close to their destination. Dripping. Squeaking. The slight shift of an officer's boot was the only audible clue that anyone was even in the tunnel, now in total darkness after Kenzy extinguished her lamp light.

It was too late.

A flash of light, and the tunnel was lit up like a hundred floodlights. Half a second before, Kenzy's nose wrinkled, and for once that familiar body odour stench comforted her.

"Dammit, Gry, you still need to wash once in a while!"

The big man laughed way too loud for the acoustics in the narrow hallway. His own squad of half a dozen troops goggled and masked with carbon-filtered tubes stood, arms drawn but untrained on the friendly forces.

"Hey now, I walked in the rain yesterday. Or was that Tuesday..."

Wall rolled her eyes and attempted to shove him aside. "If you're out, I can radio Shore to send a bar of soap."

"Nah, I wouldn't want to bother old Shore, like the mother hen he is!"

Kenzy felt her blood pressure rising. "Mother hen.

Nice."

The united squad finished the final leg of the subterranean journey without incident, apart from small talk and jibes from the hefty captain. Once reemerged into the light of the ground floor, Gry's troops removed their air-filtration masks. Animal droppings, branches and twigs, and other detritus from nature's incursion through the blown-out windows littered the lobby that was once a triage station. A steady breeze wafted the stink throughout the empty room. At least there was a breeze. The catacombs were noxious at best.

The united squad proceeded across the room following a trail of footprints to the stairwell next to the dead elevator. As Kenzy reached for the handle, a slight movement from behind the triage reception desk caught her eye.

"Stop. Someone's watching us."

Gry laughed, to her dismay. "No doubt, there is! I can already guess. Come on out, fella, the major's worried!"

Kenzy spun back to Gry, intent on delivering a slap to his fat face, when a figure rose from behind the counter, hands high in an offer of surrender. Kenzy's troops raised their weapons before it became obvious the interloper was no threat. At least in any physical sense. The man appeared to be in his early fifties, but the unkempt facial hair and greasy mane that flopped into a messy bowl cut could have been aging him. The ripped and stained tunic and ill-fitting pants tied around his waist by a rope indicated this was merely a "rat" Gry had previously met. And assessed as a non-threat.

"Major Wall, I'd like to introduce you to Mr. Allen."

The vagabond smirked, his hands shaking and still reaching up.

Mr. Allen? Does he have all his teeth, Kenzy wondered. "Hold on, you're telling me this man is—"

"Yup, he's an Allen agent, so of course I have no

authority to tell him to leave. I thought they were all suit-and-tie people too. But I have to give 'em credit—they aren't afraid to get into the trenches to protect their investments!"

Once Kenzy's troops lowered their weapons, the Allen lowered his hands. He circled in front of the desk, approaching the party but keeping a healthy distance. Clearing his throat, he nodded to her.

"Pleasure, major. Captain Gry indicated you were coming. You understand, of course, we wanted to be sure who you were."

Kenzy nodded back, still surprised at his poise despite the shabby appearance.

"No trouble, Mr.... What is your name again?"

Gry cut him off. "Allen. They're *all* Allens. Madam or Mister. Not my style, but hey, it works for them, right?"

Kenzy couldn't deny their success.

"Friendly reminder, captain, that we need to be informed of any future visitors. Are we still expecting Lieutenant Shore this week?"

"As far as I know, yes. But we will forward the information to you as soon as we get it." Gry spoke to the Allen agent with more respect than Wall could imagine he would give just any gutter rat.

"Very good. Our scans indicate you're within the acceptable power threshold upstairs. I won't keep you. I hope your stay proves worth your while."

The Allen agent smiled and left behind the reception desk into the shadows. The entire encounter could just as well have been a daydream. Wall blinked and she could have just climbed into the light all over again. Nothing more of the Allens was mentioned as the squad ascended the four flights of stairs to the safe house.

Knowing Lieutenant Shore was coming in only a few days, Major Wall accepted that she could endure Gry, as long as she could keep a fourth-floor window open a crack. And with any luck he would bring an extra bar of soap.

Parlour Tricks

Thursday, 14 June AC 0245
Holt Tower (Level 93), Capston, New Inland
Robbie Sheppard

Two weeks, and Robbie still hadn't seen all there was to see inside Holt Tower. The sequestered guests were allowed to use one of the pools but with strict supervision, and only at designated time slots to keep them from mingling with paying guests. Robbie was given time to ride in the Velodrome. As a competitor, he dreamed of having the sloped oval track to himself. Now that his dream was realized, it was anticlimactic and empty. Still, the tower held an embarrassment of riches. More comforts than he could ever dream of using.

And all this time I was happy enough to have a spare room with table tennis and some exercise equipment...

Robbie found it difficult to indulge in the entertainment of Holt Tower. The rubble had yet to settle, the smoke yet to waft away, and the embers yet to dim. Family treasures may still be salvageable, but it appeared unlikely the Sheppard siblings would have a chance to scour the ruins of the inn. How would an investigator or forensic scientist know what fragments within the rubble held any significance to the Sheppard family? How could strangers reclaim memories that were not their own?

In the room Jason Holt had called the parlour, Robbie watched Lorrie and Warren marvel at the exhibition showcasing fantastical creatures roaming, playing, and hunting in their natural habitats. The floor-to-ceiling monitors that were standard in every guest suite were windows into other worlds. Digitally manufactured images that flashed bright with swaths of colour. Projections of natural scenes from distant lands where exotic animals roamed, animals that must be long extinct. Robbie had to remind himself that the images were only illusions.

"Ever wonder if the animals are watching *us*?" Lorrie's question caught Robbie by surprise. Two weeks quarantined in the tower brought out unexpected insight from the usually nonchalant teenager. "Imagine. Maybe we're the zoo animals, and the lions and rhinos are the spectators." Warren's eyes widened as though Lorrie had just discovered the meaning of life.

Who knows, maybe he's right, Robbie thought as he leaned back into his wingback lounge chair.

Cadlen sat nestled in the corner of the big armchair, as he did every chance he got, and scrawled away on his sketch pad. Mr. Holt had provided him with a wide selection of charcoal pencils of various consistencies and shades. Robbie watched his brother's reaction to his new treasure trove. He could have sworn Cad smiled, but perhaps it was only wishful thinking. Every waking moment since, Cad drew and sketched as often as he could. Mr. Holt's only request in exchange for the supplies was that Cad draw him something. You know, to liven up that dive downstairs so the regulars have something to actually smile at, Holt had told him.

Lorrie and Warren eventually tired of watching the nature projections. They clattered their way into the adjacent games room and busied themselves with the loudest possible game they could find. Mr. Holt had turned on the bowling lanes, and the novice players were lobbing the heavy balls onto the expensive polished hardwood. Likely damaging the surface and further testing their benefactor's good will, even if Holt never seemed fazed by anything.

"So, you don't want to try your hand at bowling?"

Robbie was so deep in thought he hadn't noticed Jason Holt had reentered the room. He fixed himself a drink at the minibar, another standard feature in all the suites Robbie had seen. The bartender, who also happened to be the owner of the Jewel of Capston, poured a standard serving glass full of amber-coloured spirit, crowned with seasoning spices and a crescent-shaped citrus lemon wedge.

"I'd offer you one, but I know you'd say no," continued Mr. Holt. "They tell me the bar in your room is as stocked as the day you arrived."

Robbie blushed. Alcohol was such a grown-up thing. "Never was much of a drinker."

Mr. Holt pushed the bottom cabinet door shut with his foot and tossed the ball-tipped stirring wand into the small sink in one motion. A new program began to project onto the screen. Cadlen continued to draw, legs tucked up beneath him on the couch facing the wall-sized screen, oblivious to the programming. Robbie shifted against the backrest. Holt walked over to him, drink in hand and eyes wide.

The owner took a long first gulp of his drink and sighed. "Yeah, I can't imagine what you folks have gone through. Truly, I hope you're finding at least *some* comfort here."

"We are, Mr. Holt, of course." Robbie tried to find sincere words without coming off desperate. "Everyone's been great, and the boys don't want for anything."

"Oh, please—*Jason*. People call me by either my first or last name, but hardly ever *Mister*. I never liked it."

Robbie and Jason watched the screen. The video was broadcasting a tropical shallow that could have been in the Caribbean. The footage, if not a simulation, must have been filmed ages ago, before red tide rendered the southern climes dangerous for anyone who walked on two feet. Birds wheeled through the cloudless skies and colourful tropical fish danced in the rippled surf. The sand was white. So much life in a place Robbie always identified with disease and dying.

"I can't even imagine how you can manage a facility this big. I mean, you have to have dozens—hundreds—of smaller businesses in the tower! I could barely keep the inn afloat." Part of Robbie's discomfort came from a feeling of inadequacy.

Holt smiled and leaned forward, his elbows pushing into the cushions. "It has its moments, for sure. And I try to keep reliable people close to me. It helps that I can accommodate them right here in the Jewel—they never have to leave! Access to all the amenities, security. I have plenty of incentives to offer, I suppose.

"But really, the principle is the same, whether you run an operation like mine or a small family business like yours."

He took another drink. "You have to position yourself to succeed, and you have to love doing what you do. I mean, you really have to *live it*. This place isn't my job, it's who I am." He wasn't lying. Jason worked in the bar not because he had to, but because he chose to. Robbie never had that luxury.

"It's hard to imagine our little inn in the same world as this," Robbie said. "They're so different."

"Different? How, exactly? We both offer sanctuary to the weary traveler! Sure, our clientele may be different, but we provide the same basic service, wouldn't you agree?"

"I suppose, but I can't offer bowling, floor-to-ceiling projection screens, bars with whatever that is you're drinking—just a room with a bed, three blankets, a pillow, and maybe even a few channels if we paid the bills on time."

It was Jason's turn to laugh, sloshing his drink as he crossed his legs. "Robbie, I can assure you I've had some missed payments along the way. Only mine are a little more severe if I'm late. It's true, you know—more money, more trouble."

Robbie had a hard time believing it.

The nature program shifted focus from the shore birds to a pod of bottlenose dolphins which had begun to circle in the shallows, conjuring up a circular cloud of silt to fog up the cyan sea. Cadlen stopped drawing, his eyes drawn to the bright, sunlit paradise. Robbie watched his youngest brother purse his lips.

"Now, it helps to have your hands in a few jars." Jason continued as he made his way to the bar to pour another drink. "For example, the Velodrome, now that does fine. No lack of sponsors, because people love to watch the races. I have at least four major competitive brands going at any time. Lots of revenue opportunity.

"But the lodging, that's a little harder. When I have major events, trade shows, touring entertainers, things are good. When it's quiet, you lose ground. Usually evens out, but I'd be lying if I told you I wasn't praying for some pop idol to come through."

Robbie imagined Jason rubbing elbows with touring theater troupes, musicians, and athletes. He couldn't help imagining him in the front row while a concert blared from the stage, surrounded by teens and young adults half his age. Or milling around in the dressing room after a world-class cyclist had just broken a record on his Velodrome track. Champagne spraying and stinging his eyes while the whole gaggle of hangers-on celebrated. His guests paid him, then disappeared into their rooms, never to be seen again until they returned the pass key...

"And the clubs, they only seem to do well when

people aren't happy!" Jason exclaimed after a long swig of his amber spirit. "Big business in depression for those of us who run bars, you know."

Robbie shifted. How much money was Jason profiting from harbouring the Connellys and Sheppards? Jason changed his tone as though Robbie had said the words out loud. "Not that I want people to be sad, it's just—"

Another large crashing sound came from the bowling lanes. Lorrie cursed loudly. Robbie reflexively turned toward the sound. Cadlen ignored the commotion and kept watching the program.

"Don't even worry about it," Jason assured him. "They're not nearly making the mess you think. Acoustics are really loud in there, that's all."

Robbie couldn't imagine a bowling ball-shaped crater in imported hardwood *not* being an expensive mess.

"Sorry about the inn, Rob. I mean, I can't imagine what I'd do. Truly." Jason sighed again, swirling his drink high enough in the glass to slosh some of the seasonings into the liquid. "I've known Steven a while now. He has good people under him. They'll figure all this stuff out. We needed a guy with a strong arm for something like this, you know?"

Robbie had never heard Jason talk politics. "Not that Phil couldn't have done it—I mean, I love that guy too, right? It's just..."

Robbie wasn't sure how to answer. It was as if Jason was apologizing to someone who wasn't even there.

"Mayor Fox. What was he like?"

Jason Holt regaled stories about the former mayor for nearly half an hour. Robbie's rib cage ached from laughing as his host became more animated with each passing tale. It could have been the drinks as well. He wondered if the stories were true or dressed up to sound more impressive. Robbie had always imagined

Mayor Fox to be such a proper leader. He always appeared sharply dressed and articulate, yet relatable when he spoke on TV. Compassionate, yet pragmatic. He remembered Fox addressing the city on the evening Live Feed, how pained he seemed as he broke the news of every bombing. The mayor grew more tired-looking with each new attack. He vowed that the culprits would be found, but Robbie didn't know if the mayor believed himself.

Enter Steven Reekan.

It would have been remarkable had Fox won the election. All the policies and promises that carried him through two full terms were virtually unchanged. It was the city of Capston that had changed, suddenly and violently.

Robbie felt safe growing up in his neighbourhood when his parents were still alive. He remembered long rides on his racing bike before evening curfew. Crystal tagging along when he wanted to just stretch out and ride. Pushing the bike in through the old lobby door, the one that skidded shut before his father had replaced it, sometime around when Cadlen was three or four.

He remembered the first time Lorrie brought home the Connelly kid, how much he showed off for his new friend in front of his family, and how he still did today.

Another crash and howling laughter from the bowling lanes seemed to startle both Robbie from his daydreaming and Jason from his storytelling.

"I suppose I should wander in there and put some fear into 'em, eh?"

Jason winked at Robbie and stretched, setting the empty glass on the side table. Cadlen was still glued to the screen, his pencils by this time sitting quietly and squarely on his sketch pad on the empty seat next to him. Jason hollered into the bowling alley before the door shut behind him. Robbie peered over at the minibar. Maybe he needed to loosen up a little. *Maybe a drink wouldn't be such a bad idea...*

The screen caught his eye. The visuals had changed drastically.

In a larger than real-life scale, due to the dimensions of the wall screen, rolled grainy security footage.

From inside the lobby of the Sheppard Family Inn.

The camera angle suggested that the lens in the southeast corner, displayed in his office as Camera 4a, was the point of view. The date in the corner read May 15, two weeks before the explosion. Lorrie and Warren rolled their longboards into the lobby and straight into the vase near Cadlen's corner. His parents once told him it came from their time in Hyacynthe. He saw himself raging at Lorrie, smug in the presence of his partner in crime. Lorrie waved an obscene gesture as he and Warren turned to leave.

Robbie almost smiled before realizing that the footage he was watching had no business being broadcast on the Live Feed. This *had* to be a daydream.

The footage switched immediately to media coverage of the explosion. Camera crews and reporters had converged on the scene. Still a live event as indicated by the red bar that declared "Breaking News" scrolled past in an angry swath across the bottom third of the frame. The footage silently showed witnesses being interviewed, various members of Lieutenant Shore's first-responder team rushing in and out of the wreckage, fire crews arriving with lights flashing. Robbie and Cadlen were away at the time of the explosion, but he remembered the sound of the sirens from previous attacks. Howling in syncopation as they emerged from several directions. How many emergency vehicles had arrived too late to save his family business, his home.

Cadlen didn't need to see any more of this.

"Okay, Cad, I think that's enough." Robbie circled the couch where his youngest brother sat transfixed by the devastation playing out on the giant screen. "We've seen plenty."

Robbie reached down and patted him assuredly on the right shoulder. Entranced, Cadlen didn't move.

"Come on, little man, let's go see what your brother—"

Cadlen shook his head. Robbie was stunned by his unexpected reaction. He hadn't spoken a word in the two weeks since the explosion. Maybe the footage was providing him some sort of closure.

Looking up, Robbie saw the screen shuffle from the same live coverage of all the previous attacks. First the convenience shop. Next the office complex. On through the third and fourth targets that the terrorists had succeeded in leveling. All of which had placed a nervous city on alert. No one was safe.

No one, except Jason Holt in his Jewel.

The giant screen flashed to black-and-white feedback. The snowy image hypnotized Robbie for a few seconds, while Cad looked to his sketch pad. With nothing more to see, he reached for it as his pencil fell between the cushions. Robbie could have sworn he continued to see images of the leveled buildings, most vividly his own, like an optical illusion hidden beneath a surface of feedback. That image bled into focus, taking the shape of a familiar room. A luxurious suite from a fancy hotel, furnished with lush plants, fixtures handcrafted from exotic wood and modern art clinging to the walls. At the center of the room was a hot tub, steam hazily drifting from the foamy, frothing bath water. It reminded him of the private suite Jason had offered him and his brothers.

That reminder jarred him out of his trance when Clara Connelly stepped into the frame.

Casually, she approached the tub, turning the silver

taps off, stopping the flow of the water. A bikini top barely held up her breasts while a thick-fibered towel wrapped around her waist to her ankles. Robbie gulped, the colour in his face flushing. She climbed up onto the edge, dipping her right toes first before releasing the draped towel, baring herself as she slid into the bath and onto the seat along the near edge. Facing away from the camera, she gazed up at the giant floor-to-wall screen, like the one Robbie and Cad were currently watching, except hers was blank. Clara loosened the ties that held her top and dropped it alongside the tub as she tousled her hair, drawing it up in a ponytail so as not to let it dangle in the water.

Robbie couldn't believe what he was seeing. Embarrassed, he instinctively reached for Cad, but luckily, he was already engrossed in a new drawing, oblivious to the peep show that was unfolding live in front of him. There had to be some explanation. Jason needed to know. What if other guests were seeing the same thing?

Clara reached for a handheld. Aiming it at her own wall screen, a brief flash revealed another familiar setting.

A large room with a minibar.

A boy curled up on a couch with a sketch pad in his lap.

A young man standing over him, staring with wide eyes at the screen, then looking away in shock.

Robbie felt naked. Mrs. Connelly could see *him*, seeing...

Her!

Through the corner of his eye, Robbie saw Clara flailing her arms. Foam and water splashing as she scrambled for her towel, trying in vain to cover her breasts with her arms. Robbie heard screaming, but it came from the games room. The crashing of bowling balls had gone silent, replaced with shouting and the pounding of footsteps getting louder before Jason burst through the doors.

"What are you *seeing*? On your screen? What are you...?" Jason's voice trembled in disbelief bordering on disdain. Gazing up at the screen, he stopped in his tracks as though he crashed into a pane of reinforced glass. His expression was as though he took the impact.

Clara instinctively turned to the camera, forgetting for an instant that she had emerged topless from the water. Robbie dove in front of Cadlen, who was just then realizing something was happening. Grabbing Cadlen by both shoulders, he hoisted him up with startling ease from the couch, accidentally glancing at the screen again. By this time Clara had found her towel and covered herself from her shoulders to just above her knees. Now it was her hair bouncing as she bolted from the room. Jason appeared to be on the verge of a stroke.

Robbie didn't know where to run. Cadlen hung in his arms like dead weight, clinging to his sketch pad that had wrinkled in the confusion. Realizing the image was only an empty room, he relaxed his grip from Cadlen's thin arms.

"Sheppard, what did you see? I mean, before this..."

Robbie stuttered as he set his brother on the wingback chair. "There were video clips from the explosion. Our inn. News footage—"

Jason reached up and slammed his hands upon Robbie's shoulders, glaring full into his eyes. "You didn't see anything else? Other rooms?"

"No, nothing at all." Robbie breathed in short bursts. "Just the wreckage, then Mrs. Connelly." She had seen them too.

Jason breathed deeply, his fingers curling tighter into Robbie's shoulders. "I didn't see Clara, or you. But *we* could see the news reel. Our screen showed one of my guests downstairs. Except he wasn't alone, he was... well..."

Jason's stammering led Robbie to question if the guest downstairs was as compromised as Clara Connelly.

"It doesn't matter. Except that... this gentleman happens to be a well-known public figure who happens to have paid me a lot of money for his privacy!"

It was apparent Clara's nudity wasn't being broadcast to every screen in Holt Tower. Another knot twisted in his stomach at the thought Warren could have seen it. Or her husband. Jason immediately started barking orders into the microphone of his handheld to whoever was on the receiving end. Robbie couldn't discern the jumbled response.

In seconds, dozens of boots began to rumble around the room as security personnel deployed throughout the level. The floor-to-ceiling screen flickered again, returning the snowy pattern from earlier. The final image to bleed through the static was too much for Robbie's already nauseous stomach to handle. The contents erupted onto the plush cushions of the couch.

January 14.

Five-Cities Invitational.

Holt Tower Velodrome.

The day was fresh in Robbie's mind. His most recent race, and the last before the death of his parents in which his younger brothers and sister were in attendance. The still shot was from an airborne drone camera, focused on the thousands of spectators. The definition of the shot zoomed in, pixelating as the frame narrowed on a small group in the second level. Two boys were holding longboards. One even younger, a note pad. The other, a helmet in his lap. The pixels were too blocky to pick up the expression of defeat on

Robbie's face. He wore a similar expression now.

They know we're here. And they can get inside.

The door to the hallway flung open, and Jason screeched. "Find me Reekan, now!"

Robbie wiped his mouth with the back of his sleeve. "Jason, where do we go?"

"I don't care *where* you go, but you can't stay *here!*" Mr. Holt's pallid complexion suggested he wasn't far from vomiting either. "Reekan told me there was no danger—so what's all this!" He barged off, arms waving and muttering to no one in particular.

Cadlen retreated into a corner of the suite, out of direct view of the big screen. Robbie joined him, slinking to the soft carpet beside his shaking brother.

"It's going to be okay, Cad." Robbie draped an arm around his brother's shoulder. Cadlen straightened out the wrinkled pages of his sketch pad, the oils from his fingers smudging the pencil markings of dolphins circling a school of fish in the tropical shallows.

The Last Supper

Real men take showers, Hearn Reekan used to tell his son. Marinade yourself in scented soaps and you can expect to become soft. And because of his father's life lesson in personal hygiene, Steven Reekan didn't take his first proper bath until he was well into his thirties. Of course, Dianna Reekan would have bathed her infant son, but that was well before Steven could decide for himself that lying in warm water was the exact opposite of what his father would approve of.

That first bath wasn't voluntary. After months of physiotherapy, Steven conceded that bathing in a form-fitting tub filled with an elixir of scented oils and magnesium salt was worth a try. He admitted to no one out loud that the effect was near-miraculous. Muscles relaxed. Joints loosened. Scars even began to heel. In the dimmed light of his private quarters, where the therapeutically designed fixture was installed at his own expense, Steven Reekan was born again in the warm waters.

On the wall-mounted screen, an insipid documentary about early Reclamation Era adventures ran on the lowest volume possible without muting. He knew his history. This episode centered on the construction of the colossal demolition machines that had torn into the old cities. Dozers with five-story tracks and even wider plough blades. Excavators that could gnash high-rises in half. Dump trucks that carried away the plunder for rendering. Hearn Reekan saw to it that his young son had replica models of all of these before he could even walk.

"I want to drive one of those..."

"Ex-ca-vators." Hearn enunciated the words his son was too shy to say himself. "Slim chance you ever will. Most of those are long gone now. We rendered an old one a few years ago; haven't seen one since."

Built expressly for deconstructing massive skyscrapers, the big machines were doomed to obsolescence.

"Why are they all gone, Dad?"

Hearn Reekan grunted and shifted his portly frame in his chair. Supper was almost ready. The plates and silverware were arranged with care. Dianna shuffled in the kitchen just out of sight. Steven sat up straight so his father wouldn't yell at him for slouching.

"Because there are only so many old cities out there to tear down." Steven was accustomed to his father looking over or around him. Direct eye contact always meant he had done or said something wrong. Hearn's eyes were deep brown, like his own. Or maybe they were hazel. It had been a while since he'd seen them.

"What ever happened to the machines?"

Hearn's stomach growled and Dianna called out. Supper was almost ready.

"Most of them were taken apart and the metals were smelted. Made into new parts for new machines. That one we got last year, I think it's a farm combine now, or something."

"Watering drones." Dianna glided around the corner into the room and the conversation with a sliced pork roast on a serving tray. Garnishing of fresh parsley and sliced pineapple adorned the main course, clutched between two mitted hands. The meal looked and smelled sumptuous.

"'Bout time," Hearn muttered as he drove a fork into the largest end piece before Dianna had even finished setting the tray on the table. Steven followed suit, stabbing a portion bigger than his ten-year-old stomach could handle.

Dianna sat opposite her husband and waited until the men of the house served themselves before selecting her own piece. She always chose more green vegetables than meat. Likely because she used to work in the Hanging Gardens before Steven was born.

"The Agri-Corps needed new watering drones. They said on the news that they're finally replacing—"

"That's great." Hearn cut off his wife in between shovels full of roast. "Give all the metals to the farmers while we're down here working at half-capacity."

Steven's eyes darted between his mother and father. It was Dianna's turn to volley.

"I know when I was still up there, we weren't working at full capacity—"

"Hire more students to water the flowers. Can't be that hard."

Dianna closed her eyes and inhaled before answering. "I'm talking about crops, Trahearn. We could feed more people if—"

"Right, and we have to take care of all the lazy people who can't take care of themselves. Water your own damn gardens."

Dianna glared across the table. Steven expected her to do as she always did—frown in resignation and return to her food. Except this time, she answered back.

"And who waters *your* damn garden?"

Steven almost choked on an oversized bite. He was grateful that he wasn't looking into his father's eyes after that comment. Hearn set his fork beside his plate and returned the glare, drawing a deep breath before a long stream of fire was sure to explode from his gaping mouth.

"I'm too busy breaking my back in the smelter so ingrates like you can have all the fancy things. Where do you suppose all those gadgets come from? Machines! And they can't make those without our smelting—"

"Right, everyone owes you a debt of gratitude for all your hard work." Steven never heard his mother talk back before. "The whole dome would collapse without you. Do you ever get tired of hearing it? Because I know I do."

Instead of returning fire, Hearn picked up his fork again and continued eating. "You sound like the polymer renderers. Always whining about something."

Dianna picked up her serrated knife and carved a tiny corner off her helping of pork. She didn't look up. "You're just jealous you're still in the smelter. How many of your original crew are still there, Trahearn? Aren't you the last?"

That was a low blow. Twenty-eight years was enough for anyone in the smelter. Steven's father deserved a job in the polymer rendering plant where the work was less cumbersome and more technical. Steven never understood why his father was passed over, promotion after promotion, when he was the only one who would tell it like it is. Honesty is supposed to be a virtue.

Hearn appeared to be at a loss for words. He grabbed the sprig of parsley that was drowning in the gravy on his plate and tossed it across the table at his wife. "Here, you love your plants so damn much, have mine."

Steven looked at his own plate. The parsley was set off to the side, still as bushy and green as though it were just picked. He pinched it between his finger and thumb and tossed it in the direction of his mother.

It was at that precise moment he looked into his mother's eyes and felt more fear than he ever imagined from his father. Steven thought they would well in tears. Instead, they were cold and grey. And when she looked away, it was for the last time.

Sometime later, when no further words were said by anyone, Dianna Reekan finished her meal. She left her knife and fork neatly crossed on her cleaned plate and walked out of the dining room.

And out of their lives.

"That's life. Get used to disappointment." There were no promotions to the polymer rendering. No ex-cavators. No one going to help you when you need it. It was a lesson Steven was learning a little bit every day.

"It's not your fault, boy." Hearn reassured Steven when the water rose in his tear ducts. "She'll probably go take a bath."

The soap suds were gone, and the temperature cooled by at least a few degrees. Steven reached for the climate control switch and the jets bubbled, frothing the water back to life. If his father were alive to see him this way, he would have been as disappointed as always. At least Steven took comfort knowing that Trahearn Reekan was used to it.

As the water warmed, a mixture of floral scents wafted throughout the room. As he grew older, Steven appreciated that his father gave so much of himself for so many years, so that others could live their lives with more comfort. His heart still ached that Dianna Reekan walked away. Not because his mother was no longer in his life.

Dianna *Reekan* was dead.

But somewhere in the upper rim of New Inland, in the vast agricultural sector of the Hanging Gardens, Dianna *Langley* returned to Agri-Corps with the same name as the day she left.

Steven tired of the documentary. The bloody days of the early Reclamation when the god-sized long-haul trucks lugged reusable concrete and steel inland where a new superstructure would rise. It was supposed to be a safe place for a new, equal society to flourish. And flourish it did, only on the backs of people like Trahearn Reekan.

With his personal handheld, Steven switched the television screen off as the dim light of the wall sconces kept a hazy glow. Closing his eyes, he slid deeper until the water touched the tip of his chin. A familiar flash and the screen ignited to life, glowing pink through his eyelids.

I thought I turned the damn thing off.

Steven reached for his handheld before he reopened his eyes. The documentary was no longer broadcasting. In its place, footage of the Capston terrorist bombings flickered intermittently from one scene to the next every few seconds. He pressed his thumb on the "off" tab as though it were a button, the screen flashed to black again. This time he didn't close his eyes.

When it flashed to life again, the image of Clara Connelly dropping her towel as she stepped into her own hot tub emerged, more jarring to the senses than a thousand bombs exploding. The shriek upon realizing she was on live television throughout Holt Tower came through the walls instead of the muted speaker. Steven instinctively looked away when the camera caught full view of her shapely breasts before she squished them into her chest with her forearms.

Why am I seeing this? Can anyone else see me?

Steven swished his fingers over the control pad until

the sconces blacked, leaving only the faint secondary glow of Clara Connelly's private room emitting from his television. He continued to press the "off" tab, but the television continued to restart, each time with new footage.

A prominent businessman tangled up in the arms and legs of a woman who was not his wife.

Another pressing the tip of a long needle into his arm.

Yet another exchanging a mysterious parcel for a hurried handheld transaction.

All of these from familiar locations and rooms in Holt Tower. Jason Holt's voice began to boom from somewhere down the corridor of his floor as boots marched.

Bath time was over. *What a damn mess.*

The Apple

Jueves, 14 junio NE 267 (Thursday, 14 June AC 0245)
North End, Allentown
Private Mott Wrengel

Private Mott Wrengel ignored the rumble in his stomach and kept digging. The rubble of the office building had begun to sprout shrubs in the years it had lain in a heap. He had no memory of what the original building looked like, but he knew it had collapsed after years of abandonment. Ruptured pipes flowed freely until winter set in, freezing and expanding them until they flexed apart the walls. Nature only had to walk inside. As Mott continued to labour over the removal of heavy stone and twisted steel, he guessed it was inevitable that the bare bones of squatters would be found. The victims, having sought salvation inside the derelict old building, might have died in their sleep as the floors above compacted down on them.

Again and again, the old world reared its ugly head, bearing down upon the new.

One by one, the labouring officers finished their shifts and retreated through the maze of ruined city blocks in the direction of the National Bank. Lieutenant Colonel Desantos had sentenced the squadron to a full week of hard labour, to clear the rubble of the collapsed building. Something about a debt of gratitude to their Allen hosts. Clean up a city, rebuild a nation. *Character,* and all that shit.

All because the squadron finished last in training drills. Private Mott Wrengel was deemed responsible. As a result, Lieutenant Colonel Desantos bestowed upon them one more hour than the rest of the squadron. It was an unexpected show of mercy. Mott expected far worse given the lieutenant colonel's reputation for stiff consequences. Captain Alvara would have assigned him to at least half a day. Mott expected he would be cleaning debris until a wall fell in on him, only to become a clean-up job for his squadron mates.

The sun beat down from directly above. Sweat began to sting his eyes as soot and dust stained his forehead and cheeks. He hadn't finished his field ration breakfast before the squadron was ordered into the ruined city streets of the north end of Allentown. The overseer was a zealous sergeant, ordered to enforce rhythmic work without pause for the duration of the six-hour digging shift.

As the seventh hour began, the sergeant hollered and all except Mott stood down, retreating from the work site with shovels and picks over their shoulders. None acknowledged Mott, still working a rubble pile that looked no smaller than when he had begun at 0600 hours.

"Looks like it's just the two of us, private!" The sergeant barked as the other grunts disappeared. "One hour, and I better see the bottom of this debris pile, or I'll be hauling you away with the rest of the garbage!"

"Sir, yes sir!" Mott stiffened and saluted the sergeant before digging his pick back into the pile. He would have preferred to bury the pick into the sergeant.

As the iron tooth struck and shattered a section of concrete wall, the sergeant's handheld beeped. Mott didn't look away from his work. The overseer cursed.

"I've been summoned. Stay on task, private. I'll be back in twenty—and if I don't see progress, you better be lying dead."

"Yes, sir!" This time, he didn't stand up. The sergeant stormed off, muttering as his thumbs worked his device.

With every swing, the pick got heavier in Mott's sweaty, gloved hands. He made another half dozen swings before realizing he was unsupervised. The thought of running away flashed through his mind before reality sank in. Allentown was the most surveilled open-air space on the continent. You couldn't walk around a corner to take a piss without some camera recording you. If the lieutenant colonel wasn't watching, the Allens definitely were. Mott wouldn't have made it half a block without a bullet ending his flight.

And even if he did escape the city, where would he go?

As he lifted the pick, now ten times heavier than the first time he lifted it, a flash caught his eye, causing him to stumble. The iron fell to the ground as Mott panned around the empty streets. Not a soul was in sight, but as his gaze scanned past an adjacent building that still stood, another flash of light struck his eyes, only this time it flashed in rapid succession.

S-O-S.

Without the sergeant present to keep him in line, Mott decided to investigate. It could have been an ambush. Maybe a test from his superiors to see how he worked without supervision. Still, someone might need help. Mott's father used to tell him that there was always time to be compassionate. Gripping the pick, he crept toward the source of the light. Mott's heart pounded against his rib cage as he moved closer. Breathing through his nostrils. Swallowing anticipation.

"That's close enough, private."

A voice emanated from around the corner. Mott swallowed.

"Who's there? Are you in trouble?"

There was an uneasy pause.

"Private Wrengel." Mott's boot soles twisted in the crumbled brick and mortar. He tightened his grip on the pick handle.

"Who are you? How do you know who I am?" He tried to make his voice sound as tough as possible.

The question dangled for a few seconds before the stranger around the corner answered.

"It is hot today. Why are you still working while your brothers are not?"

The private shifted some more, and his tongue smuckered in his dry mouth. "We finished last in endurance training drills. *I* finished last."

"You are hungry, Mott."

A gloved hand reached around the corner. In its palm perched a crisp, clean, red apple. Mott salivated, licking his cracked lips. Tiny alarms went off in his mind.

"How do I know this isn't a trick?" It was a fair question.

"You don't. But it would be a pity if your brothers were enjoying a reward like this and more, while you continued to move rocks."

Mott wasn't buying it.

"I'm under strict orders. I've been away from my work long enough as it is."

Mott turned and walked back in the direction of the ruined building. The sergeant would be back any minute, and the pile was nowhere near cleared. At this point, he figured to still be digging at sunset.

A confirmation bell sounded from Wrengel's pocketed handheld. Halfway between the stranger and the pile, Mott retrieved his device. A tab flashed, indicating a transfer of fund to his personal account. It didn't make any sense—pay day was still a week away, and money never fell out of the sky like that.

As Mott rationalized the windfall in his bank account, another tab flashed. This time, a data file appeared as a tiny, square-shaped icon. He pressed the tab and the name of the folder appeared.

<NULL>

Mott tapped the screen again to open the <NULL> folder. He scanned the first document, an official order for a team of miners to continue despite reports of higher readings of methane. He recognized the date, when Garrett Wrengel went to work in the mine and never came home.

Whoever was hiding around the corner knew all about Private Mott Wrengel. The private stalked back, coming to a halt within a hair of peering around the corner. He was close enough to smell the sweetness of the apple, still perched in the gloved hand.

Mott took off his gloves and plucked the apple. He took a crisp bite and the juices leaked down his chin. The private exhaled through his nostrils as he continued to carve out chunk after chunk of apple. He didn't stop until the entire fruit was consumed, core and all. The gloved hand had retreated behind the corner.

"What if the apple was poisoned, private?"

Wrengel wiped the juice from his lip. He wanted to laugh. "What if it was? I've been away from my post too long. I'm dead anyway."

"You *are* dead. We're *all* dead, Mott."

The private sank to his backside, leaning against the wall. Tears welled in the corners of his eyes until he blinked them down his cheek. The stranger was right. When his father was killed, it was as though the poison gas had killed him too. He silently prayed that if the apple was going to kill him that it hurried before the sergeant returned.

"Dead, so long as we allow ourselves to be. Private Wrengel, do you want to *live* again?"

Mott laughed. "You think all this money you've sent me can make anything better?"

"Of course not. The money will not buy your pardon from hard labour. Nor will it buy your freedom. And it certainly cannot bring your father back from the mines."

If the stranger was making some sort of pitch, it wasn't very appealing thus far. The mention of Garret Wrengel caused him to whimper. "I told you, there's nothing left for me. That's why I took the apple."

"You are wrong, Private Wrengel. There is *everything* left for you."

Mott summoned the strength to stand back up. This man needed him, and badly enough to give him a lot of money up front.

"You need me to do something."

"It is a considerable task. Which is why I am offering you a considerable reward. Did you read the file?"

Mott held up his device and tapped the <NULL> icon once again. This time, he read more carefully. The order for the miners to resume exploration despite the detection of high gas levels had been cleared by the ranking officer of His Eminence's armed forces. At the time, he was still a lieutenant.

"You can't have your father back, Mott. But you can have justice."

Highlighted in the documents, the name of the officer who had signed off on the order burned into his brain. When Garret Wrengel was ordered to return to his post, he had been murdered. The stranger with the apple had provided the name of his killer.

Mott's energy surged, as though he could clear the pile of debris in half the time and punch the sergeant in the face if he had anything to say about it.

"What do you need me to do?"

"I need you to kill Paolo Desantos."

Breadcrumbs

Two nights and only a few hours of light sleep made it difficult for Major Kenzy Wall to find the motivation to venture back into the tunnels. Still, poring over surveillance footage for hours with sand-heavy eyes didn't lend to her best work. Cabin fever was not helping Kenzy and Gry's relationship either. A sojourn into the underground might not be such a bad thing. The major always preferred working in the field over analyzing data and paperwork.

Foregoing her beret for a black bandanna, Kenzy tucked her wavy hair and smeared the grease paint on her cheeks. Officers Lane and Swift dressed in the same clandestine attire, and the three descended the stairwell to the drafty lobby. No one appeared to be watching. Kenzy knew that didn't really mean anything.

During the planning, Gry had told her that the tunnels were directly connected to a series of underground travel conduits on the north end of the city, where the Nat Bank most likely had access. The Allens were comfortable with their presence, so long as they conducted their search within the rules. Even a ruined city had rules to abide by. Kenzy wondered how much the Allens charged Steven for access. She hoped the treasury department was creative in hiding the money trail.

"That's not to say there are no Motherland *rats* down there. It's just less likely you'll run into one." Gry enunciated the slur with unveiled contempt.

"So, if we never come into contact with them, how can we prove they're even here?" Kenzy was still trying to piece together the rationale for being in Allentown.

Gry tried to explain. "We're going to find one of them eventually. And when we do, we'll be able to prove they're here. And with proof, we can finally make the council see we've been right all along."

The plausibility of Gry's reasoning was scant, but enough to ease her mind, at least for now. Back into the tunnels, Kenzy and her officers made their way north and east beneath the surface, through stuffy narrow passages and into wide chambers. Through doors and over pipelines. Climbing ladders and wading knee-deep through drainage lines. Moving slowly, the trio estimated they had covered nearly six city blocks in only a few hours. Two sleeping vagabonds, one possibly dead, and two more escaping before they could be positively identified. By the look of their style of dress and the vein-streaked whites of their eyes, neither was likely a Motherlander. Kenzy hoped, in any case.

The trio crept onward, emerging into a vast chamber with sloped floors, partitioned in a maze-like pattern by thick concrete medians.

"Parking garage," Officer Lane observed. Her voice lilted in uncertainty.

"Yes, it must be." Kenzy flicked her handheld on. The blinking light confirmed Lane's theory. The lack of natural light indicated that they were at least two floors below ground, or the access to ground-level parking was blocked.

"Okay, we're going to stay on this level. There has to be another doorway somewhere..."

Kenzy's senses slowed as though she were waking from a deep sleep. *Damn, I know I haven't been resting very well, but this isn't normal.*

Lane spoke but the words sounded like a recording playing on shifting speeds. Kenzy turned to see both officers drop to their knees. Her focus began to lapse before she could turn on the handheld's gas detection application. She was unconscious before her head hit the concrete floor.

She was sure there was a faint silhouette sitting cross-legged on the soiled concrete. Blinking into focus, Kenzy's stinging eyes watched the figure stand, and then linger above her prone body before stepping out of her line of sight. He wasn't one of her own. Lane and Swift could have been lying behind her on the floor of the chamber, dead from asphyxiation or hostile weapons. *If I'm supposed to be dead, get on with it, then.*

Her arms could not yet generate enough strength to raise her from the floor, so her split lip continued to bleed in the stale puddle around her face. Her assailant's boots emerged as polished, thick-soled, and remarkably clean for skulking around in sewers. Then again, it could have been a trick of light, emanating from an artificial source that may as well have been another dimension. A few more blinks, and the shape was gone. It may have never been there in the first place. Kenzy's face slumped deeper as the apparition and what little hope came along with it faded away.

Kenzy Wall.

The soft tone could have been an echo of a memory. Until it repeated, a little clearer.

"Kenzy Wall."

The voice didn't register as familiar. Neither Lane nor Swift would have called her by anything except her rank. Scrolling through the voices of her colleagues, none of them spoke so soothingly. Kenzy guessed the assailant was several feet away, yet he could as easily have been whispering in her ear. Never had a voice so calming elicited as much trepidation.

"You are in an antechamber beneath the Allen streets. Your officers are alive and unharmed. You are likely concussed from your fall. Stay still."

None of this information made her feel any better. Nor did it stop her from trying to sit up, however in vain. She tried to speak, but her lungs couldn't draw enough air.

"You are not safe in your house, major."

Safe? Who is safe, anywhere?

The figure shuffled his feet as though he were turning to leave.

"Follow the breadcrumbs and you will find the fattest rat."

Several seconds passed without as much as a breath before the voice spoke one last time, before a door creaked open and closed.

"My regards to the captain. He seems a good man."

Whose regards?

Minutes stretched, and after tremendous persistence Kenzy was sitting upright in her puddle, the veins in her temples pulsing with her increasing heart rate. Lucidity led to panic.

Swift. Lane...

Turning her head too quickly resulted in a drag in her inner chronometer, and sharp pains that seemed to reach every corner of her body. The parking garage was empty. A faint light on the upper slope where Kenzy presumed her assailant exited became her beacon. Reaching for her handheld in the right thigh pocket of her cargo pants, she was confused to find it rather in the left. Relieved that it wasn't stolen, she ignited the lamp function and stumbled the hundred meters to a rusted door.

Upon arrival at the slightly ajar door, Kenzy slumped back against the wall on the open side, partially out of instinct to face any potential threat, but mostly to recuperate her breath. Every lungful of air sounded like a howling gale inside her pulsating brain. Lurching that last step up the incline may as well have been her thousandth lunge, stretching her quadriceps to the point of nearly tearing. Her coat ripped on a jutting shard of bent metal as she slid down to rest on her heels. "Here I am, "she mumbled to herself. "If anyone out there is going to make a move, do it now.

Kenzy challenged anything that was lingering in the many corners obscured by shadow to make a move. A full platoon of hostiles or a plague of rats. Her last emotional stand provided one last surge of adrenaline. She sprang to her feet and flung open the door.

Before she could process anything out of the burst of light, and before she could even lean into her first step, a gloved hand reached around her face while the opposite arm seized her by the waist.

"Kenzy, stand down."

Lieutenant Shore's grip whisked her back into the shadowed garage while another officer pushed the door back to its prior position. His whisper was the first sound that didn't feel like either a long needle piercing or a lead pipe striking. Kenzy's heart rate slowed as her legs nearly gave.

"Shore... Swift and Lane... They're..."

Shore guided Kenzy to the nearest concrete median where she slouched into the curved side. She was embarrassed that she needed to be rescued, but her concern was solely for her officers.

"We have them, and they're fine. Found them a floor down, looked like you were dragged up to this one. They're both a little woozy, but I don't think they hit the floor headfirst like you did." In the dimmed glow of his handheld, Kenzy could see his features with more clarity. The shadows made his strong jawline look more defined, but the kindness in his soft, gray eyes was unmistakable.

"The low light makes you look old." She hoped the joke was taken as gratitude.

"Older than *you*, maybe, but not *old*, Kenz!"

Suppressing laughter hurt more than if she had just let loose. As far as she was concerned, they were still in immediate danger.

"How long were you waiting in the shadows, just watching me?"

"Not long. We had to be sure we were the only ones in here with you first. And then you found your second wind, so we had to move quickly before you charged outside."

Outside, where she could have been a sitting duck. *What was I thinking?*

"I was pursuing the attacker."

Shore rolled his eyes, his forehead scrunching. "Pursuit, you say? In your condition? You couldn't have caught up to a bureaucrat on break, Kenz."

She deserved that.

"Well, I tried, anyway. Any surveillance catch him?"

Shore shook his head. "We detected movement, but as you know that could have been anyone or anything. No live eyes on this block. It's a good thing you sent your distress beacon, or we wouldn't have found you."

Distress beacon?

"I didn't send any—"

A series of connections lit up along the synapses in her memory. *Follow the breadcrumbs and you will find the fattest rat.*

She reached for her left cargo pocket and realized she had replaced her handheld back in the right side.

"Shore, we need to get out of here."

"Take a minute, will you? We're secure here for now—"

You are not safe in your house, major.

"No, I mean all of us. Out of Allentown."

Two Minutes Behind

Sábado, 16 junio NE 267 (Saturday, 16 June AC
0245)
Palacio Real, Free City of Motherland
Captain Tomás Alvara

Less than twelve hours to pack for Allentown, and he still wants me to meet His Eminence. At this hour.

Tomás woke to an awakening akin to a bucket of ice water. The colonel ripped the sheets off, leaving him naked in the darkened bunk. Within seconds he was dressed and following in long strides.

"I need you to be present for this meeting, Tomás."

Whatever you say. He suppressed a disrespecting yawn as best he could.

Colonel Tirel Desantos did not ask permission to enter, brushing past the guards and heaving the heavy doors. Tomás waited at the doorway as the colonel marched across the cluttered chamber, through a maze of sculptures and relics that were, in essence, a living timeline. Every step was designed to emulate a leg of the journey from Motherland's humblest and most desperate beginnings in the deep South. From the tropical isthmus that served as a bridge between the two western continents. Northward through the marshlands. Across the mountain range that served as a natural barrier to their silent and lethal pursuer. Red tide had forced the Motherland exodus. *La Golondriña* had guided them to their new home.

Such a marvelous collection, dedicated to the history of our people. I'm unworthy to enter.

"Captain Alvara."

Fear of reprisal outweighed his reverence for history. Tomás stepped inside.

He spied His Eminence hunched over his desk. It was cluttered with stacks of documents and hardbound tomes from his library, which occupied the entirety of the rear wall, reaching high enough that a ladder on rails had been installed for easier access to the older pieces that crowned the collection. He was dressed in his typical formal wear, even though he was not expecting company. Appearance is paramount to image, the colonel once told him. It was clear that the young ward Tirel Desantos learned from his adoptive mentor. As a result, Tomás was always expected to be professional. Because to appear common, or indiscriminate from the everyman, would imply that he was no more important than the next, no more so even than the two lifeless pillars that guarded his chamber.

Tomás wondered if Desantos felt De Léon looked pompous.

You look marvelous, Your Eminence.

No, of course you aren't overdoing it.

A full suit with bogus medallions and awards for your imagined bravery on some field of victory in your mind.

In full regalia, and at this hour for no apparent reason...

No, Your Eminence, you look every bit the man you are...

"My good man, what brings you at this hour," De Léon drawled, without looking up from his clutched handful of papers. "Don't even men of your station require some amount of *ressst...*"

Tomás stood at attention as Desantos approached the front of the desk, passing the chairs arranged to keep guests at a safe distance. Old habits. Red tide was less communicable beyond about three meters. He stood at military ease; hands cupped together behind his back.

The colonel never sat, and the monarch had long since stopped asking him if he would like to take a seat. Tomás doubted anyone before Desantos refused his offer. But then again, none before him had the courage to barge into the chamber at will without spending a few days of his life in the pillory for his efforts.

"You know, it's not in my character to rest with so much yet undone." Desantos spoke with more than a trace of self-confidence. "I felt it would be prudent to deliver a personal update, if you were still awake yourself."

De Léon peered up without raising his head. His weathered complexion betrayed his age when he did that, something he was more careful to conceal outside his chambers. The public was always expecting a strong leader, or at the very least a projection of one. Despite De Léon's weak appearance, the public would view him as strong so long as Colonel Desantos was handling the armed forces.

Still, the link between the old world and the new was important to maintain. De Léon bore the telltale signs of the red tide, that horrible disease he had survived in his youth when his own parents had not. He had difficulty standing straight for more than a few minutes. His face bore the faint lines of the never fully healed scars. His speech, if more than a handful of words or brief sentences, tended to drawl. Multisyllabic words presented a challenge to enunciate unless he controlled the intonation of his voice just so. Even in the company of the Regents, he carefully chose words to stem the fatigue.

"Does something necess...itate an update this late?" De Léon's brow wrinkled as he shifted the documents in his frail hands.

Here is where Colonel Desantos is at his most crafty.

"I wished only to keep you up to date, Your

Eminence." Tomás observed the colonel. The body language of his performance shifted depending on the audience. Posture straight, hands gently folded together, head high for clear enunciation. On the other side of the desk, De Léon was eating up the façade of formality. It was fascinating to watch.

"Yes, of course. And I can assume you've had no further *problemsss*... with your Reaper shadow?"

Nearly two weeks since Andreas was dragged out of the pillory and shipped north to Kayewat, and not a whisper. It was a stress Tomás was happy to have forgotten until De Léon brought it up. The timing was interesting.

"Andreas was taken care of, Your Eminence. I always take care of my responsibilities."

De Léon allowed himself to chuckle enough not to lose his breath. "Indeed, you do, colonel. Indeed, you do. Now, as you were saying."

"Lieutenant Colonel Desantos is dispatched to Allentown to oversee our assets. I have received word that Capstonian troops are in the city. It appears Reekan is trying to connect the spate of attacks within his city on our people."

Our people. Tomás admired how the colonel believed in Motherland as more than just a colony of refugees from a distant and disparate land. He believed in Motherland as a family. An assault on one was an assault on all.

"And if I'm not *mistakennn*... it was an operation led by your son that allowed Mayor Reekan to draw that connection?"

If Tomás had asked the same question, he knew what his fate would be. He could imagine the wooden slats clamping around his neck. Could he have survived three days in the pillory?

"It was an operation doomed to fail as a result of an

incompetent agent." Desantos spat his response with surprising restraint. "I am finished with Kayewati goons. My son was humiliated by Grant's failure—so much that he wished to oversee the Allentown operations personally."

It wasn't lost on Tomás that the more Lieutenant Colonel Paolo Desantos did outside the Motherland walls, the easier it would be to embellish his accomplishments. Nearly three weeks had passed since Andreas flashed his Reaper pendant in the overcast afternoon. The lieutenant colonel was always two steps ahead. Or Tomás was always two minutes too late.

"And your boy is in Allentown to do what, exactly?"

"Your Eminence, Paolo is there to get the job done."

Not an *exact* answer. Still, De Léon appeared to be content with the reply. The monarch kneaded his papers in his wrinkled spindle fingers as he slouched back into the plush cushions of his office chair. His darkened, tired eyes looked up at the colonel.

"And how do you suppose... the high council feels about Reekan's adventures in the ruined city?"

The colonel laughed out loud, startling Tomás. He could not imagine reacting that way in front of His Eminence. Then again, he was not Tirel Desantos.

"I don't suppose the DHC of New Inland is aware of Reekan's adventures. The mayor keeps Jennings Marribel tied up in meetings while his chief lieutenant and grunts do the dirty work in the Allentown sewers. Paolo informs me that Shore has in fact arrived."

"Your son has done well, Colonel. But I feel his *talentsss*... would be better served in Capston. I'm sure he would like the chance to... correct things."

Tomás could imagine the narrowed black holes of the colonel's glare. He was glad not to be on the receiving end of it. De Léon's thin lips were a thin line. Placing the wrinkled pages on the desk, the monarch pressed his fingertips together.

"I couldn't agree more, Your Eminence. Captain Alvara!"

Tomás' heart trembled at the barking of his name. He approached De Léon's desk in full attention, eyes avoiding the monarch.

"At ease... captain." Tomás stood down; hands clasped behind his back. "The colonel tells me you are more than adequate to oversee Allentown."

"Yes, Your Eminence." Tomás hoped his voice didn't sound as shaky as he imagined.

"Good. You will relieve the lieutenant colonel at first light."

A pit formed in Tomás's stomach. Paolo's apparent failure in Capston has now been rewarded with... yet another chance. Already passed over for a Kayewati thug. All the work Tomás had invested in his covert identity would have to wait for the next opportunity.

Perhaps he and Paolo could finally meet in Allentown, far from Motherland's gates and the gaze of the colonel and his leprous puppet.

Homesick

Monday, 21 May Ac 0245
Bay-of-Green
Phil Fox

Phil never forgot the feeling of nausea that overtook him at sea. Sure, the medication worked, sometimes in as little as half an hour, or twice that amount of time. It was always lurking, though, waiting for a rough sea or an eerie stillness to set in.

The feeling was in full churn all those years ago when Mr. Schiff, his uncle from far away, accompanied him on his first journey by sea. The pair shipped out of the Hudson, a wide bay with islands and countless ghosts, into the open expanse of the Atlantic on a southerly and westerly track. Six days until La Bermude, he told Phil. The first full day at sea was a breeze. Partly cloudy, but only a gentle rocking as the sloop cut across the caps and valleys of waves. He remembered telling himself he could get used to this. Shore birds reeling above, eventually leaving their sight as the shore receded further and further. Fishing boats became fewer until the Schiff sloop was alone, only open water in all directions.

It was around that time the feeling began to emerge.

And when he opened his eyes before sunup inside the bowels of the cabin, lurching back and forth on his bunk, the feeling was so unbearable he considered swimming the rest of the way. I can't even swim very well, he reminded himself, but I'll take my chances.

The second day was easily the worst. Running the rigging of a sailboat still had to happen and the ocean didn't care about Phil's twisting innards. The half-blue from the day before was overtaken by a darkening stratus cloud layer, low-hanging fog, Mr. Schiff explained, that would eventually overfill and leak into rain once the grey could no longer carry the load. Before that could happen, there were sails to trim, knots to secure, and hatches to batten. Phil was amazed at how unaffected his uncle appeared, gliding across the top deck from port to starboard with the balance of a cat. I'm one missed step away from a tumble into the surf, he scolded himself as he tripped on a coil of hempen rope.

By the fourth day, Phil found the seasickness manageable. His uncle remarked that his face was a little less green that morning, and Phil acknowledged his progress by keeping his three square meals in his belly for the first time since supper of the first night. Salted meats and crusty bread were garnished with wilted lettuce and vitamin pills to keep the nutrition of his cushy life in Sascota at the same level. The stratus clouds had become nimbus, teeming with an iron-grey bounty that splotched heavily on the cabin roof and windows. The rain barrels were opened once Mr. Schiff had measured the direction of the jet stream. From too far south, the rain couldn't be trusted. Red tide or not, there was too much to worry about in the water cycle south of the Red Line. But less water to lug on the journey meant more space for food storage. And other cargo.

Once upon the firm ground of *L'Isle de la Bermude*, the feelings of turbulence in his abdomen had dissipated completely. Less than 24 hours later, the pair were loading up the sloop again for the next leg of the journey, this one expected to be slightly longer due to the deviation in the course they had to travel. The longshoreman tracked the travel plan of all vessels coming into or leaving La Bermude. Officially, the pair were destined for the Azores west across the ocean, a common enough destination for the wealthy and well-connected. And the sensors would confirm that they were heading in that direction. Until the sloop was past the invisible boundary, after which the ship would sharply turn north.

It was around the same time in the journey all those years ago, when to the west on the faint horizon Phil's binoculars detected the sandbar. A writhing mass of harbour seals cavorting in the surf and along the sandy shore as the lone building leaned in defiance of gravity and ocean wind. Where he longed both then and now to steer closer if not for the long shallows that swallowed countless vessels over the centuries. To chase the wild horses, sand-matted and sea-tinged manes, and generational wisdom in their deep black eyes. Maybe one day he could stop on the north coast of the crescent-shaped island, where the sloop could moor much more safely. He would wade across the shallows to the island and maybe even stay a while. He could even imagine living out his days there.

Spruce Grove was well-guarded from the outside world. But not this well-guarded. He would wither and die in his old age, and the Reapers would not collect his bones. The remains would rest on the grassy knolls until the ocean retrieved them, as they did with all their dead. Phil took great comfort in the notion.

Rather than risk identification in the narrow Strait of Hawksport, Phil navigated east, rounding the highlands in an arc back to the west, adding an extra day to his voyage. The pod of right whales that appeared as blips on his underwater sonar screen veered away sometime in the night of the sixth day. As the Bay-of-Green approached, Phil anticipated new blips to appear, this time artificial in nature.

The grey sky of the first six days gave way to blue as the sloop switched to fuel reserves, trawling at a diminished speed so as not to generate crashing wakes along the erosion-delicate shores of the bay. Phil retreated beneath deck where the sonar screen swept in a sweeping arc around bright red concentric circles. Sure enough, a formation of five blinking dots began to converge on the sloop beneath the surface. Usually, they dispatched three. It's nice to know Albert spared no expense in the greeting party.

Phil remembered the first time the sentries greeted the sloop.

"Do you hear that?" Mr. Schiff looked over from the console.

A muffled scuffing sound along the hull followed by soft footsteps broke the uncomfortable silence in the cabin. Phil couldn't help walking to the ladder stairs, gazing up at the top hatch that remained a barrier between him and the boarding party. A click and a whoosh, and the hatch drew open, flooding the cabin with bright light. When his eyes came into focus, a diver in a skin-tight wetsuit, masqued with wide opaque goggles, stared back at him as though young Phil was an insect hiding under an overturned rock, naked, exposed.

The seasickness had given way to nervous anticipation. It had begun to creep in when he woke, only fifty kilometers from the bay. He had taken the medicine. This was something different. Familiar, but different.

Phil thought he heard the same footfalls from his first visit all those years ago, but he knew it was a memory echo. Switching off the sonar, he climbed the ladder and pushed open the hatch, that same burst of light flooding his eyes. As he stepped onto the deck and his focus sharpened, the frogman was lying casually along the padded bench seating astern. His hood drawn back, exposing bouncing wavy curls of black hair, the man smiled in his casual repose.

"Ten years is a long time, old friend!" Water ran off his Lycra costume in rivulets, pooling on the deck.

Phil smiled back. "And you haven't aged a day, Albert."

The sloop crawled into the bay, bringing the port village of Gasperro into gradual view. Rustic homes peppered the shoreline in front of a deep-green tree line, clustered around the wharf that served as the gateway to the river. Along the north shore of the horseshoe-shaped cove, the hills rose above the modest settlement, lighter green, clear-cut patches revealing grey stone markers. Phil knew Albert was following his line of sight.

"It was a beautiful service. Dad would understand why you couldn't come, though."

Phil received the news of his uncle Schiff's passing in the first year of his second term, before any of the terrorist attacks. Albert knew the impending falling out between Hyacynthe and New Inland had everyone in office on edge. All transport by sea would be scrutinized, even pleasure-craft vacationers who wished only to hide away from their problems in the forgotten coastal villages.

"I'd like to pay my respects, of course." Once he was settled in the Homestead, of course. And he had a chance to take a proper shower. And maybe have some real food.

"You seem to have made out fine with the old boat, I see. Don't suppose I have to go down below to check for contraband, do I?"

Phil laughed. "And track water through my cabin? I'd prefer you didn't."

Albert stood and the pair shook hands as the seaside village of Gasperro emerged. A small gaggle of children, glaring with scrutiny in their eyes, gathered along the edge of the wharf. One boy, maybe twelve or thirteen years old, hung from the jib crane, rocking back and forth on the chain like a pendulum as the sloop approached, before dropping into the frothy water.

"This is my stop. I imagine you want to keep on until the Grove?"

Phil nodded. About twenty kilometers upriver, the Spruce Grove would be his ultimate destination. Beyond the watchful radar of the Gasperro surveillance system, the sloop would be undetectable, if indeed anyone was even watching. The water was still high enough. If he'd come even a few weeks later, Phil would have had to travel by the wagon trails, those overgrown blacktopped roads where cars like his wooden FTE model once cruised. Either way, the solitude of the Homestead in Spruce Grove calmed his apprehension.

At least for a moment or two.

"He's here, you know."

And just like that, Phil's spirit began to sink. The sigh indicated as much.

"How long?"

Albert wrinkled a brow. "Three days, four maybe? You know how he likes to surprise us."

No kidding.

"I gave you a heads-up, at least." Kendall had made the arrangements. Albert would probably mention something about that.

"And you still haven't introduced me to your lady friend..."

"A friend that happens to be a lady, that's it." And a damn good office manager.

"Keep your secrets, then. This is my stop, cousin!"

Albert Schiff didn't bother pulling over his hood or putting on his goggles. In one motion, he drew two fingers to his temple in salutation before stepping over the edge as the children on the wharf cheered. These children were too young to remember the last time he was here. Some wouldn't have even been born. It's good to see they trust Albert enough to know I'm safe, Phil reasoned. *It's good to see they feel safe at all.*

He must have daydreamed. In an instant, Albert was leaning against the jib crane, arms folded, the Gasperro children gathered around him waving as the sloop crept past. Under the arched stone bridge, he would continue his slow crawl upriver for the next few hours.

Over two weeks, and the seasickness had gradually turned to homesickness. Phil Fox couldn't decide which was worse, but he was sure both had ebbed in the tidal waters behind him.

You had better have at least taken your boots off at the door...

Derelict

Monday, 21 May AC 0245
Spruce Grove
Phil Fox

Uncle Schiff set the motor on its slowest crawling gear as the sloop puttered up the shallows. Phil panned along the hanging tree line with wide eyes and wider wonder. He couldn't tell if the rustling movements were leaves in the faint breeze, wildlife, or the ghosts of settlers. Long past the stone bridge, the Gasperro River snaked through the thickening forest, at times canopied by the heavy brush and nurturing trees. In full bloom, the river would have appeared to be little more than a trickling stream.

Around one final bend and the remains of an older stone bridge poked out of the brush on opposite banks. The stone ramps were skeletal hands. Years ago, when they were alive, they would have met in a tender grip. Now, this freshwater river was an ocean between two shores.

Schiff drifted the sloop against the eastern side, securing the craft to the ruins. The stonework that remained made for a convenient stairway. Phil watched Schiff climb the stone with determination. Once at the top, his uncle slouched against a tumbled stone to catch his breath.

"I'm fine, Phil. Just getting a little older, need to catch my breath." Schiff didn't appear to be very old. Still,

Phil noted several occasions when his uncle seemed out of breath.

Phil passed his uncle his leather canteen. Schiff tilted it above his mouth, allowing a small trickle between his lips. A few deep lungs full of air later and the pair were on the move, disappearing into a narrow footpath that would not have been visible from the river. It would be nearly an hour's hike before they arrived in what was known on the old maps as Spruce Grove.

"The old roads from Gasperro to the Grove are still open. But I think it's best you know the river route. Just in case you need it someday."

The walking trail from the river was wide enough for two adults to walk side by side without branches whipping their faces. Phil heard a low hum that gradually grew into a rumble of engines. Within minutes, the pair stepped out of the wood trail into a wide field, high in nodding grasses as misshapen machines crawled in perfect lines. Near the eastern reaches, a few building peaks stretched into view.

"Those are the last buildings from the old times." Schiff sighed, this time from nostalgia rather than fatigue. "More and more choose to live in Gasperro, or in the settlements along the Strait. Fishing is more romantic than farming, it seems."

The vast fields were still well-managed, as far as Phil could tell. As the pair walked on, the colours changed to signify different crops. Wheat, barley, corn, even sunflowers towered in a small section. Farmhands dipped in and out of the rows, coveralls and wide-brimmed hats on every one of them. Phil smelled the sweet, dusky fumes of the diesel exhaust as the big-wheeled tractors gurgled. He sneezed, bringing tears to his eyes as Schiff laughed.

"Allergy season!" The way he said it made Phil feel like a newcomer. He was, after all.

The old settlement approached, first a tall barn with a wheel-spoked mansard roof. Doors open wide, Phil spied a pair of tractors at rest. "Do they still work?"

"One does. The other is a donor now." Schiff explained that machine parts were very difficult to acquire. It involved trading with other communities in the region and beyond, and some were not eager for commerce. "Which is why it's so important to be able to fix your own."

Schiff nodded up the bare dirt street past two tall farmhouses to a square-roofed building with two wide bay doors. An oval sign jutted from a steel pole with splotches of encroaching rust.

"*Jackson.* As in…"

Schiff smiled. "He's out of town on business, but you'll get to meet him soon, yes."

Two metal-plated pillars with rubber hoses for arms stood guard in front of the old service station. In a small parking lot just beyond, five or six autos in varying degrees of disrepair waited as though the doctor was late for their appointments.

"He still gets business?"

"Mostly from Gasperro, of course. But there are fewer and fewer autos now. Petrol is too expensive to import. And most of us don't have far to go anymore."

Young Phil understood this well. Living inside domed and walled cities meant nothing was very far away. Public transit was quiet, quick, and cheap. Whether they were magna-rail or nuclear-celled, modern transportation was always an afterthought. Here, it was an important part of any equation.

Once Uncle Schiff was sufficiently rested, the pair turned north, crossing the crops between wheat and corn until they reached the tree line. The gap between two stands of hemlock gave way to a buggy trail. The last leg in his journey to the Homestead.

"So, we couldn't travel by buggy because...?"

Uncle Schiff smiled, his stride uneven and laboured. "Mr. Jackson has the buggy in the first service bay. Says it's almost fixed now."

"Almost?" *How long could it take?*

"Almost. But if I were you, Phil, I wouldn't hold my breath. Besides, it wouldn't make it through this."

The path opened into a clearing that upon closer inspection was a swamp. Faint tractor skid tracks were still visible on the outer edges of the groomed path; lichens and dead grass matting lined the edges. Even at a cursory glance, the trail looked like it was floating.

"I don't understand. If Mr. Jackson is the shopkeeper, and there's not as much business, why would it take him so long?"

The pair walked several steps before Schiff stopped to catch his breath again. "Mr. Jackson will have to explain that himself, I'm afraid. I told you he owns Jackson Auto, but he has other businesses to tend. Sometimes he has to leave."

Phil's uncle inhaled that rich, marshy air. It invigorated him, so the pair continued to move on. The floating trail held them above the bog water, keeping their hiking boots dry.

"But as I said, it's really his story to tell. In due time, I promise."

As they moved out of the bog and into the tree-canopied final leg of the journey, several unnatural shapes began to crop up on either side of the trail. Phil recognized the skeletal remains of autos, like those waiting in the lot next to the service station. He slowed his pace in the presence of the metallic remains. A glint of light from either chrome or a mirror caught his eye, making the swath of bushes a kaleidoscope. Phil imagined the later years of the thriving village in the Grove. Mongrel buggies with half a model for a front and something else entirely for the rear scampering through the trails off the old roads.

Reapers might not be there to reclaim them, but the earth itself would ultimately leave none behind. It was against Phil's understanding of nature to leave valuable metals to rust in the woods. Had the Grove been closer to New Inland, or even Hyacynthe to the northwest, most of these would have been hauled off to the smelters. Phil vowed that one day, he would have someone send in a crew to remove the remainder of the wreckage and render what was left.

Uncle Schiff stopped again. Both he and the forest needed to breathe. The derelict autos were blights upon the land, and they needed to be cured as soon as possible.

The old barn now slouched in the middle, the open gap where the doors once met punctured by the broken crossbeam. The donor tractor, or what remained of it, was still crouching in the shadows. Both old farmhouses were long gone, but the old stone foundation of one still traced a wrinkled, grey outline in the uncut grass. There were still tractors working the crops, but only a few. They were too far afield for Phil to smell the exhaust, but he still heard their low rumbling engines.

The gas pumps continued their vigil in front of

Jackson Auto, although they had no practical purposes. A holding tank on the south side of the building was easier to fill and service now. The rust bleeding through the white paint suggested to Phil that servicing was needed sooner than later. He would have to get Albert on that. *We can't afford any leaks.*

The steel pole was gone, but the oval sign was lying against the side of the building as though it were taking a nap.

Just like the first time his eyes set upon the old Jackson Auto service station, the building was closed, and the lights were off. There were no longer any autos waiting in the empty lot. Phil sighed. Truly, it's the end of an era. He doubted there were many that would see the inside of the service bays anymore.

Well, maybe one.

Phil Fox took a sip from his canteen, the same one he shared with his uncle all those years ago. When Uncle Schiff was still alive. When the cancer treatments were secretly draining him of his energy. A pang of regret knotted in Phil's stomach. Once he was cleaned up from the trip and after a full night's sleep on dry land, he would have to make a trip to Burnside-on-the-Hill to pay his respects.

Following the trail through waist-high grasses and weeds, Phil swore he heard the footsteps of Uncle Schiff. The soft wisp of rushes brushing along his denim pants with every sweep of his feet, a whisper from an invisible spirit. The first kilometer of the road to the Homestead from the Grove fields always grew in faster than it could be groomed due to the nutrient-rich, swampy soil.

Right about here, it should start to get...

His right foot sank in the marsh mud. After a few steps, the soles of his hiking shoes grew colder from the leaking. *If memory serves me, there are perfectly good, vulcanized rubber boots in the mudroom closet. Fat lot of good they're doing me there. Mice probably nested in them anyway.*

The original trail had been built up with heavy machinery. Albert tried his best to keep it up, but it was clear the past few years had seen the swamp reclaim some of it. After about two hundred meters, the murk receded, and Phil stepped onto higher ground. His shoes squished with every step. Although the brackish water warmed to his body temperature, the hike was no less discomforting. Blisters were forming on his heels. Phil made the decision to tough it out for the final half-kilometer.

The grasses grew shorter as the tree canopy above cast a dark shade on the trail. Instead of swishing grass and suctioned steps, Phil could hear a not-too-distant snapping and crackling of twigs. A coyote, possibly. It was more likely a bobcat, scarcely seen, but always there in the safety of the deep, centuries-old forest that blanketed the old family plot. That kept the Jacksons hidden from the world beyond. Hidden from the domed cities. Hidden from other settlements and villages, from fugitives and grifters. Hidden even from the Reapers.

Pressing up the trail, Phil noted a parallel set of tracks, crushed grass, and brush merging from the east onto the main trail. It made sense that there were no buggy tracks until now. The other way into the Homestead was a wider arc circling around from Burnside-on-the-hill through a number of gated fences. The path of easiest travel was fraught with more hurdles and obstacles. It wasn't worth the effort for any chance visitors. Despite Albert's assurances, Phil was far more comfortable walking from the river, especially after all the wreckage was cleared away. Fewer eyes, fewer questions asked.

He didn't have to be an experienced ranger to know

the mud tracks that led up the trail were fresh. Phil hoped that by taking the long road in, his guest would track less mud into the house.

You've always been good at covering your tracks...

Illuvut Mitsik

Tuesday, 1 May AC 0245
6:15 AM
Illuvut Mitsik, Kayewati Free Association

The sun would only be rising close to midday, so it was still dark when my carriage pulled into view of the Ninth Circle. A winding, rocky road winds its way through the pass as the bubble-shaped covering of the Kayewat entrance grows the closer you crawl. If the sun were high, the outline of the main structure would barely be seen beyond the mountains that stood like a saw blade behind the Ninth Circle. Instead, the shape of the domed facility, windswept and snow-pasted like an igloo, managed to cast a shadow even though the sun was nowhere to be seen. Whether it was perpetual day or night, the cold was always the same.

We were greeted by sentries, bundled in insulated snowsuits so round they were almost spheres, waddling along the side of the frozen road. Arctic tractors on track wheels ground across the crusty snow as snowmobiles whined, their echoes ringing off the valley walls. The coach driver leaned outside the window and a squinty-eyed guard with frozen patches of facial hair smiled, waving as the striped barricade arms lifted, allowing us to move on. The grating squeal of iron on rusted bearings did nothing to help my headache as a light poured out of the yawning bay doors. If anyone tried to get inside Kayewat unaware of the process, the sound would have been enough to make them want to flee. If the cold wasn't enough.

And it didn't improve once inside.

The whole purpose of the Ninth Circle was to process returning citizens, as well as dissuade potential newcomers. Imagine running a marathon, hobbling on noodles for legs as you collapse at the ribbon, only to be told you still have another ten kilometers to run. The Ninth is the most unwelcome welcoming you could imagine.

With the grinding of the steel doors drawing shut behind us, we could see the light on the inside was generated from the perimeter rather than from above, giving the high arched ceiling a false shallowness. I always felt like I was standing in a cold fog, in open sky, even if it was a fraction of the height of the main structure, let alone the infinite depth of New Inland. And equally difficult to see around me, stairs and steep slopes wound in a long, slow arc downward in concentric circles—four to be exact. Shuttles whirred past, not slowing for even a second as pedestrians dodged to one side or another. There was a long walk yet. No one with half the heart to complete the journey would descend all the way to the bottom.

After about half an hour, the base of the spiral came into view. Half as wide as the topmost layer, the base of the Ninth Circle birthed a flat-roofed complex with multiple entrances. It didn't matter which you chose. The corridors inside would all lead to a central scrutineer behind plexiglass where your application would be reviewed, or your stamp would be scanned. Mine, hidden beneath a layer of synthetic skin, gave the machine a whistle as the name Walpurgis flashed on the screen on the back wall of his cubicle. Next, I entered my security code into the hand terminal to cross-reference with the Deep Databank. Another confirmation whistle, and I was on my way. No one checked my bag.

Only then did the comforts of home start to appear. As I wasn't in need of a stamp, I could take the tram through the mountain to *Illuvut Mitsik*, the core structure of the Kayewati Free Association. The substance sellers began to pop up the closer I got. One, whose name I think was Arrowhead, or Arrow_Head, or maybe just Arrow, sold me two liters of Aquavit in green translucent bottles that may not have been cleaned before being refilled. The 80-proof liquor inside would kill anything dangerous anyway. I tossed the rusty cap to the floor and took a long swig of caraway and dill-flavoured poison, saving the second bottle for later. CF would be pissed if I didn't save him any.

As I stepped out into the open expanse of *Our Home Beside the Mountain*, I sighed at the sight of my hometown. The clanging echo of steel rhythms competing against each other, punctuated by the barking voices of vendors and buyers in a dozen languages, the pungency of pickled herring and whale meat, all familiar sensations I never thought I would miss.

"Watch it, fucker!"

An overweight, middle-aged man with crossed

eyes and bad breath nearly knocked my half-drunk bottle from my hand. My fist met his jaw in one long arc, bending a tooth back as the man stumbled without falling. I noticed the gathering crowd, all in their fuzzy-rimmed hooded parkas and leather-stitched pants, waiting for my response. Straightening out his half-rotten tooth and spitting blood, he laughed, raising a fist clenched inside a woolly mitt before turning away. I heard the tittering of the crowd, approving my fortitude as they returned to their browsing, bantering, and bickering.

"Nice hook, Wally! Looks like you didn't grow soft down South after all!"

A heavy arm draped over my shoulder, nearly hooking me off my feet as I had begun to walk away. Before I could answer, CF already had the spare bottle from my bag. He was an exceptional thief. Even a double knot in the drawstring couldn't keep him from the booze.

"Watch yourself, buddy. I have more where that came from." I feigned punching CF in his unshaven jaw. He should be grateful I don't knock out the last molars in his mouth.

"More of what, fists? You keep telling yourself that." CF drawled as though he began his bender at the crack of dawn. I knew he just sounded that way, even if the Aquavit wasn't his first drink of the day.

Claw_Finger's fat face grinned under a woolen cap with a fuzzy tassel hanging over one eye. Gunshots echoed and screams and hollers boomed. A squad of police trotted across the square and a siren sounded. We made small talk and hailed a shuttle to take us to the dog tracks where a ticket got you one round of betting and a burger. I told CF to save some drinks for after. CF informed me that it was his lucky day, and we would come out of the races rich enough to retire, or at the very least, to quit working for the man. I reminded him that *the man* would have the final say, just as his pick, a scrawny mongrel of some sort, stumbled last across the finish line. When the dogfights were ready to start, I told CF I wasn't going to sit through that shit, and a good night's sleep or three were needed.

"What's the matter, couldn't catch any winks on the flight? It doesn't matter, he's not supposed to arrive until Thursday, earliest."

In the center of the oval track, a fenced perimeter served as the killing floor for whichever sport was presented on any given day. Much warmer than the outside and the Ninth Circle, the Abattoir was routinely washed of spilled blood and viscera, though the deep brown and burgundy stains never fully disappeared. The acoustics whispered like the spirits of the combatants were still there, pleading for reprieve.

Two rows down, a vagabond draped in tanned leather and wool lay across three seats, surely kinking his spine as he slept off his stupor. We both assumed it was a *he*, as there were not many homeless women in Kayewat, but his face was completely covered, so we couldn't tell for sure. CF thought he was dead based on the smell. Upon closer inspection, his torso expanded with breathing, ever so slightly, but just enough to confirm he wasn't expired. How the young couple, four or five seats downwind from our lovely neighbour were unfazed and undeterred from their heavy petting was beyond me. Two guards with rail-thin iron pikes just sat and watched while the woman grinded her hips, their heads nodding with the bouncing of her tits. At least they weren't paying attention to CF and me.

So, it's still only Tuesday morning. I have at least forty-eight hours. CF told me some bad jokes, caught me up on the dirt from the streets, and we parted ways. From out of his left mitt, the master thief did the reverse and slipped a small piece of paper into my sleeve as we shook hands and bumped foreheads. I missed the chubby fucker. We haven't had a chance to catch up since well before I moved down to New Inland, and we haven't had a job together for years. I think it was the one where we sold all those kids from that coastal town before the hooded spooks came. The boss caught a lot of flak for that one. Turns out very few are okay with child trafficking these days.

Once inside my apartment, where the cupboards were only stocked with canned food and dried meats, I opened the slip of paper. *Spleen Cavern, Thursday, 8:35 PM.*

Le Renard couldn't have picked a dirtier tavern to meet in.

After the Fire

Monday, 21 May AC 0245
Jackson Homestead, Spruce Grove
Phil Fox

The closer he got to the Homestead, the stronger the scent of burning wood curled in Phil's nostrils. A canopy of heavy tree foliage kept the chimney smoke below and the light from above out. Back in his Capston office, Phil programmed the climate controls to emit the mellow scent of a small campfire, but he rarely switched it on. Kendall hated it. Only Steven Reekan appreciated it, saying the smell of burning wood was far more pleasant than the smell of molten metal coming from the Foundries. Outside the dome, warmth is always associated with other senses. On the inside, it just happens. Someone controls it, and everyone else doesn't even have to give it another thought.

Uncle Schiff reached ahead and pulled an overgrown alder branch to keep it from whipping into Phil's face. "These things grow faster than weeds. Gotta keep them trimmed back or they'll crowd out the path."

Phil's uncle dropped little tidbits of knowledge as though Phil would have to remember them all for a test tomorrow. You have to check the perimeter sensors at least once a week. Change the oil in your buggies every five thousand clicks; three if you can. Be sure the wheat shipments are sent up the coast or you won't receive your petrol before the frost sets in. And spend time with the children or you'll run out of farmhands.

"Trim the alders. Got it." Phil wasn't sure if he was trying to remind himself or assure Uncle Schiff that he was listening.

"Easy enough job for the young ones." Gasperro had a lot of children with very little else to keep them out of trouble. Can't let them near the petrol, though, Uncle Schiff also warned. Unchecked, they might syphon off a little and go inhale it behind the old barns. The youth had enough trauma in their lives.

In the deepening shade up the trail, the faint outline of the Homestead emerged like a spirit. Phil was sure it was much larger than this. Uncle Schiff must have picked up on his thoughts.

"The Homestead today is not the original Jackson house. There was a fire."

As they moved closer, the form of a log cabin, with two dormers like eyes protruding from the steep roof, took shape. Thick moss provided further camouflage from any visibility from the air. Uncle Schiff explained that the roof was fitted specifically to allow for foliage growth.

"Mr. Jackson was never satisfied that the old Homestead was so tall. He always complained about all the extra space that had to be kept clean. Typical for him to whine when he never did any of the cleaning himself!"

Unlike the farmhouses in Spruce Grove, there was no groomed lawn surrounding the cabin. A flat stone path angled from the mud trail up to a veranda with a slatted rail. The familiar FTE logo was burned into a wooden panel above the screen door. A low light filtered out through tacky, flower-printed curtains in the windows on either side. Muddy footprints tramped up the three stairs before scuffling on the indecipherable welcome mat.

"The lights are on timers. He's not home tonight."

"He seems to be away a lot."

Uncle Schiff smiled. "Mr. Jackson has never been one to sit still for very long. Always some project on the go. You'll understand someday."

Phil wasn't used to adults speaking to him with condescension. Lucas and Elsa Fox were always forthright with him. He had questions, and they provided answers. The most confusing thing about this whole transition was the ambiguity.

Uncle Schiff had arrived one day after his mother died. The young orphan Phil had inherited property in a secret location. For secret reasons. From a secret man. Too many secrets.

The pair climbed the muddy steps. Behind the screened door, answers waited to reveal themselves. And try as he might, Phil couldn't turn the knob. There was as much a chance for disappointment as fulfillment.

"I'm tired." Phil spied the wicker patio furniture set and chose the loveseat. The woven bands creaked as he sank into the cushions, instantly feeling the dampness through the seat of his pants. The chair was rigid, forcing him to sit upright when his posture wanted nothing more than to slouch. The seat was as uncomfortable as any he had ever sat in, but he was willing to put up with it if he didn't have to open the door. Uncle Schiff sat in the rocker across from him, its runners squealing as he tipped back and forth.

"There's nothing to be afraid of, Phil. But take all the time you need. You can warm up by the fireplace."

"It's like a wet blanket here. Almost hard to breathe." Phil's chest was heavy.

"It's humid today, but not all the time. You'll see."

Phil adjusted his weight and crossed his legs. "Can we get rid of this wicker furniture?"

"You can if you like. Mr. Jackson kept it because it survived the fire. Not much did. Oh, I almost forgot..."

Uncle Schiff reached into his jacket pocket and retrieved a small wooden sun-shaped decoration.

"This survived too. It was in the shop when the fire happened. Mr. Jackson thought it was long past time to finally fix it."

The woodcraft was a barometer, Phil's uncle explained. It indicated the rise and fall of air pressure. Out here, you must be aware of the weather. Its subtleties, its quirks. Inside the domes, there's someone to do all that for you. But on the *outside*, you have to be responsible for things you used to take for granted. Phil wasn't averse to hard work. But life on the outside was becoming more complicated by the millibar.

"Maybe I'll take it with me." Phil took the wheel into his hands. "It'll look good in my office someday."

Uncle Schiff smiled. "And if you change your mind, you can always hang it on a nail inside. But you'll have to actually *go inside*, of course."

Phil's rucksack only began to feel heavy over his shoulder the last few meters of his hike. The log cabin known only as the Homestead crouched under the same thick canopy, guarded by a long row of tall spruce trees planted generations earlier as a wind barrier. Suspended from the heavy branch of one of them, a rotted rope with a shiny, bald rubber tire hung like a dead pendulum. Phil never got to enjoy swinging on it. He was already an adult when he first arrived. When he closed his eyes, Uncle Schiff was pushing his son all those years ago. Albert's already long, curly black hair bounced as he begged to be pushed higher and faster. He still had that infectious, child-like grin today.

That was a happy day. The adoption was official. Uncle

Schiff had fostered children from Gasperro before, but Albert's case was different. As a young boy, he witnessed a lot of death before the fires. Before he was rescued. Before he arrived on a wharf in a sleepy cove. Before a kind man with no children of his own gained his trust.

All grown up now, Albert did the best he could to keep the Homestead in good repair. Phil never for a second doubted that he would.

There were no muddy tracks, but a pair of well-worn boots sat outside the screen door. Above the frame, two nail holes indicated where the old FTE sign used to hang. The first thing he did after he settled into the Homestead was to take it down, prying it off himself with a rusty clawhammer from the toolbox. Give it to Albert so he can hang it up in his room, he had told his uncle.

Phil climbed onto the veranda and sat in the old wicker loveseat, just like he did more than ten years earlier. The same red cushions were now splotched with black mold, but they were dry. It was still uncomfortable. He really did want to get rid of the ugly set of furniture.

But then again, anything that survived the fire must have been destined to live forever.

The Nowhere Kids

Friday, 15 June AC 0245
Holt Tower Velodrome, Capston, New Inland
Robbie Sheppard

Twenty-five kilometers. *That's enough for one day.*

Robbie racked the borrowed racing cycle and wiped the sweat from his forehead. For the first week sequestered in Holt Tower, Robbie had rejected the idea of training on the world-class racetrack in the Holt Velodrome. The facility was closed indefinitely to the public in light of the security breach. Capston's Minister of Sport had canceled all-city track meets until further notice. That included longboarding, and Lorrie was none too pleased. As a matter of fact, he was going to see to it that Mayor Reekan, his close, personal friend, would have his job for this outrage. Robbie didn't realize his sixteen-year-old brother wielded so much power.

Of course, it was obvious Lorrie was blowing off steam. His usual outlet was Warren, who had been staying in his room ever since his mother had flashed the entire tower. Mr. Connelly kept to his quarters anyway, but now the pair squirreled away from the gawkers and pitying stares. Clara demanded her own suite, free of all cameras and viewing screens. Holt was only too eager to comply.

Through a heavy door and into the darkened, wood-paneled sauna, Robbie wrapped his towel around his waist and collapsed on a bench. "Light at 2, steam at 6." The first voice command increased the light in the room from zero to enough that he could see his hand in front of his face. The other caused the steam to hiss as the level of warm mist decreased.

"Don't suppose we could keep the steam on 8?" Steven Reekan's voice was usually sharper, as though he were forcing his syllables from the top of his chest. Robbie detected a distinct resignation this time.

"Steam at 8." *The Sheppards are on borrowed time at Holt Tower. Best to play along.*

"Steam at 7." The mayor acquiesced. "But let's not confuse the computer any further."

Traces of lavender wafted through the mist, deep into Robbie's lungs. The light at 2 allowed Steven's burly frame to sharpen into focus.

"If you think this is hot, try crawling through ducts in the Foundry." Robbie detected a hint of bravado in Steven's tone. "At least here it smells pretty..."

"The worst I've smelled is Lorrie's room after his longboard competitions. Teenager workout clothes, now that's a whole different level of stink!"

Coughing as he laughed, Steven cleared his throat. "And I can say I haven't had the honour."

Robbie shifted his posture, tightening the towel around his waist. There was a lull in the small talk. "You never had children of your own?"

In the shadow, Steven shook his head and sighed. "Career man, I guess. I wouldn't have made a great father. How many kids would want to wait around for me to come home from work?"

Robbie couldn't tell if he was serious or joking. "I'm sure you would have made a great father. You've been patient with Cadlen. And how you can make Lorrie mind, without starting a war!"

"I never wanted to start wars." Steven slid closer along the bench. "I lived through my share of them."

There was a story to be told, but Robbie didn't want to prod any further. It turned out he didn't have to.

"Since I know so much about your family, Robbie, I'll

tell you a little bit about my own."

The mayor breathed deeply and coughed again, fluid rattling in his lungs. "That's a lot of years of soot from the smelter trying to come out. Doctors say I'll be hacking it up the rest of my life. And I know this because my father had that same cough until his dying day. Thirty-five years in the Foundries and all he got was a plaque and lung cancer."

"That must have been hard on you and your mom."

Steven laughed himself into another coughing fit, hocking the phlegm onto the sauna floor. "It was hard on me. Guarantee, it had no effect on my mother."

Robbie frowned. "You lost your mother, too."

In the dimness of the chamber, Robbie watched Steven's brow crook and his eyes deepen. "You could say that. One day she walked out the door and never came back. She left my father and me, without even a word. But we were better for it."

A pang swelled in Robbie's stomach. How bad could she have been? He'd give anything to have his back.

"Before she left, Dad was angry all the time. He was pushy, impatient, and disappointed. But after Dianna left, he changed. He didn't shout as much. He stopped complaining about not getting his promotion."

Robbie kept silent. What more could he add to the conversation?

Steven sighed. "I'm sorry, Robbie. Here I am going on about my mother, and you lost yours way too soon."

Steven had called his mother *Dianna*. Robbie couldn't imagine calling his mom *Julia*. Five years ago, he watched her slip away. Withered in a hospital bed with a respirator over her face. Her natural brown hair streaked with invasive gray. Lorrie had asked her why it was changing colour so quickly. She had laughed under the mask until a machine began to squeal and the nurses rushed in. What did I do, Lorrie protested as the nurses shuffled him from the room. And Robbie saw it all from behind the glass of the observation window. Watching everything unfold from that vantage point made the hospital room on the other side of the glass less believable than a holograph projection. Or the floor-to-ceiling screens in Jason Holt's luxury suites.

"I was nineteen. Crys, a year younger than me. Lorrie was eleven, and believe it or not, just as mouthy then. Cad, he was only eight."

"Did the young fella talk before..." Steven stopped himself from completing the sentence. Robbie preferred he just say it.

"Before Mom died? No, not really. Crys always claimed he spoke to her, and I'm sure he did. But I never used to believe her. He always avoided Lorrie—but then again, Lor always picked at him."

"Light at 4." The chamber brightened enough for the pair to see each other with clarity. "I don't think I can keep you folks here much longer."

The revelation wasn't a surprise, but still dropped on him like a bowling ball on his toe.

"Is it Mr. Holt?"

Steven nodded. "Partly. He thinks that just because the police are here, nothing can ever go wrong. And I—*we*—certainly didn't think anyone could tap into his internal network. But someone has eyes inside the tower."

"Someone?" The timbre of Robbie's voice was higher than usual. The humidity of the sauna was affecting his lungs already. "Who has the ability to do something like this? Le Renard Subtil?" The infamous human trafficker and criminal mastermind featured as the subject of documentaries and news reels. The name inevitably came up whenever some cold case was mentioned, or someone went missing. Or when an explosion went off. He had deep pockets, and deeper connections. For all Robbie knew, Steven Reekan could have a mole in his midst. And if so, where on earth would the Sheppards and Connellys ever be safe again?

"Everyone likes to think that everything is Le Renard's organization, but most of that's urban legend. But let's say he *is* involved. There's no motive for him alone, so he'd have to be working for or with someone else. And we have no evidence Le Renard has anything to do with your inn, or any of the attacks, for that matter. Hell, we don't even know if he's alive anymore."

Robbie almost bought Steven's rationale. "Okay. So, if it's not him, who? I mean, who else would have a reason to target random places in Capston?"

Steven stood and tightened the towel around his thick waist. "If you ever find out, you'll let me know, won't you!" The answer was lacking. *He's holding back information.*

"So where do we go from here?" Robbie couldn't begin to imagine what came next. The Sheppard brothers, just a bunch of nowhere kids.

Holt Tower was supposed to keep them safe. After terrorists leveled their home, Steven Reekan promised the Sheppard and Connelly families that they would never have to worry about anything again. Doctors for Cadlen. School and sport facilities for Lorrie and Warren. Enough space and time for Mr. and Mrs. Connelly to mend their relationship. And for Robbie Sheppard, amnesty from his unexpected role as businessman and parent.

All of that was just a fantasy. Robbie closed his eyes.

"We have a facility." Steven's voice cut through the forced darkness behind Robbie's eyelids. "It is remote—beyond the walls of New Inland, in the Appalachian Mountains to the south. Far out of reach from whoever has done this to you. But it won't be as luxurious as this place, I'll warn you now."

Outside?

"You want to move us *outside* New Inland?" When he reopened his eyes, the figure of Steven Reekan was half-dressed, the towel draped around his shoulders.

"It would need to be top-secret. If someone who would do you harm knows you're here, we need to shake them off the trail."

"But I don't understand. How could we be safer on the outside? The whole reason for living inside a giant dome is to keep people safe inside, isn't it?"

Steven wiped his face with the towel and tossed it to the hamper in the corner. His chest and abdomen were well-defined, but pocked with scars, some long and thin and some splotches like bullet holes that half-healed.

"It's true. We live safer lives inside the dome. But Robbie, safety is always relative." He pointed at the scars. "Most of these came from the Foundries. This one, though, was a bullet. Two inches to the right and I'm a dead man. If I take that shot on the outside, I'm dead anyway. But living inside, I got medical care immediately."

Steven pulled a sleeveless undershirt over the war wounds. "Capston pays well to lease the facility from Ozarck. We have state-of-the-art medical professionals at Ap-Oz. We can still help Cadlen, too."

"That's all well and good, Mr. Reekan. But you can't protect us from what we can't see, can you?"

Julia Sheppard had died from an unseen assailant.

"If you mean red tide, Robbie, you know that it can happen anywhere." Steven was referring to Robbie's parents. Both succumbed to red tide-related illness. Neither were even aware they carried the disease, and in the end, it was a secondary infection that took their lives. Red tide only cleared the path for the lesser viruses to finish the job. The Sheppards had likely contracted red tide on an excursion outside New Inland. To a youth retreat sponsored by Hyacynthe.

Outside.

"Can we think about it first?" Robbie had no say, but asking out loud gave him the illusion that he held some stake in the decision. If he had any power to make conditions, it would be to reunite somehow with Crystal.

"I'll be away for a few days. I'm meeting with the DHC this afternoon, then following up on a promising lead. So, rest easy until I get back, then we'll sort out the details."

Steven tried to smile with sincerity, but Robbie could tell he was uncertain of anything.

"Light at 2." The room dimmed at Robbie's command as Steven opened the door, flooding the sauna for a second with artificial light. A bellow erupted before the door shut, muffling most of Jason Holt's angry voice.

"Figured I'd find you down here..."

Robbie crept over and pressed his ear to the door.

Handshakes

Friday, 15 June AC 0245
Holt Tower Velodrome, Capston, New Inland
Mayor Steven Reekan

The whole point of basking in the sauna after the workout was to relax the tension that had built up in his joints and muscles. Some of Steven's tension came from the extra reps. Most of it was the stress pulling from all sides. The media wanted answers. The people on the street wanted to be safe. Jason Holt wanted to keep his business. Marribel and the council wanted him to slip up. Hell, the Sheppards and Connellys just wanted to go home again.

You know what I want? I want five uninterrupted minutes to myself.

Jason Holt didn't give him five seconds. No sooner did the sauna door crack open than Jason's pitchy, heightened voice echoed throughout the gym. The irate owner reflected like a kaleidoscope in the mirrored walls surrounding the exercise equipment, racked bicycles, and free weights.

"Figured I'd find you down here! Only a national emergency going on and you're lying in a towel—exfoliating!"

"For crying out loud, Jason, I'm running on a few hours of sleep a night for weeks now!"

Jason waved his arms. "Fat lot of good that does my guests! Or should I say, what's left of them. Do you know how many cancellations I had *just this afternoon*?"

Steven rolled his eyes and brushed past the irritated proprietor. "Hmm, I'll say twenty?"

"Twenty-*two*, smart-ass. Executive suites, no less. Should I send you the invoice, or Marribel and the DHC?"

That last retort crossed a line. Steven spun back on the heel of his toe. "Now listen here. Businesses that make a drop in a bucket compared to you are shuttering day by day. I know how deep your pockets are—you can absorb this, Jason! Don't come screaming at me, clutching your pearls—"

"Clutching my pearls? Really, now! You think this is all about me, right?"

Actually, he didn't.

"Every day I keep the Velodrome closed, the youth of Capston suffer for it. When businessmen don't come through, the local businesses don't get to benefit from *their* deep pockets, as you say! The Jewel contributes a healthy portion of the city GDP, and everyone knows it!"

The tension that had begun to subside in the hot, humid chamber crept back. "Of course, Jason, you're all for the *people*! Greatest fucking philanthropist of our time!"

"Don't use your big words on me, hot shot. If anyone else out there is working so hard for others at his own expense, you show 'em to me!"

Steven brought his palm to his forehead.

"That's what I... Never mind. Look, do you have a reason to see me or did you just feel like ripping into me for the hell of it?"

"As a matter of fact, I do." Steven turned to walk away, and Jason followed a pace behind. "It's about the Sheppard kids."

Steven stopped. "What about them?"

Jason strode past and turned back, blocking Steven's escape route. "They're the reason for all of this. And the longer you keep them here in the Jewel, the more you're playing dice with all of our lives."

Steven hoped Robbie wasn't listening at the door. He

swerved around Jason to create some distance between them and the sauna. Robbie Sheppard and his brothers had suffered enough. They didn't need this asshole to make them feel worse.

"Jason, we have plans, but I will *not* discuss them here, and certainly not now." Storming toward the lifts, Steven suppressed every instinct to reach back and grab him by the throat.

"Oh, plans! That's encouraging! Do any of those plans involve moving the kids out of my tower?"

"I'm leaving tonight to follow up on a lead. That's all I can tell you for now."

His bag was already packed. Civilian transport arranged. If Jason Holt could leave him the hell alone, he could be in Allentown in less than six hours, provided the DHC didn't hold him up too long.

"You're leaving too? Didn't you send Shore and the big oaf on some secret mission already?"

Kenzy Wall's close encounter with a hostile agent could blow the case wide open. They could end it all in a matter of days, if not hours. This war Capston was fighting against a faceless enemy, it was going to end. Phil Fox would come back from his vacation and marvel at the efficiency of Steven Reekan's administration. Jason Holt would go back to tending his bar and cracking jokes. The Sheppard Inn would rebuild. Marribel would swallow her words.

Steven flashed his identification code at the scanner alongside the lift doors. They swished open. "If money is the issue, Jason, write me up an invoice for whatever the Sheppard kids have cost you."

Jason raised his hands in surrender. "It's not like that, Reekan. Look, they're good kids. None of this is their fault. But this wasn't supposed to be a long-term solution. I know, I'm floating just fine for now. But I gotta think about the big picture here."

The big picture conveniently never brought up the Connelly family.

"So, tell me this, then. You're in no hurry to cast out the Connellys? Spending enough time with Clara, I'm told."

The mention of Mrs. Connelly's first name caused Jason to stammer. "I don't know who's telling you what... I mean... Look, I'm worried about the poor woman. She had her privacy violated for the whole world to see. A little sympathy for her situation would be appropriate!"

"Right. Sympathy for a woman whose tits flashed all over your live feed! But how about a family that lost their home? The only memories of their dead parents? For crying out loud, Jason, they have a sister who doesn't even *know* yet!"

Jason almost choked. "You might want to send the message, don't you think?"

"Oh yes, now, because calling up Hyacynthe is so easy these days!"

"Right." Jason exhaled through his nose. "What a mess."

The two men stared away from each other in a mutual silence. Jason Holt isn't a bad man. He's naturally scared, lashing out. And it makes total sense. He's seen the Sheppards lose everything. The illusion of safety has been stripped away, and now, nowhere is safe. Steven was banking all on the secure location of Ap-Oz to shelter the three brothers until the assailants were brought to justice.

If they were ever brought to justice.

The lift doors shut, and the bell indicated they were resting behind the stainless steel, waiting for them to be summoned open again. Steven broke the silence first.

"Captain Ling is more than capable of overseeing the operation here while I'm away. Three days, tops, Jason. You have my word; we will move as soon as I'm back.

Just promise me the Sheppard boys will be treated well."

The pair locked eyes. A second flash of the handheld code and the doors swished open again.

"You have my word."

Years ago, while Phil Fox was mayor, a gentleman's handshake between Jason and Steven was enough to close the deal. Cheap rent for suites in the 90 levels, in exchange for security and first right of refusal for future developments. It would all be finalized in legal speak and ratified by Capston, and later the New Inland DHC. But it started with a handshake. A small gesture of goodwill between two strong personalities.

The time for informality had passed. Neither offered a hand.

"I'll have my secretary square up my bar tab," Steven said. Jason lowered his head. The parting shot was subtle but effective.

"It's fine, Steven. But you promise me, seventy-two hours?"

The doors slid shut before he could answer. Steven ascended the sky lift toward the Hanging Gardens. One last meeting with Marribel before meeting his team outside the New Inland dome. The decay and dereliction of Allentown would be a welcome change of scenery for a few days.

Hawks and Doves

Friday, 15 June AC 0245
The Hanging Gardens, New Inland
Mayor Steven Reekan

After half an hour of walking, exchanging shuttles, and maneuvering through crowds, Steven arrived at the DHC rotunda, only to be told that Chair Marribel wasn't present. He tried the council chambers first, only to be redirected to the offices in Marribel's home city of Heartsburg. He chose to take the stairs rather than wait for the lifts. Four floors later, Steven emerged into the open air of the upper levels of New Inland. The entire level that encircled the upper region of the dome stretched wide and out of sight into the tiered levels of the Hanging Garden Agricultural District.

Somewhere, in one of those buildings, or in between the rows of crops, or in the pastures, Dianna Langley was working. She was only one of a hundred thousand horticulturists or botanists or farmers who made their living where New Inland was closest to the sky.

It wasn't the only reason Steven disliked the Hanging Gardens. But it was the most prescient. So many years had passed since Dianna walked out on him that she could have walked past him with not so much of a hint of recognition. He wondered if she remembered her son. Her son had tried his best to forget her.

Once in the reception of Heartsburg, Steven was again informed of Marribel's absence. The DHC is not scheduled to meet until this evening, the clerk informed him through thin glasses.

"And I informed the chair that I would be absent,"

Steven replied. "My datapad tells me she has office hours this afternoon."

The clerk smiled. "Chair Marribel accepts appointments for office hours. Your datapad must not have told you that?"

Steven scowled. The smug receptionist was clearly a Marribel hire.

"So, then she must be in her garden, I take it?"

"I wouldn't know, mister—"

"Mister Never Mind. I'll find her myself."

If the conversation continued, Steven might strangle him.

Half an hour later, retracing half his steps before steering himself toward the private garden plots, Steven flexed his position of power as a sitting DHC member to the gatekeeper. Intimidated by his title, the intern stammered and gestured her hand toward Marribel's plot. Winding his way through several shades of green, row by row, as mists gusted from watering nozzles, Steven came upon a lush, exotic garden of wide, leafy plants he had never seen anywhere else. How interesting it would be to read a manifest of the variety of species she kept in her plot. If she ever decided to call him out on procedure, maybe he'd mitigate her bullying tactics with the revelation to the council about her illegal plants.

Kneeling in a row of rubbery-fronded succulents, the chair of the DHC ran her fingers through the black soil.

"I told the clerk I wouldn't be available until 1600 hours," Marribel grumbled without looking up.

"Don't worry, Jennings. Your clerk did his job. I just knew I might find you here."

Marribel stopped kneading the soil and sighed before sitting up. Her wide-brimmed hat was unnecessary in the artificial climes of the Hanging Gardens. Steven figured she was wearing sun lotion and insect repellent just for the authenticity of the experience.

"What do you want, Steven?" Marribel stood, brushing black dirt from her padded knees. She looked older in her quaint denim pants and plaid shirt. In council, she was a hawk. But here in her quiet place, Steven fashioned her more a dove.

"Pax Brien will be speaking at council this evening, and Captain Ling will be acting second. My security team has a lead that needs my full attention." Steven skirted the details. The less Marribel knew for now, the better.

"Is that so? Care to divulge how your new lead was found?" Marribel's eyes were beads beneath thin, wrinkled brows.

"No, I don't care to divulge," Steven answered. "Other than that, we obtained hard evidence at the Sheppard Inn crime scene." He was referring to Grant's handheld, which under forensic review had confirmed a money trail through the Allens to Motherland.

"Very good, Mister Mayor. It's a shame six more lives were lost before you could make your break in the case."

Six lives *not* lost, but hidden. Whomever had hacked into Jason Holt's system knew, but that was still one person too many.

"The Sheppard had a capacity to house dozens, so yes, it's a shame, but it could have been far worse."

"Dried up business actually helped save lives, it seems," Marribel said. She removed her hat and wiped her forehead with the back of her arm. "With any luck, Capston will be back in business again."

"I hope you're right," Steven answered. "Because when the chair rotates out of Heartsburg to Capston, I want to give the council one hundred percent of my attention."

Marribel reverted to her hawkish demeanor, as if she were about to launch into a council debate. "I take great comfort in knowing that when my time as chair concludes, and the mayor of Capston takes the gavel,

Mayor Fox will have returned. He will bring some much-needed tact to the DHC."

Steven smiled. Marribel still hadn't come to terms with the inevitable passing of the gavel to him in only a few short months. She could call Phil Fox mayor all she liked, but his official title would be meaningless in the chambers. He would return as solicitor for Capston. Steven had won the mayoralty, and handily. There was nothing she could do about that.

"I'll leave you to your weeding, Jennings. Could I suggest you add some rosemary around your succulents? I've read it's great for blood circulation. I mean, we aren't getting any younger, are we?"

Marribel placed her hat back on her head, shading her hawk nose. "Good luck with your lead. I look forward to your report."

Steven glanced at his datapad. Just enough time to catch a shuttle to the New Inland Arterial Causeway before rush hour. He might still make Allentown before nightfall. The real lead, from what Shore had said, was in Kenzy Wall's handheld.

The <NULL> Files

Saturday, 16 June AC 0245
The Grace Hospital, South End, Allentown
Mayor Steven Reekan

After almost four hours, Steven Reekan was within the traditional city limits of the ruined city of Allentown. If he had remained above ground, the silhouette of a downtown core would be in view by now. The Grace, the tallest remaining high-rise in the south end of town, had been spared from the bombardment of Allentown that had leveled most skyscrapers. The new inheritors salvaged what they could from the devastation that had rained on their city on and off for years. That was generations ago. The city was left for dead. But the hospital had survived, a symbol of hope in the landscape of war-torn hopelessness.

Steven saw none of this from his travel route through the network of tunnels. His driver, a shearer on an all-terrain buggy, left him outside one of several trusted entrance points in the shaggy forest canopy. Knee-high boots to slosh through the old sewer lines and a single-strapped knapsack slung over his shoulder. Steven preferred to travel light, despite the snide remarks of his inner circle.

After nearly an hour on foot, Steven signaled his homing beacon application on his handheld. Within ten minutes, a faint glow up ahead emerged into the single-beamed headlight of Shore's scooter.

"Only one bag, that's pretty light for you! Not planning to stay too long?"

Predictable. "Never change, Shore." The sun had fully

set. Without Shore's headlight, the sky would have smothered them in blackness. Nothing was as black as Allentown after dark. Not the Foundries, not Ap-Oz, not his own eyelids when he slept.

"How was your meeting with Marribel?" Shore dimmed his beam.

"Pleasant as always. I told her we found evidence in the Sheppard ruins. She was almost disappointed."

Shore laughed. "Let's get upstairs first, then we can plan our vacation itinerary." The pair straddled the two-wheeled rig and sped along the corridor. Gliding on hydro-cell power, the pair could speak quietly and still hear each other, though they kept their words to a minimum. Gry did frequent sweeps for bugs, but it was just as well to be cautious. Without question, there was always someone with an ear open.

Once inside the elevator, the pair let down their guard as soon as the doors closed. Shore pulled the face of the button control panel open, touching two wires to close the circuit and start the ascent.

"Kenzy had a close call, you say." The report was vague, and Steven was eager to hear the details of her encounter with an informant of questionable motives and methods.

"Our examination of the parking garage tells us there were no natural or accidental gas leaks. So, it seems like our guy meant to knock out Kenzy and her team, but not harm them."

The elevator came to a halt at the fourth floor and the doors creaked open on rusty ball bearings. The two stepped into the 4-West hallway, littered with obsolete machine hulks and gurneys with rotting mattresses.

"Geez, you couldn't spare anyone to clean this up a little?" Steven pinched his nose to keep the smell of mold and mouse shit from clogging his sinuses.

Shore sighed. "You sent me excellent troops, but not

one of them's a housekeeper, by any stretch of the imagination!"

"Fair enough. Kenzy and her team, they're all okay?"

"Mild concussion from when she passed out, but otherwise she's okay. No lingering effects from the gas. We got lucky."

Luck had nothing to do with it. All of this was deliberate.

"Is she well enough to talk?"

"As long as you keep your voice low, I can tell you everything." Kenzy Wall peeked out from a dim-lit triage room. "And as long as I can sit down in here. Headache's still a bitch."

The three slipped into the room and Shore closed the door behind them. Kenzy hoisted herself onto an exam table that had been fitted with a clean mattress and linens. The Allens were kind enough to provide at least a few basics. Steven chose what would have been a doctor's chair while Shore remained standing near the door.

"If I had any pills, I'd say take two and go to bed." Kenzy smiled at his terrible joke.

"It's getting better. With any luck I'll be suited up for first light."

Shore shook his head. "No chance, Kenz. We've been over this."

Kenzy rolled her eyes. "Yes, *dad*."

She proceeded to fill Steven in on the details. Shore confirmed that the testimony had been recorded while Kenzy's memory was fresh. She woke from the attack to see her assailant crouching in front of her, only to deliver a message and walk away. No surveillance footage. It was as though the guy was a ghost.

"I was confused by one thing. My handheld moved from my right cargo pocket to the left sometime while I was out."

"So, he had your handheld, but didn't take it. Was he looking for something? Was anything downloaded?"

Kenzy nodded. "Downloaded, no. But there is a new file folder, the most recent timestamped file. I had never seen it before. The folder has an interesting name."

She offered her device to Steven. The top file name was just as puzzling to him.

<NULL>

"*Null.* What do you suppose that means?"

Kenzy shrugged. "I don't know. But what's inside is a little more telling."

Steven tapped the icon beside the file name. A litany of smaller documents and picture thumbnails spread downward, scrolling into a list three times the physical length of the tiny screen. All were labeled with indecipherable code.

"Where does a guy begin?" Scrolling back to the top, Steven tapped the first thumbnail. A still shot of a surveillance camera showed an intersection in what had to be Allentown, given the state of ruin of the buildings in the frame. He double-tapped the image and it bloomed into magnification. Several men in nondescript clothes not out of place in Allentown were in the shot. Shore leaned in over Steven's shoulder.

"Magnify once more and look carefully." One of the men was three-quarters facing in the direction of the camera. Steven narrowed his eyes to focus on the pixelated, grainy image.

The wide, tinted sunglasses couldn't hide the identity.

"Desantos. So, he *is* here."

"He is, and that's not all. If you start to go through the documents, there's everything from correspondence from Motherland, itineraries, right down to the food ration lists. They're at the National Bank. But specifically, *Paolo Desantos* is there."

The Null file was a smoking gun.

"One of the files is a communiqué, coded the same as Ennis Grant's handheld from the Sheppard Inn wreckage. It details a transition of command from Desantos to Captain Tomás Alvara—another prominent figure in the colonel's retinue. It appears Paolo is being relieved so he can finish a job he didn't complete the first time."

Finish the job...

The three words wailed in Steven's mind like a siren. He had promised Jason Holt that he wouldn't be gone more than seventy-two hours. That window of time had shortened drastically.

"We have to move on this, now." Steven rose from his chair. "Shore, mobilize the troops immediately, we're moving out within the hour."

"You mean all of us? Kenzy shouldn't be moving."

"All of us. We're not leaving anyone in the Grace."

Kenzy sat up. *"You are not safe in your home, major.* The informant had made it a point to say that."

Steven's eyes widened. House? The Grace was Capston's safe house in Allentown. They were not safe.

"Scratch that, captain. I want all personnel out of this building in ten minutes."

Eleven minutes later, a convoy of heavy boots tramped up the main arterial tunnel from under the Grace beneath what was on the surface a parking lot, fissured and overgrowing with invasive trees. Steven and Shore nearly came to blows over who exactly was going to stay in the rear with Kenzy during the evacuation. Gry volunteered before anything irrational could be said or done. Steven noticed Kenzy groan. He wasn't sure what bothered her more—the notion that someone was babysitting her, or that said babysitter was the fragrant John Gry. Still, Shore appeared satisfied, and he lapsed into command, charging off to lead the team deeper underground. A plan needed to be devised. Paolo Desantos may still be in the city. And if so, this was the best chance they were ever going to get to bring him in. The Null files contained enough evidence that even Jennings Marribel would have to listen. Explaining their presence in the forbidden city would have to wait.

The tunnels were, for the most part, wide enough for several people to walk abreast, with enough head clearance to jump without hitting the ceiling. Shore directed the twenty-strong Capston squad down a lesser tunnel to avoid any surprise encounters. Gry had only scouted so far into the lesser-traveled passages. It was obvious why.

Movement was agonizingly slow. Shore and the head of the line stopped frequently to clear obstacles. Steven shouted up the line to quicken the pace.

"We can't fit two side by side up here," Shore yelled back. Steven wasn't used to taking up the rear. He was less used to being helpless. A promise to keep an eye on Kenzy's wooziness justified the inconvenience.

The only sounds in the narrow duct were dripping water and sloshing boots in puddles. The squad only spoke when necessary, to direct someone around an obstacle or to offer a hand. According to the most reliable maps, Shore figured the squad would come out in a boiler room about two blocks northeast. Decommissioned before the bombardment, it was likely sealed off from the above building's street-level access. Steven eyed the scanning application on his handheld. No gas detection. Live electrical conduits ran parallel to the tunnel. Oxygen levels were stable. This might just work.

Kenzy stopped in her tracks, pressing her hands to her ears. "Do you hear that?"

Steven waved the troops on. "What are you hearing?" As the squad disappeared up the blackened corridor, he held his breath. A faint hum emerged from the silence in the form of a vibration. Closing his eyes, Steven concentrated on the sound. It could be a moving vehicle on the surface, likely several blocks away.

"I hear it, but it's faint. You must be feeling the vibration, concussions will do that to you."

Steven placed a hand on her shoulder and gestured Kenzy to kneel. Reaching into his knapsack, he retrieved pain medicine in the form of small white capsules. Kenzy swallowed three and took a long swig from her canteen.

"These should act quickly. Take the time you need, but when you're ready we need to catch up with the team."

The major squinted her eyes and nodded. "I can walk. Come on, Shore will be wondering where we are."

The lieutenant was a mother hen in the best of times. Steven motioned for Kenzy to follow close behind him. The hum was growing into a buzz, indicating the moving vehicle was approaching their position. Something wasn't right. The Allens never showed themselves topside, least of all in any moving vehicles without cover of night. Anyone occupying the city was likely doing so illegally, and therefore traveled as discreetly as possible. Whatever was moving up there was far from discreet.

"I don't like this." Steven pulled his handheld out and keyed his screen link to Shore. "Hayward, you hear that up above?"

Shore's voice didn't respond, but a texted reply appeared.

We hear it. 20 from the boiler. Clear way ahead.

Steven estimated he and Kenzy were about twenty meters back. "We're on our way, don't wait for us."

Copy that.

The buzz morphed into a rumble as the vehicle closed in, within a block of their current position. Kenzy moaned under her breath despite her best efforts to stay strong. A piercing alarm screeched in a high frequency, doubling the major over as she collapsed to her knees. Steven thumbed the tabs open on his handheld to determine the cause of the alert.

A surge in electrical power spiked on the status bar. Steven didn't have time to figure out the cause.

A muffled boom from the direction of the rumbling shook the tunnel enough for Steven to stagger, dropping his device into the puddle at his feet. Ahead, panicked screams echoed the length of the hallway. Kenzy released a pained cry before the shouting from up ahead turned to panic.

"Shore! Gry!" Steven hollered, unconcerned about the element of stealth for the moment. Incoherent barking and shouting were interspersed with cries for help.

"Collapse..." The only discernible word he could hear sank Steven's heart into his stomach. The tunnel was in complete blackness without his handheld lantern light. Homing in on Kenzy's cries, he lunged toward her position. His boot caught on some debris that still cluttered the hallway. Steven tumbled forward, instinctively reaching his hand to catch himself. In so doing, his right hand slashed across something as sharp as broken glass.

"Son of a *bitch*!" Rolling to his side, Steven clutched his right wrist. The slice was deep. Without his light, there was no chance he could keep the laceration closed, let alone clean.

A flash of light lit the hallway. Kenzy Wall was kneeling beside him, his dropped handheld in her gloved hand. "You looking for this?"

Steven nodded his appreciation. Kenzy fished the med

kit from his pack and wrapped his entire right hand in clean white gauze. "We're gonna have to get that closed up topside. Here."

Covering the cloth bandage with a rubbery water seal wrapping, Kenzy tied off the bandage and reached to help Steven to his feet. The pair looked at each other and silently agreed to press on. Within seconds they caught up to the rear of the squad.

"Steven! Kenzy!"

The booming voice of John Gry up ahead was a welcome noise. "Gry, what's happening up there?"

"Something went off on the street, enough to collapse the tunnel ahead of us. We're cut off from Shore. I think he has Swift up there with him. Can't hear anything."

Steven beckoned for his handheld. Toggling through the menu with his left hand proved difficult. With reluctance he allowed Kenzy to take it back. She was able to find the link to Shore with ease.

"Hayward, do you copy?"

Nothing.

"Lieutenant Shore? Do you copy? Acknowledge."

Still nothing. No text, no voice.

Ahead, the foremost squad troops clawed into the fallen debris. In the glow of his light, Steven saw several of his forces seated or kneeled while others tended to their head wounds. It would be a miracle if they all made it topside alive.

"How's your head, Kenzy?"

"You weren't kidding, those pills work fast." Kenzy typed with her thumbs.

```
Shore, if you receive this, make a noise.
We're coming. Hold on. K
```

"Somebody knew we were down here." Steven rested his injured right hand in the crook of his left elbow. The street above had fallen silent. "*Desantos*. He was tracking us."

Kenzy's informant had tried to warn them. A hundred photos and documents proved the Motherland lieutenant colonel was here in Allentown. This reeked of his handiwork.

And when I find you, Paolo Desantos, I will hurt you.

Creaking metal and crumbling stone echoed in the tunnel behind them. Whatever had exploded on the street above had caused more damage than Steven realized. Forgetting his lacerated hand, he grasped Kenzy by the arm as pain spiked up his own. The light on his handheld flickered, the electronics suffering from too much water exposure from its fall into the puddle. Sections of the wall loosed and caved as the ceiling split. Terror from his team members ahead reached a hollered crescendo before a massive section of the tunnel ceiling collapsed. Instinctively, Steven tugged Kenzy toward the wall.

He couldn't tell if his eyes were open or closed. There was indeed a blackness deeper than the Allentown night sky.

Ranger Man

Saturday, 16 June AC 0245
Holt Tower (Level 92), Capston, New Inland
Robbie Sheppard

After an extra-long lounge in the sauna, Robbie's legs were still tight. He was grateful that the lifts saved him from climbing thirty flights of stairs from the gymnasium level to the suites on Level 92. It was all he could do to stumble from the lifts into the living room. The minibar on the opposite wall was tempting, but the plush sofa halfway there would give his tired quadriceps some respite.

Just as he was before Robbie left, Cadlen was still curled up in his preferred corner, sketch pad in his lap while he gazed up at the floor-to-ceiling screen. The lights in the room were dimmed by half, as was the volume of the feature film he was watching.

"Mind if I watch with you for a while?"

Cadlen glanced at his brother and nodded. Robbie willed his tired legs to make it to the near end of the couch before flopping into the cushions. With one final effort, he swung both legs onto the middle space between them, his toes brushing against his baby brother's knee.

Robbie noticed the sketch pad was open to a blank page, and Cadlen's hands rested upon it without a pencil. "Movie must be good if you're not drawing!"

Cadlen raised his eyebrows. The look loosely translated to "I suppose."

The identifier bubble in the bottom right corner indicated *The Adventures of Ranger Man* was half over. It was just as well. Robbie didn't have the energy to start a three-hour show from scratch. Of course, he had to see the ending after five minutes of the titular hero in a gunfight with a Death Monk in a crumbling old building somewhere in the midwestern badlands.

Amazing how Ranger Man almost had a sixth sense, as if he knew where the bad guy was lurking around every corner. His pistol always had just one more bullet which never missed its mark. Robbie didn't bother asking Cadlen what happened earlier in the film. He got the gist of it. Agent Ranger Man was in hot pursuit of a gang of marauding criminals from the ranges of Sascota east toward the Great Lakes. The villains worked for a well-connected crime syndicate operating in the wilderness outside the safety of the Sascotan Federation.

What struck Robbie as Ranger Man closed in on his quarry was how dangerous the world outside the domed walls could be. Within an hour, the agent needed to administer a cocktail of medication to combat airborne viruses, fend off bandits wielding clubs and spears, and even fight a ravenous, scraggly lone wolf. Sure enough, just when the jaws of the mad dog were about to gnash his face, the bullet from his smoking gun saved the day. At least that day.

"Ranger Man has it all, doesn't he, Cad?"

Cadlen had begun to sketch the hero of the film. In his drawing, the swashbuckling agent wore similar cargo-style pants, his trusty gun holstered in a leather strap dangling below the waist. His shirt was slashed from the wolf attack, revealing a cut physique replete with scars from his previous adventures. The eyes were fierce, as though he could stare down any threat.

"Ranger Man saves the day; in case you were wondering." Lorrie sauntered out of the lifts and over to the edge of the couch. "This has been played twice today already."

"Thanks for spoiling it for me. Where have you been?"

"My last booking for the longboard track was today. Figured I'd take advantage since Holt's probably gonna kick us out."

Robbie was surprised by Lorrie's comment. Did Jason tell Lorrie what he had overheard him saying to Mayor Reekan?

"Who told you that, Lor?"

Lorrie crooked his neck. "What do you mean who told me? I was just saying, he'll probably want us to leave after all that crap with the video cameras."

Robbie sighed to himself. There was no point in his brothers worrying about something they couldn't control. It might have only been just Jason blowing off steam. Robbie had been behind the heavy sauna door, and he only heard a few words before the pair had moved out of earshot.

"Hold on, Robbie. What have *you* heard?"

Robbie tried to feign ignorance, but Lorrie was on to him.

"Spill it, brother. What's going to happen to us?"

Ranger Man had the villain at gunpoint, back against a wall. Robbie sympathized with the bad guy.

"I overheard Steven and Jason arguing. Mr. Holt wants them to move us out of the tower. Mayor Reekan told me that he wants to move us to a secret base somewhere down south."

Lorrie opened his arms wide in disgust. "So, you can't trust either of them! Figured as much. Just wait till Clara Connelly finds out, she won't be too happy about leaving."

"Jason didn't mention the Connellys. Just us."

Lorrie exploded. "Just the Sheppard kids! Because *of course*, he wants to keep Clara around. I mean, no one would recognize her with her clothes on, right?"

Robbie stood, the ache in his thighs shooting as soon as his feet touched the floor. "Calm down. We don't know anything yet, it's all just hearsay."

"That's right. But not for long. I want some answers—and I bet my longboard I know where to find that asshole."

Lorrie stormed to the lifts. Robbie made to pursue him, but the stiffness kept him from reaching his furious brother before the lift doors slid shut.

Back on the big screen, Ranger Man had taken into custody the villain who had confessed his sins in a last stand hailing in bullets. Robbie was glad Lorrie didn't carry a gun. He didn't like the quarry's chances otherwise.

Less Than Nothing

Saturday, 16 June SC 0245
Holt Tower (Level 91), Capston, New Inland
Lorrie Sheppard

Nobody is looking out for us.

Lorrie Sheppard charged down the wide arterial corridor of the 91st level. Uniformed officers emerged from and vanished behind doors, some to offices and others to unmarked suites. The Connelly family, after a major ruckus, were moved from the 92nd level into the smaller cluster of living suites when Clara Connelly had insisted they be stationed closer to the security level. It didn't add up to much. There, the hacker still managed to cut into the video feed in Clara's private suite, broadcasting her goods for all to ogle.

Through a set of double doors, Lorrie pushed into the living quarters on the south wing. The corridor narrowed to one that reminded him of the Sheppard Inn. He could have laid across the floor and touched both the odd and even door number sides. 9188N was the destination.

Toes to the edge of the door frame, Lorrie pounded his fist three times without even trying the handle. After a few seconds, he repeated the rhythm. *I know you're in there.*

From the inside, a latch clicked and a bolt slid. Lorrie turned the handle and shoved the door inward. Clara Connelly was dressed in a snug-fitting evening dress, her hair curled on the ends and loose over her plunging neckline.

"Where is he?" Lorrie barked and Clara backed a step away.

"Warren and his father are upstairs, you know that." Clara appeared confused. Lorrie brushed past her into the suite.

"I'm not here for Warren." Lorrie panned around the room. The scene was all too familiar. "They really mean it when they say it always looks bigger on camera."

Clara blushed and crossed her arms over her cleavage. "There's no one here, Lorrie, so if you don't mind—"

"I don't mind at all. If Holt's not here now, he'll be coming soon, won't he? You're all dressed for the part."

"How dare you barge into my room and talk to me like this? Maybe your brother puts up with that, but it doesn't work like that with me!" Clara tossed her hair to the side and gestured to the open door. "Now get out before I call Captain Ling."

"Call Captain Ling! Just as well she be here for the show!"

The en suite door opened. "That's about enough, Lorrie."

Jason Holt stepped into the main living space; his sport coat tucked under his arm. "If you have something to say to me, let's have this conversation elsewhere. Mrs. Connelly has nothing to do with any of this."

Lorrie's mouth began to dry as he searched for his opening salvo. The words he rehearsed all along the way to Clara's door were jumbled and fragmented when he needed them to be clear. He cleared his throat.

"I know what you said to Reekan. You want us out of here."

Jason sighed. "I don't know who told you what, but there's a huge misunderstanding."

"Is there? Because it's pretty clear to me that you want us out of your ivory tower—but you're in no hurry to throw your new toy away, now are you?"

Clara Connelly swung her open hand and slapped

Lorrie in the cheek, nearly sending him to the floor. "You little bastard!"

Jason lunged forward, restraining Clara from following up with a second swing. Lorrie backed deeper into the room, holding his hand to the stinging skin of his face.

"Call Ling! I'll have you charged with assault!"

"You're not going to charge anyone with *anything*, you little shit!" Jason shielded Clara as he stepped to Lorrie. "That's the problem with you. Always shooting your mouth off, but it's all a bunch of nothing! Well, let me tell you, Sheppard, you're *less* than nothing—outside my building, *you're not even alive!*"

Lorrie's eyes welled and his fists clenched. He came this close to throwing punches only once before, when Troy taunted him for losing in a city-wide two years ago. He knew he wasn't going to hit the tattooed longboarder that day. But this was different.

"Leave him alone, Jason!" Robbie's voice broke Lorrie's focus. His big brother was standing behind Clara in the doorway. Captain Ling bustled into the room and around everyone until she was standing directly between Jason and Lorrie.

"That's enough, you two. Lorrie, you're done here."

The captain was several inches shorter than Lorrie, but she wielded an immense presence. Disarmed by her command, Lorrie loosened his fists as a tear slipped from the corner of his eye.

"This isn't done." Lorrie seethed over the captain at Jason, himself disarmed by the commotion and unwanted attention. Robbie moved into the room and reached for his arm. Lorrie shook his brother's hand away.

"I need to pack anyway. Might as well take my chances out on the street—if I'm already dead, what's the worst that can happen, right?"

Captain Ling motioned for Clara and Jason to retreat

into the living room away from the exit. She turned to Jason. "We have a deal. Seventy-two hours. I can't do anything here until I talk to Steven."

"I don't give a shit where Steven is, the deal is off. You do what you have to do, Ling, but I want this little fuck out of here this time tomorrow!"

It was all coming apart. No point holding back now.

"You gonna send Warren too? And Charles, so you can have your piece of tail to yourself?"

"Get him out of here!" Clara shrieked, and Ling summoned a guard to restrain Jason who was frothing at the mouth. Robbie grabbed Lorrie by the shoulders.

"Enough, Lorrie!" His brother shook him, making his neck buckle. "Not another word!"

Lorrie never heard Robbie holler with such anger before. Of all the things he had said and done without consequence. It came as a surprise when Robbie released him and turned back to Jason Holt.

"Mr. Holt, this *little fuck* isn't going anywhere without me." Lorrie's eyes widened at the sound of his brother swearing.

"Suits me fine. The three of you are gone this time tomorrow, or I'll remove you from the premises myself."

Clara began to protest. "Jason, let Cadlen stay. He's no part of this."

"Cad's seen enough of *you* for a lifetime. We all have! He's better off with his family!"

For the first time in the commotion, Lorrie's thoughts turned to Crystal. There had to be a way the Sheppard brothers could be sent to Hyacynthe. Monsieur Laurent could make it happen. Lorrie's grudge against his sister paled in comparison to his loathing of Jason Holt and Clara Connelly.

Hyacynthe would have to be a safer option than wherever Steven Reekan was planning to move them. Secret base down south, Robbie said. *Outside,* where diseases, criminals, and wild animals were waiting. Ranger Man was only a character. He didn't exist. He never existed. What chance did they have on the outside?

Lorrie imagined his body heaped on the back of a Reaper salvage wagon. Robbie lying in the mud, covered with sores. Cadlen in shackles, stuffed in a shipping crate by Le Renard and sold out West. The reality of the situation was beginning to sink in.

"I'm sorry, Robbie..."

Robbie glowered at Jason one last time before turning back to him. "Come on, we have to pack."

The Panic Room

Monday, 18 June AC 0245
The Catacombs, Allentown
Private Mott Wrengel

<NULL>
The way is filthy, but the reward will be worth it.

The man with the shiny apple had transmitted instructions to Private Mott Wrengel's handheld device. He was to take a winding path through a labyrinth of tunnels, some narrow enough he had to crawl through stagnant, muddy water and rodent shit. Mott imagined has father, clutching his throat as he suffocated to death on invisible toxins, writhing in worse, deep below ground. Paolo Desantos was responsible. According to the information the stranger had sent him, anyway. It didn't really matter, in the end. Mott quaked in fear whenever the lieutenant colonel walked by. So did everyone else. A lot of good men didn't come home from the march west, and Mott still had to carry water by the gallons every day.

As a young ward, Mott held Paolo in reverence. By the time he had enlisted, that had changed to fear. As he wiped muck from his face, crawling on his belly toward Paolo Desantos's private quarters, it had distorted into hatred.

Emerging from the narrow crawl space into a corridor through a broken duct grate, the private stretched his fingers until they were tangled in cobwebs. Dim, yellow lights allowed him to see the length of the hallway, which ended at a steel door, slightly ajar and emitting blackness. Every step closer quickened his heart rate. He closed his eyes and remembered the directions.

Once through the steel door, shut it tightly behind you.

Expecting it to creak on heavy, rusted hinges, Mott was surprised and relieved that it closed silently. The bolt clicked, and a silence he had never experienced before took his breath away as he fumbled for his handheld. There was a light switch somewhere near the entrance. In a panic, he dropped his device to the floor. It clattered in a tinny echo. Mott waved his arms around, smashing his right wrist into the door. Collecting himself, he slid his uninjured hand along the smooth wall until the switch met his fingers.

The room lit up like a sunspot burst, causing the private to squint until he could refocus on the small chamber. It was a tin box big enough for one occupant, confirmed by the single cot adjacent to a tiny kitchenette and a privy, open for anyone to see. Granted, there wouldn't be any need for extra privacy in a room so small.

Mott imagined that this space was nothing like Paolo Desantos's private quarters.

The privates used to speculate what they looked like. Most expected them to be lavish, decorated with art from his many travels all over the countryside. Some guessed he slept in hyperbaric capsules instead of a bed. Mott always expected a more modest design, with exercise equipment, cupboards stocked with high-nutrient foods, and maybe a small fireplace.

But this was little more than a temporary shelter. It was deep enough underground that bombardment wouldn't be able to penetrate it. There were enough supplies for one person to wait out whatever forced them to hide for weeks. Mott had heard of bomb shelters like these existing throughout the maze of tunnels beneath the ruined city. What better place to stage his next move?

In the closet, you will find a pressed uniform. Put it on.

Fortunately, his handheld hadn't shattered; only the outer covering had come apart when he'd dropped it in the smothering darkness. Mott set it on the edge of the cot and opened the double-doored closet. Sure enough, Motherland military fatigues, neatly pressed, hung on hangers. The patchwork of camouflage would offer little protection in the deep gray and black of the catacombs. He would have been better off wearing all black.

He wasn't being paid for his opinion. Mott peeled out of his muddy, soaked cargo pants and shirt, removing his undergarments until he stood naked in front of the wardrobe. He closed his eyes and breathed, using the calming exercises he was taught as a ward. It was the first thing he did when he learned his father had died. The pangs of loss always returned, but the gentle, rhythmic breathing allowed him to stay within himself until the pain subsided. Three deep exhalations through his lips, seeping like a gas leak, and he opened his eyes.

Once he put on the uniform, he would no longer be Private Mott Wrengel.

First the underlayers, light and snug-fitting, then the pants, buckled at the waist. The jacket was next. The buttons slipped through their holes, and the fabric, creased from pressing, conformed to his body shape as though it were measured for him. A beret worn in ceremony by the higher command enveloped his tied hair. Last, boots that shined better than he could ever make his own. He crisscrossed the laces up his shins until he tied them in taut bows.

Mott turned to the mirror on the inside of the left door of the wardrobe. As he met his own eyes in the reflection, he swallowed hard. From beret to boots, the image in the mirror caused him to shiver. The family name strip above the left breast pocket wasn't *Wrengel* reflecting backwards. He doubted that anyone who wore the *Desantos* name struggled with as much anxiety.

The rucksack by the door is packed. Read the map. Leave your device.

Mott slung the rucksack over his arm. One more round of rhythmic breathing, and he would exit the bomb shelter through the silent steel door. He knew he had to leave his handheld behind, in the event he was apprehended before he could finish the job. Failure wasn't an option.

The last message Mott Wrengel read before he switched off the device was the last nudge he needed.

Your father would be proud.

Harbinger

Tomás never liked traveling through the Allegheny foothills pass. Too much exposure. Bottlenecked between two plateaus, Motherland troops would be prime targets for any snipers worth their salt. He would have preferred to travel through the snaking foothills, but it would have been on foot. His Eminence De Léon was insistent that the transition of command in Allentown happen right away. Tomás agreed. Whatever it takes to get a face-to-face meeting with the lieutenant colonel.

The procession of three all-terrain rigs crawled over the uneven trails, sloshing fresh mud into twin tire tracks. The fat, deep-treaded tires pushed over protruding boulder points, jostling Tomás and his driver in the caged frame open to the elements. There was safety in staying in the middle of the pack, but he could have done without the exhaust from the lead rig blowing into his face. The cadre of armed escorts in the trailing rig monitored movement within view of the pass, which made Tomás feel a little safer. This journey was anything but stealthy. Motherland shouldn't have to lurk in the shadows, anyway.

With the narrowest stretch behind them, the road smoothed out somewhat, and the caravan doubled its speed. Winding through sparse communities, they encountered few people. Most were gawking from run-down cottages or from behind ruins. Motherland had exerted its influence along the pass, occupying or looting communities that posed any threat. The few towns that resigned to Motherland hegemony in their regions were left intact, usually vassals to the foppish sovereign of the walled city north and west beyond the Alleghenies.

"Sir, one mark dead ahead. He's not moving."

Past the desolation of a settlement overgrown with vegetation and sickly spindles of dead trees, one man stood, his back to the approaching caravan. Hooded by a long overcoat that dragged in the mud, the unidentifiable figure was indifferent to the approaching motorcade. Tomás raised his right fist and the three rigs stopped about a hundred feet from the cloaked figure.

"Scanners, report."

"Nothing, sir. Just this guy. Your orders?"

He's alone, it would seem, anyway. Tomás angled over the side of the buggy, his boots sinking past the soles and into the muck. Motioning his two fingers to his eyes, the snipers raised their sights on the figure in the road. Halfway between the lead rig and the stranger, he called out.

"We wish you no harm, villager. Kindly step off the trail so we can pass without incident."

The cloaked figure did not respond and did not turn to face him. The earbud buzzed. "On your mark, sir?"

Tomás raised an open hand signaling the snipers to wait. "My good man, if you please."

The figure turned then, revealing he was not in fact a "he" at all. A woman with chin-length, neat brown hair drew back her hood.

"Greetings, Captain Alvara, to Allentown city limits."

The city itself was still out of view, if only because the towering buildings of long ago lay in ruins below the tree line. Tomás estimated it would be another three hours at reduced speed before they'd reach the Nat Bank block. So long as their greeting party didn't hold them up much longer.

"Madam Allen, I presume. To what do we owe this welcome?"

The Allen agent strode toward Tomás, whose hand was still in the air to keep his itchy-fingered snipers at bay. "You can tell your shooters that I am unarmed. I'm sure your scanners can confirm I am alone, as well."

"Stand down." Tomás heard the relaxing of the guard behind him and he dropped his arm. "I am ordered to relieve the commander of our garrison. I trust our arrangement is in good standing?"

Madam Allen smiled. "I am happy to hear of the exchange, captain. Your predecessor has conducted himself in a... concerning manner."

Tomás raised an eyebrow. "Is that so?"

"Lieutenant Colonel Desantos has been an exemplary guest, until recently. He ordered a drone strike against your foes in the south side. As you know, this violates the Allen agreement with Motherland within our territory."

This bit of news came as a surprise. Paolo was very meticulous in everything. If he launched an offensive in violation of an agreement with the Allens, it had to have been necessary.

Or was it finally a lapse in judgment? A kink in his unassailable armour?

"I can assure you that my mandate is to surveil, not to strike. When I speak with the lieutenant colonel, I will learn of his motives."

Madam Allen smiled again, something agents didn't often do. "*If* you speak with him, you should say. Paolo Desantos enjoys his solitude."

That's an understatement. The man is antisocial.

"He remains in the city, does he not?" Tomás felt his bile rising. He had better not be gone already.

The agent nodded. "He does. Paolo keeps to his private quarters in the Nat Bank sublevel, as I'm sure you're aware. You should know, captain, that you are not the only one seeking him lately."

Really?

"Could this be the reason for his offensive maneuvers?"

Madam Allen shrugged her caped shoulders. "Perhaps. I'm not at liberty to say."

Her answer was as good as an affirmation. "A preemptive strike against Reekan, I would guess. Casualties of the drone attack?"

"Unknown."

Leave it to Paolo to plan an attack, only to fail. At least a drone wouldn't result in Motherland casualties.

"Unless you have other news to deliver, Madam Allen, we would continue on our way in all haste. I have many questions for the lieutenant colonel before he leaves."

"Indeed. But I would ask that you retreat below ground before you enter the city grid. We implore all our guests to refrain from surface travel."

It was just as well. The sublevels in the city's north end were easily passable for the motorcade, directly to the blocks surrounding the Nat Bank. Besides, Tomás was nervous to rankle any further feathers with his hosts. The Allens were uncomfortable business partners. Colonel Tirel Desantos's vision of a Motherland strong enough to rid the consortium from the ghost city made the temporary arrangement acceptable.

"Very well, madam. We are grateful for your information."

"Safe travels, Captain Alvara. May you relieve Desantos quickly. I fear for his safety."

The Allen agent drew her hood and strode off the trail into the dead heath. As the caravan continued on its way, Tomás nodded his appreciation to the agent. In her draped trappings, she almost looked like a Reaper, skulking in the dying thicket of a forgotten settlement. This assignment was beneath him. At first, he was to keep Paolo's seat warm. It had become a clean-up job.

Once below ground, Tomás was more assured of the rest of the journey. The access to the sublevel was through an old garage bay, built after the Allentown bombardment as a clandestine point of entry. Dozens of such access points were available if you knew where to find them. What appeared to the unexpecting eye to be a service bay for petrol automobiles was in fact a ramp that led beneath the ground into a complex system of old sewers and service corridors. As in the ransacked villages along the pass, some meandering vagabonds poked around corners, the high beams of the lead rig exposing their dirty faces and saucer eyes. They skittered away like the rest of the tunnel rats.

The caravan crawled to an idling stop at the checkpoint of a junction in the tunnels. The guards raised their flashlights to confirm the identities of the arriving squad. Emerging from a windowed office, a ranking officer strode toward the second rig. Tomás climbed over the door as the sergeant saluted.

"At ease, sergeant…"

"Staff Sergeant Sylvio, sir. Welcome back to Allentown."

Tomás hated small talk, especially with inferior officers. "Direct us to the National Bank. I will speak with the lieutenant colonel immediately."

"Yes sir. He spends most of his time in his quarters. We have not seen him for several days, but I can confirm he is there."

Several days?

"Who authorized the drone strike in the South End, Sergeant Sylvio?"

The staff sergeant tilted his head. "Drone strike, sir?"

His instinct was to chastise the officer for his ignorance. Tomás considered the source of his intelligence. A lone, hooded Allen agent in the middle of the road, a harbinger of the misdeeds of Paolo Desantos.

And yet, Sylvio here was oblivious. There's no way even the lower-ranked officers wouldn't know about it.

"Listen, sergeant. I want confirmation one way or another that a land drone did or did not detonate in the south side of Allentown somewhere near the Grace Hospital complex. And I want that scrolling across my handheld within the hour. Now, point me to the Nat Bank."

Sylvio straightened into a salute. "Sir, yes sir. Left flank, five-point-five kilometers north-northeast, sir."

Tomás climbed back into his rig and signaled for his driver to proceed. "One more thing, sergeant. Has anyone else gone down the left flank recently?"

The officer shook his head. "Not that I have been told, sir."

It didn't mean much. There were more narrow tunnels and ducts ranging out from the bank that anyone as small as an adolescent boy could wriggle through, if they were so determined. Tomás nodded and returned a salute to the guards and the sergeant before his cavalcade continued down the left flank of the junction.

Not five minutes later, the corridor shook hard enough for Tomás to fall out of his seat. A deafening boom caused his heartbeat to throb in his chest and his ears to ring as though he had been struck with a blunt object. All three rigs ground to a halt as the lighting in the corridor flickered into darkness. Falling dirt became raining pebbles of concrete before chunks of the ceiling dislodged in the quake of the explosion.

"Full retreat!" Tomás waved to the rear rig which had already shifted into reverse. The tunnel was not wide enough to affect a three-point turn. The three vehicles whined as their transmissions strained to reverse at the highest possible escape speed. Tomás glanced behind to see an increasing orange glow. They had seconds before a wall of fire would rush upon them, incinerating every unfortunate soul still below ground. It wasn't supposed to end this way. He would have held the Allentown garrison steady for a few months, little more. Colonel Desantos would praise him for his command, and the promotion he deserved would finally be bestowed. Tomás Alvara was not meant to die like a rat in the sewers of a ruined city.

Closing his eyes as the rig buzzed in its retreat, another colossal boom echoed through the corridor, only this time the orange glow fell into blackness. The soldiers in the rear rig began to holler more loudly. Tomás opened his eyes and turned again to face the lead rig.

It was gone.

A massive section of the tunnel ceiling had collapsed, flattening the rig and all but sealing the corridor from the surging flames. Rays of natural light strained into the tunnel as wafting smoke billowed through the debris pile. Heat washed into the conduit as Tomás pulled his jacket over his head.

As the rumble settled and the rigs slowed, flashing beams of light from the guards at the junction darted alongside the remaining two vehicles. Staff Sergeant Sylvio jumped into Tomás's rig, enveloping him in a heavy blanket.

"Sir, can you hear me, sir?"

His ears rang, but he could make out the sergeant just fine. As he looked up, his head spun.

"Report, sergeant!"

Sylvio swallowed hard. "Sir, it's the National Bank. *It's gone!* The whole city block. *It's all gone!*"

Strange Bedfellows

Wednesday, 20 June AC 0245
The Catacombs, Allentown
Mayor Steven Reekan

Steven Reekan felt the goose egg on his forehead for any trace of blood. In the sheer darkness of the collapsed chamber, he could only guess how close he came to being flattened by a chunk of the ceiling. As he shifted his legs, relieved that his extremities all responded, broken rocks clattered around him. He pulled the collar of his undershirt over his nose to filter the remaining air of the chalky dust. Slow and steady, he breathed through his nostrils to calm his heartbeat.

After a moment, Steven called for the major in a croaked and parched gasp: "Kenzy?" He remembered grabbing her wrist and yanking as the ceiling cracked and the walls split. Whether or not she was able to dodge the collapse was too heavy for him to guess. Flexing his fingers, he felt a shot of pain sear from his right hand. Kenzy had bandaged his hand as best she could after he'd fallen and lacerated it on a piece of glass or sharp rock. He never did figure out which. It was meant to be a temporary fix. By now, the team should have been blocks away, in a subterranean chamber John Gry had already checked and secured. Steven and Kenzy had been separated from Gry and the rest of the team after the second collapse. There were screams of horror ahead of them in the tunnels before the blackness washed over him and the major. They could all be dead.

Touching the bandage with his free index finger, Steven felt liquid pooling. The entire wrapping was soaked. Touching the tip of his finger to his tongue, the rusty tang of blood made him wince. The laceration needed stitches. He had never performed an emergency suturing in the field on anyone, let alone himself, but it was moot without his backpack. It had fallen as he lunged, and with no light source, he had to assume it was lost. Along with the emergency first aid supplies, his rations and gas detection reader were gone, as well.

Steven closed his eyes. If the wound continued to bleed profusely, he'd be gone sooner than later. He wondered if it was better to survive the loss of his team than to join them in the blackness. A pang of sorrow welled in his belly, drowning out the pain of his injuries.

"*Steven.*" A voice echoed as though it were whispering into an open barrel. Kenzy must be dead. This had to be his mind playing tricks on him. He had heard that those close to death often hallucinated.

"Steven!"

That was no hallucination.

A rustling sound no more than a few meters away snapped Steven out of his pessimism. She was alive and moving freely nearby. It sounded like hands and knees shuffling.

"Kenzy, are you hurt?"

"There's no time, we have to move. Now."

A hand felt around on his arm until fingers gripped the tattered sleeve of his uniform. She tugged in a gesture for him to help himself.

"Gas levels are rising quickly. If we stay here, we'll suffocate." Kenzy's voice was determined, but there was a hint of panic in her words.

Cradling his injured right hand to his chest, Steven leveraged himself to his knees. "Lead the way," Steven acquiesced to the major.

"There's a breach in the wall, small but not too small for you to make it. There's a duct on the other side. It leads deeper beneath ground, but away from the gas." Kenzy's voice rattled from inhaling too much concrete dust. Without another word, she shuffled through the breach. Steven dragged himself with his good hand into a narrow crevasse, feeling his shirt rip, just beneath the breast pocket, on a jagged edge.

Shimmying into the duct, he vowed to himself that he would lose ten pounds if they survived.

The duct was a tube, its diameter just snug enough that he could crouch on three of all fours if he didn't arch his back. Keeping his injured hand elevated as high as possible, he leaned into the curvature of the tubular duct and pull himself forward, awkwardly at first before establishing a rhythm. Kenzy's boots were never more than half a meter ahead of him.

"Keep going, Kenzy, I'll catch up." Steven leaned his upper body weight into his shoulder as he tore the fabric from his uniform from the breast pocket. Wrapping what he could manage around his bad hand, he breathed deep and pressed on. Kenzy hadn't moved forward without him.

"The duct is pretty clean, at least as far as I got," Kenzy answered. "Keep moving, we have a way to go yet."

The pair slogged forward for what felt like an hour before Kenzy came to a halt and Steven's forehead collided with the sole of her boot. "There's a grate. This is our stop!"

In the black, a metallic rattle gave way to a squeal of snapped hinges. Kenzy grunted before a clattering beyond the exit echoed in the distance. Steven had seen people demonstrate surges in strength in moments of desperation. He wasn't sure if his lack of eyesight was causing him to feel disoriented, or if the gas was slowly poisoning him.

Kenzy wriggled through the broken vent feet first, her

boot soles falling to a floor of some sort. "I'm standing up straight, Steven. Find the opening and reach, I'll guide you through."

"You're the boss, major." As he maneuvered his legs backwards through the hole, Steven smiled. Kenzy Wall had grown so much since she joined his security team. She was small, but fit. Quiet, but insightful. Compassionate, but strong. Men and women with twice her experience and training could learn a lot from her.

Steven's boots hit the floor with a thud and his knees buckled. Instinctively, he reached for the wall to support himself with his injured hand, opening it wide and spreading the laceration apart.

"Son of a *bitch*!" Steven groaned, closing his right fist and tucking it back to his chest. Staggering in the darkness, he teetered forward, each step of his thick-soled boots stamping onto the concrete floor heavier than the last.

"Steven, be careful." Kenzy's warning came just as his shins smashed into an iron brace of some sort, toppling him forward. As if it mattered, he closed his eyes. He imagined stepping over the edge of the Hanging Gardens, plummeting through the artificial atmosphere as buildings whisked past, crashing through the ground level into the Foundries where he would surely burn in the molten smelters. Time stood still for half a second.

He kept his wounded hand close to his heart and scrunched his nose, expecting it to break upon impact. He didn't know what to think when, instead of the fires down below, his face was greeted with a plush mattress.

Steven only knew he was waking up because a faint, pinkish hue filtered through his closed eyelids. They twitched, unwilling to part for the invasive light. He moved his toes, free to wiggle without heavy boots on. Inhaling, he shifted his shoulders in the mattress before realizing he was under a thin but heavy blanket. Steven flexed his left hand into a fist and relaxed it again, not daring to do the same with his injured hand.

"It's about time you woke up, lazy bones!" Kenzy's voice was much cleaner and calmer than the last time he heard her speak. His eyelids opened like Velcro straps as the light in the room assaulted his senses.

"How long..." Moving his head side to side, Steven shifted beneath the blanket. As his vision came into focus, he saw that the light was much dimmer than he expected. He was lying down on a narrow cot, covered almost to his chin. He peeled the blanket aside, revealing his injured right hand completely cleaned and bandaged, fastened in a sling to his chest.

"Whatever you do, don't tinker with your bandages." Kenzy sat on a small stool at the side of his bed. "It took most of the clean gauze to clean that up. If you're lucky, the infection stabilized—but I'm no doctor."

Steven dropped his legs over the edge of the cot and forced himself upright. "Where are we?" He scanned the room. The walls were deep gray and riveted panel to panel, floor to ceiling. There was only one cot, leading Steven to assume Kenzy had slept on the concrete. The room was lit with sunken pot lights, only half of which had working bulbs. He spotted a small kitchenette with cupboards, open shelves with jars and boxes, and what looked like a cooking surface with two coiled burners. Moving adjacent, an armoire with one door ajar revealed hanging clothes. A thin, wrought iron ladder climbed the wall beside it to a round hatch in the ceiling.

"I'm not sure, but I think it's a bomb shelter." Kenzy looked up at the ceiling hatch. "And before you ask, I tried, and it's barred shut. Too much corrosion in the hinge, maybe."

"But the gas levels—"

Kenzy shook her head. "The power cells I found were

low but had enough juice to top off my reader. We're safe here. There's enough ventilation—from *where*, I don't know, but we've been here almost forty-eight hours and the air is still coming."

Steven made to stand up, but Kenzy pressed down on his shoulder. "Stay put, you've still got a lot of medicine in you, and you just woke up."

"Bomb shelter," he muttered. It made sense. Allentown's turbulent past only made it logical for people to prepare for the worst, which of course had arrived with a vengeance over a lengthy conflict. How long this particular shelter had remained intact was the question.

"How did you manage to find an unused bomb shelter?"

Kenzy laughed. "Who said it was unused?" She reached under the cot and retrieved a human skull so clean it could have been a model. Startled, Steven flinched.

"Meet your roommate, Steve." Kenzy levered the jaw up and down. *"Why do you have to hog the sheets, roomie!"*

"You mean..."

"Yup, our friend here was on the cot. Don't worry, I flipped the mattress and changed the linens."

"Lovely." Steven forced himself to his feet and immediately regretted it.

"You really are stubborn," Kenzy said. "Between the gas, the loss of blood, the medicine, and the lack of food, I'm amazed you can even stand up."

Food. His stomach grumbled. "What have you been eating?"

"Freeze-dried rations, without water. A little dry but at least nutritious." Kenzy walked to the kitchenette and retrieved two thin packets. "Your choice—beef stroganoff or chicken gumbo. I'd pick the chicken, personally."

Tearing the top seam free, Steven funneled the

chicken gumbo packet above his mouth and swallowed the contents. Powdered broth and bits that had the consistency of cardboard stuck to his tongue and the roof of his mouth. He summoned as much saliva as he could.

"No water, eh?"

Kenzy shook her head. "There's enough humidity that we can make condensation. That'll be enough for us to get by for now. There was a jug, but I tested the water. No good."

There were enough ration packets in the kitchenette to last several more days. The prior occupant had consumed some, evidenced by the litter he had left behind in a wastebasket. He must have died from an illness of some sort. Steven wondered if it was red tide, and if the virus was strong enough to survive without a host all these years.

"So, how do we get out of here?" Steven thought about the rest of his team. Shore, Gry—all of them were surely dead. But then again, here they were, he and Kenzy, not only alive, but on the mend, if only trapped underground. The fact that the Allens hadn't found them almost three days later dampened his spirits. If *they* hadn't found them, no one would.

"Still working on that." Kenzy pulled her handheld from her pocket. "I tried to bring yours back to life, but no luck. Mine, though, has a little life yet. I'm working on the homing beacon, but it's still offline."

Three days, and no one had found them beneath the streets of Allentown. Not Shore, not Gry, not the Allens.

Not Desantos.

Desantos. He must have tried to blow up the Grace Hospital, but the bomb went off early. "Kenzy, can you still access the <NULL> files?"

"I think so, but I need all the power I have left. Why?"

Steven reached out his good hand. His bandaged right hand tingled from the antibiotics doing their job. "That guy who attacked you, what did he say again?"

"He said, *you're not safe in your house,*" Kenzy murmured. "Whoever it was, he gave us all the evidence we needed to go after Paolo Desantos. He must have known that Paolo was going to take out the Grace."

Steven tore the seam of the beef packet. "He was warning you. Not safe in your *house*. What does he mean by 'house' though?"

Kenzy squinted. "I mean, the Grace is our safe house in Allentown. What else could he have meant?"

Steven's police and security headquarters were the only safe house he could think of, on the 90 levels of Holt Tower. Yet, a hacker had proven quite effectively that the Jewel of Capston might not be as safe as anyone thought. Jason Holt was certainly spooked.

He titled the packet back and swallowed the brown powdered ration. "He meant just that—we weren't safe in the Grace. So, what does he do? He sets off a bomb nearby to scare us away. Does that sound familiar?"

Kenzy gulped. "Holt Tower."

For the first time since he woke up on the dead man's cot, Steven felt a wave of panic. It was starting to make sense. "How do you flush someone out of a place as big and secure as Holt Tower? You hack into the closed circuit and *show* them that you can." The footage of the Capston bombings, leading up to the Sheppard Family Inn—that was a warning.

Seventy-two hours. That was Jason Holt's ultimatum. Steven nearly wretched the years-old powdered rations onto the floor.

"Kenzy, Holt gave us three days to move the Sheppards, and that would be *today*! What if Ling doesn't think we're alive? If none of us survived, she's in command!"

"And if Jason follows through, she'll have no choice but to move the Sheppards and Connellys to Ap-Oz..." Her words trailed off as though she forbade thought of concluding the likely course of action.

"Which is exactly what someone trying to silence witnesses would want to do. *Get them out of Holt Tower.*"

The bomb shelter, which had saved their lives, at once became a prison. "We have to get out of here, major, or at least communicate with the Allens. Or else the Sheppards and Connellys are as good as dead."

Promise

Friday, 22 June AC 0245
Holt Tower (Level 93), Capston, New Inland
Cadlen Sheppard

"Cadlen... Cadlen..."

There was no light to strain through his grainy, sleep-encrusted eyes. The very act of opening his eyes came with the pressure of a headache, as though he had only slept for an hour or so. At 3:00 AM, he couldn't imagine anyone being awake by choice.

Recognizing his sister's voice made it painful. Realizing why she was waking him was worse.

"I'm so sorry, little brother. I don't have much time, so I wanted to say goodbye."

Crystal was sitting along the edge of his mattress, lumpy and uneven yet contoured to his small body shape. Cadlen arched his shoulders and stretched as he blinked to consciousness. His cotton pajama shirt was rumpled under his arm. Robbie had given him one size too big. He was still figuring out how to be a dad.

Cadlen propped himself on his left elbow. He thought it was tomorrow...

"Monsieur Laurent had to move the date forward. Things like this are hard, Caddie. I don't know why he changed the time, but he wouldn't have unless he had to."

Cadlen's expression was blank, his eyes now wide. He understood.

Crystal placed her hand on his pointed shoulder, the cotton shirt's collar half-hung down his arm. "I promise, little brother, when I send Robbie the first payment, I'll make sure he gets you some PJs that actually fit!"

His smile was enough to make Crystal's eyes water. Cadlen looked at the photos of his siblings on the wall across from his bed. As soon as his eyes came to Lorrie's picture, it was as though she could read his mind. In a way, she had to.

"And Lorrie..." Crystal sighed. "He doesn't want to talk to me. And I don't know what to say to him."

Neither do I, Crys. Neither do I...

He looked at his sister, trying his best to remember every detail. Her dyed blonde hair pulled back into a tight ponytail. Her round, plump cheeks that created the soft contour of her face. Hazel-blue eyes that were hard to discern in the darkness of his room in the wee hours. She smelled like baby powder, just like his mother. The scent lingered around his sister like Julia Sheppard's memory in his mind.

And as suddenly, that would fade as well.

"I'll be away for a long time. We talked about that, remember?"

He analyzed her words and expression without blinking.

"I left a letter for Lorrie to read. But I don't want you to give it to him until he's ready to read it. I trust you to decide."

Crystal tucked an envelope folded into itself under his pillow.

"I trust you more than anyone, little brother."

Cadlen's sister leaned forward and kissed him on the forehead, pressing her lips against him for an extra-long moment. He prayed it didn't have to end. Her lashes brushed his chin as she pulled away. A tear trickled down his face. He wasn't sure if it was his or hers.

Crystal sat up. "I'm going to write you letters as often as I can. I want you to keep drawing and send me your pictures! And when I am all done, I will be able to come home. Monsieur Laurent promises I can come home, and he never breaks his promises."

Crystal's promise was reassuring. He remembered how fondly his mother and father both spoke of the man who was like a second father to them while they were younger. When they met at the Retreats in Hyacynthe. His mother had promised Cadlen they would make a trip one day to the dome on the great river, and that Laurent would love them just as much. In his mind, he was a kindly older gentleman with neat, cropped greyish-white hair, a face wrinkled from smiling so broadly, and a twinkle in his eye. It was in this image he placed his faith, and it helped him feel a little better knowing Laurent would be watching over his best friend left in this world.

She hadn't said her last words to him before his eyes blinked heavily, jarring him awake. Before the scene could play out like it did so many times in his dreams.

"Cadlen... Cadlen..."

Robbie was shaking him, not nearly as gently as Crystal had shaken him awake so long ago. This time, he snapped to attention. The bed in the Holt Tower's 93rd-level apartment suite was far more comfortable, yet he never slept as soundly.

Cadlen swung his feet over the edge. This time, he knew what was happening. After Lorrie's tirade against Jason Holt and Clara Connelly, he knew it would be swift, and soon.

"Cad, we're leaving earlier than they scheduled. We have to move quickly, and Captain Ling told me we can't say a word..."

Cadlen caught his brother smiling to himself.

"Well, that won't be so hard for you I suppose. But keeping Lorrie quiet at all... That might be harder!"

The corners of Cadlen's mouth turned up in a smirk.

"They're bringing us to a place outside Capston—outside New Inland, even. Captain Ling calls it Ap-Oz. It's a secure fort, high up in the mountains, not far from Ozarck. We're finally going to see the mountains! And she told me one other thing..."

Cadlen followed Robbie's gaze, and his heart skipped a beat when it stopped at Crystal's picture.

"Monsieur Laurent contacted Captain Ling. They're going to bring her to Ap-Oz, too!"

It took the silver-haired man four years, but Crystal was right. He did keep his promise.

Secrets

Thursday, 21 June AC 0245
Le Niveau-des-Nuages (Cloud Level), South Side,
Hyacynthe
Crystal Sheppard

One last look, to be sure no questions are skipped. And to change her mind for the umpteenth time on that thirty-sixth multiple-choice question. Crystal had filled in and erased all four options at least once. She settled for "c."

The fifth examination always ended up being the most difficult. Year four, five courses over eight months, leaving the remaining one-third of each year to recuperate and earn some money to send home to her brothers. Laurent insisted that the mundane work at Lacraie during her study period was in the interest of self-preservation. Opportunity would present itself once the fourth quarterlies were complete. There was enough to worry about without taking on added responsibilities in the labs.

Crystal rose from her seat halfway up the auditorium rim and descended the sloped aisle to the invigilator's desk. The protocol was strict. Turn the examination booklet upside down. Initial from the witness and yourself, then feed into the narrow slot of the electronic processor. Forty-eight hours later, a grade would be provided. An 800 was necessary for her to retain her scholarship standing. Of the possible 600 points she received from chemistry, bioethics, and geo/calc, 496 was cutting it a little too close for comfort. Biology should be fine. It felt like a clean sweep, and Crystal's instincts were usually spot-on. Physics, on the other hand, always worried her most. Most students were happy to achieve 100 of 200. Crystal was aiming for 150. She figured to land somewhere in between. One way or another, it was done.

With a little over a week before she was due to return to Lacraie, where her work rotations increased to fourteen days from ten for the next three months, Crystal planned to sleep uninterrupted for the next few days. That would of course depend on whether Mireil and Druna would let her. Mir was struggling with the pre-med science load, but still had one more year to bring up her average. Druna, on the other hand, would likely need to re-register for intermediary sessions. She would have scored above the other two in socializing, without a doubt. Unfortunately for the party girl, that never appeared on her transcript.

Back at the apartment in *Le Niveau-des-Nuages*, Crystal threw open the window to allow the swift breeze of the river to cool her room. No sign of Druna at all. Mir was writing later in the afternoon, so she wouldn't be home until well after supper. Crystal had warned both her roommates in a terse handheld message:

```
Finished. Home and in bed. Sleeping. Would
like to keep sleeping as long as possible.
Hugs, C
```

The "hugs" comment was strictly for Druna. It had become somewhat of a term of endearment in the two years she lived with Crystal and Mir. As much as she drove them crazy, they still loved her irrepressible naivety.

"Light at 2." The room dimmed and the tint of the window glass deepened to a slate grey. The hush of wind in the upper level of the Hyacynthian south side lofts soothed Crystal. She missed it in her cramped room in

Lacraie. Down to an oversized T-shirt, Crystal slipped under the sheet, folding the comforter over onto the unoccupied side of her double bed.

She woke to the persistent buzz of her handheld on the bedside table. It went off enough to vibrate itself against the brass lamp base, where the buzz made a metallic echo. It had better be an emergency, she muttered to herself.

"Answer."

The voice command activated the microphone and wireless hub speaker.

"*Crystale*. Laurent here."

The old man's voice strained more than usual. He must have known she was fresh out of the last quarterly. Crystal rolled onto her right side, wiping the sand from her eyes.

"Monsieur, I'm awake. What's going on?"

It was a response she would have preferred to deliver a little less forward, but it was the best she could manage in her half-awakened state.

"I need to speak with you. It is urgent, *chère*."

Crystal's heart sank. "Okay, I can meet you in... maybe twenty minutes?"

"I am at your door. Take the time you need."

He's already here. Mir and Druna must be out, or they would have let him in and awakened her. Swinging her feet to the floor and into a waiting pair of slippers, Crystal reached for her bathrobe. She didn't bother looking in a mirror or brushing her tangled hair.

"Unlock front door." The handheld command released the electronic lock allowing Laurent to enter. She came into the common room just as he latched the door behind himself. The old man turned to reveal a deep sadness in his soft, wrinkled face. His eyes were normally bright, especially when he was talking to Crystal. Today they were narrow, red-streaked from either a lack of sleep or some deep worry.

Laurent stood still, back to the shut door, hands clasped in front of him. Crystal stared at him, refusing to accept the horrible news she knew he was about to deliver.

"What's happened, monsieur?"

"You should sit, *Crystale*. There is a lot to discuss."

Crystal shook her head as her knees began to wobble beneath her. Laurent walked up to her and gently motioned for her to sit on the couch. She couldn't help shaking her head, as though it would dampen the impact of the news.

"Your brothers are safe."

She felt her breathing settle into a rhythm and allowed Laurent to guide her to the soft cushion of the couch. He sat next to her, taking her hands in his own. Veined and spotted, Laurent's hands were a cool and soft dome of protection.

"The inn was struck by an attack, but your brothers were not there when it happened. The building, however, is a total loss. I am so sorry, *chère*."

Tears leaked from Crystal's eyes, still stinging from the sandy sleep. One of her greatest fears upon acceptance to Hyacynthe was that she would never be allowed to go home again. It never occurred to her there would be no home left if she ever did. Laurent's words were soft, but their impact crushed her as though the whole of Hyacynthe's arching dome came down.

"Was anyone killed?" Her thoughts immediately turned to the potential for many victims. She never prayed so hard for no business.

"The inn was vacant. One body was found in the ruins. It was one of the attackers, who somehow couldn't escape before the explosion. The investigation is ongoing."

"Wait, ongoing? When did this happen?" Laurent's tone left her feeling as though it had been some time ago. He sighed.

"It has been... some time." Laurent lowered his head. Crystal pulled her hands away.

"Some time? What are you saying, days? Weeks?"

"Almost three weeks."

Three fucking weeks.

"That was near the end of my first rotation at Lacraie! Why didn't you tell me?" Crystal's sorrow shifted to anger. The server had told them about a fifth attack in Capston. Even then, it would have been old news. "You didn't think I could handle it?"

The old man sighed. "When I received the news, it was the official press release, which indicated there were six killed. These included your three brothers, and the Connelly family, whom I'm sure you remember."

Yes, she remembered them well. Warren Connelly, at least. She couldn't remember meeting his parents. The kid was annoying, but he kept Lorrie busy.

"So, the press reported that they were killed... But you're telling me they're all alive?"

Laurent nodded, his dry lips tight. "I was able to confirm that all six were brought into safe custody by the police. I wanted to tell you immediately, *Crystale*, but it appeared to be a targeted attack. Specifically, Lorrie and his friend. I didn't want to compromise the investigation."

What did those two get themselves into this time? Lorrie must have had something to do with it.

"So, what happens now? Can we bring them here? There's still an embargo."

"I don't think it would be in their best interest—or yours—if they were to come here. Where Captain Ling is sending them, they should be well-protected."

Crystal had no idea who Captain Ling was. There were

many questions. "Sending them? Where are they now? And why send them elsewhere?"

"It is a lot to process," Laurent said. "From what I have been told, your brothers were being kept in Holt Tower, under the direct care of Mayor Reekan's security corps. Captain Ling sent correspondence through the Allens, which took several days, as you would understand." He wasn't wrong.

"So, what did Ling say?" Crystal didn't know if the captain was a woman or a man.

"She was spare on details. But she did tell me that they were concerned about a security breach. She feels your brothers would be safer away from Capston. Away from New Inland entirely."

Laurent's breath shortened the more he spoke. Away from New Inland. What did that mean?

"When are they leaving?"

"Captain Ling did not say."

"Where?" The more the old man revealed, the shorter Crystal's questions became.

"She called it Ap-Oz, but would not elaborate. It is a secured facility, much like Lacraie, except for biotechnology research. Your brothers will be far out of reach from whomever is threatening them."

It was at least a little comfort, but Crystal still had a hundred questions. "But they can't stay there forever! Will the insurance on the inn be able to pay for their living arrangements?"

As though it were buzzing again, Crystal's eyes darted to her handheld, nestled in the robe fabric in her lap.

Ian Null.

"It couldn't be..."

Laurent crinkled his brow. "Couldn't be what?"

Crystal shook her head. "It's nothing, monsieur. I just—"

The old man shifted to face Crystal directly, retaking her hands. "Please, what is on your mind?"

Crystal replayed the encounter between the mysterious, handsome client who caused her to miss her shuttle back to Hyacynthe Station. A stranger who overcompensated for her loss with an exorbitant transfer of funds.

Enough to rebuild an inn.

She confessed in a long string of run-on sentences, digressions, and jumbled memories. Laurent listened intently, processing the information as Crystal babbled.

"Why didn't you tell me about this before?"

Crystal laughed as she wiped her eyes with the back of her robe sleeve. "I meant to tell you, but the money was just so much. I haven't spent a dime of it, Laurent, I swear! I figured someone would come looking for it eventually—it had to be too good to be true."

Laurent offered an arm for her shoulder. Crystal rested her head against him and let her emotions pour. "I have to stop crying on you, monsieur, I'm sorry."

The old man rocked her back and forth as though he was trying to lull a newborn to sleep. Laurent never had children of his own. He would have made a wonderful father. "You've done nothing wrong, *chère*. We can investigate the money transfer later. But it seems like quite a coincidence. Do you remember what the client purchased?"

Crystal looked up. "I just wrote bioethics this week, you know I'm not supposed to say."

Laurent shook his head. "When we open the investigation, I will be on the forensics team. You can tell me."

She revealed, with a little lingering guilt, that it was a prescription for radiation poisoning treatment. Laurent received the news with a look of puzzlement. It seemed irrelevant to the Sheppard Inn attack. Still, there appeared to be plenty of moving parts in the case.

"What did you say was his name again?"

"Null. Ian Null, according to the requisition. His handprint checked out. There was no reason for me to suspect anything, apart from the money, anyway."

She proceeded to describe him in great detail, although the surveillance cameras would have had a clear view anyway.

"So, you're telling me he's a handsome fellow?"

Crystal blushed. "I mean, sure. That's not what I was trying to say."

Laurent smiled. "You didn't have to say anything. Your eyes say it all."

"He was just really... nice. He was kind, patient. When he realized he made me late for my shuttle, it looked like he was really sorry. But there was something..."

Ian Null didn't seem comfortable. In the waiting room. In his new clothes. In his own skin.

"And you're certain you've never seen him since?"

Crystal closed her eyes and Ian Null's smile appeared. *Who am I kidding? I see him all the time...* Her thoughts snapped back to her brothers. How shameful that she allowed herself to be distracted by a stranger's money and charm. For a moment, she was as angry with herself as Laurent.

"I will speak with Lacraie. I'm sure it is a coincidence and nothing more. But let us not keep secrets from each other anymore, *Crystale*."

Secrets? Crystal kept the contents of her bank account from the old man. The old man failed to tell her that her home was destroyed and her only surviving family members were in witness protection. Big difference. Laurent's embrace had cooled as her tears dried.

"How am I supposed to go back to Lacraie, monsieur?"

She released the frail man and turned away from him. The more the news sat in her gut, the more it festered.

"Until we can arrange for you to travel to Ozarck, the

safest place you can be is Lacraie. I know it won't be easy—"

"Nothing is easy," she interrupted. It was time for the old man to leave. "Nothing ever is."

Running the Rails

Sunday, 24 June AC 0245
Hyacynthe Station
Crystal Sheppard

The thought of working at all sent Crystal's mind reeling. Working in an internship at a nuclear medicine clinic was overwhelming. The magna-rail ride from Hyacynthe to Lacraie was usually smooth and quiet. She could dim the tint of the windows from grey to pitch black if she wanted to sleep. With the touch of a button, she could blast cool air or increase the temperature of her seat cushions. But after Laurent's news about the inn, no comforts on the face of the earth would be able to distract her. The train may as well have been a covered wagon.

In the days since her mentor revealed that her brothers had narrowly dodged assassination and were effectively confined to witness protection, Crystal had grown increasingly bitter. Maybe there was nothing she could have done. Maybe if she was still home, she would have been on shift at the reception desk. Maybe she would have been buried in the rubble.

No matter how she analyzed it, her trust had been betrayed. Laurent's reasons and his words didn't change anything. She had a right to know about her brothers, her home.

Three hours and change after the bullet train slid out from Hyacynthe's arched dome, Crystal stepped onto the platform of Hyacynthe Station like she did before she knew what had happened. Nothing around her had changed. Commuters rushed past her to meet their connections or their shuttles. Barking attendants called out the next departures. It was early afternoon, and hungry travelers still crowded around the food kiosks. The last time she was here, she saw her brothers in the strangers around her. Not this time. Everyone was faceless.

Crystal's shuttle wasn't expected for another hour. Two more hours across far less forgiving ground before she would arrive at the Lacraie facility. Guards would still be on duty, sentinels heavily armed and disciplined in the event of unexpected guests. Laurent had assured her that Lacraie was the safest place she could be. That reassurance had since lost most of its credibility.

A cup of java and a crusty bread sandwich later, and a small crowd had begun to accumulate at the various platforms in the station. All except the shuttered New Inland gate. Crystal glared at the lifelessness of the abandoned platform. She had always felt a pang of homesickness every time she looked at it or walked past it. Today she could have jumped the barricade and run the hundreds of kilometers of magnetic railway, all the way through the badlands, past the junction, and straight to New Inland. She was from Capston. They would have to let her back in. Her family needed her.

Cadlen needed her.

Crystal's handheld buzzed and she snapped back to reality. There would be no running the rails today. Or ever.

An incoming message blinked on her screen.

Hi Crys, just checking in. Worried about you and your brothers. Message me when you get to Hyacynthe Station. Mir

Crystal didn't want to keep anything from Mireil. It was harder to trust anyone after Laurent, but she knew deep inside her flatmate wouldn't let her down. It didn't make it any easier to open up to her, though.

Hi Mir, just had lunch. Departure in 30 min. C

There would be no airwave connection beyond the station, and communication in or out of Lacraie was kept to emergency transmission only. Emergencies like the destruction of a home and family in mortal danger apparently didn't apply.

Laurent stopped by but you already left. I know you're mad but he seemed so upset. M

I just need time, okay? If he's that worried about me he knows where to find me. C

Why was Mireil bringing up Laurent now? An usher hollered the fifteen-minute warning for the Lacraie shuttle. Below the green bubble of text from Mireil, a second bubble emerged in a light yellowish hue.

Laurent. He's there with her.

Crystale, I am sorry I kept the information from you. I hope you can forgive me. L

She had forgiven him, at least with her words. Both she and he knew it was a lie. Laurent had offered to defer her next rotation, but Crystal had rejected the suggestion outright. Now more than ever she needed something to keep her mind off clinging memories of her brothers. From Robbie's tired eyes. Lorrie's sharp tongue.

Cadlen's soft words.

⌁

She was at the New Inland departure gate. Robbie was

there, and her dad. Cadlen's sketch pad was in one hand while the other clutched Robbie's. He was only eight years old. Crystal set her travel bag on the concrete platform and knelt in front of her baby brother.

Cadlen let go of Robbie's hand and dropped his sketch pad to the ground. His hair was getting longer without his mother to make sure he got it cut. Kind, soft eyes peered through the wisps.

Come home soon.

Crystal blinked tears and pulled Cadlen into her arms, kissing him on the top of his head.

"I'll see you again soon. I promise."

"Five minutes. Lacraie!"

The barking attendant interrupted a memory Crystal had tried her best to keep in the corners of her mind, where it couldn't corrupt her with stinging nostalgia. Too late.

After your rotation, I will bring you to them, Crystale.

A queue had formed at the shuttle dock. Crystal turned her attention to the magna-rail platforms once again, only this time she looked past the New Inland line. There weren't as many people waiting at the Ozarck platform. For a second, she wondered if Ian Null had come to Lacraie on a magna-rail train, or if he had hiked along the empty rail lines. Wherever he was, Mr. Null never knew that she was going to spend even more of his money on travel.

They will be safe in Ap-Oz, he had told her. *Appalachian-Ozarck.* It was a research facility, sort of like Lacraie but for biotech studies, high in the mountains down south...

Mir, tell Druna to let Remy down easy. I love you and I'll see you as soon as I can. Please water my plants. Xo C

Passengers began to climb onto the magna-rail coach at the Ozarck tunnel. Once they had left, even Laurent couldn't turn the train around. Her New Inland identification wouldn't permit her to make the transfer to the New Inland line, but she wasn't going home anyway. There wasn't a home to go to anymore. Once she arrived in Ozarck, she would find her way to Ap-Oz, and she would hold Cadlen in her arms again, no matter how much taller he had grown, no matter how long his hair hung in his face.

Crystal stepped onto the Ozarck platform as the last call for the Lacraie shuttle bellowed.

PS. Tell Laurent I'm sorry too. C

Dying Flowers

Le_Renard_Subtil is never late. Twenty minutes past our agreed meeting time at the Spleen is more than cause for alarm. It's a fucking crisis.

I waited until my handheld turned over to 9:00 PM and decided I wouldn't wait a minute more. The last mouthful of water was boring, but Aquavit isn't something you can casually drink all day without suffering the consequences. I started drinking water to dilute the liquor as soon as I realized Le_Renard was late. These kinds of hurdles require clarity of thought.

The *Spleen* is an appropriate name for such an establishment. As the organ is situated behind the tenth rib, the tavern of ill repute was found on the tenth deck of the Third District. And as its name would suggest, it is a haven for the ill-tempered. Like most watering holes in Kayewat, the lights are kept dim all day. The proprietors do their part to provide cover for their clients' shady affairs.

Before rising from my whale-skin chair, I scanned the room as far as my eyes could without moving my head. I had chosen a booth beneath arched stonework, my back to the wall as best I could manage without appearing too obvious. In half an hour, several patrons had come and gone, but most were sloths, slouched over the ivory-trimmed bar or plugged into the wire tubes for their sedatives. The Spleen offered dialysis and detoxification as some sort of phony "public service." Not once did I ever jab one of those intravenous needles into my arm. I have no desire to trade my own substance abuse for hepatitis!

9:01 PM, and I left the relative safety of the booth. Nothing of concern from my earlier blind spot set off any alarms. Confirmation of payment with the barkeep blinked on my handheld. His thugs outside wouldn't be chasing me down for drinking-and-dashing today. I nodded toward the bar. The tender didn't even look at me.

It was at that moment the patron slumped on his barstool caught my attention. Bundled up in typical Kayewati outdoor gear, he would have been anonymous to anyone else. Except he was strangely familiar to me. As I delayed my departure by checking the correspondences on my handheld, I strained through my alcohol-clouded memory. Where have I seen this guy before?

It was best to make my way to the door

without drawing any undue notice. There were maybe a dozen others in various states in the Spleen, and any of them could have a sharpened blade in their coat sleeves with my back written on it. Most didn't appear like they could even stand up, let alone lunge at me. Somehow, they were the ones who worried me the most.

As I neared the door, a smell met my nostrils as though a bucket of rotten chum was hurled on me. All of Kayewat has a certain bouquet, like diseased or dying flowers. Of course, invasive stenches here are normal. But just like the other senses, we remember smells based on our experiences, like voices, or the sound of steps on wooden floors. Memory is a powerful thing. And even in my semi-inebriated state, it only took half a minute to place this one.

Earlier this week in the Abattoir, CF and I smelled that same smell off a homeless guy a few feet away. At the time, we weren't sure. But here he is, definitely alive, and there are no coincidences in Kayewat.

Our homeless friend was following me. First Le_Renard no-shows. Then this guy appears again. It's a terrifying feeling to realize that between the Abattoir and the Spleen, he and I likely crossed paths several times.

I hailed a shuttle and returned to my

quarters back in the Second District after several diversionary detours. I didn't explain it to the driver, and he didn't ask. I apologized for making him circle the block twice. "I'm paid all the same, buddy. I'll drive you to the North Pole if you have the money and the time." I'd just as soon go there.

Wednesday, 9 May AC 0245
4:05 AM
Narrows Block, Second District

I double-checked all my security measures. Le_Renard paid for the best. Once I was home, I usually never gave my own safety a second thought. I poured a hot bath and sprinkled some salts into the steaming water. Once I was submerged up to my chin, I could feel the tension and all the stink from Kayewat dissolving, rising from the water in the steam and being sucked out the exhaust fan. It rattles as though it's trying to cough out a flu.

I have to admit, it's hard to come back into the decay of Kayewat after being on the outside for so long. Even the most decrepit buildings in Capston were like flower gardens in comparison. I stayed in this abandoned hotel for most of my time there. The security system was armed, but easy enough to decrypt. Capston doesn't allow for vagabonds to squat in vacant properties. So, I was surprised to learn that I wasn't alone.

And it was the information I stumbled upon while bunked down there one night that was the reason for my trip home to Kayewat. Le_Renard needs to know.

My handheld buzzed.

CF: We need to meet right away. Emmanuel is compromised. Ninth Circle, 0600, Friday. Clawfinger.

The message was sent from CF's account, of that I'm certain.

But CF did not send it. The missing underscore between words gave it away.

The bath water was suddenly as cold as the arctic sky. 1:00 AM, and only a few hours before the person on the other end of the message expects to meet me. There's no point going to sleep now.

I spent my last few hours poring over my documents and journal entries. All that I have is newly encrypted. At 5:59 AM, the contents of my files will appear in an Allen account with instructions. It may take several days, maybe even weeks to reach Le_Renard, but it's the best I can do. Claw_Finger is probably dead. But I owe it to him to see for myself.

As this could be my last entry, I look back on a life and career with few regrets. I do, however, wish I could have been able to save the Sheppard kids. If I hadn't left the alley door open when I fled, maybe they wouldn't have been caught up in all this shit. Anyway, it's too late for them. Maybe for me, too. I just hope my information can save the exiled girl in Hyacynthe.

Messrs. Allen, please expedite the correspondence in haste.

Respect,

Walpurgis

Heroes Die Hardest

"Lucas Fox was a hero."

Sixteen degrees and overcast. A light breeze lifted fine-granulated silt from the badlands and carried the cloudy dust for leagues across the cracked and parched plains. The Council of Sascota would have preferred to hold the memorial for Captain Fox inside the dome. Phil's mother insisted it be held in the open air. Fortunately, the forecast didn't call for any southeasterly gusts, which would have blown in unwelcome radiation from the Midwestern Seam. An outside service offered more cons than pros, as far as Phil could reason. There would be far fewer guests. Everything was at the whim of the churning winds. And obviously, more risk of outsiders appearing. It was because of outsiders Phil was mourning his father's death in the first place.

The Sascotan mayor spoke to the modest crowd of less than two dozen through a veil mask usually worn during dust storms. It was an obvious critique of the decision to leave the city's walls. Phil looked around the crowd occupying the front third of rows of foldout chairs. When the mayor stepped onto the dais, about half of the spectators applied their own face coverings.

Elsa Fox covered her face with a traditional widow's veil. The days since Lucas's murder aged her years in

Phil's eyes. Already weakened by the red tide, she moved a little slower every day in the best of times. Before the news was delivered to the Fox family door, Phil watched his mother slowly descend into her own grave. Now, she'd opened her arms wide and allowed herself to free fall into it.

"Mrs. Fox, I apologize for the lateness of the hour. I have some awful news."

Phil closed his eyes. He was at the dining room table, books opened and strewn. The climate was set for "tropical dew," whatever that was meant to emulate. It flooded the room with gentle water-trickling sounds, a sweet dewy scent of fresh-watered plants, and a warm, soft light. She always told him that this setting reminded her of his father, ranging across the vast Continental Divide. Lucas Fox was a national hero. He risked life and limb to drive the magna-rail trains over thousands of kilometers of unforgiving terrain and hostile territory.

It all came to an abrupt halt earlier that day.

The officer from the Sascotan Guard, cap under arm, explained what happened. Phil closed his book and listened through the trickling water to the recount of his father's killing. The train arrived at its scheduled stopover at the Badlands Junction, destined for Hyacynthe Station later in the afternoon. The most dangerous leg of the journey was the Lake Region. There was little unrest around the junction in recent years.

The killers were waiting for him.

Emerging from the station terminal, Lucas Fox was walking back across the staging to the train. Three men approached him from behind and, according to witnesses, asked if he was the captain. No sooner did Lucas answer yes, the man in front of him thrust a concealed knife into his stomach. The brigand behind him wrapped her arm around his forehead and slid her blade across his throat. The entire incident was over in less than twenty seconds. The three strangers, dressed in jumpsuits and low-brimmed caps, walked away with a brisk determination as the magna-rail captain and national hero crumpled to the dirty platform in a heap.

The gory details were provided by the official investigative report, and Phil only read them when he was older. In real time, the officer only got to say half of what he had planned before Elsa Fox crumpled from her own wounds to the carpeted doorway. Her cries were muffled by laborious wheezing as the red tide stifled her reaction with heaving convulsions. Phil ran to his mother. No sixteen-year-old should have to hold his widowed mother in his arms as she gasps for breath.

And in that sense, standing for an hour in the outside air was a minor inconvenience for the attendees. Phil did not sympathize with any of them.

The mayor offered his condolences to conclude the service. Phil and his mother remained seated in front of the grave marker, a modest slab of marble with a fine engraving of his smiling face above a description of his life and accomplishments. The stone would be moved back inside Sascota to be displayed outside City Hall next to other recipients of the Order of the Plains monuments, where the dust of the badlands and the inevitable radiated plumes couldn't desecrate it.

One by one, the guests stopped and stooped to offer a hand and an awkward condolence to Elsa and Phil. As the final guests moved along to the line of shuttles waiting to return to Sascota, Phil inhaled and prepared to steady his mother as she made to stand. A final guest emerged, his nose and mouth covered with a mask and his eyes shielded by deep, black-lensed glasses. His hair was deep brown, but it was obvious he was colouring premature grey from his mussed mane.

"I'm sorry for your loss, ma'am."

The man bowed as he clutched his hands in front of

his waist, twiddling his thumbs in circles. Phil watched his mother squint to recognize the well-wisher.

"Thank you for coming." It was all she could manage to say.

The man turned to face the monument. "I never met him. But I was once told he was a great man. Turns out, he was. Huh."

Phil couldn't interpret the meaning of the stranger's spasmed exclamation. *Huh.* It sounded like a cross between a chuckle and a hiccup. After a silent moment of paid respect, the man turned to Phil, again keeping his hands to himself.

"Your old man, he was indeed a hero. And when heroes die, they always die hardest, don't they? Huh."

Instead of walking toward the waiting shuttles, the man turned and walked in the exact opposite direction, into the open plains as the wind conjured more dust into the air. Phil stared at the man as he vanished from sight. Elsa told him later that she didn't know who he was. He didn't believe her.

Phil dropped his knapsack at the door and hung his coat on the old three-pronged hat rack. There were no climate controls in the Homestead. The natural scent was nothing tropical, only burning wood laced with faint must. The open-concept cabin was adorned with furniture from several different sets, all donated over the years from friends in Gasperro. The love seat looked like the companion piece to the armchair in Albert's office. It had a tacky orange and brown swirling print pattern. Albert could have it back.

The fireplace was lit and burning well through the hardwood chunks that were glowing red in the embers.

The chainmail screen was half open. Phil prodded around the fire with a cast-iron poker and closed the curtain. From the bathroom in the back of the cabin, the shower was hissing.

You better not drain the hot water tank.

In the adjoining kitchen, he selected a glass from the old hutch. He poured himself a drink of green spirit from the dusty bottle in the liquor stash. It had been there as long as he could remember. The label was half peeled and worn, and the original screw-on cap was long gone, replaced with a spongy cork that would likely have altered the flavor at that point. Phil wasn't concerned.

"Aquavit. Huh! A glass of that stuff... It'll either kill you or make you live forever!"

Phil winced from the strong after bite that brought to life the caraway and dill flavour that had been subtly influenced by the cork. The voice from the bathroom behind the loft stairs felt like an echo from a dream. From another time, when he first opened the door and walked into the bay of Jackson Auto. In the memories he tried so hard to stifle as Mayor Fox of Capston all those years.

Phil turned to see the old man in his plush robe, carrying a few more pounds and his hair a fair bit grayer. At least he had given up trying to dye it.

"*Le Renard Subtil.* More like *Le Renard Argenté...*"

The old man ruffled his hair, trying to fashion a reasonable style without the convenience of a brush and mirror.

"Huh! Good to see you too, my son..."

Self-Immolation

Lunes, 12 marzo NE 267 (Monday, 12 March NE 267)
Motherland
Lieutenant Paolo Desantos

Paolo didn't even have time to shower or change his clothes. For eight days he had led a doomed march through cruel badlands, under an unforgiving sun to an empty promise of potable drinking water. His Eminence De Léon greeted the broken squadron outside the city gates. There was no parade, no cheering crowd, no ribbons or music or ale. The figurehead of Motherland, dressed in his unblemished military fatigues, didn't reach for Paolo's hand. As the defeated survivors trudged through the city gates, His Eminence instructed Paolo, through his hissed slur, to immediately meet the colonel in the chapel.

The chapel. Parched with thirst, he would need to trek another four hours outside the city walls to another place, without even a chance to fill his canteen.

Through the spindly, sparse undergrowth west of the city, Paolo cut through dead and dying growth, the dust beneath his boot treads wisping into the air with every step. The mission had been expected to take longer. Despite arriving early, there was nothing to do when it was determined that the water table was tainted. Nothing, apart from cleaning up Commander Yael's mess. A whole squad of sappers, a decorated commander, and dozens of good soldiers had lost their lives. Under

Paolo's command.

There would be consequences. Except no one would see it. The only witnesses would be the colonel and whatever spirits were trapped in that cursed hovel.

It was early evening when Paolo passed through the stone remains of the village of Jude. He tasted the dust on his tongue as he passed the covered stone well that was once the center of the fledgling community. His father told him of the day the village council agreed that the well had to be filled and capped for good. It meant long hikes outside the village to springs that remained drinkable, massive gallon jugs hanging on the ends of poles that pressed down on the shoulders. It meant rations. Bathing only when it rained, which was less and less common. It meant deteriorating health for the young and early death for the elderly. Jude was dying.

Under the shadow of the setting sun, Paolo spied the frame of the last bastion of prior life in the doomed village. Through the sparkling, kaleidoscopic windows, a faint light blinked.

Closing the heavy oak doors behind him, Paolo saw his father, the colonel of Motherland, kneeling in the nearest wooden pew to the altar. A sweet scent caused his nose to twitch.

"I would offer you a drink, son, but you know that would be impossible." Colonel Desantos bowed his head, arms rested on the armrest. "But of course, if you had been successful, there would be enough water for everyone."

Paolo's throat was scratchy. His words were gasps. "The tests indicated the water may have recently been contaminated."

"Perhaps if you had arrived sooner, you might have been able to secure the water table before the locals poisoned the well." The colonel waved his hand, motioning for Paolo to come closer. Every step Paolo took was laboured as though he were approaching the pillory in the center of Motherland.

"We arrived two days early," Paolo whispered. "Yael had no better luck."

"Yael was an outstanding commander, Paolo. Explain to me how he was killed."

He stopped adjacent to his kneeling father but did not look at him. "The commander had gone mad. I made the decision myself." He couldn't bring himself to say he summarily executed the commander in the midst of committing crimes unbecoming of a Motherland officer.

"Gone mad, you say? From the red sickness?"

Paolo didn't answer. Red tide caused people to behave in unusual ways. Most didn't become rapists. Paolo wanted to believe that red tide didn't change anyone, but revealed their true nature. Unless it killed them first.

"You know the consequences, son."

Paolo turned to his father. The colonel's tool kit, a rusted rectangular metal box with two clasps, waited for the punishment to begin. The sweet oil smell strengthened close to the altar, giving Paolo watery eyes and a headache.

The lieutenant dropped his rucksack and removed his shirt. The fabric skidded across the scar tissue on his back. He leaned forward, resting his hands on the wooden table that served for generations as an altar. Paolo was ignorant of religious ceremonies. He was only a boy the last time his father brought him to the chapel for a service. He remembered hooded priests; their faces hidden in shadow. A holder with four candles, flames dancing atop the wicks before being snuffed out. Words echoing in his child brain in languages he didn't understand. Paolo had never told his father that he couldn't sleep through the night for years. The water in his eyes began to bead and leak, but he would be damned if he allowed himself to taste even a drop, no matter how thirsty.

The crack of a leather-tipped whip and a razor-like slice across his shoulders brought him back to the present. Paolo tightened his hands into fists as his father carved a new incision for every day of his journey to and from the failed water source. Eight lashings were the most yet. After the final blow, Paolo heard his father drop the whip to the chapel floor.

"I'm sorry, son. I wish it didn't have to be like this." Colonel Desantos retrieved a small bottle and a cloth. As his father dabbed disinfectant on the open slices, Paolo bit the inside of his mouth and tasted the blood as the liquid stung. If he weren't weakened from dehydration, he would have torn the surface from the altar. He spit away the tears that passed over his lips.

"I know it burns. One day soon, this chapel will burn too." The sweet smell of petrol permeated the building. Much of it had been spilled throughout the sanctuary, likely more than once. "This is the last time you will see this place, Paolo."

That was untrue. Paolo saw this place when he closed his eyes.

The colonel placed adhesive bandages over the scourge marks. "I am proud of you, my son. You marched on through the bleakest of conditions, only to be failed by Yael and the sappers. To come home with as many as you did—Alvara would not have fared so well."

Indeed, Captain Alvara would have ended up in the pillory. He would have gotten off easy that way. Paolo gritted his teeth. His temperature was rising.

He turned to his father. They were the same height. In Colonel Desantos's eyes, Paolo saw yellow in the corners, faint red streaks splaying from his widened irises. The pair held the gaze for several minutes.

The colonel broke the stare first and turned to his seat. Paolo retrieved his shirt and reached his arms through the sleeves, wincing as the lacerations under the bandages creased and splayed. The injuries seared, but they would heal. One of his sojourns had once led him to a settlement with a rather skilled apothecary. The creamy balm he had purchased would heal the wounds in half the time. It meant for a lot of nights sleeping face down in the meantime.

"I am promoting you to lieutenant colonel, Paolo."

No one would *fail* into a promotion unless they were the son of the colonel. The taste in Paolo's mouth was more bitter than the blood of his bitten tongue.

The colonel turned one last time to his tool kit. Retrieving a small canteen, he stretched his hand to Paolo.

"Drink, son. You have a long walk home."

He took the small plastic bottle and walked back up the aisle without a word or a nod. Once outside, under the twilight Jude sky, Paolo looked east. Motherland was four hours away by foot.

He would make it in three.

Paolo unscrewed the cap of the canteen and poured its contents to the parched earth, which needed it more than he did.

Monday, 18 June AC 0245
27 Kilometers, 239° West-Southwest of Allentown
Ian Null

The hike was a full day on foot to the gentle slopes of the Allegheny foothills. The mountain chain extended south into the Appalachians and Ozarcks. Null had no desire to follow them. Once over these hills, it was generally level land for most of the way to the West Coast. He would deal with the Rockies when he got there.

Ian Null couldn't stand to be in the costume for even a second longer. He had to stay in disguise until he was safely beyond the Allentown city limits. But that wasn't enough. There were too many hidden cameras—in trees, behind rocks. Sensors that would log the movement of anything the size of a rabbit and up. Heat tracing, and the technology to predict who or what the orange blob on the screen could be. And then there were other people. Anything that stood on two legs could be an Allen. Or a clandestine Motherland operative. Or a New Inland spy.

Or someone who had erased their identity and started a new life.

In a sparse clearing high up the slope, grown in for years with poplars and alders, Null found refuge in a collapsed cabin. The gable ends remained triangular, but the center was caved into the floor. The remains of a fire pit were easy to spot. Clearing away enough grass and branches, Null built a small fire. He didn't need one to cook or to keep warm. All he needed was enough to immolate the traces of his former self. A small fire that would release minimal smoke. Twenty kilometers removed from the Allen frontiers was comfortably far from any ground-based heat signature sensors.

Null removed the hairpiece first. It itched his scalp as though the fibers were made from baling twine. Next, the plastic teeth with decayed, black gaps. How many times did he cross paths with big John Gry, only for him to scoff and dismiss him? It would melt within seconds in the fire he was about to build. The disguise had allowed him to move around Allentown without detection, but he would not be going back again. As he stripped off his stained and torn shirt, the fabric rubbed the healed scars of his father's whip across his back. He stood naked as he fished a fresh set of clothing from his knapsack. The shirt and pants were fresh off the loom, creased and crisp as the day he donned them for the first time. He had wanted to appear professional for his visit to Lacraie.

It was always possible that Crystal Sheppard had alerted the Hyacynthe authorities. They may be investigating *Ian Null* right now. Slava Allen's diligence ensured that any forensic trail would lead instead to Private Mott Wrengel. Null felt sorry for his doppelganger, the orphan who marched proudly to his own demise believing Paolo Desantos had been responsible for the death of his father.

Paolo hadn't killed his father. But he *had* killed Mott Wrengel. That was the cost of his freedom.

After half an hour, Null doused the embers and stirred them into a thick, black paste.

It is dead.

With his knapsack packed and secured, Null pulled his handheld from his cargo pocket before gazing towards Allentown one last time. In the north end of the city, a giant black plume continued to billow into the sky. He was still incognito in the city limits when the land drone went off outside Grace Hospital. The smoke from that first explosion had exhausted into the wind, just as the Nat Bank would in due time. He had winced when the explosives detonated in the Motherland stronghold. Mott Wrengel wouldn't have felt a thing. When they reached the epicenter, the forensics would find DNA, maybe even teeth, which would be identified as Paolo Desantos, thanks to Slava Allen's handiwork. They may even find that the uniform, or whatever remained of it, was worn by the lieutenant colonel the day of his promotion. The news would find its way back to Colonel Desantos. And it would destroy him.

Paolo Desantos is dead.

Paolo Desantos had to die so that *Ian Null* would be free.

Satisfied, he slung the knapsack over his shoulder and

opened his handheld. Before nightfall he would be past the highest ground and well on his way into the valley below. All calculations indicated that he would not need his first dose of radiation medicine for a few days at best. Without any unforeseen delays, he would have enough to make it through the Midwest Seam, that stretch of contaminated earth that left a swath hundreds of kilometers long, at its narrowest point. Beyond that, he had all the time in the world to reach the western townships. So long as he crossed the Rockies before the snow fell.

Null opened the tab on his handheld to the transaction receipt of his Radiogardasse prescription. *Crystal Sheppard.* His only regret was that he hadn't met her in a different place and time. Maybe one day Steven Reekan would put it all together. The <NULL> files contained enough information to prove that Paolo Desantos had blown up the Sheppard Family Inn. He regretted involving Wrengel in his plans, but he felt no remorse in killing the Kayewati agent. In Grant, he saw Yael. And in himself, Paolo had seen his father.

It only seemed right to give Crystal Sheppard the rest of his father's money. It was at least compensation for the loss of her family's home. When they had met that day, he had stared into the same eyes in the drawing that he had held in his hands in the Sheppard Inn lobby. Null had intended to keep it, but knew he couldn't look into any of the Sheppards' eyes again. Maybe someday Reekan would find where he hid it.

Ian Null walked into the brush, away from the black and gray ashen remains of his former life. All that he took with him were Paolo's handheld, Paolo's scars across his back, and Paolo's regrets. Null hoped they would recede in time.

It didn't matter. He knew he would never forget Crystal Sheppard. The first time his eyes had met hers, it was already too late.

Epilogue: A Time to Sow

Friday, 25 May
City of Moab, Midwestern Seam
Brother Simon

As clouds began to creep across the sky of a sunny spring morning, Brother Simon toiled in his freshly tilled garden. He and his kin believed that in the heart of the swath of poisoned earth, one parcel of land remained untainted as though the Light poured over it. The Ansati city was a fable. It was known by many names. Most carried unfavorable connotations.

The City of the Dead.

The Leper Colony.

The Radiation Zone.

Among the Ansati druids, it was known as *Moab*. To Simon, it was called home.

Crouched in rows of dirt mixed with black soil and compost, Simon pulled the drawstring of his shawl tighter as the wind picked up. One at a time. Form a small hole, measure up to the first knuckle for proper depth, and drop the seed. Cover, and repeat the length of the row. Ansati harvests were bountiful, in large part due to the attention to detail and knowledge of the crops. It was too early yet to plant beans or leafy vegetables. But not too early for pumpkins, squash, or rutabagas. Raël always complimented Simon on his full, plump vegetables. As long as he could continue to trade for Raël's preservatives come fall.

Simon shuddered as a chill descended over him. Straightening his posture as he knelt, he closed his eyes and breathed. The world always slowed down a little when he reached out to it. The last, straining rays of sun fighting through the emerging cloud cover warmed his cheek. In the stillness of the late morning, Simon rested his hands on his lap. He could feel the warmth of his tilled garden beneath his feet and knees.

Footsteps.

Could it be?

Simon kept his eyes shut. "Welcome home, brother."

The steps continued, a little less faint with each soft, deliberate step. The rhythm, the subtleties of the footfall moving onto the stone walkway from the street, it was all familiar.

It is. He has returned.

"Isn't it still too early for squash, brother?"

There was a softness in his voice that was missing when he left. Simon prayed this was a good sign.

"According to my records, it is the best time to sow. The last frost has passed."

The man stood behind Simon, who opened his eyes and continued planting. He would like to finish the row before rising to his feet and greeting his guest.

"Are the Forty angry with me?"

Simon shook his head. "The Forty are worried about you, Andreas."

One last seed dropped into one last hole, and Simon stood, stretching skyward as he turned to the returning prodigal son of the Ansati. In his absence, the Catholic Forty dispatched brothers and Sibylline across the land when it was learned Andreas had fled. He was so angry that day. His red episode was more heightened than ever before. *And he was doing so well learning how to manage it.*

"They were never going to find me." Andreas drew the hood back to hang behind his neck. Carefully, he pulled the draping right sleeve of his robe up to the elbow. Simon felt the pain in both his own skin and his heart at the sight of the Kayewati glyph carved into Andreas's forearm. A deep red line outlined the stone figure, crusted over with deep scabs that oozed liquid.

Simon motioned for Andreas to follow him back to his house. "I have medicine that can soothe your stamp wound. You've been scratching it."

Andreas smiled and pulled the sleeve down. "It's true what they say. When they stamp you, it's forever."

Yes. It is.

"At least allow me to make you a meal."

Andreas nodded. "Thank you, brother. I've had my fill of rotten fish. A warm stew, perhaps?"

Simon smiled. "I think I can arrange that."

The pair stared in silence at each other for a moment. Each was analyzing the other.

"Simon, I have a favour to ask of you."

"Anything, son."

Andreas licked his chapped lips. "I would like to speak with Sister Esparánza. Can you bring me to her?"

Simon swallowed. "Let us eat first."

He turned for his house in the sparse suburb of Moab, the city's downtown rising in the grey sky to the west. Andreas followed at the same pace, keeping a three-meter gap between them. As Simon opened the door, he turned.

"How are you *feeling*, Andreas? You seem... different."

Cool drops of rain began to patter on the front stairs and cobblestoned walkway.

Andreas scratched his cheek. "Never better, brother."

Acknowledgements

In early '92, young Brandon was tasked with writing a short story for a creative writing class. That story far surpassed the page limit, but a kind student intern encouraged him to write the story the way it was meant to be written. The final submission was 54 double-spaced, dot-matrix printed pages. It read about as well as could be expected from a sixteen-year-old Grade 11 student. But the story stayed with him.

Today, the seed that was planted with a story called *The Fifth Sector* has blossomed into *Chronicles of the Reclamation*. The world and the characters who live in it have inhabited my mind most of my life. I'm proud to finally introduce them to everyone!

I have so many people I wish to acknowledge:

My parents, Joan and John LeBlanc. Mom has been an author, freelance writer, and editor for many years. I grew up watching her pursue her dream, and she taught me that I could do the same. My dad is the hardest working man I've ever known. He built the house my sisters and I grew up in. He planted trees our own children now climb. Together, my parents shaped who I am. I love you, Mom and Dad!

My sisters, Marcie Hayman and Brianne Marcoux, brothers-in-law Alan and Dave, and nephews Rohan, Piersen, Alexandre, and Leo.

My sons, Kieran and Colby. Being your dad is the greatest privilege I could ever have. I am proud of you both, and I love you more than anything in the world!

Christina Jones, for unconditional love and support. You were the first to read my entire story draft front to back—that was no small task! I couldn't have handled any of the business and marketing without you. Love you!

No writer is an island, so I would also like to acknowledge my writing friends, whose influence on me has been invaluable:

Audrey Doyle, my copyeditor, for your diligence and enthusiasm for my story; Robert Williams for designing my cover; Erika LeClair, for formatting; Jeff McLennan and Tom Bowser for concept sketches that were crucial to my world-building.

The Monday Night Writing Group, who adopted (kidnapped?) me after a chance encounter at Second Cup. You all treated my characters like your own, and they're better for having met you.

Terry Armstrong, for countless hours of developmental editing, feedback, and guidance. Every author would be lucky to have you in their corner.

The Eleven, my novel-writing course mates. Every one of you made the lockdown of 2020 so much brighter. I am privileged to have worked with you, and I cherish the friendships we've developed.

The Stanley Consolidated School Writer's Workshop, for your dedication, honesty, silliness, and boundless imaginations. I'm proud of you, Writerz! Never stop creating! Thank you to the students and staff of SCS for welcoming me into your community.

Kim Doucette, my long-time friend and spiritual guide, for supporting me in those early university days. You understood me when I didn't understand myself. Thank you for the Kimspiration!

Em Whelly, for reading my drafts multiple times without complaining, appreciating my sense of humour, and patiently explaining the publishing process—some things more than once. Cheers and Writer's Tears!

Mrs. Betty Davis, who offered me a safe space in the Port Elgin town library and fostered my love of reading and writing. I will never forget your kindness, and I am eternally grateful.

And thank you, for taking the time to read my story.

Brandon J. LeBlanc grew up near Port Elgin, New Brunswick. Now an educator in the village of Stanley, he teaches students from grades six through twelve. He lives in nearby Penniac, New Brunswick, with his sons Kieran and Colby, and his bunny Lily. Brandon is known for his lifelong passions for music, trivia, geography, and Star Wars. He enjoys spending time and listening to records with his partner, Christina.

Exiles is his first novel, and the first of three that will comprise the *Chronicles of the Reclamation* series.

www.ingramcontent.com/pod-product-compliance
Lightning Source LLC
Chambersburg PA
CBHW061346190726
48288CB00005B/1614